About the Author

Ashley Sorrell, author of the *Fatal Prophecy* series, is a Canadian who loves cheesecake and spending time with her son, James.

The Fatal Prophecy Vol. 2: Carter Blood

Ashley Sorrell

The Fatal Prophecy Vol. 2: Carter Blood

Olympia Publishers
London

www.olympiapublishers.com
OLYMPIA PAPERBACK EDITION

Copyright © Ashley Sorrell 2023

The right of Ashley Sorrell to be identified as author of
this work has been asserted in accordance with sections 77 and 78 of the
Copyright, Designs and Patents Act 1988.

All Rights Reserved

No reproduction, copy or transmission of this publication
may be made without written permission.
No paragraph of this publication may be reproduced,
copied or transmitted save with the written permission of the publisher, or in
accordance with the provisions
of the Copyright Act 1956 (as amended).

Any person who commits any unauthorized act in relation to
this publication may be liable to criminal
prosecution and civil claims for damage.

A CIP catalogue record for this title is
available from the British Library.

ISBN: 978-1-80439-488-5

This is a work of fiction.
Names, characters, places and incidents originate from the writer's imagination.
Any resemblance to actual persons, living or dead, is purely coincidental.

First Published in 2023

Olympia Publishers
Tallis House
2 Tallis Street
London
EC4Y 0AB

Printed in Great Britain

Dedication

For Bianca Korva, my getaway driver, and Bradly Parent, my bad hair day savior.

Acknowledgments

Thank you to my boyfriend Dylan for encouraging and helping me write this book.

CHAPTER 1

Ace, Krum, John, and Lewis followed the red-haired woman into the dining hall of Galdorwide's memorial. They took a seat, and a waiter arrived, pouring each of the Scaasi men a single cup of angelic delight. The waiter placed an extra two cups in front of the small woman. He began to pour lavish punch into each of the two glasses. She smiled, and the waiter walked to the following table.

"How are you alive?" Krum asked forwardly.

"Dad told us you died," John added. "That you killed yourself. He explained it all… pretty graphically."

"I did," she admitted, "but… my brother Daemon had taken precautions that if I were to die, it would only be temporarily; perks of Arcane magic, I suppose."

"Kind of like a resurrection spell?" her youngest son, Lewis, asked.

She tilted her head. "*Hmm*, sort of. Each time I die, my aging is slowed. When I return, it's like my body ages as a newborn's would."

"So you were reborn?" Ace asked.

"Nope, I remain in my adult body, but I don't age as quickly. The more I die, the longer it takes for me to age. With that being said, as much as I love my youthful glow, I'm hoping that I never experience death again, which is why I've returned to Galdorwide. The death you are all aware of, where I committed suicide, has not been my latest death. I felt like it was time to return home… to my children."

"Over twenty years later," Ace reminded her. "Why now?"

Their mother, Aisley, threw her head back as she knew that her boys were not taking her simplified explanations so well. "Years ago, your father had put a binding spell on me. He knew the aspects of my magic, how I didn't stay dead. He did whatever he could to make me less powerful, to tame me, even if that meant killing me every once in a while. So I got away, ran away with a man, who turned out to be similar to your father – not as bad but still a slag breath. I have returned to visit my sons as well as mourn the death of my sixth child: Mark."

"Wait—wait... Mark? Mark Bisterne?" Krum asked with disbelief. "That scrawny uncanny guy was our half-brother?"

She nodded. "Mark was more like you than you know. Anyway, I can't stay here long unless I have protection."

"You have us," John said, sincerely. "You also have your brother Daemon. He's still youthful. He looks to be about your body's age. Plus, his friends still talk about you as if you had died yesterday. We could have protected you... all along."

"I didn't want to come so forward about you guys helping me when you were younger. I didn't want to be a burden."

"You wouldn't have been a burden – and you could've come with me when I ran away. Why didn't you at least tell me?" Krum asked.

"I-I don't know... I was a mess. I was worried about my own shadow back then. But I'm stronger now if you guys do decide to help me. I can help you with whatever you need."

"We don't need a promise of your help to help you," Krum said sincerely. "We're men now, and we've faced many beasts before."

"But there's one thing... none of us have successfully conquered, so I'm still worried." She took a sip of her drink with a shaky hand.

"And what's that?"

"Your father."

A war cry came from the entrance of the dining hall. They looked over to see a tall, athletic, blond-haired and blue-eyed seventy-two-year-old man wearing a pinstriped suit. The man running jumped up onto Alizeh's family's table and attacked her uncle, throwing himself and the man onto the floor. Krum stood up, throwing the napkin that had been on his lap onto the table so that he could watch on and see if he would have to intervene.

"What's that about?" John looked at his mother.

"That is your father attacking my ex from high school. It looks like some things never change. Tell me, has your father remarried?"

A lanky man in his upper sixties broke up the fight. He had dark, spiky black hair and blue eyes. He had grabbed Tony Scaasi from off of Eric Nguyen before whispering into his ear. Tony's eyes traveled to where his ex-wife sat. The man turned to look at her as well. They both smirked.

"We best get going." Aisley threw her glasses back on. She reached to the floor where her purse and umbrella sat.

Krum put out his hand to halt her from standing up. "Who's that guy?"

"Mark's father. The man I divorced eight months ago. How about we go visit Daemon?"

The Scaasi brothers grabbed their belongings and headed out with her. Before they could exit, Krum stopped them. He ran back into the dining hall and returned with Benjamin Black, boyfriend of Queen Bella Carter. They then proceeded to walk out of the memorial dining hall onto the sidewalk browned from the rain. Aisley lifted her umbrella and opened it. The umbrella stretched out long enough to shield her, her sons, and their friends as they walked.

"So, who's your friend?" she asked.

"I'm Benjamin Black."

"Well, Mr. Black, it's a pleasure to meet you. I'm Aisley Soleil. As you probably couldn't tell, I am the woman who birthed these men."

"I would never have guessed." He smiled. "But I do remember you from back when I was in high school. I was in my final year when Lewis was starting his first year."

It was a long journey, but they had finally arrived at the isolated school of Arcane Magic. They strolled up to a high chest gate. Beside it, there was a wooden sign that read:

Python Seger School of Arcane Magic
New members and walk-ins are welcome.

Behind the gate was a blue house-like building that had a red rooftop. On top of the roof were two points where gargoyle statues sat. Two wooden steps led up to a porch near the left of the house that stretched to the building's front entrance – arched and circular white windows were located on all three floors. Three deadened, twisted trees sat on the property. The rain began to fall harder as lightning began to strike. The sky became a mix of blue and black.

The gates creaked open upon their arrival. As they walked up onto the porch, they took note of the vampire molds on the four corners of the doors. The door squeaked open slightly, and a disembodied hand with long, pale nails motioned them inside. Spiderwebs hung from the entryway. Inside the building, the floor was tiled with black and white squares. A pillar stood beside the doorway where a statued bat sat upon a crystal ball. Bats were carved along the bottom of the stone walls. Along the far wall were five suits of armor. The armor was similar to that of the royals, except the purple trimming was black.

A tall, averagely built man with a graying blond beard walked into what appeared to be the school's training room. Around his head, he wore a pale blue headband.

"No – it can't be." His jaw dropped, and he spoke with a gritty voice.

Aisley didn't recognize the man's face, but she'd recognize that voice anywhere – her brother's friend, Aaron Silvermaul.

Behind the man stood another pillar where a statue of a vampire bust was placed. Beneath it was a plaque that read: *Tassos Rudd the Famine of the Galdorwide Crossroads.* Spiderwebs hung from the ceiling to the midline of the walls, statues, and door frames.

"Please tell me you plan on staying here. We have extra rooms available. Ais – oh my Merlin, it's been too long." The man walked up and hugged the girl whom he had spent all of his high school years helping Daemon protect, as she had a knack for getting into trouble. They could hear a wolf howling in the distance.

Suddenly, the door opened. A tall, averagely built boy who looked to be in his mid-twenties walked in. He had strawberry blond hair and blue eyes.

"I don't know." She pulled away from her old friend's embrace. "I don't even know if I'm staying in Galdorwide. I was hoping Tony would be dead by now."

A bat flew in from the window. Before they knew it, it had transformed into a young boy. He was tall, of average build, with deep dark brown eyes. He looked to be in his mid-teens.

Aaron turned to the boys. His eyes focused on the young vampire. "It's about time. Water was getting in." He groaned as he walked over to shut the window. "Go upstairs and make yourselves presentable. We have guests."

The two boys nodded. Before the red-haired boy could walk up the stairs, Aaron grabbed hold of his arm and brought him to Aisley. "Aisley, this is Coby; Coby, meet Aisley."

Coby's blue eyes widened. He looked at Aaron. "You mean this is Aunt Aisley?" Aaron nodded. Coby turned to his aunt. He went for a hug until he realized that his gray V-neck sweater was drenched and muddy. He extended his hand for her to shake. The woman smiled and embraced her nephew, who was much taller than she was.

"And you're staying." Aaron narrowed his eyes with a smile. "That's final. Anyway, I want you to meet the gang. I'll start with my children. Here's one of them now." He looked over to the stairway where a tall boy with curly red hair and green eyes walked down. The boy who looked to be in his early twenties wiped his tired eyes.

"What's going on?"

"It's about time you woke up! It's dinner time. You'd think that you were a vampire. Anyway, you know the Scaasi brothers; this is their mother, Aisley!"

"Man! Really! Wow, Aisley! It's fantastic to meet you finally! I'm Chris, anyway, before I continue and converse with all you people" – he looked to the Scaasi brothers and Ben – "I'm going to make myself a cup of caffeine quake. Does anyone want some?" The men shook their heads politely.

"You bet!" Aisley smiled. Her eyes widened. Chris winked and headed through the doorway that branched off just behind the stairs.

"Stephen! Brad!" Aaron called. "Come down here! There's someone I want you to meet."

Stephen was the first to come down. He was averagely built with long, blond hair and looked to be in his upper teens.

"Stephen, this is Aisley Soleil, Daemon's sister," Aaron presented the red-haired woman.

"Hello!" he said with a wide smile.

Brad followed shortly after Stephen. They were almost identical, except Brad looked more mature. "Hi, I'm Brad," he introduced himself as he pointed to his chest with his thumb. All three of Aaron's children had his delicate round-faced features and cleft chins.

"You guys must be tired. It's been a long day. Let's head to the kitchen." Aaron motioned them over.

The kitchen was extensive, with an oak wood table long enough to seat twenty people. The chairs had unicorn hair as cushioning. The backs were wooden with carvings of unicorns and trees. Chris was standing by the counter, pouring two mugs of caffeine quake. To the right were a dishwasher, stove, and fridge. Near all the appliances was a grand piano where a teen girl with short, blonde hair played. If Aisley hadn't noticed the girl's breasts and soft facial features, she would've thought that this was another boy. She wore a black vest, a white tank top, and baggy jeans. On her hands were red leather gloves with their fingers cut off. On her head was a pair of black shades. She turned around after hearing the rustling of feet.

"Mamie, this is your Aunt Aisley. Aisley, this is your brother's daughter Mamie," Aaron introduced.

The girl stood up. Her mouth was agape. "Wow – it's you! My father had told me bedtime stories about you! You're one of my heroes." The girl approached her aunt in awe.

"It's very nice to meet you, Mamie. You're a very talented girl. Music was never one of my strong suits. I wish I could play the piano as you do," Aisley complimented the star-struck girl. Mamie blushed.

They all sat around the table when a handsome brown-haired teenage boy walked in; this was Ken. Chris yawned.

"Sorry, we woke you." Aaron rolled his eyes. He then looked to Ken. "Aisley, this is your brother's youngest, Ken. So, now you've met all of our residential students."

"Are these the new teachers?" Ken asked innocently.

"No, you've met these boys before. They're your cousins: Ace, Krum, John, and Lewis. And this is their mother, your aunt, Aisley," Aaron explained. "And of course, Lord Benjamin Black."

"Oh, sweet." The right corner of his mouth raised into a smile. He joined his friends and family at the table. The front entrance door creaked open.

"Horus!" A deep, groggy, breathy voice boomed from the other room.

Light steps patted quickly down the staircase. Two men entered the kitchen. One was the boy who had made his entrance as a bat just a half-hour ago. The man who accompanied him was almost as tall as the door's frame. He had pale skin. Aisley could see red veins extending from his face's edges. He had pale blue eyes that almost looked white with long, black hair down to his shoulder. He wore a black velvet trench coat and a black pinstripe suit; Tassos Rudd, the vampire whose statue was out in the training room beside the suits of armor.

Aisley's eyes widened, her heart fluttered. When her eyes met his, she panicked, knocking her cup of caffeine quake over. The liquid spilled down onto her lap. Aaron immediately got up and reached for all the napkins that had been placed out. Chris had picked up the mug and brought it over to the counter so that he could refill her drink.

The man smiled, walked over to the delicate, trembling lady. He lifted her hand and kissed it. Her sons tensed as they realized who this man was – the head vampire. They had never met him before, but they had seen memorials and pictures of him in the newspaper. He comes from the only bloodline where vampires are birthed. They assumed that the young boy beside him was his next of kin.

Krum had brought Ben on this journey as he remembered that his uncle's friend, Michael Tuskroar, was a vampire, but he hadn't known that the head vampire, who had been the one to turn Ben, would be making an appearance.

"It's a pleasure to meet you." Aisley bowed her head as Aaron began to pat her lap dry. Any girl would have been embarrassed in a situation like this, but Aisley had lived long enough to know by now that life was too short to get hung up on the little things, especially as a true legend stands before you.

"The pleasure's mine." The man smiled as he released her hand and took the empty chair beside the red-haired woman. At the end of the table, this specific chair had a higher backing with a vampire bat's brass face. Next to the face were two arches of wood that had been carved to look like bat wings.

Ben sniffed and straightened, clearing his throat. He squeezed his eyes shut, then glanced around the room. Ben furrowed his brow then shook his arms out. He quickly headed down a corridor and turned to the first door on the right, a bathroom. His movements slowed, his legs began to tremble. He brought a hand to his chest and straightened himself again. "Oh, no. No, no, no, no. No. *Mmm.*" He tilted his head and closed his eyes. "Ten," he exhaled. "Nine," he exhaled. "Eight." He opened his eyes. "Sev—" His right leg began to shake. He rubbed his eyes. "*Um*—" Ben felt around in his pockets. He moved to the mirror, his breath shaking rapidly. He pulled out his wand. "Okay, okay… it's okay." His breath trembled. He raised his wand to his head. He began to wiggle his fingers. "Breathe, just breathe."

Behind him, Mamie entered. She slowed.

"Mary? Mary, please call me back. I think it's… *Uhm.* I think it's happening again." He sniffled and panted. He put down his wand.

The teenage girl gently touched Ben's back. She lowered the toilet seat. "Hey. Hey. Hey, come on, sit down. Sit."

Ben sat. She took a seat across from him on the ledge of the bathtub. "I know what's fun. Naming the most annoying people we've met, *huh*? You go first," she encouraged.

Ben, shiny-eyed, took a gasping breath as he scanned the floor.

"Come on, it's easy, *huh*? Everybody is annoying, right?"

"*Uhm.*" He dipped his head and nodded. He sniffled. "*Um...* Lat... *Mmm.* My friend's pup, Latte, does that count?"

"Yeah. Weirdo. Who else?"

"*Um...* my girlfriend – my girlfriend. She drinks with her pinky out."

"I'm sure that's not the only annoying thing she does." She chuckled. "I hate my boyfriend sometimes."

"And, *uh...* and Adelaide. She never stops calling her boyfriend 'honey.'"

"Honey is a horrible nickname. It makes everything sticky. Tell me another thing that annoys you about your girlfriend." She chuckled. "I know you want to. If not, can I tell you a story? I slipped on ice in front of my class on a trip – I was in my last year at Galdorwide Training School. Everyone laughed, including my elderly teacher. I needed sixteen stitches." She pointed to a scar down the length of her arm. Ben chuckled with a smile. "There it is, there it is, good." She smiled. Ben exhaled deeply. "There you go." She patted his knee. "There you go, okay? You got this. Just keep taking deep breaths."

Ben nodded and closed his eyes. Mamie got up. She glanced toward Ben, who sat up and placed a hand on his forehead. Ben wiggled his fingers and opened his eyes. He looked at the girl then wiped tear stains from his cheek. "*Um...* How did you know?"

The girl leaned against the sink and faced him. "My dad has panic attacks."

Ben raised his eyebrows. "Oh."

"If that's what happened here, *huh*? Unless you're always looking to get attention from women in the washroom."

Ben grinned with a chuckle. His wand began to vibrate. He answered it as the girl stepped aside.

"Hey, Mary. No. No, I'm okay. Really. I promise. *Mm-hmm.* Yeah, I got help from a friend." Ben cleared his throat. The girl glanced toward him. "Okay, I don't know when I'll come by, but hopefully soon. Yeah, I love you too. Okay, bye," Ben put down his wand.

Mamie leaned on the sink. "*Huh.* You called me a friend."

Ben smiled. "It's just faster than saying the girl who slipped on ice on her field trip."

Mamie smiled back.

***

"Dad's here." Coby's eyes widened.

"How do you know?" Aisley asked.

"I can hear him." His ears perked.

Daemon's eldest child ran to the training room and peeked out the window to see Michael Tuskroar shielding his father with the wing of his green cloak from the rain. Coby furrowed his brows. He began to think of how soft the four men who raised him were becoming. As they walked up the porch, Coby began to brainstorm what he would say about his sister being here. Before he could say anything after they entered, he noticed his father's face drained. He could see Daemon's body rocking to his heartbeats.

Coby turned to see where his father was staring. It was at Aisley. She stared almost in awe and was not sure what else to do. She swirled her mug in her hand. She took a sip after the awkwardness in the room began to make her sweat. Michael clanked the door behind them, also unsure what to do. He, too, had known Aisley; they had gone to the same high school, and though he'd never tell anyone, he once had a crush on her.

"Aisley?" Daemon asked in a clear tone.

"Congratulations," Aisley began confidently. "Your spell of keeping me alive has saved me from more deaths than I can count." Daemon took a step closer to better look at the woman who looked the same as he remembered. "You did what you promised you'd do – protect me."

His eyes widened. It was Aisley! The sound of his heavy pants filled the silence between the voices.

"I'm back home. Back where I belong. Everyone believed I was dead. I'm surprised you believed it too. I mean, your golden locks should've been replaced with gray ones. It's the law of nature. We're twins; we age together and die together. They no longer saw you as a threat. They thought your courageous, fearless spirit died with me," Aisley continued.

Daemon was shaking in his shoes as he held back tears.

"Tony and many others tried killing me. They thought they got what they always wanted, but now they'll see, our reign has only just begun." She embraced her brother, whom she had been far away from for far too long.

***

For the billionth time, an argument during breakfast had broken out between Ace and his patients later that morning. Ace was furious after being kept awake all night by Spencer's cries. Her bedroom was located right beneath his. The vent made it sound as if his weeping niece had been in the room with him. He often had his son, Eion, use a spell to sound proof the basement when guests were over; however, at night he liked to hear his patients.

"That's the third night this week that you've kept me up." Ace's voice boomed as he handed each of his seven patients plates of beautifully displayed eggs, oysters, and crayfish. "Your crying will have to stop eventually. It's only going to make your condition worse and keep you here longer."

Spencer opened her mouth to explain. "I'm bored. I hate it here. We can't even step outside for fresh air. You just lock us in your basement and let us out for meals!"

"Are you questioning my methods?" He managed to sound both professional and intimidating. He snarled, allowing the eggs he scooped up with his fork to fall back onto his plate. "None of you can go outside until you're fully healed. We can't impose any threats to your health. You get your monthly shopping trips if I think you're healthy enough."

He shot a dark look to his three children – Eion, Abigail, and Freyja. Spencer had never met the two girls, and before becoming her uncle's patient, she had never known that they had existed. Eion was now sixteen, Abigail twenty-one, and Freyja nineteen. Eion didn't talk much. He had lost most of his mental and physical abilities back when he had been injured playing Crash Ring back in high school. Spencer didn't see much of Eion, but their paths would cross at a Scaasi family get-together. The girls would've been old enough to go to these events, but Ace claims they were too sick to leave the house. There wasn't much resemblance between Eion and his sisters. He had blue eyes like Freyja and dark-brown hair like

Abigail. However, Abigail had brown eyes, and Freyja had short, black hair. Spencer had never met her cousins' mother, and neither had her father, Ace's brother, John.

Spencer tried to argue back. She didn't believe that being locked up was the best cure for them. Before she could say anything, a loud belch came from Lena Baxter. She was a patient of Ace's who had been there before Spencer's arrival almost one year ago. Lena was quite odd with big, brown expressive eyes and exotic features. She was slim with dark brown hair.

"Did you make any bacon today, Doc?" Lena asked.

Spencer looked down to the girl's plate. Lena had already finished the food before Spencer had even taken a bite.

Ace's dark face turned admirable as he looked from his children over to Lena. He smiled. "I made some just for you, on top of the stove." His eyes turned misty. "I'm glad to see you're eating. You grow more beautiful each time you do."

"Bullspit." Spencer pushed her plate away from her. "You think that compliments from you are going to make me cured like her?"

Ace grinned. "You're right, Spence. Why don't you get some more needless workouts in and fetch Lena's bacon?"

"What's the *magic* word?" Spencer asked as she folded her arms.

Ace did not allow magical use, and the *m* word had seemed to become a curse word. The only times they were allowed to conduct magic were if Ace had been testing them to see their magical progressions and limitations or if he were instructing his children to handle something he could not without magic.

The effect on everyone present in the room was incredible. How in Galdorwide were these once-powerful witches allowing this man to have such control over them to the point their magic had become more of a curse? Ace had backed away so quickly, he had almost knocked over himself and his chair onto the floor. Lena looked over to Ace. Her wide eyes had nearly doubled in size. She smirked, hoping Ace would give Spencer what she deserved. The veins on Ace's temples throbbed.

"We all can relax." Spencer laughed. "We were all taught at a young age that the most powerful, polite word in all of Galdorwide is *please*."

"I don't care what you meant!" Ace boomed. "I had made it specifically clear to all of you that the *m* word must not be used under this roof!"

Ace had an earthshaking, frightening yelling voice. It lowered Spencer's confidence, and she didn't know why, but she began to hold back tears.

"I warned you, again and again, Miss Scaasi, and I have had enough of your rebellious behavior!" Ace pounded the table with his fist, spit sprayed from out of his mouth.

Spencer looked around the room. Everyone looked just about as scared for her as she was – except for Lena, who wore a giant smirk on her face. "I'm sorry," she mumbled.

Ever since Spencer had arrived in Ace's home care, Ace had been threatening her. It was as if he and Olly had switched their shoes for the time being. It was all because she was his brother's daughter. However, her father had always been a kind, gentle, caring man and had no idea why his older brother Ace would have ill feelings toward him and her. She knew that she was different from her father. Her mother had made that very clear. Her mother would often scream at her during a fight and say, 'You're a bad-blooded Scaasi!' It wasn't like Spencer was outrageously rebellious or dangerous. She just had a temper common to teen girls, especially those who were food-deprived.

Spencer was a Scaasi – a Scaasi who was more evil than good. Spencer imagined that even if she were to go back home, her mother would be unhappy, and honestly, Spencer could say that she had those same ill feelings for her mom. She wanted to be back home with her dad, who would tell courageous, uplifting stories, and her twin brother John Jr., who would lighten any situation up with a joke, even if that meant annoying her every so often. Of course, as bratty as her three little sisters were, she missed spending time with them and playing some of the strangest games with them.

Spencer missed home so much, she had constant aching pains in her stomach, and it wasn't from the lack of food. She missed her family, she even missed attending school, she missed receiving letters from Tris, she also missed her mother's home-cooked treats, she missed sleeping in her real bed (despite how similar the one here was meant to be), she missed going to the café with Tris. Spencer missed her mischievous nights with her two cousins Aldaricus and Caden. Spencer longed to train for Crash Ring with her cousins finally. The most dangerous sport ever allowed to be played on the school's ground, with two teams floating on a spiraling ring with their brooms as they cast spells on the opposing team.

Ace had locked Spencer's and the other patient's magical belongings up in the crawl space of an attic of his home. Their wands, brooms, spellbooks, and cauldrons had all been confiscated upon arrival. Ace didn't care about his patient's skills or grades, for that matter. Spencer was the only student, and no matter how much she insisted on needing her items to practice and study, he denied. Upon release, she'd return to school with none of the homework done. Spencer feared that if she missed out on any more reading, she'd be held back another grade. Her Uncle Ace was a Nullum, born from a witching family but born without a drop of magic in his blood. Unfortunately for Ace, this meant that he was a disappointment to his family. Luckily, his son Eion and his two daughters were gifted with magical abilities, despite their mother being a Heofsij. During her stay, Spencer's familiar had arrived. She had never known what her familiar was, but she was excited to learn that it was a raven; this meant that she was an imaginative, observant, and philosophical witch. It also indicated that she enjoyed complex ideas and was often daydreaming, finding wonder in the stars. Overall, one would say that a witch with a raven familiar is a talented one. Unfortunately, Spencer didn't spend much time with her feathery friend as Ace had locked the bird up in the cage and had a separate room in the basement where the familiars were locked away.

Spencer looked over to Freyja, whom she felt closest to in this institution.

Freyja was unlike her siblings. She was quiet and shy and didn't feel much like a Scaasi at all. New guests often confused her as a male. Hence, another reason why she didn't feel like the typical Scaasi woman. Sure, she was hot-headed and witty, but she was humble and would mark the first Scaasi woman ever to be a lesbian; this, of course, was something she kept to herself. Not even Spencer knew of this secret.

It was her sexuality that made her different from the rest of the Scaasi family. She had hinted it to her father, expecting that him, being a Nullum, would understand being a not-so-typical Scaasi. However, with the mention of her being attracted to the same sex, he grew a temper.

Upon meeting Freyja on the first day, Spencer noticed a scar going down Freyja's left eyebrow. Considering that they had spent a lot of time together, they had grown very close, and Freyja later revealed that it was from Ace drilling into her skull during one of his experiments. Freyja grimaced and held back tears as she spoke. Ace had lied about the scar, saying that she had fallen off her bed when she was younger, bumping her head off her nightstand.

She had only been a year old, and she couldn't remember, but Abigail had explained the event to her. At one point, Abigail wasn't so sure that she'd live through the procedure, and sometimes she wished that she hadn't. Abigail recounted her father taking a sliver of tissue from the toddler's brain, comparing it with his own. Adam, the first non-familial patient, had been asked to do the same to Ace. Being new to Ace's world of science, Adam didn't question it, but now, he would do anything to go back and drill further into the doctor's skull a year later. After almost twenty years, Ace was finally able to compare the brain cells. The test had ultimately failed when he saw no difference between a witch's brain and a Nullum's.

Freyja and Abigail had lived a life hidden from the rest of the world. They were raised in a basement and were only allowed upstairs for mealtimes. They had spent their whole lives in a basement, never understanding why they couldn't go out to play or go to school like Eion.

And, exactly one year ago, Eion had been hurt at school playing a game of Crash Ring. Only the apparent damages were temporary. Ace had convinced Eion that he was still too ill to go out into the real world. But, now, almost everyone – except for Lena – was getting sick and tired of his lies. Eion craved the summer's sunlight on his skin and wanted to go back to his everyday life where he wasn't treated as a lab rat. He missed going to the lake by the school, its water would glow a bright blue where he would sit on the neon grass.

Today was Eion's birthday. Everyone had seemed to remember except for his father. His hopes were high, only for them to be crushed, and he thought back to last year when his hopes had also been destroyed. He swore never to expect anything nice from his father now that he was just like all of the other witches under the roof.

Just as all their thoughts had wandered, especially onto Eion, who had not touched a single crumb on his plate, Ace cleared his throat and said, "Now, as we all know, today is an extraordinary day." They all looked to Ace eager-eyed, hoping that he had finally remembered his poor son's birthday. "This day could very well be the day I find out how I – a Nullum – can become a witch."

They all looked back to their plates, fearing who would be today's test subject. Every morning, Ace would say that *today is the day!* As if believing in it would make it come true. The patients' thoughts immediately became bitter. They had almost forgotten that three new patients were coming in. Two anorexics and one patient with a broken leg and neck. Anorexics were Ace's favorite patients as their illness was mental, and their stay here could be as prolonged as he wanted without drawing any suspicions.

"We can't scare the new patients, so we must welcome them appropriately," Ace continued. The room was silent as if he had been alone in the room the whole time. "We will have spread out along the house. Abigail, you will stay out here in the living room, lounging on the couch. Lena, you will be my main greeter." He winked. Lena blushed.

"I'll take their coats," Robbie Black said in a lusciously sarcastic tone.

"Excellent!" Ace cheered. He believed that Robbie wanted to help cover up his lies.

As much as they hated the idea of covering up Ace's secret and luring the three patients, they knew that they couldn't trust Ace. They feared what he might do if he caught them doing something out of line. They had no magic and no defense. Ace had his frightening scientific tools and a black belt of a Heofsij martial art called Karate.

His smile faded as he turned to Spencer, the most rebellious of the group. "I suggest you stay in your room. We will tell them that you were fatigued and needed a nap. Understood?" Spencer nodded. "Great. After Robbie takes their coats, I will lead them through the house and introduce you to each of them. We will all enjoy the night, welcoming the guests, drinking wine, and feasting on an array of desserts. When the night is done, you will all go to your rooms, and I will lead them to the laboratory. Understood?" The rest of his patients nodded. "Oh! What a perfect little family we have here," the mad doctor mused. "The three guests are girls. Abigail and Freyja, I'd like you to make friends with them. We want them to have a perfect evening."

"I don't know how to make friends," Freyja quietly rebutted as she smirked at Spencer. Luckily, the girl's soft voice went under her father's ears.

"We also can't have any awkwardness or suspicions, so that may even include you guys throwing in a few compliments toward your doctor," Ace continued brewing his plan.

"I'll tell them you're my hero," Robbie said lusciously.

That earned the twenty-five-year-old a pat on the head. Spencer snorted before holding in her laugh. She covered her mouth and pretended that she had briefly choked on a piece of food. She and Robbie had grown close considering their relatedness, and she knew for a fact that Robbie hated Ace just as much as she had.

Ace turned to Spencer. "Are you all right?" he asked sincerely.

She turned, trying to keep a straight face. She nodded before making an 'okay' sign with her hand. "Throughout the night, can I come up for a cup of caffeine quake?"

"You will do no such thing! Do that, and I promise it'll be you whose head will be drilled into."

Robbie and Eion tensed, Freyja's face reddened. "I'll bring it to her," Robbie said calmly, patting his hand down as if telling Spencer to relax and that she was safe as long as he was there. "Ten?"

Spencer stifled a smile and nodded. "Triple triple."

"Good, getting some sugar and calories in you." Ace took another bite of his food and smiled, proud of the young girl.

"Black." She changed her mind.

Robbie grimaced and inhaled deeply. He'd do anything to get Spencer out of Ace's care because then maybe she'd get better.

Ace rolled his eyes. "If you keep this up, you'll never leave." Spencer bit her tongue.

Lena batted her eyes. "So, Ace, the first of the month is coming up. Does that mean shopping day?"

Ace nodded. Spencer didn't allow herself to get too excited. Last month, she was not allowed to join, and that was when he liked her a smidge better.

"We can go tonight, get some outfits for tonight's dinner. Spencer, you will stay here. I'll give Robbie the task of buying you new clothes." He turned to Robbie.

"Oh, Merlin!" Spencer couldn't help but laugh.

Last month, Robbie had returned with a raven-feathered trench coat, assuring her that no ravens had been harmed in its making. He had also grabbed her a lengthy, black leather skirt, a tied dyed tank top, and a pair of black leather tights that had cut-outs along its sides.

"Child's section will do best. That tank top you got her last year is far too baggy."

Spencer was wearing that shirt. She grew increasingly self-conscious as everyone looked at her shirt as if it wasn't already eye-catching enough.

The group left through the back door that afternoon. It was a bright, sunny day. Everyone spun around, delightedly, as it was the first time the sun had kissed their skin in a month. They passed the backyard's glowing green lawn. Past the garden was a lovely black bench.

Robbie slowed his pace to stand next to Eion, whom he had never seen so sad besides his last birthday. "Cheer up, it's your b-day. I asked Spencer, and she said I could use some of the money for her clothes to get you a gift. You're out on your birthday." Robbie widened his arms. "What more could you want?"

Eion shrugged. He thought of thousands of other things he'd want. Like birthday cards from friends, a pile of gifts he'd typically receive from his family and friends at his birthday party. And here he was spending it on a shopping spree that would happen once a month. Sure, it was a special day, but it wasn't *his* special day. He never cared much for his birthdays until he stopped getting them. He'd never felt so lonely on his birthdays. He wished never to obtain them again. All they brought him was misery. He gazed miserably as the bright sunlight's rays pierced his eyes. They began to water. He couldn't tell whether it was from the pain that was being emitted into his eyes or from the depression his father had diagnosed him with just a few months ago. He missed the freedom he once had in the house that was now a prison. He missed playing Crash Ring. He missed his friends Clancy Scaasi and Nicholas Snowball. They, however, hadn't seemed to be missing him at all. Not once had they written or visited him after his accident, even though Clancy said he'd stay overnight if he wanted company knowing that he wouldn't be able to leave the house for a while.

Countless times, Eion, Robbie, and Spencer tried unlocking the attic crawlspace to open all their familiars and magical items, but all times had been an utter failure with damning consequences. Ace had zero tolerance for any actions that were out of his order. Eion hadn't told the others, but he was sure he found a foolproof way to get into the crawl space. He wanted to give the plan further thought before getting his friends' hopes up. Eion had to admit there was a time when he liked the isolation. He hated school, and his part-time job as a servant at the castle. Bella, for some reason, had taken a liking to him despite his Scaasi/Nullum father. Eventually, his father's tests and the silence before the new guests had arrived became overwhelming. He felt so cut off from reality, and his father always put him down and babied him as if he had permanent brain damage. For a while, Eion believed this.

He would do anything for a relative to stumble upon him in the store and realize that he wasn't a vegetable as his father had proclaimed. He would do anything for someone to find them locked away in his father's basement. He would do anything to be back at school and work, even if that meant cleaning the queen's shoes and vouching for all of her desires.

He'd miss his father, strangely, but he always dreamt of being saved by someone, anyone who would take him from out of his father's home and into a safe and free one. Eion had once had things going for him before his accident. After coming face-to-face with the terrifying, cunning, powerful king, he stood up for the queen he was wrongfully harming. Eion knew that he couldn't overpower the king, but he also knew that he couldn't stand by and watch, even if that meant his death. Eion had been able to slip through the king's clutch. It was a narrow escape, and he feared that at his next shift, the king would end him. However, that next shift never came as the following morning was his accident. Even now, he still woke up in the cold, drenched sweat, worrying about the king, especially after the blood moon. His father explained that the king and his followers were back. He could still see the king's livid, mad face, and he could only imagine what fear the ghost of the king would bring him. During bouts of sleep paralysis, he could see the king staring at him from the corner of the room before approaching him and pulling his long, brown curly hair from off of his scalp, or so it felt.

Before walking entirely off of his backyard lawn, Eion could've sworn that he saw someone in the bushes. The teenager lifted his fingers to his lips as if to hush Eion. Eion squinted. The teenager looked eerily like his cousin, Aldaricus.

"Listen," Robbie walked back after noticing that Eion had stopped following him. "All that matters is that we know what day it is." Robbie placed his arm over his friend's shoulders, breaking him out of his trance. He led him over so that they could continue following the group. Eion looked back only to see that Aldaricus was out of sight.

"What?" Eion asked as he had been transfixed on what looked like his cousin to hear him.

"It's your birthday!" Robbie reminded him for about the ninth time that day. "Maybe we'll bring it up tonight, at the dinner with the new girls. Maybe they're cute. Oh and before I forget," he reached into his pocket and pulled out an envelope. "It's nothing much, just something I was able to make with what Ace allowed me to keep in my room. Boy, does that man have trust issues."

"Well, you've tried to break out twenty-eight times – I counted." Eion laughed as he took the card from the man whom he considered his closest friend. "Not to mention that time you purposefully set off the fire alarm and tried to convince him to let you out even though he had been in his office watching you do the whole bit with the match near the alarm. Best not to try any more reckless acts until you think up a well-organized one. The more he trusts you, the more privilege you get. If anyone is to break out of this joint, it'd be Lena."

"Yeah, right, your father's got that girl so dickwhipped. I mean, what does she see in him besides his tall, athletic figure, deep raspy voice, or striking chiseled features… and who can forget about those big, almond-shaped hazel eyes."

"Now who's more dickwhipped, you or her?" Eion laughed.

Robbie looked away nonchalantly and lifted his black leather tights. Eion knew Robbie had a crush on his father as he didn't care to deny it. However, he did not care how attractive Ace was. Robbie knew he needed to escape.

"What were you staring at back there, mister?" Robbie asked, dramatically changing the subject.

"Just daydreaming, I guess," Eion lied. He didn't want to risk getting up Robbie's hopes because he knew that Robbie would hope for the same as him, that they were there to unlock Spencer, who would later reveal to the kingdom the truth behind Ace's wooden walls.

"What's stopping us from running away right now?" Robbie asked as they crossed the street. He took note of Ace in the lead. He wouldn't notice if they ran off.

"You do know you've tried that before? Or did he give you too much brain damage after the incident?"

Robbie rubbed his head. "I did?" Eion laughed.

Ace looked over his shoulder, taking note of the two boys at the back who kept whispering to one another before laughing aloud.

"Should I try it again?" Robbie asked.

"What? No—" Before Eion could object further, Robbie stepped away from Eion to show that he was not a part of what would take place next.

"HELP! HELP!" Robbie howled. He started to run back where he had come from to get as far from Ace as possible. He tripped over his own feet. "HELP! ACE HAS BEEN MOLESTING US!" Robbie lied.

As you could guess, Robbie paid enormously for what he had done. Any onlookers were charmed by Ace explaining how Robbie was a previous drug user and mentally ill – all correct. However, because of this, they believed that Robbie had gotten confused or hallucinated; this became even more valid as Ace had his fellow patients, especially Lena, tell anyone concerned how great of a doctor Ace was.

As they approached the backyard's lawn, Ace grabbed hold of Robbie's arm, squeezing it as he speedily walked into the house and threw him into the kitchen, against the fridge. Ace turned to the stove and picked up the pan that still had leftover bacon sitting in it. He raised it before blowing it across Robbie's head. Chunks of bacon fat became entangled in his wild, curly hair. Ace gave Robbie the task of cleaning the house on his hands and knees before sending him downstairs, where he would spend the night alone with Spencer, with no dinner.

While all the other patients sat around waiting for the guests, Robbie had finished cooking kiwi surprise and licorice donuts as per Ace's request. He began to wash the windows. Robbie was then put out in the backyard with his foot chained to the far wall, where he would have to mow the lawn. Once finished, Ace went outside and supervised him as he cut the front yard. Robbie was then chained up in the backyard once more to trim and water the garden. He was also given black paint to touch up the garden's bench. The sun beat down on him, and he was beginning to regret wishing for the sun's touch. He'd do anything for a drink. Robbie knew that he shouldn't have tried even though he couldn't remember his failed attempt, but it was worth a shot. He'd sell his soul to Mania to be free from this place finally, so that chores and a frying pan to the face wouldn't seem so bad.

His back ached, and sweat dripped down his forehead as he tended to the garden. The sun was beginning to set, and he had never felt so exhausted. Ace began to call him in. Robbie mustered enough energy to rush into the shade of Ace's home, where a loud machine supplied air cooling on the Nullum's wall. Robbie had not finish his chores yet as Ace told him to bake a nutmeg pie and blueberry bonbons. Ace laid out all of his treats on the table like a buffet. He went to pick up two plates, one for him and Spencer, but Ace smacked his hand.

"Sweets aren't dinner," Robbie protested. "Plus, you're the one who wants Spencer to eat more."

"Yep, she's probably starved. You'll be the one to tell her that her one piece of candy and a cup of black caffeine quake is put on hold on the night for your actions."

"But—"

"Go downstairs!" the doctor snapped.

"Can I at least take a shower?"

Ace and the other patients had already been washed and placed in fancy dresses and suits.

"No! Downstairs!"

He walked out through the living room, passing all those who seemed excited to have a feast and a night unlocked. He opened the door that led to the basement and headed down. He had only reached the bottom of the stairs when the doorbell rang. Ace reopened the basement door and stared down at his two most rebellious patients. "Remember! You're ill and napping, so not a word!"

Despite Ace having his magical daughters place a soundproofing spell throughout the home, he was still worried about any possible sounds getting out. Robbie and Spencer tiptoed to her bedroom and closed the door. Robbie collapsed on the bed, and Spencer took a seat beside him. She gasped as a tall figure emerged from the dark corner of her room.

CHAPTER 2

Robbie sat up on the bed and immediately stood to his feet. In the dark room corner was a tall teenage boy with blue eyes and light brown hair. Spencer knew who it was – Tris Smith, her crush from Galdorwide High. Despite how pleased Spencer's eyes were, she was still startled by his presence. She and Robbie stared at him silently.

"Come on in!" they could hear Lena exclaim from upstairs.

Tris took another step closer. She now noticed that her friend, whom she had not seen in months, was sporting a mustache and goatee. He wore a jean button-up shirt and black jeans. Below his left knee, there was a hole in his pants, revealing scraped skin. She could see a little pinprick hole just above his right eyebrow.

"Hi," Spencer nervously said as he was acting quite peculiar and dazed.

"Hi, Spence." His head and eyes traveled around her room.

Spencer worried that this was an escape mission, and she feared Ace finding out. She patted her hand down as if to tell him to hush his voice to a whisper.

Tris obliged as he continued. "It's been a long time. It's nice to see you."

Spencer stifled a smile. She stood up, inching closer to her Uncle Robbie whose brow seemed to be placed in a permanent furrow for the time being. "What are you doing here?" she asked. She had a bad feeling but wanted to try and act as normal as possible.

"Same as you. I've been feeling ill lately," Tris said almost robotically.

"Oh… really?" Spencer asked slowly. "What's wrong?"

"Sedated chills. I haven't been myself lately. I feel as if I'm in a constant trance where all I want to do is sleep, and I always feel cold. May I?" Tris motioned to what would've been Lulia's bed, where a fluffy baby blue blanket sat.

Spencer nodded. Tris sat on the bed and wrapped the blanket over his shoulders as he shivered.

A loud ruckus of fake laughter sounded from upstairs. Spencer rolled her eyes.

"It's nice to see you." Spencer smiled after heaving a sigh of relief. She took a seat back on her bed. Robbie sprawled his exhausted body back onto the bed as well.

However, Tris didn't share a smile. Instead, it looked as if he was holding back tears. His eyes left Spencer's and traveled over to Robbie. "I didn't think you'd be the kind to fornicate during your hospitalization."

Spencer's eyebrows raised, and her mouth dropped in shock. Her eyebrows lowered to an angry furrow, and she gritted her teeth. "This is my uncle! Not that it is any of your business!"

The laughter from upstairs seemed to have come to a halt. "*Shh!*" Robbie sat up, placing a calming hand on Spencer's shoulder.

"I'm sorry," Tris apologized. "It's just I've been thinking about what it'd be like to see you again finally. I guess my mind wandered when I saw you two in here."

"I have never been so offended in my life!" Spencer yelled.

"*Shh!*" Robbie pleaded. He widened his eyes as he gave his niece a stern look.

Spencer began to weep. She looked at her uncle. "Where's my caffeine quake?" Her eyes darted to him, almost filled with hope to make her night somewhat better.

Robbie shook his head solemnly as his eye contact with her remained. "I tried escaping while we were out on our shopping trip. I failed miserably, and Ace punished me, making me do all his baking and chores. When I went to make a plate for us, he smacked my hand. I begged him, Spence. I did."

Spencer snapped out of her weeping and began to smack her uncle repeatedly on his chest. "How could you!"

"Don't—Spencer," Robbie fought to catch the girl's tiny wrists. He toppled over as Spencer continued to attack him.

Tris got up and pulled Spencer off of him. He pulled her up to her feet and held her tightly in his hands. She tried to fight out of his grip.

"I'm sorry," she said as she finally calmed herself. "I'm sorry. I can't control myself sometimes. Mix the survival instincts of a starving witch with the blood of a Scaasi, and you get a wild Spencer."

"I know." Robbie sat up slowly. He began to pat his hand where Spencer had once been seated. "Scaasis," Robbie snorted with a shake of his head as he attempted to lighten the tension.

Spencer smiled as Robbie wrapped his arm around her and gave her a little shake. She turned to Tris. "Does Ace know you're here? He didn't mention your arrival or a new patient with your illness."

Tris shuddered. "He does. I've been here for a few days now. I had been in his laboratory. He's finally going to make a room for me tonight."

"Did he hurt you?" Spencer asked, taking further note of his skidded knees, a hole above his eyebrow, as well as what looked to be a burn on the tip of his left ear.

"No," Tris said, almost humorously. "He's my doctor. Why would he? I'm here so that he can find a cure."

"We've been trying to escape, Tris…" she tried to explain.

"Escape?" Tris furrowed his brow. "Why would I escape?" he asked.

Both Spencer and Robbie stared at him in disbelief. "He said that I'd only be here for four weeks. His tests have been going well. All you need is to be cured, and he'll let you go home. One of my sisters, Regina, is being admitted upstairs and he said she'll be out in no time."

"Listen, kid. I've been here for six years. The year before that, I was in Skogen prison. I was treated much better there and was set free in a shorter amount of time." Robbie tried to show Tris how leaving this place wouldn't be as easy as he thought. "But, kid, if you do go free, you have to go home and tell them that we need help."

"Whatever you think is wrong with Ace, you're wrong," Tris tried convincing him. "He has saved my life." Tris placed a sincere hand on his own chest. Robbie felt his face grow hot. "Ace is one of the greatest people I know, and he's a Nullum. He's a skilled scientist, yet he is so humble and modest about his skill. You act as if he is Mania's incarnate."

"No one here likes Ace," Spencer tried to explain.

"Lena does," Tris said. "She sees what I see."

"Yeah, well, that girl," Robbie began, "belongs in the Clockwork Sanitarium. I know the Baxter family. I was in prison. They were all alcoholics! I wouldn't be surprised if that girl had vodka every morning in her orange juice. She used to be a harlot."

"And how do you know that?" Tris asked.

"Her procurer was my dealer."

"Dealer?"

"He used to sell me Haunted."

"The drug?"

"No, the house," Robbie replied sarcastically. "He was a good man, helped me fix my broom once during a deal. Anyway, we have our beliefs about Ace, and you have yours. But what have we missed in the outside world?"

"A lot," Tris snorted. "The ghost of the king returned, summoned dragons, and killed like half of his followers on purpose. There was a blood moon that day."

"We heard, but Ace didn't tell us much. Was anyone in our family harmed?" Spencer asked.

"Your Uncle Krum had been injured throughout the battle, but as you'd guess, he managed finely."

"What about the Black family?"

"All good," Tris reassured. Robbie leaned back on the bed as he heaved a sigh of relief. "Your father" – Tris looked to Spencer – "was pretty bold and valiant that day, along with your Uncle Krum. I mean, I'm sure they'll be legends. Especially Krum, I mean all the adventures he's been on, he should write a book. I'd love to read it, and I'm sure all of Galdorwide would. Once I'm out of here, I'd like to join the ministry, as my grandfather once was."

"That'd be a death wish." Robbie lifted himself onto his elbows. "Her father, Krum, and Ben are all crazy. I mean, why fight danger when others will do it for you? I mean by right, royals should have to, so why not just leave it to the queen and her knights?"

"Aren't you a royal?" Tris asked.

"Oh yeah, you're right." Robbie tilted his head as he recalled his Pure aura that'd make extravagant sparks, twirls, and streams of purple magical energy exit his wand during spell casting.

The three of them could hear the sound of cutlery getting passed around upstairs. Spencer and Robbie's stomach rumbled.

***

Gower approached Bella, who sat on her throne yelling orders at her servants as they began to prepare for the yearly royal feast where only ministry members and those of Pure aurae or those related to pure aurae could attend. Gower cleared his throat, trying to gain the queen's attention.

She waved her servants off as well as the choir, telling them to take a twenty-minute break so that they could leave her alone with her fellow ministry member.

"What is it, Gower?" She meant to be kind, but her words came out as if she were annoyed by his presence, a thing that happened to her tone of voice more often than not.

"*Uhm...* well... Your Majesty. I hate to be the bearer of bad news for the second time, but you see... my crystal ball has shown me yet another revelation," his voice stuttered and squeaked as he could tell the queen had already been having a less than an enjoyable day. "The kingdom may, once again, be in grave danger. The feast may have to be called off."

"Why?" Bella asked through gritted teeth as her green eyes widened.

"In my crystal ball, if I have seen correctly, the king is scheming up another terrible plot to bring a great tragedy to our kingdom."

Bella was about to rage until she saw her friend tremble. She calmed herself. "What did you see?"

"Terrible, terrible things," the red-haired man shook his head as he looked down to his feet.

This morning, while he held his crystal ball, maggots had crawled from out of it. He had gasped, dropping it, and that's when the visions flashed. Blood smeared the hands of a short, slim young girl with light brown eyes, women dressed in black hung from trees with ropes around their necks. In the background of the vision, he could hear distant, distorted screams. The young girl backed up into dangling feet. A bright, yellow light shone through the forest, and she could see that ropes bound the women's hands and feet. The tree in front of the young girl began to crackle. The tree's trunk thumped as the large, old tree cracked along its center, and the girl watched on as a shadow of a large being sheltered her from the yellow light. The young girl backed away from the unseen creature. It approached, crackling the leaves beneath it. The yellow light and the images disappeared from Gower's room. As he stood in the castle, he looked out to the old tree that could be seen outside the throne room's window.

"Are you sure it was my father?" she asked. Gower made a choking noise as he held in his sobs. He nodded. "All right," Bella said as she reached her tiny, pale hand for Gower's forearm. She rubbed it in an attempt to comfort the man whom she had never seen this saddened before. "You don't have to say any more. I understand. Can I know exactly who or what it is I have to worry about?"

Gower looked up. His eyes were shiny as he fought so hard to keep his tears from dripping down his cheeks. "The king, he will summon giant creatures. I heard him say that his final creature won't be so easily defeated in the vision. It will be impossible."

"Creatures," Bella repeated before looking to the throne room's door that sat twenty feet from her throne.

She felt utterly lost with the new information. She brought her fingers to her chin as she grew lost in thought. Her father was powerless, but with the help of his followers, it was as though he had never left. He had just switched from protecting the kingdom to trying to destroy it.

"I have faith." Gower nodded as he regained his strength. "You are the greatest ruler our kingdom has ever had. I know it even though not all may see through your child-like appearance but what the kingdom doesn't know is that the more they underestimate you, the more you can use that against them. Your father underestimates you the most of anyone." Gower smiled.

Bella's heart fluttered at his flattering. Maddox, the queen's right hand, entered the throne room. He turned to Gower and stared at him.

"Gower, can you give us a minute, please?" Bella turned to Gower and gave him a sweet smile, something she had never shown him before. Maddox's eyes followed the werewolf ministry member as he exited the room. He waited until he had seen the door shut before talking to the queen.

"It's Benjamin Black, Your Majesty. He has sent the message that he has gone away to take care of his new condition at an Arcane School called Python Seger, where he will be trained by the head vampire himself on how to control his impulses."

Bella gritted her teeth. "Why couldn't he tell me this news himself?"

"It was a spur of the moment, he claims. He says you can visit anytime."

With that, Bella hopped off the black, metal throne and began to stomp out to the room where Gower had been waiting. She sighed. After standing still for a moment outside of the throne room's door, she noticed that her body was shaking. Bella couldn't tell if it was the news of her father or her boyfriend.

"I need to get out of here," said Bella, exasperated. "Maybe we should hold a ministry meeting and tell them of the news if you are up for it." They shuffled out of the large castle with a nod as Bella alerted Gower that Ben would not be attending any ministry meeting any time soon.

"You shouldn't be mad with him. He's getting the help he needs. Without it, he may go rogue," Gower said encouragingly. "It truly is for the best that he gets the help before the new hormones kick in."

Bella breathed in deeply and exhaled for an extended period, hoping to relieve the tension in her chest. It failed.

They arrived at the tall, narrow building whose exterior and interior were blanketed with black, shiny mirrors on the walls and the floors. Except for Ben, all ministry members arrived. The office was the only room in the building at the top where the staircase led.

Gower nimbly stood as he was the one who would address the news to the ministry. He pulled out a paper from his red cloak that he would read. It'd be more comfortable if he didn't have to look them in the eyes as he revealed that the king's next strike had been foretold a few days after the king's attack, meaning that it would occur within the year. Gower rarely read off of papers when announcing to the ministry. He often had no problem speaking in front of people. Gower was a teacher, after all. But today, he looked scared, as if he had not met another witch before. The dim light behind him shone through the paper. They could see the chicken scratch that he would be reading. They guessed that it hadn't been his writing. It couldn't have. He was one of the neatest writers and often wrote letters to the kingdom on behalf of any urgent news.

Before reading, he looked up from the paper and blinked repeatedly. Gower looked back to his scroll.

"I have unfortunate, maddening news," he began. His body rocked to his heart's rapid beats. "I had hoped... that the king would've realized that we are not a ministry to mess with; however, this—this is not the case." He pressed his lips and shook his head as he held back tears.

He handed Bella the paper and asked her to read it. She cleared her throat. She was nervous as she had never seen Gower act so bewildered. She stood up in front of the ministry.

"The kingdom will suffer at the hands of the king once more. As the ministry, we must keep an eye on the forbidden forest as the king has created monstrous beasts that will rise from within the trees in my – Gower's – crystal ball. In particular, one creature may be the doom of the kingdom as according to the late king. It is impossible to defeat as he has placed a protection curse, and only a male Carter can defeat it."

Bella's jaw dropped, and her eyes traveled to her younger sister, Angel. She lowered the paper and addressed the ministry, shaking her head. "There is no male Carter, not after my late father and brother's death."

"I'm sure we'll find a way," John, the usual optimistic, said with a sure nod of his head.

"No," Angel began. "What about our cousin?"

Bella rolled her eyes. "Anahita may act like a man, but she's not a man."

"No, not Ana. Rabbit."

Bella stared at her younger sister for a moment, trying to make sense of the few words she had spoken. "Rabbit?" Bella asked when nothing came to mind.

"Yes," Angel nodded.

"Rabbit?" Bella asked. Angel nodded once more. "We have a cousin named... Rabbit? Who also happens to be a male?"

"Yes."

"Doesn't ring a bell."

"He was born with an Alet aura, has a sister named Maria," Angel began to give her sister clues. "He came to my eighth birthday, and we went around telling everyone that he was my secret twin because of how much we looked alike. His birth name is Benjamin Carter, but he changed it to Rabbit."

"Oh, I remember him. And he chose to have the name Rabbit?" Bella scoffed.

"Ever since he and his friends made the band 'Imaginary Kings.'" Angel nodded.

"Didn't he drop out of Galdorwide High?" Bella asked.

Angel looked down at her hands. "I think so."

"And he's our only hope?"

Gower felt as if he was going to be sick. He sprinted to the door and ran down the stairs. His three closest friends, John, Arthur, and Olly, followed.

His heart was beating rapidly, his mouth had gone dry, and his stomach began twisting on both ends. His friends slowly approached, trying not to crowd and scare him off. While trying their best to be quiet, Olly had missed one of the shiny black steps that blended so closely together that it looked like a giant slide from the top. He came tumbling down, landing on all fours.

His once tidy blond hair had become a rattled mess. Gower turned around, startled by the crashing and grunting. His stomach dropped, startled by the sudden appearance of his three friends as he had wanted to be alone.

John smirked and lifted Olly onto his feet. "Go on, Olly, tell him that hilarious joke you had told me earlier. Gower will get a kick!" He attempted to stray from the serious conversation that would rise eventually.

"What's the difference between a rabbit on a treadmill and a laughing rabbit?" Olly asked. "One is a fit bunny, and the other is a bit funny!"

Angel walked down the stairs. She, too, had been a close friend of Olly's. In her hands, she had a bag full of Gower's favorite treats, mainly because they were her son Thomas' favorite as well. They could see cups of pudding with chocolate drizzled whipped cream pressing against its lids in the transparent bag. Adelaide, Dorothy, and Alizeh followed closely behind her.

"I just want to be left alone," he had said to his friends before noticing the young blonde woman who stopped in her tracks. He immediately regretted his harsh tone. "I don't want to hear any jokes, but I can use some pudding," he managed with a smile.

The six friends ventured off to the Echor Erkling Bar, where they would enjoy a meal and discuss the grave future ahead.

"Galdorwide is too risky. I say we alert the kingdom, and we make our way to Gimmian," said Gower.

Adelaide's eyes glazed over with a dreamy hue. "As much as I can go for their licorice gems, Bella would never run from her home, especially when the threat is her father. She'll go down with a fight whether we like it or not. She's our friend, and we can't just leave her to fight on her own – not to mention, this is our home. We can't run. We need to stop the king once and for all."

Gower shook his head. He was still not on board with trying to beat the impossible.

"We may not be able to kill the beast, but I'll do some research tonight with Dorothy and see what we can find. There are other ways to overpower the king's plan." Alizeh nodded.

"Can we please stop calling him the king?" Adelaide raised her hand as if to halt Alizeh. "He's not the king any more. His name is Delanie." They all nodded in agreement. "Just have faith," Adelaide turned to Gower. She placed a comforting hand over his.

Gower gave them a tragic look. They hadn't seen what he had.

"If you feel uncomfortable here, Gower," Angel began, "you can leave. Don't ever feel like you have to do what we do."

Just then, a loud crash came from a few tables down. Pink syrup had splattered on the windows of the bar. Pieces of sliced, boiled carrots streamed down the wall. The waitress Ann's face, apron, and blue uniform shirt had the particles of food and liquid splattered all over it. She had been staring furiously at the three burly men who sat at the table. As quick as the crash had come, two of the men vanished.

The other man wasn't so lucky. Ann lunged at him. Her oldest brother, Adam, emerged from the kitchen. Her other brother, Owen, had run from behind the bar. They pulled her off the man, who looked rigid and in shock. She struggled against her brothers' grips. As soon as she had broken free, the man had vanished.

She turned to her brothers. They raised their brows in questioning. They tried to hide the smirks on their face.

"They were utterly disgusting, disturbed men talking about all kinds of perverted things. One said he had told his daughter not to wear pigtails because they were handlebars! I know his wife and their daughter is seven! He's lucky I didn't fillet him alive! It would've done him some good. He could afford to lose a pound or two hundred!"

Adam shook his head with a smirk, walked away, returning with a mop. He handed it to Ann. She took it, still shaking with anger.

Owen went back behind the bar and took their customer's orders. Adam had grabbed a bowl, went to the freezer, grabbed a scoop, and began to make his younger sister a bowl of ice cream. It was a kind gesture he had done for as long as he could remember – she was forty-five now, but she was still his baby sister no matter how old and fierce she was. She was still mopping and scrubbing when he returned, bearing gifts.

"Call it a night." He stretched out his arm revealing it to his sister, who scrubbed furiously at the pink stain on the wooden floor. "I'll work in the kitchen and serve." He smiled before leading her to the back.

Everything in Echor Erkling had seemed to be back to its calm state. That is, however, until the blue and green flames in the lanterns blew out. Ann screamed and dropped her bowl to the floor, another mess she'd have to clean. Things got worse when two strange men in black trench coats entered the bar. Lightning struck, and the lanterns relit. They took a casual seat on two of the free bar stools. Ann ran into the kitchen, fearing that these men had caused the power outage. Owen, who always seemed calm and almost emotionless, told the men that his sister was deathly afraid of the dark. Then, as a joke, he asked if they had done it.

One of the men, a handsome fellow with long, blond, curly hair down to his shoulders, who wore a purple witch hat, gave Owen a demonic look. Owen was taken aback. He was often the type of person that everyone enjoyed talking to, even if it was only to spill their guts.

"No," he hissed evilly. "Don't you know who I am? You've surely read my books. *Made for Error: The Call of an Empire.*"

"Can't say I have," Owen ruthlessly said as he continued to wash a glass.

The man reached into his trench coat's pocket, pulled a pocket-sized book, and handed it to Owen. "Well, soon, you can say you have just as the rest of the people in the twenty kingdoms have." He winked as he gave a broad smile that revealed his pearly white teeth.

Angel and Adelaide approached the man with the tilted royal hat in awe.

"Kenneth Riley?" Adelaide asked, quaking in her heels. Arthur watched on curiously from his seat.

"The one and only." He spun around dramatically. He reached for Adelaide's hand and kissed it. He turned to Angel and honored her the same. "And whose lovely presence am I in?" he asked as his friend he entered with kept his eyes straight, staring off into the distance as he took large sips of scented slammer.

Alizeh rolled her eyes as she stayed seated with Arthur and Gower. "At least now they can stop drooling over Krum."

"They?" Arthur asked, almost angered by the revelation. He looked back over to his fiancée, who looked like an absolute fool, or at least that's what he told himself.

"I-I-I'm Adelaide Nillag," she stuttered, bringing her hand to her chest to make sure he knew who Adelaide was.

"And I'm Angel Scaasi." She bowed. Adelaide followed as she had forgotten whose presence they were in – the son of the newly crowned Emperor Peta Riley.

"*Ahh*, Angel Scaasi." His eyes widened with an exaggerated admiration. Adelaide couldn't help but be jealous despite her fiancé sitting at the table behind them. "The rebellious princess, all for love, I presume?"

"Once upon a time, yes." Angel grew sad as she remembered her husband that she had not seen for about a month now.

"*Ah*, have a seat." He pulled out the barstool beside him.

Angel smiled and gladly took a seat by the devilishly handsome man. Adelaide stood, unsure what to do.

"Joining us?" He turned to the redhead, whose face was now a deeper shade. She blushed further as she took the seat beside Angel. His eyes then traveled to the table where the girls' other guests sat. He looked to Alizeh. "And how about you, darling?"

She shrugged as she took a final sip of her caramel passion before grabbing her purse and taking a seat beside Adelaide. The four men looked to one another. Arthur stood up angrily, pondering whether he should strike the flirtatious man, but he decided not to. Instead, he took the open seat beside Gower, where Angel had been sitting, closing the gap between them.

After Alizeh's gracious introduction to the man, she asked him what brought him to Galdorwide.

"Well, you see, I've heard many complaints about missing persons, this man being one of them." He nudged the man beside him, causing the liquid he had just sipped to spill from out of his mouth.

The man gritted his teeth and turned to face the girls. "Bliant Cherish," he introduced himself to the girls with a two-finger salute after he swallowed.

"Wait, are you related to Maddox Cherish?" Angel asked the tall, averagely built man with blue eyes and light brown hair. The man nodded. "Oh wow! He's my sister's right-hand man! But I guess you probably already knew that."

Bliant smiled, revealing a kindness in his eyes that she had never seen in anyone before and especially not his brooding, scary, guard-dog-like brother.

"Anyway," Kenneth brought the attention back to him. "Bliant's son has been missing for almost a year now. Bliant had brought Crispin to his school's hospital ward after suffering from his severe case of Sanguivoriphobia, the fear of bloodsuckers. I have come to help out this kingdom's ministry to help solve this case."

"We are part of the ministry," Angel gestured. She then brought her attention back to Bliant. "How come you didn't come to us?"

He shrugged and gave a shy smile. "Well, my brother had told me how busy you guys all were with the dragons and the king. I just didn't want to disturb you."

"It wouldn't have been a disturbance, really," Alizeh reassured. "Next time, feel free to tell us about any problem. Okay?" she asked. The man gave a kind, shy smile and nodded.

"Anyway," Kenneth said, this time through gritted teeth. "So, you're the ministry? Great, I'll be joining you on all other cases until we find the whereabouts of Crispin Cherish. From there, we can hopefully find the other missing persons in your area."

"I'd like to join too," Bliant barely said.

"Welcome aboard," Alizeh smiled.

Arthur looked to Gower with a frown. He turned to the smiling bunch who sat on the bar stools. "Don't they need to pass some kind of training?" He spoke through gritted teeth. "Like how I had to despite everyone in the ministry knowing my skills?" His anger soon made him shake his head and scoff like a maniac. His face had grown a deep, bloody red.

The following day, Angel and Bella donned their cloaks and walked over to their cousin's farmhouse. He lived two miles outside of Galdorwide's village. They had sent a letter to Rabbit last night explaining that they wanted to meet with him and for him to be alone and outside waiting for them. Angel knew of his housemates and thought it best to leave it up to Rabbit on whether or not his friends find out that it's his shoulders that the kingdom rests upon. There was a row of five houses. The middle house had red, wood-paneled walls and wooden, chipped shingles for a roof. The two houses on either side were made of red bricks with black shingles. Each of the homes looked to be about two stories tall. A giant, black ladder extended up to the window of the middle home. They approached the last house. The homes were located right in the woods and opened toward the vast field. The view was magnificent, even on a cold, cloudy morning.

Behind the last building was a brown, brick barn with two wooden doors. Bella questioned the doors as pigs, sheep, and chickens roamed freely along the five lots. A young, tall, athletically built man exited the last home, closest to the barn. His eyes caught theirs after he turned to close the door, but soon his eyes had fallen on something more fascinating. A chicken had managed to get on top of the low brick wall that divided each of the houses. The man with long, blond hair that fell just slightly below his shoulders approached the chicken in awe.

Bella was already unimpressed. His outfit to meet with the queen was a long, brown fur coat, bell-bottom jeans, a yellow shirt, and brown sunglasses.

The girls stopped at the end of the driveway, waiting for him to meet them. He turned to face the brick wall and extended his hand, reaching for the chicken, trying to pet it. The chicken fluttered its wings. Rabbit quickly pulled his hand away and jumped back from the tiny creature.

He looked to his cousins with a reddened face. He straightened himself up and ironed his hands down his coat as he walked toward them.

"To what do I owe this rare pleasure?" he asked, placing his hands in his pocket lined with werecat fur.

"This." Bella reached into her purple cloak pocket and pulled out the scroll that Gower had brought to the ministry's attention.

Rabbit took his hands out of his pocket and opened the scroll. As he read, he glanced up at the girls every so often, wondering what any of this had to do with him, and then he read the bottom – a male Carter. His eyes widened.

"So this means me?"

"You are the only male Carter," Bella replied monotonously.

A slim young girl with long, curly, tangled blonde hair and blue eyes passed by them. She leaped forward onto the ground as if she were trying to catch something. She crawled quickly to a hole in the bottom of the porch of the house beside Rabbit's. She stuck her head in it. It was quite an odd sight as the girl looked to be in her early teens, far too old to be acting like this. She was also wearing attire too lovely to be rolling around in. She had been wearing a pale, pink sweater and a neon, pink skirt. Her pink nylons had holes in them. The young girl wore shiny black shoes and white socks that were topped with lace. Her head remained in the spot.

"So, what kind of creature are we talking about?" Rabbit asked, taking the attention off of his young neighbor and back onto him.

"We know just as much as you do," Angel said solemnly.

"Let's hope it's not a giant chicken." Bella rolled her eyes.

Rabbit's face reddened further.

He took off his glasses, revealing green eyes. He still resembled Angel as much as he had when he was younger; they had blonde hair, green eyes, thick eyebrows, and full lips. He turned to look behind him when he could hear his neighbor's door swing open. A tall, slim man stood with his hands on his hips. His blue eyes were wild as he stared at the young girl whose bottom half was the only thing he could see as she stuffed her head beneath the house. His dark, brown hair was a mess. It looked as if he had just rolled out of bed.

The man stomped down the steps. "Diana!" he shouted. He grabbed hold of the young girl's legs and began to drag her out of the porch. He flipped her around with an angry thrust. She looked up at him, a smile of excitement on her face. He bent down, grabbed her shoulders, and stood her on to her feet.

"There's a mouse under the porch!" she exclaimed. "Can you catch it for me? Please!"

He began to shake the young girl. She looked like a doll in his grip. "Stop chasing mice!"

"Do it again!" she exclaimed after he had stopped shaking her.

With a shake of his head, he stomped back inside the house and slammed the door behind him. The young girl noticed her audience and ran toward Rabbit. She was jumping with excitement, and Rabbit couldn't help but smile back at her.

"Raby! There's a mouse under the porch! Can you catch it for me?" She jumped around, pulling on his sleeve.

His smile immediately faded. However, it didn't entirely fall when he saw Diana's other brother, Amara, approaching. "I'm not a fan of mice, but Amara will probably be able to get it for you."

Her head snapped to look at her older brother as he approached. He had long blond hair reaching down to the middle of his back. It flowed graciously behind him as he slowly neared with a kind smile. He was wearing a leather jacket and black jeans. He carried a large, green gym bag over his shoulder.

"Amary!" she shouted. "There's a mouse under the porch!"

"For real?" he asked with a smile.

"Yeah! For real! Can you catch it for me?" she asked as he had already placed his gym bag on the ground along with his leather jacket, revealing pale arms covered with self-harm scars. He and the young girl ran toward the porch. He bent down, soiling the knees of his jeans. He reached for the porch's paneling and pulled it out of place. He began to crawl inside. Diana stood clapping with excitement.

"Looks like that girl belongs in Clockwork," Bella scoffed.

Rabbit, who had been smiling at the young girl as he always had as her happiness was contagious, slowly turned to face Bella. "I don't think it's brilliant to talk lowly about someone I care about, especially when you need my help."

"She's sorry," Angel replied.

"Yeah," Rabbit kept his eyes on Bella. "I'm sure she is."

Amara pulled quickly out of the porch. He stood to his feet and dangled the mouse by its tail.

"Oh no! It's dead!" she exclaimed.

"Do you still want it?" he asked his sister genuinely.

"No," she replied with a frown.

"Can I keep it?"

"Sure," she shrugged.

With an excited smile, he sprung up the steps of the porch and ran inside.

Amara's room only he, Diana, his brother Seppo, and his best friend Clancy could enter. Stuart didn't have a problem with being excluded. He was pleased. Every time he would pass his younger brother's room, he would catch a whiff of a rancid, foul, and putrid smell. He didn't know why and he didn't ask. But as for the rest, they knew. He often hunted small animals and brought them home. He would place them in his bed and sleep beside them. Luckily, the stench of death never seemed to follow him. The Johansens were all quite strange in their way, well, maybe not Stuart.

Amara's strangeness stemmed from his love of the dead. He often fantasized and had visions of the afterlife. It was as if the afterlife was calling to him, but he couldn't leave his friends and his family – not yet. His love of the dead began to blossom when he had first heard of Pool Jr. Scaasi's travels and read journals that he had written as he lived with vampires for nine months back in 2007. He was torn between dying and between becoming the undead. Either way, he had time to think it over.

"Anyway," Bella crossed her arms. "We don't know if he chose male Carter because he forgot about you or because he doesn't believe that you'll be able to stop the creature. Either way, when the time comes, on the battlefield, you will need to wear a disguise so that there's no target on your back."

"What kind of disguise?" he asked.

***

Ace had thrown Robbie into his room. He had bought some supplies and began to bar his door. He would remain locked and secured in for a total of three days before being let out for food and water. He had given him a bucket where he could relieve himself for the time being.

Three days later, during breakfast, Spencer had noticed that Robbie had not come up to eat. When she asked her uncle where he was, he explained that he had lengthened his punishment after giving the incident further thought. After all, he had tried to escape, all while trying to spread a nasty rumor. Spencer tried to convince him to let Robbie have a meal, but he was not budging. Instead of hanging out in the farthest room in the basement where a decently sized living area was located, Spencer decided that she'd stay in her room. If he were going to punish Robbie, he would have to punish her. Ace would know that Spencer couldn't last on such a restrictive punishment. She lay on her bed staring up at the baby blue ceiling with white, fluffy clouds floating about, not literally as it had been in her true home. Absolutely no magic besides the magic used to create the replica of her room was allowed. Spencer rolled her eyes as she realized how it was okay for Ace to break the rules. The more time she spent with herself, the more her thoughts wandered. Spencer wondered if this would be the house in which she dies. Not from a beast or anything magical, just a Nullum doctor experimenting on her as if she were some rat.

If he had spent his high school years sober, he might've been able to be a brilliant wizard like his three brothers, but here he was barely able to remember a spell which only required the aid of a wand. His time here at Ace's home had hit an all-time low. Now that he was sober, he felt utterly lost and brand new to just about everything. Maybe one of these new girls would be the cure for Ace's Nullumness, and they can finally be sent free even if Ace uses his newfound magic to brainwash them all. However, even if there were to be a cure, if Ace kept him locked up like an animal, he'd surely starve before his captor's victory.

The room rattled slightly, a plate of the asparagus-stuffed bear appeared near the bottom of his door. Robbie, whose body had been weakened, immediately jumped off the bed, grabbed onto the plate's edges, and squatted where he could see another set of feet on the other side. The food was cold, but he had finished it almost as soon as he had received it.

"You're welcome," he could hear Spencer whisper from the other side of the door.

"But how?"

"I'm your sister's daughter, remember?" She laughed. He could hear Ace's heavy footsteps walk down the stairs. Spencer's shadow hastily disappeared from Robbie's view.

Robbie immediately crossed his room and laid back on his bed, hiding his plate beneath his blanket. His door flung harshly open, slamming hard into the glass desk that had sat on the opposing side of the door. A crack formed along its top.

Ace stomped over.

He ripped off the blanket and took the plate. Robbie laid back, defeated and feeling hungrier than ever; he couldn't fight. Each time he stood, his vision would go black as his blood pressure had reached its lowest surviving point.

Supposing he was still alive when someone or something would save everyone from this monster, he tried to dream of his life back to the way it was, without making the promise of staying clean. Ace seemed to only care about himself as everyone's conditions before admission had become worse – all except for Lena, who had fallen for his charms. He knew that his entire family knew that both he and Spencer were under Ace's care but hadn't they been concerned about not receiving any letters or any communication for that matter? If they could all just realize what Ace had going on here, they'd be out almost immediately as both Ben and his brother-in-law John had been part of the ministry.

His room was completely black. All the rooms were, no matter what time of day, as the room's windows only revealed the dirt around them. But for some reason, Robbie felt as if his room was growing even darker. Exhausted, his stomach growling, he found enough strength to roll on his side to make himself more comfortable. His mind turned, and his eyes rolled back as his body tried to shut down to save Robbie from further torture. He quickly fell into a deep sleep.

He had a horrible dream, one that was similar to his reality. He was trapped in a small, dark room with no furniture and absolutely no light. He couldn't see anything, just blackness. He could hear the deafening silence and feel his body tremble as his hungry stomach turned, he wanted to scream for help, but no voice had come out from his lips. His head pounded furiously as his blood pumped with fear.

"Help," the real him was able to moan as he lay in bed.

When it was time for dinner, Spencer feared her uncle's wrath. She heard the basement door unlock, which was their cue to head up. Spencer walked up the stairs with the others. She tried to blend herself in the middle of the crowd as if this would help her hide. Upstairs, it looked somewhat peaceful as the full moon shone through the windows and illuminated the room along with dim Heofsij light fixtures called lamps connected to electrical lines Ace had created from stuff he had brought from the Heofsij land. The screen door was open as Ace's Heofsij air conditioning system had been broken. For a moment, as Spencer looked to where a breeze strolled in, she could swear that she could see a tall, athletic boy with big, doe hazel eyes with dark brown, long, and wavy hair.

She was almost sure it was her twin brother, John Jr., looking through the screen door.

CHAPTER 3

The plate that sat already filled in front of Spencer was filled with round, crunchy, stinky food.

"Go on, eat," Ace said harshly. "I've realized I've been harsh on you lately. This food will be your last punishment so long as you don't act out again. You must eat every single piece of cat food. It's part of your punishment as well as your treatment. Maybe after this meal, you will learn to appreciate the luxury of food we all have."

"And if I don't?" Spencer tested.

"If you don't, you will remain here, on this chair, with no sleep and no water. You will starve as this is your only food option until it's completed. If you do finish, you and I can enjoy a cup of tea outside, on the porch enjoying the night's cool air."

Spencer's eyes lit up, but soon her eyes squinted as she became lost in thought. Her brother had seemed to disappear from the door window, but maybe, if she didn't eat and she'd remain in the living room, then perhaps when her uncle went to bed, she could call for help. This seemed to be a better option than allowing her brother to see the two of them enjoy cups of tea as if everything was all right. She pushed the plate away from her.

Everyone was sent back to their rooms, all except for Spencer. Ace left to use to the washroom and said that he'd return shortly. Spencer slid between the small crack between her chair and the table as not to make any noise. She walked over to the kitchen stove, where her attention had been lying all dinner time. He had used a large kitchen knife to prepare his other patient's fine meal of onion ostrich.

Her fingers danced along its blade as she quietly reached for its handle. But soon, her eyes traveled to something else, fudge balls with chocolate sprinkles, a family recipe she had not tasted in a long time. Her hand left the knife, and she reached for a fudge ball, closed her eyes, raised it to her nose, and began to sniff the dessert. Ace peeked from out of the hall; he had placed the knife there intentionally to see if Spencer would act as Robbie most definitely would've. Instead, he caught the heartbreaking sight. Her eyes remained closed as she finally exhaled after breathing in the food's sweet aroma. She opened her eyes; Ace inched back from view slightly as he kept his eyes on his niece. She looked around and reached for the knife. He tensed. She looked back to the fudge ball and lowered the knife cutting it into halves and then quarters. Ace stood, not knowing what to do. His eyes traveled over to the girl who looked so different as she took part in one of her previous eating rituals. She then looked around, hoping that no one was seeing her. She reached her fragile, pale arm to the kitchen cupboards and began to open and close them as quietly as she could as she started her search. Ace's brow furrowed, and his heart quickened. He felt something inside him that he never felt before, something he didn't exactly know what it was. She found it, icing sugar. She brought it to her nose, closed her eyes, and breathed in its aroma before placing it onto the kitchen cutting board where her one fudge ball laid in four separate pieces. She reached into the drawer beside her and pulled out a teaspoon. The icing sugar collected in the spoon's dip; she brought the spoon to eye level as she took her left index finger and brushed off the excess sugar until she could only see the outside of the scoop. She then poured the remaining sugar on her dessert. She reached beside the sink where a tiny, blue plate sat, recently washed. She took the plate and placed her dessert on it. As she walked back to the kitchen table, Ace made back to the bathroom to allow his niece to eat in privacy. Before he could close the door, he heard a sweet, kind, familiar voice call to him.

"Uncle Ace?"

He cleared his throat. "Yes?"

"Come here," she replied simply. He hesitantly approached. "This was your mother's recipe, wasn't it?" she asked. He nodded slowly. "Share with me?"

Ace nodded slowly once more. He gently pulled the seat away from the table as if he still needed to be quiet. He took one of the four pieces off of the plate and placed it in his mouth. He looked up at her and smiled. He held in tears; he had forgotten the final ingredient, something that had been missing all these years, the icing sugar. Spencer smiled before looking at him cautiously.

"I know, I'm on a strict feline food diet, but may I?"

"You may."

She reached for one of the remaining three pieces. She placed it in her mouth and held it in there until it completely dissolved as she tried to savor its taste for as long as possible. Ace took another piece. Spencer laid her hands in her lap.

"Go on, eat," he said gently.

"Can I give it to Robbie?"

"Yes, if—if you have one more full one," he croaked, unsure of how she would respond. This time, he was looking for her best interest, not trying to challenge her.

"Won't I be eating someone else's portion?"

"Take it; I'll make more tonight. I don't care, go on."

After eating a whole fudge ball with icing sugar, she brought down one full one and the quarter from the previous ball down for her Uncle Robbie. Ace unlocked Robbie's door with a long, bronze key. He pulled the door open. Robbie, like a wild animal, seized the plate from Spencer. Ace pulled Spencer from out of the room then proceeded to relock Robbie's door.

"You may want to show some gratitude!" Ace shouted from behind the closed door. Spencer stood next to him humbly. "This won't be a regular occurrence." He grabbed Spencer's wrist gently then walked her back up the stairs.

"I'm going to hop in the shower; you can go in after me, then we can spend the night on the porch," Ace explained as they returned to the dining room table. He grabbed Spencer's bowl and brought it over to the garbage by the basement door that he had locked with eleven different keys.

Spencer smiled as she stood with one hand holding her arm. He left and went to the bathroom, where he turned on the shower. With the noise of running water, Spencer walked hastily to the door with light footsteps.

"John," Spencer breathed through the screen door that had the same amount of locks as the basement and back door. "John?"

John Jr. appeared into view alongside their two older cousins Caden and Aldaricus. They were grinning as if a plan had come together.

"Are you all right?" Aldaricus asked.

"What's been going on?" John Jr. began to interrogate. "You haven't been yourself lately; your letters, they worry me. Are you not getting any better? Are you? I've asked you to come over for a few nights, and you say that you'd rather be here!" he whispered angrily.

"I haven't written or received any letter!" Spencer whispered in the same tone as her brother. "It must've been Ace!"

"It was your handwriting, Spencer; it's not like he can use magic to copy your writing."

"I said it wasn't me," she whispered sternly. "He must've made one of his children do it; that wasn't me writing to you. Look, can you tell Dad and the ministry that Ace has us all locked up in here like animals? He stole all of our magical objects. I can't even magic myself out! We're practically Nullums like him in here! Please! He's been experimenting on us and making me eat cat food! He won't let us go home until he figures out how he can obtain magic himself! Please, tell the ministry!"

"Stop blabbing. We'll get you out," said John Jr. "We'll get you home." He gave a nod of assurance.

"You won't be able to magic me out either; magic acts strange in this house, I've only done one magic thing properly, and that got food on the other side of a door."

"Why don't you try that then, but for yourself?" John Jr. asked.

"Oh, geez, wish I had thought of that!" she whispered sarcastically.

"Okay, we don't need to use magic. Have you forgotten who I'm with?" He nodded to their cousins.

Caden reached into his Viridi varsity sweater and pulled out a lock pick kit. Grabbing a hook-like tool, he stuck it in the bottom of the first keyhole. Caden then took out a device with three ridges and stuck it into the top of the keyhole. He began to move the bottom tool side-to-side and the top tool back and forth. The lock clicked, and he moved the tools clockwise with ease: one down, ten more to go. Spencer stayed chatting with John Jr. and Aldaricus through the small, circular window.

"If we all get caught, we're all dead," Spencer said as Caden successfully opened the second lock.

"Don't worry," Aldaricus tried to assure her.

She remained quiet. She even hesitated to breathe as she focused on the running water coming from the shower. Before she knew it, Caden had successfully unlocked all eleven locks. Spencer ran to the door to see the outer door hanging freely while the inner side seemed to be glued onto the frame. Caden, breathing heavy with fear, tried pulling the door open, only for it to remain shut. Spencer listened anxiously; the water was still running.

"Did he lock himself in here too?" Caden whispered, only to slam his palm against the door frame.

"No," Spencer cried. "There's a code he uses," she explained.

Caden leaned close against the glass door, defeated. "We'll get you out," he promised.

"Can't you try opening the attic hatch where your wand is?" John Jr. asked from the window.

"I've tried everything!" Spencer cried loudly.

"*Shh*," the three boys ordered.

"Try and fit through this window," Aldaricus suggested.

"Yeah, right," she scoffed as she folded her arms. "Like I could fit through that."

"Have you looked in a mirror lately?"

"Well – no."

"Come over here," he waved her over. He then looked to Caden. "You brought the glass cutter, right?"

Caden nodded and walked over. He slightly tapped the window and began to rub his hands along it. Caden took out a black suction that resembled a tiny plunger with a metal handle. He placed it on the window. On the end of the handle was a point that pressed against the glass. He began to turn the handle; the pointer made a slight scratch around the window's edge, creating a perfect circle. Once Caden completed the process, he pulled the suction off. He reached into his varsity jacket and pulled out a metal rod that had a small circle at its end.

"This is going to get loud," Caden warned.

With each tap, he became more desperate as he increased the force, increasing the noise. He brought the suction to the window once more and was able to pull it out successfully. Only to be disappointed once more. It was a double glass window, and only he would be able to get to the second glass from the inside as the tool couldn't reach the other side. She had to hand it to them; they had tried everything in their power to help her escape.

"Told you it was a waste of time learning Heofsij tricks," Aldaricus smacked the back of Caden's head. Caden let out a low growl and slowly turned to face his older cousin, who was a few inches taller than him.

Caden and Aldaricus began shoving each other. John Jr. tried to break them apart. The water turned off.

"He's coming!" Spencer warned.

The boys, who had already been panting with adrenaline, fear, and anger, hesitantly began to run off. "We'll get you out," they said once more. Spencer ran to the kitchen, where she took her usual seat, trying to act casual.

She heard the bathroom floor creak. Her heart began to press hard against her chest. She was sure she would faint. The bathroom door creaked open. Ace was shirtless, wearing only the bottom half of his pajamas. He was drying his face off with a green towel. Once he removed it, he roared.

"What the hell was all that noise?"

She looked to the window, he wouldn't be able to tell that Caden had taken out one side of the window, but when her eyes trailed to the door, she could see the moonlight shine in from a large opening at the bottom. She quickly looked back at him.

"I had forgotten to work out this morning. I was doing some jumping jacks; the vibrations were rattling your medals and trophies." Her eyes traveled to the bookshelf where trophies sat at its very top. Medals hung alongside the wall. One award caught her eye in particular; it was the tallest one. Its base had a gold plaque that read:

Ace Scaasi
California Taekwondo Championship
1984
First Place

Three pedestals rose from the base extending to a triangular top where a gold cup statue sat. On its top was a golden statue of a young Ace whose leg was high above his head.

For a second, all Ace did was stand still. While Spencer had been distracted by the trophy, his eyes had laid upon the front door. He lunged toward his niece, grabbing her by her wrists. Spencer tried to pull herself out of his grip to no avail.

"Who tried to get in here? Who?" he roared as he shook the tiny girl.

Spencer pulled herself out of his grip, which led her to topple backward with her chair onto the floor. Her body slammed against the wooden bars on the back of the chair.

"Who?" he yelled once more. Loud bangs came from the door. Ace sat Spencer up in her seat. "Not a word."

He angrily huffed as he approached the door. He punched in an eleven-numbered code and pulled the door open. The night air whipped in through the door. Spencer looked behind the four shadows to see the outlining of the world she used to be a part of. Her father, John Jr., Aldaricus, and Caden had all rushed inside. There was a panic in her father's face while the three boys looked different somehow; they looked lost and dumbfounded.

"Dad?" Spencer called.

John's eyes traveled to what used to be his daughter. She was a skeleton; she was pale with dark circles under her eyes. Her hair had thinned. She had looked worse than she had when she had been first admitted. If she hadn't called him dad, he would've thought she was merely another patient.

"Oh, honey." He left the boys as he approached his daughter to hug her.

He then turned to Ace. "She looks worse, Ace. I brought her to you to help. Now I wonder if I should bring the boys under your care," he snipped.

Caden's head had been roaming the room; he rested his hand on the side table for support. Aldaricus hung his head, his hand over his mouth. His face was red. John Jr. squinted his eyes in confusion as he looked at his father and uncle.

Ace gave a charming grin to his brother's insults. As they spoke, Spencer looked to her brother and mouthed, 'Let me out!' John Jr. scowled and brought his finger to his mouth; he looked to Caden and Aldaricus and his uncle nervously. After seeing they were still in the midst of a conversation, he let out a sigh of relief.

To Spencer's fear, her father locked hands with his brother and went in for a hug. He was leaving them all here.

"So, what brings them here?" Ace folded his arms before turning to look at the three boys, who seemed quite humbled for once as they stuck together, close to the door.

"Well, I'm not quite sure what happened. They were at the school's hospital wing when an explosion overcame them. You see, they weren't hurt but… Caden has lost his vision, Aldaricus lost his voice – well, sort of." John turned to Aldaricus. "Go on."

Aldaricus shook his head in a wild objection. Caden's hand reached out, missing Aldaricus, who stood beside him. His hand floated around until he finally got hold of his bicep; once he had, he gave what looked to be a weakened punch. Aldaricus yelled angrily, and the voice that came out wasn't a human sound. A rush of 'Hee-Haw's' came from out of his mouth. He had the voice of a donkey. There was a long, shocked silence. Spencer looked very confused, she usually would've laughed, but he sounded like a real donkey; she feared that they weren't joking around. Ace's eyes widened with surprise; it was nothing he had seen before.

"And Junior – he has lost his hearing."

"How odd," Ace seemed both intrigued and convinced. "But why have you brought them to me? I'm sure this is more of Notleaf and August's situation."

"They referred me to you," John explained.

"*Hmm*, all right, I'll see what I can do. I can never turn down patients," he turned to Spencer and gave a wicked smile. He looked back to John. "Follow me downstairs; you can add rooms for the boys." The charming man ushered him toward the basement stairs.

John took note of the code and the eleven locks. "A lot of precautions you have there."

"Oh, yes, I have some new admissions with outrageous fears and schizophrenia. Best not have them roaming about until their conditions are controlled."

As John and Ace entered the basement, all the patients, except for the weakened Robbie, began banging their fists against the doors, a sound that didn't quite travel through the spell Abigail had placed on the thick walls.

Upstairs, Spencer confronted the boys. "Why couldn't you have just lied about your conditions?"

"Well," began Caden, who was looking slightly over her shoulder rather than her eyes. "Put it this way; it's more believable. We magicked our conditions; only Aldaricus' didn't go quite as planned." He raised his hand to pat Aldaricus' shoulder only to pat the side of the blond's head. "Sorry." He lowered his hand before attempting to look back to Spencer, this time looking at her shoulder. "We transported to the hospital wing and discussed the issue with Notleaf. He had his suspicions; he told us that we should become patients under Ace's care but to be careful because he had sent Tris here only for him to leave completely loving the man. So we schemed up a plan, I'd become blind, Junny would become deaf, and Aldaricus would become mute – well, he can't communicate now."

"So there wasn't an explosion?" she asked. Caden shook his head. "Why didn't you just tell my dad?"

"He's been away at the ministry's mansion. The king is plotting something big once again. But Notleaf got hold of him after the incident."

"Well, you still could've told him!"

"True, but we didn't go through all this for nothing. My eyes burned for a good ten minutes to save your ass!"

"I'd tell Dad now, but who knows, Ace might overpower him, magic doesn't work in here properly, and... Ace is considered a lethal weapon in the Heofsij land. You guys just should've sent a letter to the ministry; this isn't a joke. This is serious. We're going to need someone on the outside to help us; any ideas?"

"We don't need anybody else; we have each other," Caden assured.

Spencer rolled her eyes and folded her arms before staring at Caden; only Caden couldn't tell as he was now looking at her neck.

"Yeah," John Jr. piped up. "I'm terrible at reading lips. Can you guys re-speak but this time more slowly?"

Spencer slammed her face into the palm of her hand. She then looked back to Caden. "Seems like they're having a grand ol' time downstairs; I'd ask you to pick the inner locks, but well, you're blind."

Caden's mouth dropped. He hadn't thought of that. "*Aw*, shit. This is why we need you while we make plans." He gave a thumbs up but ended up poking Aldaricus' shoulder. Aldaricus stepped away, realizing the hazard his cousin had become.

Downstairs, John and Ace sat in the living space. "Roman's disappeared again; indeed, he's supporting the king. You know, you'd think having Mom back, he'd stay on our side."

Ace shook his head. "He's always had darkness in him. He became fascinated with the king by the end of his high school time. Daeva didn't help his psychosis; she's worse than him. We should've brought it up to Mom; she would've set him straight. Could you imagine if she found out her son is in the king's inner circle?"

"When this had all started, I had wished that it was just a rumor." John sighed. "But I can't say I was surprised. I can barely remember how close we once were. He used to be sweet and sensible, a bit odd in others' eyes, but nothing evil was in him. I wouldn't say it's too late for him. He did seem reluctant during the battle of dragons."

"Well, the king offers his followers immortality and loads of money; that's enough to make anyone loyal."

"If only we had a kind, positive leader." John sighed. "Don't get me wrong, Bella's heart is in the right place, but she scares even me, and she's no Saint Merlin."

"Where has Roman been staying?" Ace asked.

"A manor in the forest, of course." John laughed. "Living the dream."

Ace became silent. All of his brothers had been living the dream, whether they knew it or not. Roman was filthy rich with a disturbing yet sexy wife, Krum had traveled the world both in this realm and the Heofsij one, John had a gorgeous family full of dotting children, and Lewis was married to a princess who sacrificed her crown for his love. However, Lewis was now without Angel and his son, so maybe Ace didn't have it too bad now. Growing up, Ace had it the worst, and now here he was, widowed with patients entrapped in his basement. If only he could obtain magic, then maybe he could live the dream too.

"Does Roman and Krum know that their sons will be staying under my care?" Ace broke the silence.

"No, I'll see Krum... Roman, I'll just write him a letter."

"You remember the rules, don't you?" Ace asked.

"No visitations, only letters." John smiled. "Merlin, I missed Spence. Will she be discharged anytime soon?"

"That'll be up to her; she's approaching recovery quite bitterly. I got her eating today, though; I made some of Mom's fudge balls." Ace sugarcoated the truth. John's mouth began to water.

Spencer aided Caden over to the kitchen table where they would sit until John and Ace ascended from the basement's glow. "I'm glad you guys are here, even though if you guys had just listened to me, we'd all be free."

"I'm glad my suspicions were correct," John Jr. said louder than he intended as he couldn't seem to align his pitch to average volume. "Man, those letters. I knew that wasn't my twin."

He still hadn't mastered lip reading so all Spencer could do was smile. She turned to her cousins. "I'm glad you guys got here when you did. Ace was going to kill me, honestly. I didn't know how crazy he was before I was admitted here. I mean, how dare he keep me here and forge my writing? I always liked locking myself away from my family and people in general, for that matter, but now I've been cooped up in my room – well, what looks like my room – with no other option. I can't bear to stand it any longer. I mean, there's only so long you can be left alone with yourself before going completely mad. So does anyone besides Notleaf know what's up here?"

Caden shook his head. "No, not that I know of; hopefully, we'll find a way out of here soon. We honestly would've gone to the ministry if they weren't in the forest. The forbidden forest is no longer forbidden. It's prohibited, illegal to enter without the badge of a ministry member."

"What's the ministry dealing with, anyway?" Spencer asked.

Caden shrugged as he stared directly in front of him, making Aldaricus, who sat across him, feel uncomfortable. "Something about crazy giant creatures not like giants or trolls but like animals that have grown ten times their original size. Boring, really," he said, unfazed.

"*Boring?* That's terrifying," Spencer shuddered.

"I mean, the king has all kinds of followers, and that's the best he can come up with? Does Ace have any tea or caffeine quake or alcohol?"

Spencer shrugged. She stood up and walked over to the fridge, where she found a bottle of saffron eclipse, an alcoholic beverage mix of black and red liquid. Spencer pulled it out, walked over to the cupboard, and grabbed out four glasses. She served them to the boys as well as herself, damn the calories.

"So, how did the spell go wrong when it came to Aldaricus?" Spencer asked, wondering how a simple spell to mute someone could've gone so wrong. "It's not a complicated spell. All you have to say is, Forsuwung."

"Yeah, well." Caden reached to find his glass. Spencer, in fear that he might topple it over, placed it in his fingers. "Fart piper over there said 'Forsuburro.'" He pointed to John Jr. when he meant to imply Aldaricus.

Spencer laughed. "Oh, Merlin, how have you guys lived this long without me? You guys are crazy." She then turned to Aldaricus, who pouted cutely. She had never seen him so humble before, and she had to admit, it was a better look for him. "Ace won't be of any help, but once we get out, I'll put you back to normal. But for now, we're under house arrest. Hopefully, I'm not completely mad once we escape. Oh, I'm feeling faint." She rested her head in her arms.

Caden went to pat her back but ended up petting her hair. John Jr. and Aldaricus looked to the window and saw the small circle of what they could see of the world.

John said his goodbyes. Spencer held on for as long as she could. She didn't want to let go, but she knew she couldn't say anything; it'd put both her and him at risk. She'd risk the four on one but Caden was practically useless blind and Ace was a skilled combat fighter. Spencer wiped her tears as she watched him exit through the door that Ace had punched the code for. Ace showed his new patients to their rooms.

Caden bumped into his nightstand as he tried to find his way to bed. He fell to the ground. His room was made of wood and the ceiling was short; his father always had to walk in hunched over. The wood on the logs had been painted green; the paint was old and chipping off. A crooked sign sat on the floor beside his nightstand that read 'Viridi Vipers.' Beside his door lay his pair of muddy work boots. He had just gotten a job as a digger at Galdorwide's memorial graveyard. After the attack of the dragons, they needed all the help they could get.

It wasn't much. Caden and his father didn't have the luxury of a lovely house. Instead, it was made of logs and had three bedrooms, one bedroom that Krum never let anyone enter. After talking to his Uncle John a few months back, Caden learned that his mother had had a miscarriage, a baby girl they had named Anneliese. After a heartbreaking conversation with his father, he knew that the room was her nursery, one she never got to see. Since then, Caden had wondered what it would've been like to have a sister one year older than him. He reached up for the edge of his bed and pulled himself up.

Later that evening, Ace let his patients roam about in the basement. Spencer, Eion, Abigail, Freyja, John Jr., Caden, Aldaricus, Robbie, Lexi, Regina, and Ellen gathered in the living area while Crispin, Lena, and Adam roamed about the halls.

"We'll be quiet," Eion suggested. He had revealed his escape plan. "We will wait for Ace to call us up for breakfast tomorrow. Robbie, if he lets you out, you will have to make a scene. I'm sorry, but you would be the most believable. While making a scene, you will be on the staircase, angering him, he will come down, and we will shut the door behind him. We will have to break the code system down here first."

"Right," said Robbie. "Woah, woah, wait, you're telling me I'm going to get locked in with that douchewaffle badger?"

Eion made a face that showed that he wasn't going to change his mind. Robbie turned a sickish green. They couldn't tell if it was from his lack of food or his dread of the following day. His eyes fixed on the ceiling.

Their hearts all stopped as they heard Ace's heavy footsteps march down the stairs. Lena, Crispin, and Adam saw the anger in his eyes and moved out of his way as he approached the living area. The tall, athletic man had bloodshot eyes, making his gaze look fierce. His brown hair was in a messy bunch as if he had been wearing a hat. His striking chiseled face only made him look more demonic-looking when mixed with his fury. His almond-shaped eyes fixated on his son.

"Hello," Robbie said with fake enthusiasm; despite everything, he still didn't fear the Scaasi man.

"Oh no," Spencer said under her breath.

Ace came to a halt beneath the doorway. His hands were on his hips, displaying his great posture that came with years of Taekwondo. He stared at all of their faces one by one. In his pajama pocket were the boys' three wands sticking from out of it.

"*So*," he said in his usually raspy voice.

"Evening," Robbie said in a sarcastically winning voice.

"How stupid do you think I am?" he replied in a deadly whisper.

Eion knew that his father knew. "I'm sorry." He looked to his feet.

"All your whispering, I may not have magic, but I hear everything in this house! What do you think? I'm lying? You want to break the code box, Robbie is to distract me, and you'd all lock me down in here."

All their mouths dropped, including Robbie's. "Wow," Robbie muttered to himself, both amazed and startled.

"You're damn right, wow! I am more capable than you know! Being magicless has made me smarter, stronger." He approached Robbie. He then looked at the rest of his patients, who sat like scared rabbits on the two large couches. "I could kill you all right now if I wanted to. You're all weak without your little wands." He reached into his pocket and grabbed out the three new arrivals wands and snapped them in half.

Ace's threats had seemed to go on for hours. His throat had become scratchy as he had worn down his voice. He let out a long exhale before turning to Spencer, who flinched. "I'm very disappointed in you, Spence. Come with me."

Ace turned and stormed out of the room. Spencer looked to Robbie, who looked just as worried as she did. He gave her a nod of encouragement as he rocked his fist. Spencer slowly stood up and followed Ace.

She was relieved to find that Ace had passed the laboratory and headed up the stairs. When they got upstairs, Ace shut the door firmly behind them. Spencer looked around at the small kitchen that would be even more cramped the following morning now that he had a total of fourteen patients. She looked at the wooden table whose color seemed to fade with each day.

Spencer took her usual seat and looked around, unsure what else to do. Her breathing trembled. The room seemed so different now that she feared the wrath of her uncle.

The clock on the wall that hung above the counter seemed to have stopped. Spencer looked at the bookshelf, where books were cramped next to the trophies. She wanted to read some of the books on the shelf but was too afraid to ask – especially now. One, in particular, stood out to her – *Tapped for Evil*.

Ace sighed and turned on the small radio that sat by the fridge. A song unfamiliar to her began to play. Her eyes traveled to a CD case whose cover was quite exciting and read *Teddy Bear Metal*. Yes, its performers are animated teddy bears that decided that helping sick children with jokes and lollipops wasn't their passion.

Ace then clattered around the kitchen. Each clashing of pots and plates made Spencer jump. He was tossing things everywhere. Ace didn't seem to be in his usual state of mind, which was already hazardous to begin with. Ace gave her a dirty look as he threw pickles and quail meat into the frying pan.

"Don't ever try to fool me again," he said sternly. "Now, I don't want to blame you." He took a plate from out of the cupboard and placed it in front of his niece. He walked back over to the stove and carried the pan over, placing a pile of fried pickles and meat onto her plate. "I do want you to get healthy. I was talking to your father, and nobody wants to lose you. At this rate, with your lack of nutrition, your death can happen at any moment, and I fear your disorder may already have done some damage to your kidneys that may be irreversible if we do not get you better now."

Spencer wished that she could grab her wand and magically make her food disappear, but she had no choice but to eat it here. "I'm sorry, Uncle Ace," Spencer only apologized because she thought that that was something he'd want to hear.

"Eat," Ace snapped. "You can't starve yourself any longer. I won't allow it." He walked to the fridge and pulled out a tub of butter. He grabbed a spoon from the utility drawer and plopped a heaping tablespoon onto her food.

At that moment, a slight knock came from the basement door. When Ace opened, the girl squealed. It was Ellen. "I can smell the food. I didn't eat any of my other meals. I only eat dinner, may I?"

Ace smiled and allowed the girl to take a step inside. Ellen took a seat beside Spencer. Things hadn't been the same, both of their thoughts became more and more obsessed with food that conversation wasn't on their mind. Ellen eyed Spencer taking in her new weight; she couldn't help but be jealous despite how sickly she looked.

"On second thought, I think I'll pass," Ellen stood up from the seat.

"Ellen," Ace narrowed his eyes and gave her a charming smile that had always seemed to work on Lena. "You're a beautiful girl."

Ellen blushed. She sat back down. Anyone else in the world could've told her this, but Mr. Ace Scaasi was a strapping man; her heart couldn't help but flutter.

"You deserve to be on the cover of *Witches* magazine," he said with a charming grin. Nothing more was said until their three plates were cleared.

"I'm tired," Spencer stretched before letting a loud yawn. "I'd like to go to bed."

"No," Ace snapped but then lowered his temper. "Unfortunately, you two and all those who had conspired against me will spend the night doing chores."

"You just wanted to feed me for energy, didn't you?" Spencer accused.

"No," he said before merely shaking his head. "Lena, Crispin, and Adam will all get to enjoy their soft beds tonight." He turned to Spencer. "I saw you admiring the books. Once you finish, you can pick a book from the shelf, and it'll be yours to keep."

Once the eleven rebellious patients had finished the list of chores to do around the house, Ace brought Spencer over to the bookshelf. Her hands immediately pulled out the heavy book, *Tapped for Evi*l, written in fancy gold writing on the cover. Behind the title was the photograph of a handsome man with flowing blond hair. He wore a tall, purple witch hat and matching robes. His bright blue eyes were almost surreal, yet the photo didn't seem to have been tampered with; Spencer beamed down at the image.

"I didn't know Kenneth Riley wrote this." Spencer practically had to hold in her drool. "A son of the emperor, leader of the peace, and writer? This man truly is marvelous."

"All the girls fancied him, and back in the day, they fancied his father too," Ace explained.

"Really?" she asked, trying to picture the emperor Peta Riley young;

she could imagine it quite well; aged fifty-seven, he was still quite handsome. Ace nodded. "Have you read this book?"

"Yes, he's a brilliant man. He has influenced some of my experiments. Unfortunately, he has yet to discover how to turn Nullums into wizards." He frowned. Spencer yawned as the sun was beginning to rise; she and all the others sent to do chores would have to eat breakfast before heading down to their rooms.

***

Bella wandered out to the backyard of the ministry's mansion, Angel followed. There was a garden outside that they hadn't seemed to remember; after all, the ministry's villa was usually the last resort when chaos neared. However, the ministry members had taken precautionary measures this time. There were plenty of weeds in the garden bed, and the yard's grass needed some cutting. She decided that she'd assign one of her servants to do the yard work as she and the ministry didn't have any time for such things. The trees in the forest had gnarled their branches in position after going back to their normal state after the event weeks ago. There seemed to be new flowers that Bella had never seen before growing along the edges of the forest square before the mansion's lot. Frogs began to hop out of the forest wildly. The sisters looked to one another.

"It's spring," Angel suggested. "Maybe they just want to bathe in the sun."

"Yeah," Bella replied, unconvinced. She walked to the garden and decided to sit in front of it, keeping an eye on the surrounding forest. Angel joined her.

Suddenly, from the bushes along the forest square, the two sisters heard a loud scuffing noise. Bella and Angel, startled, rushed to their feet, wands in hand. From the bushes emerged a massive centaur. With its lower body resembling that of a horse and covered in dark brown fur, the beast reminded Bella of her childhood nightmares of being turned into one. The hair on the human half of his body was the same color, flowing beautifully down to his neck.

"Yes?" Bella asked grimly; she was almost disgusted by the creature. Growing up, she feared she'd wake up to find the legs of a horse beneath her. Angel, however, found herself quite mesmerized by the creature's big, doe eyes.

"My queen," he said gallantly. His front hoof lifted, allowing himself to bow.

Bella's father, years ago, had banished the centaurs. She had to say, she was quite offended to see one lurking around. His coat was shiny, Angel wanted to reach out and pet him, but she knew that that was an offensive act. A child centaur approached; he had the same dark brown hair. However, the horse's body was a cream color. Its legs were knobbly. He almost looked precisely like the centaur in front of him. Angel had lowered her wand while Bella stood holding hers out at an arm's length.

Before the creature could say any more, Bella attacked. She dropped her body, grabbed its legs, and tossed him over onto his back. She held onto his front ankles firmly while his back legs frantically kicked as he told his son to run. Krum had been watching from the window; a small smile appeared on his face when he saw the tiny woman flip over a full-sized centaur.

"My father banished your kind!"

He raised his head to look into the queen's eyes. "I'm sorry, just let me go; I thought now that your father's reign was done that we could come back. No other kingdom wants us."

Bella tightened her grip. His back legs began to kick once more. Bella looked at Angel and saw the shock on her young sister's face. "Help me!" she said through gritted teeth.

Angel shook off her empathy for the creature and went to help her sister; she was sure Bella had a good reason for it. The centaur was able to break one hoof free from Bella's grip. He quickly turned his head and bit her hand. Bella let out a scream as she shook her hand, not from pain but in fear that his condition was contagious. She continued to scream as her thoughts raced about her turning into one. The centaur broke free from Angel's grip and ran back to the forest. Krum raced outside. Bella could see her vision fading as all her energy was being put into her screams.

"Let me see." Krum offered his hand. Bella calmed her screams; she stretched out her hand. "He barely got any skin." Krum tilted his head before looking back at her. "Did it hurt?"

"No!" Bella snipped, pulling her hand back. Krum held his hands up in surrender. "I'm not going to turn into a centaur now, am I?"

Krum tried to hide his smile. "No, ma'am, you won't." He looked off to the forest. "Hopefully, they left Galdorwide; if not, they're looking for trouble assaulting the queen like that."

"In all fairness, Bella assaulted him first," Angel piped up.

Just then, the back door slammed. It was John who hurried over to Krum. He had taken off his glasses. His eyes looked reddened as if he had been vigorously rubbing his eyes clear of tears. He was wearing his usual, nice suit, but his clothing looked messy with wrinkles this time. His tie was crooked, and one side of his white dress shirt was untucked.

"What a night," John said finally, looking to his brother Krum. "I need to talk to you."

They went into the tiny, dark kitchen only lit by a few candles. The walls were made of stone. A long, wooden table with built-in bench seats sat in the middle. Empty, wooden plates, bowls, jugs, and spoons had been scattered from the ministry's breakfast earlier this morning. There was still some caffeine quake in one of the jugs. John poured himself some and another for Krum. He took a sip before taking a seat across from the pirate. He sighed.

"What happened?" Krum asked.

"It's our sons. They got in an accident at the school's hospital ward. I brought them to Ace's. Notleaf tried to get a hold of you yesterday, but you never came," John explained.

"I never received a letter. Is Caden all right?"

"He's gone blind; Notleaf tried magic, but it didn't work. He suggested I bring him to our brother. Ace wanted me to inform you that your only way of communication while he's under his care is through letters, no visitations."

"All right," Krum said as he took a sip from his mug. He didn't like it, but he trusted his brother; after all, he was just a Nullum. He looked to his brother John and saw that his unease was still present. "How's Junior?"

John's eyes flicked up to Krum before looking back down to his drink. "He's gone deaf." He shook his head. He took in a deep breath as he still looked lost in thought.

"What else is bothering you?" Krum asked.

John sighed and looked to his older brother, this time with tears in his eyes. "It's Spencer." He shook his head once more. "She looks sicker than ever. I can't bear the thought of losing her, especially for her to die under Ace's care. I want to be with her, but Ace insisted that he was going to make her better."

"I'm sure she'll be all right. Ace won't let us down." He gave a nod of assurance. "We don't have to pay him for his homecare, do we? I mean, if we are, worst-case scenario, you threaten to stop paying him, he'll throw her back to you in no time."

Adelaide appeared in the kitchen. She halted when the two men stopped talking and looked at her. "Oh, I'm sorry, I'll come back later," she apologized and also held back the need she felt to bow. They weren't royal, but they were practically famous – infamous.

"No, it's all right." John waved her in.

"A-are you sure? I don't mind waiting; I just wanted to make some pancakes," she rambled.

"Yes, it's all right." John smiled.

Krum couldn't help but stare at the girl. Her red hair was vibrant as the sun shone in from the window by the sink. More freckles had appeared on her face as the warm weather approached. She was wearing high-waisted black shorts that showed off her long legs, and he snapped out of his daze when her fiancé, Arthur, walked in.

His eyes were flashing despite not even noticing Krum's admiration toward his fiancée. "Imagine my surprise when" – Arthur's loud voice boomed throughout the small room, sending Adelaide's heart beating wildly; she jumped to look at him – "it wasn't enough that you were gawking at Kenneth, but Alizeh tells me you had been drooling over Krum as well."

Adelaide's eyes widened. She quickly looked at Krum, who was in their presence, then back to Arthur. "Well, darling, Kenneth was a childhood crush of mine, seeing him on the magazines and all and well, Krum, he saved my life when I was a little girl, so yes I crushed on him, but that was… then. And with Kenneth joining the ministry, you still mustn't worry. I mean, it's not like I stand a chance with him."

"And if you did?" Arthur challenged.

"I wouldn't," she replied quickly. "Arthur, what has gotten into you?" She decided to no longer feel small, so she began to shout. "It's not like I'm sleeping with anyone else! And for your information! I was excited to tell you, but now I'm not, and I don't want to tell you until you're no longer frinxing me off!"

"Tell me what?" Arthur asked blankly. Then his eyes widened as a puzzle of information went into place – Adelaide had denied drinks last night, and she had been sick these past few mornings. "Good Merlin, are you pregnant?"

"Are you calling me fat!"

His eyes widened even further, further than thought to be possible. "No, no, it's just you've been sick lately, craving strawberry pancakes, and you refused drinks last night."

"Oh." She calmed herself, then folded her arms. "Well, you're right." She didn't seem too excited, but Arthur assumed that was just because of his rude greeting this morning.

"Really?" Arthur asked eagerly. "Are you all right? Is the baby all right? How'd you know?"

"Ian," she replied simply. "And yes, I'm fine, and so is the baby. Ian said he'd be keeping a close eye on me during our stay."

"Well, shouldn't you go home and rest?" Arthur suggested. Her eyes sparkled with fury. Before she could open her mouth, he changed his mind. "Well, maybe not. After all, we will need your brain."

"Come on, let's leave them to it." John stood, Krum followed.

They both congratulated the couple before leaving them to bask in what should've been a happier moment. Maybe with them gone, they could.

"We can finish talking in my room," John suggested.

They slipped out of the kitchen and down a narrow hallway where torches flickered along the walls. They went up the many stairs, zigzagging until they reached their desired floor. The door beside John's bedroom stood ajar. John saw Bella snap the door shut after hearing their footsteps approach. John furrowed his brow. It looked like Bella was back to her old self, not wanting to be around anyone else besides herself and sometimes Ben.

They reached the room where John would be staying until their case would come to an end. The paint on the door had been peeling like the rest of the house had been. A small, golden plaque had been placed on John's door that read, JOHN SCAASI. It was something new added to each bedroom's doors, now that the ministry was beginning to grow in numbers.

They stepped inside. Krum's head was almost touching the ceiling as he was a few inches taller than John. The room was what you would expect in an abandoned mansion that no one cared enough to repair. There were large, mullioned windows on either side of what looked to be the remnants of a brick fireplace as now there was just a squared hole in the wall. To the right was a white armchair that had one of its arms broken off. The tiles on the floor had all been torn off, leaving the crisp cement beneath their feet. Above them, wooden pieces pricked out of position. They walked over to the dusty bed where they would finish their discussion.

"Your daughter," Krum began.

"Anorexic; Ace diagnosed her with anorexia nervosa, something Mary and I had already feared to be true," John replied as he picked dirt off of the white sheet. "But she seems to have only gotten worse under his care."

A pile of spellbooks sat in the corner of his room, including the one that helps witches unlock their powers. Just a few months ago, the book gave Gower the power of mimicry that didn't require any abilities. You only needed proper thought and concentration. John himself had received the gift of breathing underwater. John Jr. had been given the gift of precognition; Lovetta, one of Gower's students and close friend of John Jr., received the power of super-strength. Aldric, another of John Jr.'s friends, had been given the ability to work all elemental magic at equal strength – the strength he naturally had in fire became the strength he had in the other three elements. Caden, John's nephew, was the last to receive the book's final gift, magic mimicry, which gave him the power of all four auras. Maybe if Caden had met with John for training sessions, he'd be able to unblind himself, but for now, that was Ace's job.

John's wand was lying on top of the windowsill, something Mary would've smacked his hand for as it would leave pale sun marks on the wand's precious wood. Krum reached to the bedside table where a pack of cards sat. He picked it up and stared over at the window. Krum kept an eye on the hedges making sure a pack of centaurs weren't making their way through. He then turned to John, who was looking at him nervously.

"What are you looking at?" John asked, rubbing his hands together. "See something? Any of the king's giant creatures."

Krum smiled. "No, nothing like that." He patted his younger brother on the shoulder. John smiled.

CHAPTER 4

Life at Ace's was significantly different than life back home. Caden often had the house to himself as his dad was away, but now he was living in a place where he could always hear people chatter. Everyone was getting on his nerves. Ace's place was strange. He could tell without even looking – it wasn't just the structure but the doctor himself. He had all his patients locked away like animals, yet he expected them to be clean and proper every second. This morning, when Caden walked up the stairs, with Spencer's help, Ace had ordered him to tuck in his green dress shirt at once.

Loud noises would come from upstairs during the night. It was as if Ace had purposefully thrown something whenever Caden was beginning to fall asleep. Ace often did his experiments during the night. Caden could hear the screams and explosions going off down the hall. However, Caden could say a few good things about staying at Ace's because he had a familial bond with his fellow patients. Only one didn't seem to like him much, and that was Lena, Ace's pet. Other than that, everyone seemed to like him. None of it was fake because they feared him, which was usual at Galdorwide High. During lunch, Ace fussed about the state of Caden's socks.

"Sorry," Caden said as he plopped his fork filled with lime chicken into his mouth. "I would've done a better job dressing if I could look into a mirror."

Caden, unfortunately, saw some similarities between his Uncle Ace and his father, Krum. Like his father, Ace instructed that Caden eat three times the amount of food after saying that he had finished, which must be a Scaasi thing. Spencer sat next to him during his meals so that she could help him eat as well as bombard him with whispers of how angry she was that he had got himself blind instead of going to the ministry.

"None of us should be here right now," she whispered and then pulled away before Ace grew too suspicious. Once Ace would move on to chat with another patient, she would lean back over to him. "You're a genius. Now we have to find a way out without using magic."

After the patients finished their meal, they were all ordered to bring their dishes to the sink. It was Adam's turn to wash the dishes. While attempting to place his plate on the counter, Caden's silverware crashed onto the floor. Ace swung around. Spencer dived to the ground and began to pick up the plate's broken pieces that looked as if he had licked it clean. Ace saw this and decided to let it go.

It was a sunny morning when Mary received letters from both John Jr. and Spencer. She brought them to her chest and held them tightly after they had flown in through her window. It had almost been a week since John Jr.'s arrival at Ace's home care. She had just woken up her three daughters for breakfast. They rubbed their eyes as they slumped their way down the hall. She sat at the table, waiting for them to join her.

"What's that?" Olivia asked as she took her usual seat between Lulia and Harriet.

"Letters from the twins." She held up the yellow envelopes addressed in their handwritings, both of which were awful, as usual. John Jr.'s was circular, sloppy, and large, while Spencer's was undersized and looked as if they had been written by a shaky hand. Everything seemed ordinary to Mary as the writing looked just as it did on their homework scrolls. "I hope they're doing okay. They better be listening to all of Ace's suggestions. We all know how stubborn they can be."

She could still picture the twins walking into the kitchen wearing their plaid pajamas and random band tees. They were so similar yet so different. It baffled her.

For a few moments, they were all silent as Mary read from the letter. John Jr.'s first.

Dear Mom,

I am writing to both you and Dad. Uncle Ace has alerted me that there is no quick fix for my condition. My recovery will be a long journey. As Ace explains, my condition is like a candle: sustained in one moment and blown out to smoke the next. I will have to be very precautious to heal as soon as possible. It will be hard work, but it will all be worth it once I get my hearing back.

I will stay in bed most days and be isolated for my healing to go as scheduled. I wish I can say that I will be back to normal soon, but Ace said that I might get my hearing back, but just not to its fullest potential. Sometimes, when I am alone, I think I hear my breaths. I get excited and call for Ace, only for him to enter the room and not hear a word he says. Through writing (as I have yet to master lip-reading), he explained that sometimes what I think I am hearing is just myself feeling vibrations or possibly even hallucinating, reminiscing on the beautiful sounds I was once able to attend. I need you to find strength and keep believing in me. I need all the positive thoughts and vibes I can get. Spencer and I are fine when Ace allows me to roam freely and Spence dances to 'Babe, You're Strange' by The Imaginary Kings, just like old times. Ace said that as much as I need silence and isolation, I need fun and relaxation, which is best done with my twin. She's less annoying here.

I will be okay. Spence will be okay.

I am sending my love, John.

Olivia leaned over the table, stretching to get a better look at the letter. "How's Junny doing?" she asked. "Must be having fun not having to go to school." At this point, Olivia got her mother's eye and knew that at once, she should sit back in her chair like a proper lady. She quickly busied herself with her dark chocolate and a ginger roll.

"I assure you that being sick and deaf for months on end is way worse than going to school for seven hours," Mary said with a quick look to Olivia. "Ace's care is more expensive than schooling, so I hope he treats them promptly."

"He will," Olivia tried to assure her mother.

Mary smiled before looking at Lulia. "So, Lulia, are you excited to start Galdorwide High in a few months?"

She nodded as her face lit up, her red curls bounced off her shoulders. She rested her head in her hands as she began to daydream. Mary was happy as her twins had been far from excited for their first year, and she had to fight them every morning to get them out of bed. Just then, one of Mary's younger brothers, Jadon Black, walked in with his son Dallas. Jadon was wearing a purple and blue plaid buttoned shirt. Dallas, now eighteen, wore a jean jacket with a gray shirt beneath. Mary had almost forgotten what day it was.

"Good morning," the tall, athletic man with sunflower eyes said in a deep, baritone voice as he entered. He smiled, which showed off his dimples that sat beneath a triangular, pointed nose. He had long, flowing hair down to his shoulders and sideburns. "Lovely spring day outside." He looked so different from when he was younger, but Mary could always recognize his puppy-like eyes.

He and Dallas walked in, taking the open seats next to Mary. Dallas pulled out three tiny boxes from out of his jean jacket. They were presents for the girls from both him and his father. They did not see them much, but they always wanted to show their love each visit.

"Is that for us?" exclaimed Lulia as she pointed at the tiny blue-wrapped boxes. Dallas nodded. He slid each of the boxes along the table toward the girls. Lulia snatched it into her hands immediately. "Did I ever tell you that you're my favorite cousin?" They ripped open the presents.

Once the wrapping had been removed, the boxes were enlarged to their proper size. Inside Olivia's was two t-shirts that were both black. One read 'Stay at Home' in white writing. The other read 'Pajama Girl,' which was a nickname they had given her because all she did was stay in her pajamas if it was a day off from school. If it were not, she'd be dressed nicely for school, come home and take a shower, just to put pajamas back on. Inside Harriet's box was a black tote with white writing that read the names of the four goddesses: Astradung, Sophia, Carina, and Aisling.

Inside Lulia's was a tiny sword that was as long as Jadon's hand. Her eyes lit up as she held it up in front of her face.

"A lot of damage that sword can do," Dallas began. "It's been in the Black family for generations. Now that I am eighteen, Dad said I could pass it on to someone else. And who other than Lulia? You're going to be the next 'it' witch, you just watch."

Lulia abruptly stood up, knocking the chair behind her over as she ran to hug her cousin. Mary usually would've been angry about the chair but decided to let it go as she saw how happy her daughter was.

"Those are all lovely gifts." Mary smiled. "And, girls, don't forget to thank your uncle, I'm sure he had a part in this too." The girls all thanked him. Mary offered her brother and nephew some of her breakfast, which was more of a dessert. They nodded. Once they all finished their meals, Mary began to clear off the table.

"So, what's the plan today?" Mary asked.

"Well, we were thinking of heading to Heofsij land, not too far, just to a London coffee shop Justin and his family went to. They loved it. It has a view of the park. He said their caffeine options are great, and maybe we can even buy some bikes while we're there," Jadon said.

"The girls haven't been to the Heofsij land. They do not even know what a bike is, let alone know how to ride them. I'd love to go, but John has gone to the ministry castle for work, and I can't leave the girls home alone."

"You don't have to," Dallas piped in. "I'll stay with the girls, just as long as Dad brings a caffeinated drink back. And I think you should let Lulia go. She is old enough. She is going to high school in just a few months after all." He winked at the redhead.

***

Aldric and Lovetta were outside on the school's lawn off to the side by the lake, where they usually went to practice their new skills. They had to be hidden and extra careful when discussing and performing their crafts. The last time they were caught, they had to add Caden into the group. It is all tough to explain, and the two of them didn't even know if they grasped the entire concept yet. Still, all they knew was that they had split and gained powers to keep from becoming corrupt and, more importantly, keeping the queen from gaining all its control, becoming the most powerful sorcerer ever to have lived. If Gower did not trust the queen with the book, they knew that it was best to lie and keep this book from her.

"*Hmm*, how else can you work on super-strength if we can't draw attention like the trees?" Aldric had asked.

"Well… I can fight you," she suggested.

"You want to fight me?" Aldric asked with a laugh. "You want to fight me?"

Lovetta knew that if Caden and John Jr. were around, they would be telling her, no, not to, for her safety. It was as if they didn't even take her power seriously despite knocking a tree down with only one good kick. The more Aldric laughed, the more she wanted to. Not for anger but for the respect she demanded.

"Right now?" He laughed again.

She stood up, and so did he. She bowed, and he did as well. A few weeks ago, she attended an arcane class at Daemon's school, where she took part in a duel, not with magic but with her fists and legs. Daemon, as well as the other instructors, were immediately impressed. They asked her to join their school full time, but she only declined because she knew that Aldric and Gower's training was more critical. In one class, she felt that she did learn a lot from Daemon, and she felt like she had known enough to take Aldric down. Lovetta wanted him to treat her as Daemon had.

"You're very strong," Daemon had observed. "But your full strength hasn't even reached its full potential. You must unlock and set free the strength you're holding back inside you!" Little did he know, she was holding her strength in, and she had done it purposefully as she did not want to injure his student, Jiselle, severely.

Aldric was still smiling as they prepared themselves. She nodded and promisingly smiled. "Lovetta," he began. "This is embarrassing, but okay." He turned instead of getting in stance; he patted his cheek, wanting her to strike. "Give me your best shot."

Before she could, he raised his elbow, hitting her, she fell to the ground. As she remained on the grass, she kicked out her leg, sweeping him from beneath his feet. He fell. She raised her other leg and kicked his face before standing up. She raised her leg over her head and shot it down, striking his back. He immediately got back up. She grabbed each of his wrists, and with her newfound strength, she was able to flip him over. She then remembered more of Daemon's advice – *slow down, focus your strength.* He got back up and approached her. She kicked him straight in the chest. With her other leg, she kicked his face. She spun around and kicked his face once more. He fell.

He reached out for his wand that had fallen out of his red cloak pocket. He spun it around and pointed at Lovetta. "*Brynewelm!*" he cast beneath his breath. He pulled himself up onto his elbows than to his knees. "That was good, Lovetta," he said as he rubbed his jaw. "It was. Again?" he asked.

She tried to punch him, but he blocked it with his arm. She reeled back in pain. His arm had burned her. She did not care because they both had to work on their skills, even if that meant him using magic during their fights. She went for a kick, but he caught her leg. Steam emitted from her baby blue uniform slacks. He held onto her, twisted her, and brought her to the ground. She stayed down for a bit. She needed a break as her leg and arm pulsed with pain. *Focus*, she could hear Daemon's voice, knowing what he would say if he were here. She rubbed her leg, which now sat beneath a black mark in her pants. She focused on her strength as she would for a spell. She slowly rose to her knees. Aldric went for another kick, which she blocked with both her hands, pushing his leg down. Her hands bubbled, but she did not pay any attention to it. Instead, she stood up, jumped, and kicked his face sending him back to the ground.

"Again?" she taunted.

***

Aldaricus, Caden, Spencer, Robbie, Eion, Lexi, Ellen, Regina, and John Jr. all sat in the basement living area.

"I had a job offer for when I graduated. The Galdorwide Stable was looking for a horse trainer. I aced the Art of Taming Animals. I was so happy," Regina began. "My life was finally coming together, I was slowly becoming happier, my appetite was coming back, but Notleaf took note of my pale skin, dark circles under my eyes, and my decreasing weight and sent me here. Do you think he knows what Ace is up to?"

"He had his suspicions. That is all I'm allowed to say. Who knows if Ace is listening," replied Caden.

Aldaricus wanted to join in the conversation, but he feared the embarrassment of his new voice, especially around Regina, a beautiful girl from Ixicia. He had not noticed how pretty she was until he got to know her. Everyone at school made fun of her. She was pale with stringy, brown hair that surpassed her shoulders. Her lips were often cracked, something she had tried to fix with spells and even herbal remedies, but nothing seemed to work. Despite his new fondness, there was nothing different from how she looked now and how she looked while at school. Regina was even wearing her school uniform as it had been what she was wearing when she was admitted, and she had not found the energy or confidence to wear the clothing her father had packed her. Her father was embarrassed by her, usually looking at her in disgust every morning. He hated the lack of effort she put into her appearance. Because of this, she felt truly alone. She couldn't explain how she got the bruises. She could not bear to tell him how students tripped her in the halls. The worst part of the bullying was that it didn't stop at school. Her father would call her 'screwed up.' And girls from Ixicia were practically treated like slaves, and her and her family moving to Galdorwide didn't change her father's view of her. He could see that she had no friends. Sure, she had Spencer, Ellen, and Lexi, but that was only at school. She never tried to see them outside of lunch, but neither did they.

On good days, her father would tell her that she needed more confidence as if by saying it, she would be gifted it. However, personalities cannot change with a simple wish. She was admitted to Ace for anorexia, though it was not like Spencer's control or Ellen's self-consciousness but more because she didn't have an appetite. How could she when all she wanted to do was cry?

Regina grew uncomfortable as Aldaricus continued to stare at her. She lowered her forehead into her hand as she thought that he was staring at the bare spots in her eyebrows that she had plucked out during a manic episode. Her eyes looked back up to Aldaricus, who gave a sweet smile before reaching into his pocket and pulling out a pocket-sized notebook and pencil. He scribbled some words and handed them to Spencer to read.

"Aldaricus says: I too was offered a job for after my graduation day as an acolyte at Galdorwide's chapel; like you, Regina, I'll be missing out on a great opportunity."

Regina slowly sat back up, still unsure if she should continue to cover her eyebrow. She smiled when her eyes met his dimples. She lowered her hand.

Spencer looked to Aldaricus. "Doesn't the chapel stand against your parents?" Aldaricus nodded. "The church has objected to the late king's behavior, even claiming that he is a worshipper of Mania. Do your parents know?" He shook his head.

"Well, I'm proud of you, a true good Scaasi." Spencer smiled. "Looks like our generation may change how the rest of the kingdom looks at our family."

***

Mary could not help but be anxious. Traveling to the Heofsij world was no simple spell. Teleportation was something a witch needed a license for, something her thirteen-year-old daughter did not yet have. A single mistake could send you somewhere on the opposite side of the universe. She walked down to the basement, where all their magical supplies were stored. She grabbed out nine white candles. She handed three to Jadon and three to Lulia.

"Place them on the ground around you," Mary explained.

Lulia had to admit, she was nervous too. Hands shaking, she placed a candle in front, then one to her left and the other to her right.

"Light the candles," Mary instructed.

Lulia grabbed out her training wand. "*Ad*!" she cast as she pointed to each candle. Several bolts of blue fire exited her wand and lit each candle with a blue flame.

Mary reached into her purple coat pocket and pulled out a postcard of London. In the picture were tall and large buildings. "Look at this picture," Mary began. "Then close your eyes and vision this – nothing else, understand?" she asked. Lulia nodded.

"For this spell, it is crucial that you focus. A single slip of thought can send you to a different time or different place. I want you to continue to vision London and repeat after me – 'sé.'"

"*Sé.*"

"*Cristendom ic andgietléast.*"

"*Cristendom ic andgietléast.*"

"*Be isrbodung, crístesmél.*"

"*Be isrbodung, crístesmél.*"

"*Mec andstandan ablawting columba! Estmere ic ambyhtsecg and sted ic ambyhtsecg! Awendendness mec columba nú!*"

"*Mec andstandan ablawting columba! Estmere ic ambyhtsecg and sted ic ambyhtsecg! Awendendness mec columba nú!*"

"*Dette sy min eyre, swá.*"

"*Dette sy min eyre, swá.*"

"*Egl hit isrbodung!*"

"*Egl hit isrbodung!*"

The world around Lulia began to spin out of control. It was a wonder she remained on her feet. She could feel the pressure in her head grow. Her eyes struggled to stay open as her vision took in too much stimulation. She looked around as the spinning colors were light, then dark, then back to light. The world stopped spinning, and she fell backward and hit her head. She opened her eyes to see a spider crawling in its web. The light faded. The room she had fallen into was dark. A pink light came from out of the tiny, wooden window. She looked beside her and saw a shelf filled with dancing flowers – which was odd; she was almost sure there was no presence of magic in London. She felt alone and scared. Her mother and uncle should have appeared beside her by now. She reached into her pink, frilly dress' pocket and pulled out the sword Dallas had given her.

Dizzy and bruised, she stumbled up onto her feet. Lulia lifted her sword, fearing that she had not traveled to the right place or time. She was sure she did not think of any time zone except for the one she was in. She had no idea where she was. How could she send herself somewhere that she didn't even know existed? There were plenty of shelves along the walls, and in the middle of the room, it looked to be a dimly lit store.

A purple candle was lit inside of a glass jar that sat on what looked to be a clerk counter. Behind it was what looked to be an actual skull with intricate designs carved into it. Beside the candle and the head was a small basket where vials of potions and powders sat. She approached the counter and read some of the labels. The label on the basket read: *Only .03 feohs each!* One read: *Desire Me Powder*, a mix of pink and red powder in a glass vial. *Good Luck Powder* consisted of dark and lime green powder. Lulia made a disgusted face when she read the vial: *Dog Saliva*.

Wherever she was, she knew she could not stay here. The back of her head pulsed where it had struck the cement floor. She made her way quickly and silently to the door. Before she could open the door, she heard heavy footsteps approach from outside. She ducked and looked out the window to see the last person she would ever want to see in her dust-covered dress and messy hair that had tangled from all of the spinning – Ike Bernard, the principal of Galdorwide High. He was the real reason that she was excited for Galdorwide. He was short and either wore a big smile or a scowl – something many would say about her.

He had blue eyes and short, brown hair. He wore his blue Galdorwide High staff polo shirt and black slacks. Lulia had the hugest crush on him ever since she looked through the twins' yearbook; seeing him now was like seeing a celebrity she had always dreamed of meeting.

He was not someone that most girls crushed on. He was often referred to as 'The School Dad.' He was a coach for Galdorwide's Advenvolley team. It was Lulia's dream to become his top player. It mostly was because she wanted to impress him. However, she did have to admit that the game did look fun. An enchanted white ball would bounce around the Advenvolley field. It could travel as far as the forbidden forest. It hops from team to team, and the teams have to make sure that the ball does not hit the ground. If it does, they lose.

She looked around the store quickly, and only one place looked good to hide in – a black coffin. She ran to it and swung the door open, revealing a red, velvet interior fit for a vampire. She shuddered before locking herself in. She heard the bell above the store's door ring. She opened the door of the coffin just a crack so that she could look at him. A small boy walked in closely behind Mr. Bernard. *Does he have a son?* she asked herself, almost feeling betrayed. Her face grew hot. The boy had the same blue eyes and pudgy nose. Mr. Bernard walked in. He almost looked bored. But, how could he? The store was filled with strange things like ancient skulls and coffins. He tapped the bell on the clerk's desk that sat beside the head. He looked down to his young son, who looked to be about seven. "Don't touch anything," he said just as the young boy was reaching for an arrow that had a ghostly silver outlining.

"You dragged me out here on the weekend. Can you at least buy me something?" The young boy rolled his eyes.

"Yes, but not from here," Mr. Bernard replied. He peered out, looking to the back at a doorway shrouded in a purple rag waiting for the clerk to come. He impatiently rang the bell once more.

"Can it be an Advenvolley ball?" The kid's eyes lit up.

"Sure," Mr. Bernard replied. He seemed distracted. "But you can only use it around your mother or me."

Mother? her inner voice screamed.

Mr. Bernard looked to be in one of the aggressive mood swings that Spencer mentioned. He looked angry but kept himself calm and composed. Lulia admired that.

"My friend got one for his birthday last week. He says by high school, he'll be better than me, and I can't let that happen."

"Doesn't sound like a friend to me," Mr. Bernard replied in a monotonous voice.

A man with wild eyes and messy brown hair with thick sideburns exited from the back room. He approached them, almost hunched over.

"Mr. Bernard, always a pleasure seeing you," the man greeted with a raspy voice. "Is that your boy?" the man asked, peering over the principal's shoulder.

"Yes." Mr. Bernard smiled. "My oldest, Chonen." *Does he have more children?*

The clerk smiled at the young boy before looking back up to Mr. Bernard. "How can I help you today?"

"Well, not the usual," Mr. Bernard said harshly. "However, I think you can be of assistance."

The clerk's smile faded as he raised his brows. Mr. Bernard reached into his pocket and pulled out a scroll. He handed it over to the clerk, who unraveled it and began to read the long page intensely.

"That is a list of everything I need." Mr. Bernard's lips curled. "My boss requires a certain discrepancy, and he has asked me to collect these objects. He is up against some meddling witches and is only taking precautions. I know those objects combined can be quite alarming. There are rumors – you see, people are out to harm him seriously."

The clerk's face turned red as he debated whether he should allow such objects to be bought off him. He precisely knew what spell these ingredients were for.

"I assure you that if I did not trust my boss, I would have declined this errand."

The man looked up and nodded, hoping that his instincts were wrong. If they were right, the whole kingdom could be in danger. The man reached beneath his desk and grabbed out a brown paper bag that read The Withering. Two dying, red flowers were painted beside the fancy lettering.

Ike Bernard was the principal at Galdorwide High. Who would his boss be? wondered Lulia.

"I will see what I can find," the man said as he reached for one of the vials in the basket on his counter – Lulia was sure that it was the vial that had the thick, creamy consistency labeled: Dog Saliva.

"What's that?" Chonen pointed to a pair of shoes surrounded by a similar eerie, silver glow that the arrow had.

Mr. Bernard looked to see what he was pointing at. "Those are Haunter's Shoes. When you wear it, you get to walk in the steps a deceased person took moments before their death. It is a recent discovery, and many do not know of its existence," he explained.

"Why would anyone do that?" Chonen asked with an almost disgusted face.

"You can see everything as if you were them and there at that time. You can see exactly who or what killed them. It gives some people closure and can give others proof to a mystery." Mr. Bernard then looked to the clerk, who grabbed a leather-bound notebook and placed it inside the paper bag. "I don't mean to rush, but I am in quite the hurry."

Chonen began to roam the store. He waltzed around the shelves and was now in the aisle Lulia had been in. He looked at all the objects very closely, all while keeping his hands behind his back to make sure not to touch something that would curse or hurt him. A glowing green bracelet had seemed to attract his attention. Three other bracelets were similar; one blue, one red, and the other purple – the colors of the four primary auras.

After growing bored of the sight, he looked over to the black coffin. He squinted his eyes toward the small open crack. Lulia backed away, hoping that he had not caught a glimpse of her eye. Lulia heard the rustling of the paper bag.

"Come on, Chonen, I can't keep my boss waiting," his father called.

Lulia's body relaxed. The moment she heard the front door close, she looked out of the crack once more to see if the clerk had left his station. She was growing hot and sweaty and could not bear to be in there any longer. She had looked just in time as the man disappeared into the back room. As quietly as she could, she slipped from out of the coffin, passed the aisles of strange objects, and exited the store.

She clutched the bottom of her frilly dress as she looked around. She was in a dark alleyway surrounded by stores that seemed to hold just as many strange objects that The Withering had. The store directly across from her had flashing black lightning bolts displayed within the window. Two witches wearing black cloaks muttered to one another. The men's greasy, long hair shielded their faces. It was as if they did not want to be seen in such an area. She noticed the strange stares coming from those who whispered to one another as they looked at her. She could not blame them. Her dress looked practically neon in the poorly lit street where the stores and their objects were almost entirely black. She began to run past the two witches, who gave her a kind smile. One of the men had a cut along the bottom of his chin.

Lulia knew she was in Galdorwide, but she knew that it was a part of the kingdom she had never traveled to before. She looked at the people and the stores as she ran. Nothing looked familiar, and none of the store's names had rung a bell. Lulia wondered how she could have possibly imagined herself coming to a place like this, and then it hit her. For a moment while she was picturing London, her mind drifted off to all the magic she would learn in high school, and then her thoughts traveled to Mr. Bernard, whom she was most excited to see in person. She paused as she tried to catch her breath.

Suddenly, a lady with messy, brown hair emerged from the corner of the shop Lulia had stopped in front of. "You lost, dearie?" the woman asked in a high tone before cackling.

Lulia jumped back.

"She's with me," a familiar voice stated firmly after the woman had tried to reach for the young girl's shoulder.

Lulia turned to see Mr. Bernard looking down at her. Her face reddened even more, her heart began to beat faster, and she could swear that she could just about faint at the close sight of him. The woman bowed her head almost as if she feared him.

"What are you doing here?" Mr. Bernard asked as he crouched to her height, which seemed to be the same as his son, who looked strangely at the young girl. His blue eyes sparkled like the blue light energy in the lantern above them that shone down.

"I-I was supposed to go to the Heofsij place called London, but I ended up here – somehow." She looked to her feet.

Mr. Bernard stood to his feet and wrapped his arm around her shoulder, guiding her past the witch. Her surroundings were slowly becoming familiar. They were just along the edge of the forest. After making their way to the school and the office, Mr. Bernard decided that he and his son could make a short trip with the young girl to London to make sure she arrived safely. He performed the same ritual. Instead, this time, he, his son, and Lulia all stood in the middle of the candles. Lulia wiped her palms along with the skirt of her dress before Mr. Bernard held on to her hand.

They now stood outside a tall, yellow building. Tallgrass and flowers surrounded the mesmerizing building. It was nothing like Lulia had seen before. Mr. Bernard took the palm of his hand and began brushing off dirt and dust that had collected on her dress. "Make sure to tell your mom next time to keep you in her circle; quite odd you were sent to a whole place you had never heard of."

"Yeah... strange," Lulia mumbled but also glad he didn't bring up the fact that she was underage.

"Your mother and uncle should be here." Mr. Bernard looked around. "Let's go and find them." The three of them headed inside the building. "How old are you, Lulia?" Mr. Bernard tried to make conversation.

"Thirteen," she replied almost breathlessly as her body was fighting hard against the anxiety racing through her. She met her crush, who turned out to have more than one kid and a wife. To make things worse, she had to meet him with messy, tangled hair and dirty clothes. "I'll be fourteen soon."

"Ah, so I will see you soon," Mr. Bernard smiled, still holding his bag from The Withering. He did not trust it alone in his office.

"Lulia! Lulia!"

Lulia looked up and saw her mother and uncle. They had been sitting inside, and as soon as she entered, Mary stood up and ran to her daughter. Her dark, brown hair bounced around frantically as she approached her daughter. Jadon had jogged behind her.

"What happened to you?" Mary asked, her hands locked around her daughter's arms.

"She had teleported to the series of stores just behind the forest. She said she had never been there, so it's quite odd Lulia would teleport to a place she was unfamiliar with," Mr. Bernard explained.

"Thank you," Jadon said with a grin.

Lulia looked around at the café that did not look much different than the ones at home. Except here, you had to place an order rather than wait for it. The clerks here didn't have any psychic abilities to tell which food their guests craved.

"Goxrough, that's a dangerous place," Mary panted. She brushed her hair out of her face. "I was so worried."

"How was it?" Jadon asked his niece almost eagerly. "Growing up, Mom—I mean, Mary" – he rolled his eyes with a chuckle – "never let your three uncles or me into that city. I obliged her rules, and I've always had this itch to know what was beyond those trees."

"It wasn't nice," Lulia groaned.

Mary stood to her feet, adjusting her purse that she only wore out when visiting Heofsij land. Lulia felt embarrassed as her mother still held on to her hand.

"Oh, Lulia, you're so lucky Mr. Bernard found you. Goxrough is filled with dangerous people." It was as if as soon as Mary processed the words she spoke, she slowly turned to Mr. Bernard, the principal of her two eldest children. "What were you doing in Goxrough?"

Mr. Bernard paused as if pretending not to hear her, then as if his answer had processed through his brain slowly, he turned to Mary. "I was just showing my boy around, curious little one he is."

"You still owe me an Advenvolley," the boy moaned.

Mary, satisfied with his lie, looked to her daughter and began to brush her fingers through her hair, trying to take out the tangles. Mary had to hold in her instincts to pull out her wand and clean her daughter off right there and then.

"Yes, I do. We must be on our way." Mr. Bernard said his farewell. Mary and Jadon thanked him once more. Mr. Bernard had shaken Jadon's hand while taking Mary and Lulia's hands to his lips to kiss it. If she didn't faint now, she knew she never would. Mr. Bernard strode away.

Lulia followed her mother and uncle outside. She could not help but think that Mr. Bernard had lied to her mother. Mr. Bernard did buy stuff from Goxrough. Was he up to something dangerous? Why would he be showing his son around a dangerous place if he had not felt entirely comfortable around the people who worked and shopped there? Lulia's gut told her to tell her mother and uncle the truth, but her heart told her not to. She went with her wrenching heart. After all, he was still holding onto his shopping bag, so maybe they just weren't concerned.

Mary had gripped the hands of her daughter with relief. She would not know what she'd do after losing another child. "Oh, I'd love to get Mr. Bernard a gift when the school season returns, Lulia. You'll be the one to give it to him as thanks."

"Careful now." Jadon laughed. "I think you're falling in love."

"We all know, no one is a match for my John." She smiled happily as she thought back to how she married the kindest man.

They began to walk throughout the city, giving Lulia a tour. Lulia looked around nervously; she feared that she and her family would get pointed out as witches and that they would be detained and eventually burned, or at least that was the fear that John Jr. had put into her head.

They visited a restaurant in London where her mother and uncle ordered fish and chips and pina coladas, while Lulia ordered a full breakfast complete with eggs, sausage, ham, and bacon. Lulia was relieved that the restaurant had an all-day breakfast menu because all the other foods sounded quite strange.

After dinner, she and her family took a walk in a park with tall trees, but the open area was not covered by trees, unlike the kingdom. They also stopped for ice cream. It was nice spending one on one time with her mother and uncle. Most of the time spent with her uncle was also spent with most of the Black family. And for once, she had alone time with her mom, whose thoughts were not rambling about the twins. Lulia understood her mother's pain, heck she even missed her annoying brother, but Lulia did not stress like Mary. She didn't doubt that they'd return home.

Her mother insisted that they must stop at the market, where she had picked out an oversized, brown fur coat. It did not quite suit her personality, but it did look good on her. She somehow even looked posher.

Mary promised to buy Lulia a gift, but she immediately regretted it as her daughter ran toward a shiny, silver jacket. But as she promised, she bought it for Lulia, who had immediately thrown it on, taking off her pink cardigan. Mary picked up the cardigan that her daughter had thrown carelessly over her shoulder and onto the ground. Mary placed it in the bag where she had swapped her new jacket for the old.

The next stop in the market was dessert. They each got a donut. They began to pass by pastel-colored buildings and headed to a Heofsij royal residence. To get there, they took another walk through a different park. Lulia stared at the houses just along their edges and saw that the world was not too different from her own, despite the large vehicles used for transportation in place of brooms and carriages. It had taken a while for her to get used to their loud noises, but Jadon insisted that she was lucky that they had not gone to a city in this land called New York.

They were just about to leave when Jadon saw a poster of Ren Nillag announcing a book signing at a library. Before moving to the Heofsij world, Ren was quite close to the Black family, making sure to visit them after celebrating holidays with his own family. Lulia, after seeing his face on a large poster, grew excited as she missed him and his holiday gifts. Growing up, Ren was her favorite person in the world. She grew up calling him uncle due to his close friendship with her mother and uncles. However, despite this title, Lulia had a crush on him. She always thought that she would grow up to marry him. However, now that she was older, she realized that this was an unattainable dream.

"Can we see him?" Lulia squealed.

A crowd led to the library. A person at the door allowed a few people in at a time. He seemed to struggle at this as people pushed their way past him.

Luckily, Jadon was the tallest person in the crowd, and he was politely able to pass by as people made way for him. He held Mary's hand, who held Lulia's, creating a simple train as they made their way to the front of the crowd. The lineup did not end upon entering. Instead, it stretched to the back of the store. Along the tables were displays of his book titled: *Girl of Wind*. They eventually made it to the front of the crowd. Both Mary and Lulia began to fix their hair.

"Where is he?" Lulia asked as she stared at a long desk with piles of his book displayed.

"He'll be out soon," Jadon explained.

Jadon looked down at the book that he held in his hand. He furrowed his brow before opening it.

Ren Nillag came into view as he approached the table with a steaming mug of tea in his hand. There was a square, white object that he placed his cup on. The library had provided it. It was a device that would keep his drink warm throughout the meet and greet. He took a seat at the desk. On either side of him sat two posters, one of the book's cover and the other of his face. He was wearing a red suit. Mary looked to Jadon, who was flipping through pages intently. Mary looked down at the copy she had in her hand then looked to Lulia. Photographers raced to the front of the crowd and took pictures of him. He smiled, revealing shiny, perfect teeth. Mary looked behind her, where she saw women of all ages practically drooling over the sight.

As Ren turned to face the final photographer directly, his eyes drifted to Mary and then to Lulia. He immediately stood up from his chair. "It can't be," he said as his smile grew impossibly more gigantic.

The crowd looked to the girls whom he had been staring at. Ren waltzed around to the front of his desk and approached them. He reached for Lulia's arm and pulled her up onto the heightened ground where his desk sat.

"I want you all to meet the young girl who inspired the young protagonist Lily!" The crowd fell silent as he started to talk in his deep and pleasant voice.

Lulia's face burned a bright red, half because of embarrassment and half because Ren had written her as a main character. She began to wonder what was so special about her. Lulia knew that she would not make it for the leading role if there were ever a book written about her life. Her life was boring. School and homework were all she had going for her, and that would make quite a boring book. The photographers flashed their cameras wildly.

"Smile, dear," Ren looked down at the girl whose face looked frozen in stone with what looked like frostbitten cheeks. Once the cameras stopped, she looked over to her mother and uncle, who looked anything but pleased.

"What an extraordinary moment this is!" Ren looked above the angry faces and over to the crowd. "I have not seen the young Lulia for almost a year now, and here she stands before us all."

He rubbed his hand on top of Lulia's head, which only made her bad hair day worse. The crowd applauded the young girl. Lulia left for her mother and uncle since she was feeling a little overwhelmed. She staggered. Mary took her daughter under her wing as she continued to stare, frightening the man. Lulia looked down at the book. The cover illustrated a painting of a young girl who looked her age, had the same red curly hair and wide grayish-blue eyes. The girl in the picture was sitting. Only her torso was visible. She looked to have been wearing a pink silk dress with a blue jewel decorated in the middle of her collar. Was this picture supposed to be of her?

Jadon shook his head before trying to make his way toward the man. Mary grabbed the back of his arm, trying to stop him from approaching any further. Her attempt failed. Jadon stomped toward the man, who put his hands up in surrender.

"I bet you're getting a lot to exploit us," Jadon sneered.

"Exploit you?" he asked loudly. "This is a book about magic. Who could I be exploiting?" He let out a chuckle for the crowd to hear but widened his eyes in a warning that only Jadon could see.

"You were always greedy, looking for any way to make a fortune."

Ren blushed. He was not expecting this reaction from a long-time friend. His green eyes strayed to Mary, who looked just as angry as Jadon. He wasn't sure which wrath of theirs he feared the most.

"You know me, I'm your friend." His voice shook in fear. "Any misgivings you think I wrote in my book, I'm sorry."

Mary began to flip through pages to find the exact quote she had found earlier. She had seen her brother's anger waver, but she knew that he needed to say more than sorry. Once she found the passage, she read it out loud, "An introduction to the Brown family. Lily was a nasty young girl, the nastiest I had ever met. Her temperament is why I had chosen her to be my main character, so full of bitterness and anger, something most teenagers can relate to. However, The real-life inspiration for the character Lily, whom I am writing about, is currently around twelve years old. However, we can't blame the girl for her anger, resentment, and temper. She was raised by a shrewish mother whose past is far darker and twisted than one can imagine. Who knows the dirty secrets that will unravel as time passes? When they do, I want to be there when it does. The mother who inspired my character Emma had a dark past that began when her parents died, leaving her in control of her four younger brothers. Now, this may be the reason why Emma is who she is. She had two brothers tempted by evil, one who made bad decisions as those around him walked all over him, and the worst brother of them all who had been in and out of rehab since the age of nineteen. And I can't bear to read the rest," Mary threw the book to the ground, holding her tears back.

That was all Jadon needed to hear to rev up his anger. He lunged toward Ren, tackling him to the ground. The crowd of people stepped back, watching the two men roll around. Mr. Bernard and his son strode beside Mary. It looked like Ren was being bludgeoned to a pulp. "That's enough. He's had enough," he said as he lifted Jadon to his feet.

Jadon wiped his bloody lip, the only visible injury that Ren had inflicted. Ren, however, looked like he needed medical attention. Sirens could be heard approaching the building in the distance. Jadon straightened his clothes before brushing his hand through his long hair and out of his face.

"You should've ignored him," said Mr. Bernard. "Trust me. I was angered, too, when I read it. There is no more honorable family than yours. Your aura proves that," he whispered after noticing the wide eyes staring up at them. "It was a rotten thing for a Nillag to do. He's a disgrace to their good name."

The five of them headed for the door. Though many felt as if they should stop them as the police sirens grew louder; however, none of them wanted to stand in the way of a man who stood four inches taller than six feet. They hurried down the street. Mary was shaking with both anger and fright as they turned a corner.

"What? Heofsijs can't fight without the ministry getting involved?" Jadon scoffed.

"They're called police," Mary corrected as she straightened out her blue dress and fur coat.

"He better not write about us again," Jadon warned.

"I doubt he will. Did you see him?" Mr. Bernard cackled longer than any of them would have liked.

"I thought you left?" Lulia asked.

"I decided what's the rush." He smiled. "Then I saw all the posters all over the city and had to come by. I did not know what he had written until I had arrived at the library early today. I had to stop after just one chapter." He shook his head.

The sirens approached. They ran to the woods where they laid out the candles and, as a group, left at once. They did not want to risk getting detained in this city. Who knows how the police would respond with five people unknown to the Heofsij database starting a brawl in the middle of a library?

CHAPTER 5

The conclusion of summertime happened too swiftly for Aldric and Lovetta, but John Jr. and Spencer would have done anything to be able to head back to school away from Ace's care. It was hard not to be jealous of all their friends that were going out buying new clothes and materials to prepare for the new year. Lulia had confirmed, when she woke up this morning, that it was the happiest day of her life. However, the only thing that would have made it better was no school uniform like her training school. She would've swapped her blue dress shirt and kilt for a pink and white pin-striped suit. She decided that that would be what she would wear when the first monthly school dress-down day took place.

Last night, Mary had made a special dinner to celebrate Lulia being an official Galdorwide student. The dinner was one of Lulia's favorites – mint pork. Mary had gone out of her way to grab all the ingredients that usually came out around time for Saturnalia. Jadon and Dallas had come over to celebrate with them. Their mouth watered as the smell of mint floated throughout the kitchen. After dinner, besides Olivia and Harriet, the family had stayed up drinking hot temper around the fireplace. Mary and Jadon had shared tales of their high school experiences. However, some stories that Jadon began were quickly stopped by a stern look from her mother. Lulia knew that one day Jadon would tell her all the stories when she was older, without her mother knowing, of course. Dallas then went on to talk about school and how he met the troublesome love of his life, Elisa. Lulia had never met her, but Dallas explained that she would be at this year's Saturnalia dinner. Dallas explained how the school had helped get his dream job which, to Lulia, did not seem so dreamy – he had gotten a career as a food worker at a local restaurant. If all went well based on his credentials, the owner would pass the restaurant down to him and it would be his own. Still, for now, he oversaw the whole restaurant.

Lulia had woken up at dawn and began to prep everything for the day. She laughed, knowing that if the twins were home, they would be asleep until precisely an hour before going to school, giving them only a few minutes to eat before walking to school. No teleportation was allowed as they were unlicensed. Besides, under-age children had a high risk of falling out of line with the spell and ending up somewhere completely different. After a horrible incident between Bella, a princess at the time, and her older brother Aidan as they traveled from the forest back home with the horrifying sight of him missing, never to be seen again, a lot of kids learned to play magic safe. Lulia shuddered at the thought.

Shortly after Lulia had awoken, Mary rushed out of bed and stormed about the house in a bad mood. Mary had stayed up late with her brother and had forgotten what it felt like to wake up in the morning to wake her kids and make sure they were all up, fed, and off to school. The last time she had not awoken, Lulia and Olivia had walked to school, and the twins had slept in. She looked around the house after Olivia complained that there were no socks in her drawers. The three girls raced around the house, bumping into one another as they ran up and down the stairs. Lulia looked at Olivia with envy as she wore a white dress, a cute top hat, brown shoes, and the new glasses prescribed to her by doctor Notleaf. The most that Lulia could do to make herself look somewhat better was white hair clips to hold her curly hair from falling in front of her face. Olivia had almost slipped down the stairs wearing her squeaky new shoes.

Lulia and Olivia headed down the porch stairs waving goodbye to their mother. Olivia's brown handbag held only her training wand and a few snacks. Lulia had a giant bag with four back-breaking textbooks, a rod, and a compressing cauldron inside.

They had just stepped from their front yard when Lulia raced back inside. There had been a notebook in the bag from the Heofsij world. Assuming it was bought for her by her mother and uncle while she had been too busy looking at her surroundings, she ran inside and grabbed it. She wanted to make sure that she had absolutely everything she needed for her first day of school. No surprises.

They had finally reached the training school when Olivia and Harriet went their separate way. Lulia hated to admit it, but she missed the twins. She would have done anything to have John Jr. and Spencer walking by her side, helping her find all her classes. Lulia deeply inhaled as she approached the running kids, who all looked to have clusters of friends. The bell rang, summoning the students to hurry inside and grab their schedules and uniforms if needed. Lulia decided she felt more comfortable wearing

Spencer's uniform. She felt more prepared this way. She dashed across the street and over to Galdorwide High.

Lulia nervously looked up to the clock that hung at the top of the pointed roof. She had five minutes to get in line, grab her uniform, schedule, and find her class. Lulia did not even have her dad, a teacher, here to show her around as he was at the ministry's mansion for work. Her mother usually replaced his opening at the school, but this time it had been occupied by an eager new teacher who was yet to be revealed publicly.

She stepped onto the pale, dirt path that forked into two different directions as a pond stood in the middle of the way surrounded by bright, green hedges. The school looked like a castle with its three turrets. She looked around and had not found anyone from her training class. It was the same eight people in each of her subjects. She didn't make any solid friends there. She never felt the need to. She would hang out with Olivia at recess, but she did not have the twins or Olivia. Here she would need to make friends. Lulia briskly headed toward the school.

Inside, she saw four long lines of scared-looking kids. They were the rest of the first years still waiting in line for their uniforms and schedules. Lulia felt as if she stood out from the rest with her bright, red hair. Everyone else seemed to have blond and brown hair. Her eyes widened as Mr. Bernard stood in the middle of four professors. Each of the four professors represented each of the four magical auras. It was the auras that would help teachers understand how each student can strive in each class. All auras had different abilities. Pures were good with cauldrons, Viridis were good with using natural tools, Caeruls performed magic best at nighttime which often meant extra school hours for struggling students. Alet auras excelled in fire magic. So often, spells were reconstructed to involve fire magic when an Alet student experienced some struggles.

Lulia stood in the line in front of the professor, who wore the Caerul blue cloak. The professor was gorgeous. She was athletically built and had blond shag-cut hair and blue eyes.

Lulia hated the anticipation of arriving at class. She was petrified of who might be in her class. She was often intense and described as a bully to some back in the training school, but she was now in high school, and things would be different. Caeruls were often looked at as lesser witches due to their limited abilities during earlier hours of the day. She wished that she had been born a Viridi like many of her other Scaasi relatives. The

Viridi word struck fear in many.

A very short, slim boy stood in front of Lulia. She could see him quake in his white dress shirt and black slacks that were held up with suspenders. His dark brown hair had been parted as if his mother had wanted to take an embarrassing family photo with him. Her eyes quickly grew bored of the boy and traveled back to Mr. Bernard, who stood watching the new students arrive, greeting each of them personally after receiving their uniforms. He was wearing a gray sweater and blue slacks that matched his eyes. Lulia looked further down the rows of teachers and noticed that the Alet aura's headmaster had changed since her school tour last January. The new one was young; he had long brown hair and blue eyes. A daisy stemmed from the breast pocket of his red cloak.

Finally, Lulia had gotten to the front of the line. She told the headmaster that she needed a small size. She then waited to have her hand shaken by the one and only Mr. Bernard. She wiped her sweaty right hand along the side of her dress before approaching him.

"Welcome, Lulia." He winked.

Her eyes widened, and a broad smile spread on her face. She felt like a complete idiot, but she could not help it. He handed Lulia her schedule.

"Room 59, can you give directions?" she asked.

"Straight down the main hall, make two lefts and the room will be the last door to the right." He gestured.

"Thanks." She smiled before pushing her way to the Caerul girls' dressing room that was to the left beside the large gym that had windows for walls.

She feared gym class, especially if all the people in the hall got front-row tickets to Lulia flinching during pyroball. It is just as scary as you are thinking. Pyroball consists of twelve rubber balls lit on fire. Each team player (twelve on each team) controls one ball and another on the opposing team. With all their wands raised, they must push the ball closer to the other team player. Luckily, the fire on the ball does not harm the students, but it is a frightful visual and gets the students' blood pumping as they try to keep the pyro ball as far away from them as possible.

She hid in one of the stalls instead of stripping in front of her classmates. She threw Spencer's tight uniform inside of her backpack and headed toward room 59. Her heart was trying to fight its way out of her chest. She saw the number above the door and turned inside to find students lined up at the front of the class.

The professor was a short woman who was averagely built. She had dark brown hair and matching eyes. She wore a red, sporty sweater and Lulia was sure that that was the only thing the young teacher was wearing on her torso. The zipper hung down mid-chest, and her cleavage was the first thing noticeable about the woman. She was looking down her attendance list as she stood at the back of the class.

The bell rang, and she looked up from her sheet to find a few of her male students gawking at her. She smiled. "Well, first years, welcome to the Art of Musical Magic. I am professor LaRusso. I have you standing at the front of the class because…"

Please don't be some dumb ice breaker. I do not want to meet people or be their friends. If I need a friend, maybe I will be friends with that kid. Lulia's eyes focused on the young boy who had stood in front of her in the uniform line. She had not seen his face, but she recognized his short stature and parted hair. On his face, he wore thick glasses that made his eyes look twice the size. He was now wearing a blue suit jacket, dress shirt, and slacks.

"I will be assigning you to your seats based on your surname."

All the muscles in Lulia's body relaxed. She got herself comfortable as 'S' was far down the line. Eventually, she got to 'S.'

"Beau Scaasi," the teacher read as she pointed to the far seat in the last row. The short boy, who looked frightened by his own shadow, approached the seat. The teacher stepped toward the seat in front of him. "Flower Scaasi."

A girl with light brown hair pulled away from her face with a white headband approached the table. She was wearing a green dress shirt with her sleeves rolled up just beneath her elbows.

The teacher tapped the seat in front of Flower. "Lulia Scaasi." Lulia approached the seat. "Great, three Scaasi," mumbled the teacher.

There were more Scaasi's in Galdorwide than any other family. It was hard to keep track of them all. Lulia had never met these two, but she was sure they'd get along just splendidly.

A smile cracked on Lulia's face as she turned to Flower, who shared a smile. Their smiles turned to smirks. Flower looked back toward Beau, who slid down on his chair and covered his face with the red textbook with musical notes printed on it.

***

Ken kicked his feet off Python Seger's front lawn and flew into the air on his broom. Coby, Chris, Stephen, Brad, and Mamie followed. Horus, however, took to his bat form and flew up into the air beside his friends. In a blink of Daemon, Aisley, Michael, Tassos, Ben, and Aaron's eyes, they set off out of sight.

Mamie made sure that the cage had been safely locked in place on the front of her broom. Horus was known to get tired on flights, so she left the cage door open so that he could fly in with ease and take a break. Horus, however, was confident and told Mamie that her action was utterly unnecessary. He was a vampire, born to take flight at night. They lowered their aim as they broke the barrier between Galdorwide and Gimmian, a kingdom whose residence mainly included dwarves, elves, and pirates. An odd pairing, but with a town covered in gems, the elves and dwarves thought it best to keep the pirates on their good side.

They all successfully made it through. They looked down below and saw a forest of trees. It twinkled purple, white, blue, and pink as glowing bulbs of flowers blossomed throughout the trees and bushes. Gimmian was unlike Galdorwide in many ways. There were no streets or castles, only treehouses. There were a few hammocks for the traveling pirates that came in through the kingdom's surrounding sea. Pirate ships floated in the ocean beneath them. Fairies, elves, and dwarves peeked out from their doors in the trees and up in the sky as they watched the witches and bat soar past them, heading toward the head elf's home.

***

"I don't understand," said Robbie as he, Eion, and Spencer stared at her bedroom door that had been sealed shut from the outside. The three of them had fallen asleep in Spencer's room and woke up two hours after they should have been awakened for breakfast.

Spencer looked down to the mail slot, an addition made by Ace on all his patients' doors for food if they had been punished and needed to stay in their room for several days. The pit in her stomach grew more prominent. When Robbie and Eion paid attention to the door's edges, Spencer secretly reached her dry, scaly arm for the slot's flap only to find that, to her fear, it had also been sealed.

Robbie reached for the doorknob, wrapping both his hands around it. He stepped back from the door and lifted his leg onto the wall. Robbie twisted and pulled the knob while his foot pushed against the blue wallpaper. After no avail, he turned to Eion. "You're the sporty one."

"Who has a brain injury," Eion added. "We've already tried everything."

"What if this is it?" Spencer chewed at her brittle nails. "What if he doesn't open the door this time? What did we do?"

"Nothing." Robbie turned to Spencer. "We did absolutely nothing, which gives Ace just the right amount of reason to do this kind of thing."

Eion pressed his ear against the cold basement door. "I can't hear a thing," he said tensely.

"Noooo," Robbie said, exasperated. "Soundproof." He circled his finger next to his head. "No reason to press our ears against doors, walls, or the floor." He slumped onto Spencer's bed.

"We have to do something," Eion objected. "Who knows when he'll let us out." He turned back to the door and wrapped his hands around the knob before aggressively trying to open it once more.

***

Creatures continued to stare up at the broom-flying witches.

"We should fly higher," Coby stated in a way that left no room for objection. "We're attracting too much attention. The last thing we need is word getting out that a group of witches are in town. We're not the most loved beings."

They tilted their brooms upwards and soared higher into the night sky. Chris looked below. His eyes gleamed as they caught sight of a cave; its inside glistened red and silver. He stopped flying. Those behind him passed in front of him. Chris lowered his broom and headed straight for the cave. If Gimmian lived up to Galdorwide's tales, there were tons of diamonds, rubies, and other gems unknown to Galdorwide, worth tons of Feohs. Even if he could snatch one jewel, he would have enough money for a nine-day supply of food for every Python Seger staff and student.

"What are you doing?" Coby, who usually took charge, shouted down as he stopped mid-air. The rest of the students came to a halt.

"Money grab!"

"But—Chris!" Coby lowered his broom down, catching up with his brother, as did the rest of those around him. "How will we get to the head elf in time if you go off track?"

"We have plenty of time. All we do is tell our dads that we had a great chat and lost track of time," Chris explained his concocted lie.

"We'll miss class tomorrow," Coby reminded through gritted teeth.

"Let's take our time then, shall we?" Chris lowered his broom and flew ahead of his nagging friend.

Coby shook his head and looked at his brother. "What if what we have to collect is urgently important that needs to get to Dad right away?"

Ken shrugged. "I'm sure if it were dire, he would have said it." Ken, along with everyone else, sped past Coby, including the usually well-behaved Stephen and Brad.

"We don't have time!" Coby roared impatiently. He sped up his broom. "There are gems in Doryu Edjer's museum! Only consequences are dragons, and that'll be impossible to happen again!"

"Everyone's raided it already." Mamie looked back toward her brother.

"Well, I'm going to the head elf's now." Coby made a sharp turn and headed North. His feelings of anger immediately turned worrisome.

The others landed on the ledge of the cave. They parked their brooms and hopped from them.

"Can we just walk in?" Mamie asked.

She took a step forward, but Chris lifted his arm, stopping her in her tracks. He shook his head. "If people could just walk in, you'd think there would be people swarming this place. What we're doing is… illegal."

Brad and Stephen stepped away from their brother. Their hands in surrender.

"We're going with Coby," said Stephen.

The two of them hopped onto their brooms and kicked their feet off the ground. Chris looked to Ken, Mamie, and Horus, who had turned himself back into witch form.

"You sure you know what you're doing?" Mamie folded her arms.

"Of course not." He smiled. "Come on, if we hurry, we should be able to sneak in through the back before the dwarves leave." He nudged to the side of the cave.

There was a path along the side of the cave that the four of them followed. There was a small door fit for dwarves. Chris knelt and reached into his red cloak pocket and pulled out his wand. He was able to unlock the door with a few taps of his wand. Chris crouched down and walked in. Ken, Mamie, and Horus followed.

Before walking any further, Chris turned to face Horus, who was at the end of the line. "You stay here and make sure that no one comes in this way. It'll be our escape route," he whispered.

Horus looked behind him. The ground beneath him began to rumble.

"They're almost done with work, the perfect time to sneak in," Chris added.

Horus gave a late 'okay.' When he turned, he realized his friends had ventured off inside.

Chris raised his wand. "*Dunnian*!" All four of them turned invisible. They would be safe in this form if they stayed quiet. The ground continued to vibrate beneath them. It was a weird feeling, being invisible, hence why many witches chose to go about other ways of sneak attacks and burglary. "Let's go," Chris said in front of them.

A loud bang caused Chris to fall over. Ken tripped over his fallen friend. They had popped back into sight.

"Uh-oh," said Chris as he saw the shadows of two hairy dwarves approach as their mumbling grew louder. He reached back into his cloak for his wand. Mamie, not knowing what to do, stood very still. She even began to hold her breath, allowing her chest to fill with pressure. She could feel her face grow hot as she grew woozy.

"*Dunnian*!" Chris cast. They successfully vanished but suddenly reappeared once more. He looked down at his wand and saw that it had broken in half. "Go! Go!" Chris, in fear, whispered; he had looked to Ken and to where he imagined Mamie stood.

Stephen and Brad had finally caught up to Coby. Curious creatures still stared up at them. They took their flight even higher. Down below, they could see pirates riding horses and elves and dwarves riding carriages. The treehouses drifted in view as they soared closer to the clouds. When they looked down, all they could see was the twinkling lights of decorative gems, caves, and flowers.

"We have to hurry," instructed Coby. He leaned forward on his broom, allowing himself to speed up. He had become concerned with the rolling clouds approaching quickly. They soon found themselves in a sea of cloud fog.

"Now what?" Stephen asked in a panic as he blinked rapidly.

"Just keep going straight!" Coby lowered his head, shielding himself from the instantaneous wind that rushed into his eyes. "Head down. Maybe we can get away from the clouds, damn who sees us."

They dropped down from beneath the clouds. The three of them squinted their eyes as they looked ahead.

"I can see it!" Coby pointed to a stone castle perched on top of a mountain. From afar, it did not look like it amounted to much. The sun was beginning to rise.

As the sun lit up the kingdom, it looked like a whole other realm compared to its appearance at night. Pale, blue, fluffy clouds skimmed their heads. The sky was bright, and the domain was an endless sea of blue and green.

"All we've got to worry about now is pegasusses. They aren't too friendly of sky intruders," Coby explained.

"There's pegasusses?" Brad asked.

"Yep, and despite their beauty, those purple, winged stallions are quite vicious."

Brad made a horrified face as his head spun around, looking for the daytime creatures. On his face was an expression that made his brother Stephen laugh – a lot.

Coby looked around. He had only studied Gimmian culture but had never seen pictures or had ever visited before. It was as if he plummeted into a young girl's dream. Blue snowflakes began to swirl around them. The weather, despite the snow, was quite warm with the help of the blazing pink sun.

Brad reached into his pocket and pulled out some peanut snacks, and began to eat. He often found himself struggling to maintain composure on an empty stomach. Brad feared interactions with strangers, especially if it was an elf, a creature he had never spoken to before. Stephen looked over to his older brother with a jealous face as he eyed the snack.

"Head down," Coby instructed.

They landed on the green lawn on the top of the mountain smoothly.

***

Chris, Ken, Mamie, and Horus took flight, hoping to catch up with the others in time. They had flown high, away from sight, but they dipped down below them when the clouds became too thick. The green sky was beginning to rise slowly. The kingdom was evolving into a whole different appearance. Now, with the sky clear, Coby, Stephen, and Brad were still out of sight. They must have been quite a while still behind them. Mamie looked down in awe at the green and blue structures and plants. She was even more impressed by the specks of purple that dotted the kingdom beneath them. Down below were elves wandering about in bright colors. From here, the elves, dwarves, and pirates looked ant-sized.

Chris had to admit, the fun and thrill he had felt when he found out about their mission to Gimmian were beginning to wear off, especially now that he did not have any precious, expensive souvenirs to bring home. Now that their adrenaline had worn off, they noticed how thirsty they had become. The sun was scorching.

Mamie wrapped her legs tightly around her broom, keeping it at a steady pace. She reached for her leather jacket. The leather stuck to her sweaty skin. She ripped it off and tied the arms of her jacket around her waist, revealing her white tank top beneath. She was beginning to wonder how much longer she could go without water in this heat. She had stopped noticing the glorious kingdom and its fascinating colors.

"Can we stop for a drink somewhere?" she asked. "I'm sure there's a market nearby."

"Can't be much longer now," said Ken. "Let's just kick up our speed."

Despite the warm climate, snow fell around them and onto the tops of the treehouses below. The cold of its touch provided a hasty release from the heat that quickly faded once it melted on their skin. The city's colors faded beneath the white, but the shine had only grown stronger as the sunlight reflected off the snowy surfaces.

They gripped their hands tighter around the brooms, sending more energy into it. Their speed quickened. Horus' beady eyes looked to Mamie with distress; she gave the nod, and the bat flew into the cage that hung from her broom. A little latch hung from the top of the cell, Horus flew up, wrapping his toes around it. He turned upside down and wrapped his wings around his body.

"See, it's all right to be tired. We all are." Mamie patted the cage.

They all tried not to pay any attention that the head elf's castle was still nowhere in sight. Black stars were beginning to blossom in the green sky as the sun started to descend. Mamie reached for her jacket and threw it back on. The wind was starting to pick up. The snow started to whip around wildly. They all went into their pockets and pulled out their riding goggles. They all tried not to pay any attention that they should have met the boys halfway by now if things had gone successfully.

"Shouldn't be far now," said Chris.

"There!" Mamie shouted as she pointed ahead of them. Her shout had startled Horus, and he flew out of the cage. Silhouetted in the now purple horizon, high on a mountain over a black lake frosted with ice were the turrets of the head elf's castle.

They gripped the edges of their brooms tightly, aiming their brooms downward. They flew over the lake, dropping the nose of their brooms. They all landed just before the stone wall. Horus turned back to his standard form, wearing a buttoned-up blue shirt, a color that brought out his brown eyes.

Suddenly, blush pink and sky blue-colored worms emerged from the ground. They swarmed around the guests' feet rapidly.

"What are these things?" Mamie asked in a panic. She began to smack a few that had started to crawl up her legs.

Horus gasped as he looked across the yard behind them. The ground had been covered with swarming worms all coming toward them. The terrain continued to crack as more worms emerged from the surface. They covered every inch of the lawn.

"*Aargh!*" shouted Chris, who had a worm crawl inside his pants rather than on top. He began to smack wherever he felt the slimy tickle.

More worms crawled up their prey. They began to take bites of their skin. Their heads began to cave inside of the bite wounds. Hail rained down from the sky. Unsure what to do, they all started running, stepping on as many worms as they could and hoping the movement would swing them off of their bodies.

"We're done for!" Chris exclaimed. "They must've got the others too!"

The ground beneath them began to rumble, starting to sag. A hole beneath each of them appeared. They were sucked inside. They fell for what felt like ten minutes. The soft opening above them had sealed. Few worms remained attached to them until the rushing air had swept them out of the wound burrows they had created. They reached a cement bottom.

"That," Chris panted, "was close. Well done, everyone."

With a sharp clunk, a steel gate opened. Small, plentiful thuds suggested that the elves were heading toward them. The ground beneath them was damp. Horus burst into his bat form with a screech and flew up to the corner of the room. He would fly throughout the castle, find his way out, and fly back to Galdorwide, no matter how strenuous the journey.

Bite marks covered the kids. They were all sweaty as they anticipated the elves' arrival. Light blazed through the door. Chris reached into his cloak pocket and pulled out his wand only to find that it had now completely broken in half from the fall.

He looked over to Mamie and Ken. "Dad's going to kill me. I have broken so many wands that I can't keep track any more."

The footsteps continued to approach. The three of them looked up to the corner of the dungeon. Horus had disappeared.

"Can you believe our luck today?" Chris looked back to Mamie and Ken.

This was not how they pictured their grand arrival.

Five elves entered the dungeon. The elf in the middle was a female with black eyes and pointed ears. She had medium-length hair that flew upwards. She was wearing a royal blue cloak and not much else besides green leaves to cover her privates. The other elves wore the same coverage but wore matching dresses beneath. There was one male who wore a blue robe beneath his cloak. He had long, gray hair that went down his back. In his hand, he held a staff whose tip glowed a bright white. The rest of the elves had lanterns that held blue flames.

"Follow us," the middle elf screeched.

Chris looked up to the corner of the room, to where Horus was, and gave a nod.

Stiff, hot, bleeding, and bruised, they followed the elves through the castle. Outside of the dungeon was a grassy slope that led to two large oak doors.

A wonderful peachy smell wafted from behind the doors. Chris peeked through a bright mullioned window that sat in the stone wall of where they were heading. It was a large dining hall with long, cherry wood tables and benches. It looked as if over two thousand elves had been dining. Distant from all the elves, on the closest table to the window were Coby, Stephen, and Brad, who sat numbly staring at their food with their arms crossed.

In the air, candles hung above them. The silverware glistened from the candles' flickering flames.

Horus had flown out of the dungeon and headed toward a breeze. He saw a tiny hole in the stone hall. He flew out of it and entered the forest that sat behind the castle. He flew up and over and headed back toward Galdorwide.

The half-naked elf pushed open the doors. They walked in, passing by their friends, who gave them longing looks. They then pushed open another set of oak doors which led to a vast, echoing hall whose walls were lined with flaming torches. Even from here, they could smell the sweet aroma of the stuffed peaches. They continued to walk away from the warmth and the light of the dining hall. They now walked down stone steps.

"In!" shouted the elf as she opened the door that stood at the bottom of the steps.

Inside was an office. A tall, averagely built elf with blue eyes and long, light brown hair down to the curve of his back was standing in front of a wooden desk with his arms folded. He was wearing a white satin shirt and red velvet cloak. On his forehead was a circlet that wrapped around behind his pointed ears. The front of the circlet dipped just above his nose where a green jewel sat.

The office walls were made of black stones. On top of the shelves in the room were jars filled with different types of flowers and fungus. There was a fireplace to their right, but it was left unlit. The elves behind them had shut the door, leaving the three kids alone in the room with the head elf.

"So," the elf spoke with a soft voice, "you boys decided that you wanted to disrupt my cottandy worms, did you?"

"First of all," Mamie piped up in a rage, "I'm a chick, and second, all we did was step foot in your yard. They devoured us. Look at my face!" She circled her finger in front of her face, pointing at all the bite marks.

"Silence!" shouted the elf. "What brings you to my castle?" Chris gulped. "It better be of importance; after all, I've already had enough intrusions today," the elf hissed.

"You've already met my two brothers and our friend Coby. They were dining in the hall. I'm sure they've told you everything."

"Oh, so you're the ones he spoke of… they said there'd be four of you." The elf raised a suspicious brow.

They all felt as if they had been punched in the stomach. "My servants reported having seen another boy with you in the yard. Where has he gone?" He decided to pose his last statement as a question in hopes of receiving a response.

"I think the worms hurt him badly," Mamie piped up. She always had been the compulsive liar in the group to get them out of situations.

"Silence! My worms do not do any damage besides biting. Anybody attacked by my worms lives and walks immediately afterward."

The three of them looked at one another with white faces. They all felt extremely sick. If their parents did not get here soon, they would surely suffer. All they had to do now was stall. Mamie looked to the ground beside the desk. Two mini reindeer were resting on the gray rug. Around one's neck was a red collar where a charm of a gold heart hung.

"Can I pet it?" Mamie pointed to the sleeping animal. She went to take a step forward.

"No," the elf replied.

They had stayed in the office explaining how they had no idea where Horus had gone off to. They bounced lies off one after another. It was almost natural.

The half-naked elf walked in. Her mouth was thin as her face grew hot with fury.

"Fuck this." Mamie raised her wand. "*Bord*!" A green shield formed around her, Ken, and Chris. "*Elektrisk casul*!" A tangled, green ray exited her wand as she pointed to the ceiling. The green magic struck the roof and dispersed throughout the room. Green, electrical energy rained down, hitting the two elves down.

"Mamie!" Chris squeaked.

"Oh, come on, they're not dead."

"Yeah, well." Ken wiped his hands down his brown sweater. "We weren't sent here to start a war," he criticized his sister.

"Yeah, well, we didn't come here to get bitten by worms and interrogated."

"It's not like they were hurting us." Chris brought his hands to his head. "Electrical rain! That is not a normal response!"

Mamie smiled. "I know, thanks," she said with gleaming pride. Ken and Chris looked at her, unimpressed. "What? We are taking classes at Python Seger, not Galdorwide High. We're not meant to be cookie crumbles like everyone else in our goddamn kingdom."

Horus, Daemon, Tassos, Aaron, and Michael rushed through the office door. They looked at the two fallen elves then back over to the group of kids who still stood inside a green shield. Brad, Stephen, and Coby could be seen out in the hall trying to peek inside.

"Explain," said Daemon, his attention focused on his daughter.

Mamie launched into the story, starting with their arrival to Gimmian and their sidetrack at the mines.

"You guys were sent on a mission. You guys all should have arrived here together. The elves were expecting seven to arrive, not three and not four. They thought you were intruders and treated you as such." Daemon pinched his nose. He kept it there as he prepared to ask, "Why are the elves blackened and on the floor?"

When Daemon did not hear a response, he looked up to see his daughter giving a broad, cheesy smile. He shook his head with a smile. "You know they're gonna hate us now, right?"

"Then the feeling's mutual." She hid a smile as she brought the shield down.

"Just wait in the hall, we'll deal with the elves, and maybe now we can get our cowls." Daemon brushed the kids out as he and Aaron tended to the two fallen elves.

Cowls are a breed of owls whose feathers are either pale pink or baby blue, depending on their gender. It was supposed to be a surprise gift for Aisley as it had been her favorite animal since she was a child. She had never seen one in real life but had heard of stories and seen pictures, and that was all she needed to fall in love. Gimmian is the natural habitat for cowls, but they could quickly be brought to Galdorwide if provided with proper care. Daemon knew his sister needed something colorful and happy in her life, and he thought this would be a good start. He had gotten two which could be a handful when flying as they tended to get distracted quickly and fly off, hence why he sent all of them to retrieve them.

***

There was a rap of knocks on Principal Bernard's door. On the other side was Lulia, who immediately hid her smile as soon as she heard the doorknob click. There in front of her was Mr. Bernard, and if she wanted, she could see him every day.

Her whole body went numb. All the confidence she had was now gone. Mr. Bernard was looking unusually grave. He stared down from behind his button nose at the young girl. Lulia wished she could go back to class and not have gotten herself in trouble.

There was a long silence after they each had taken a seat. "So, what brings you here?" His voice seemed disappointed. Maybe he was tired of the Scaasi like the rest of the teachers. Lulia could not look up at him any more. She stared at her hands that lay in her blue kilt. She could see her knees slightly tremble.

"I got bored in class. Everyone was reading books, and the teacher said today was free time, and I did not want to spend it reading, so I turned around to Flower – a girl somehow related to me. I smacked her hand and said tag. Then we went back and forth for a bit, and then we ran around the classroom, and that's when the teacher sent me here. If you're wondering, once I'm done here, I'm going to tag her, then she'll be coming in." Lulia looked up to see that he was staring at her. "I'll take whatever punishment you think I deserve. You can suspend me, expel me—"

"Expel you?" Mr. Bernard chuckled, but his mood still seemed quite upset.

Lulia's eyes widened. "Are you going to brand me?"

"Brand you?" He laughed harder, tears beginning to stream out of his eyes.

John Jr. had always told her horror stories of high school and the teachers. One day, he said that the worst students were branded. Based on her principal's laughter, she now knew this to be a lie.

"You're too funny, Lulia," he said as he wiped his eye with his gray sweater sleeve.

"So you're not going to punish me?" she asked.

"No, not today, Miss Scaasi," replied Mr. Bernard. "But I must press that what you did was wrong and should not happen again. I will be writing to both your and Flower's families tonight. I must also warn you that this being the second day is not a great start for you. Students have been suspended for this kind of behavior before. However, I will only be sending you two to detention."

"Understood." She gave the nod, sending her red curls flying forward. It was still better than her other guesses. However, she was more worried about her parents receiving a letter than about her detention. Her mom would indeed send an army of spoons at her while her dad would most likely just be disappointed, which was always a disheartening sight.

"What happened to your forehead?" he asked.

Lulia lifted her pale hand where she felt the hot liquid. She pulled her hand down and saw blood smeared across her fingertips. She looked up at him and gave a wide smile as she scrunched her nose. "I may have also tripped while playing tag."

Mr. Bernard shook his head with a smile. "You should go to the hospital wing to see the doctors."

"No, it's not bleeding much." She shrugged.

"I was just on my lunch break," he began, lifting a plate filled with lime and mango shrimp that was most likely prepared for him by his wife. "Then shortly, I have to give an announcement. Care to join me since the class is free time anyway?"

"Sure." Her eyes lit up.

Mr. Bernard raised his wand and pointed it at the space on his desk in front of Lulia. A salty piece of lamb appeared in front of her, along with utensils and some napkins. Lulia took a napkin and wiped her bloodied hands. "My wife had made this for my lunch, but the shrimp has me almost full," he explained.

A white mug appeared with a steamy, red liquid, Hot Temper Hot Chocolate. She was flattered.

"Once we are finished with our food and drinks, we will get back to our daily duties." Mr. Bernard raised his mug of caffeine quake.

She smiled. "I was anxious coming here," she said with a shake of her head.

"Yes, I wasn't expecting to have any visitors today." He laughed. "It is only the second day of school. Usually, the riots begin on the second Monday of the school year." He laughed again.

Lulia brought her fork filled with lamb meat into her mouth. She swallowed and took another bite. She loved her mother's cooking, but boy did Mrs. Bernard beat her when it came to lamb.

"I'll be sure to behave from now on," said Lulia as she took a sip of her hot chocolate. "So why are you so nice to me? I'm sure you don't share meals with all of your troubling students."

"Well, I want to make a good impression on your teacher. The longer you are here, the more they'll think I'm lecturing you." He winked. "We all get bored sometimes."

***

The ministers took the familiar path down the mansion's narrow, stone steps. Everyone kept quiet just as they had during the dinner. The only person who seemed to talk was Kenneth, and when he spoke, he only talked about himself.

They walked past portraits of the extinct Behemoth family. The Behemoths were a royal family that resided in this mansion before the last family member, Joseph, died alone in this house.

Suits of armor welcomed them at the bottom of the steps that led them to the mini classroom where all the adults would take a seat besides Bella, the ministry leader. Bella stood in front of them all wearing a stunning, silk, purple dress, but before she could speak, there was a knock on the castle's front door. Bella smiled and said that she would see who it was and that Gower could begin the meeting. When she opened the door, she was anything but pleased. "Password?" she asked.

"Password, are you joking?" Lewis, Angel's estranged husband, stood on the front porch.

She did not realize how much she took not seeing the tall, slim, blond, green-eyed man for granted. Lewis hurriedly passed the queen and entered the castle.

Downstairs, they could hear the quick feet approach. Angel looked to see her husband pacing toward her. Her heart dropped, and her legs felt non-existent. Besides Kenneth and Bliant, all the males puffed their chest at Lewis' sight.

"There you are!" he began. "Where have you been? This whole thing has been ridiculous. Are you ready to come back home?"

"Well, I've been here, you know that. There is another high-importance case. I can't go back home," Angel replied with little confidence.

"So, you're saying when this is all done, you will come back?" he asked. He always did have a way of hearing what he wanted as well as receiving it.

"No." Bella came down the stairs, her arms crossed.

"Eternal anguish!" Lewis angrily turned to Bella. "We were doing so well before you came back into our lives!"

"Yeah, definitely, it's not like there was a bruise on her chest that night we stumbled upon you guys in the forest. When you were trying to kill Alan."

"Everyone here has tried to kill Alan!"

"Who's Alan?" Kenneth asked as if he had any relevance to the conversation.

Bella bit her tongue, she could not stand Kenneth, but she knew she had to be polite as his father was the emperor, the man in charge of all kings and queens.

Lewis turned to Angel and grabbed her arm to stand her to her feet. Krum pulled out his wand. A storm clapped outside of the mansion. Everyone stood up from their desks and backed away from the two men as Angel stood in the middle of the circular room. Now that Krum had stood up from his chair, it was evident that the desk made for a child was now lopsided.

Gabriel and John had reached out for Krum and held him back. Gower and Bella escorted Lewis out of the basement. The man whose blond hair was now down to his shoulder blades kept looking back, shouting his love for the woman. She reached for her stomach as it began to turn. She wanted to run upstairs and check on her son, who was fast asleep on the top floor. She looked around and noticed that everyone in the room was looking at her. She slumped into her desk as she waited to stop hearing her sister and Gower argue with Lewis.

***

"What a brilliant second day!" Flower exclaimed. "Detention already! Living up to the Scaasi name, we are."

Flower, Lulia, and Beau were walking home from school, heading to Lulia's home. Tomorrow, you'll have to get in trouble, Beau." She looked to her wimpy cousin, whom she had yet to know how she was related with. "So you can join us for detention Friday night. There's no better way to spend a Friday," she said with a wide smile.

His eyes widened. "No way! You guys are crazy, honestly," replied the young-looking boy. He was slowly beginning to talk more and more to them. Lulia and Flower could tell that they were growing on him. Who wouldn't they grow on?

Flower patted Lulia's shoulder. "You're more than everything I wanted in a sister."

"I thought you had like two sisters?" asked Lulia.

"Yeah, but Guinevere is always locked up in her room dreaming about our neighbors while Comely is too busy doing boyish stuff like Titanrally and Airnet. I get along best with Clancy, my brother. He is twins with Guinevere. They're the oldest," she explained.

"Oh wow!" exclaimed Lulia. "My oldest siblings are twins too! A boy and a girl. Our families are identical except that I have three sisters."

"Wow, we really are related." Flower laughed before turning to Beau. "How many siblings you got, Tiny?"

Tiny was Beau's nickname given to him by Lulia and Flower. A boy outside walking around called Beau tiny after hearing the girls call him that. After seeing that this had hurt Beau, Lulia and Flower stood up onto their feet and approached the more senior student.

"Call him that again and see what happens." Lulia stomped over.

"Yeah!" Flower backed her up.

The boy laughed wildly. Flower laughed along with him, making the boy stop in confusion.

"Do you know who my brother is?" Flower asked as she bounced her head with confidence. When the boy didn't reply, she answered for him, "Clancy... Scaasi."

The boy's eyes widened, and he backed away. His slow steps turned into big sprints.

Clancy was fifteen years old and was well known among the school as he and his friends had appearances scary enough to send grown witches running in the opposite direction. Clancy had long, greasy black hair that surpassed his shoulders. He wore studded bracelets and black combat boots. Clancy was relatively short, or he looked short amongst his friends, some of whom were already six feet tall. Everyone at Galdorwide High was scared of them. Other students were convinced that they all killed animals and witches for fun. Still, they could just be thinking that because of their song lyrics from his band 'Chaos.' He hung around with two other bands, 'Imaginary Kings' and 'Misfit Crew,' whose members were all already graduated. Despite being older, they got along with Clancy's band as its members ranged from fourteen to nineteen.

Flower smiled as she looked to her brother, who stood around his friends smoking bone dust, a cigarette that no person in their right mind would smoke. Yes, they were smoking legit bone dust. Their supplier resided just outside of the forest near their homes as they were all neighbors. They looked over since they saw the two girls approach the more senior student, but now they smirked with pride as they saw the boy run off.

"I don't have any siblings," Beau replied.

"Well, you got us, Tiny." Flower nudged the young-looking boy.

Lulia stopped in her tracks as she saw her mother whip the door open when she arrived home and paced over. Flower and Beau had stopped as well. Their eyes were on the averagely built, tall woman with dark brown hair and gray eyes. She was wearing a blue dress, and her hair was done up nicely. There was no special occasion, and Flower had to admit she envied the woman because of this.

"You!" She pointed to her daughter with a wooden spoon. "You go upstairs. No friends tonight."

"Mom!" Lulia whined. "These aren't my friends. They're my family." Mary glared at Lulia. "Mom, please," she begged.

"You should've thought about that before you got detention, now shouldn't you've!"

"*Uhm*, excuse me," Flower piped up. "We told our fathers that they would have to pick us up here. Can you just punish Lulia once we leave?"

Mary went to speak but paused until she got her thoughts in order. "You guys can come inside and eat." Mary turned around and stepped inside.

Flower stepped inside and took in the beauty of the home that sparkled with fine furniture and decor. They walked over to the tall kitchen island table where Mary handed them plates of breaded bear.

"What time did you tell your parents to come?"

"For eight," Flower replied with a smile, one that looked familiar to Mary, but she couldn't quite place her finger on why.

"Fine, homework only, under my supervision, here, in the kitchen." When Mary turned, Flower turned to Lulia and winked.

While doing homework, Flower's eyes couldn't help but wander to the blue, velvet curtains that looked more expensive than her whole house. The velvet curtains hung around high, narrow windows.

Precisely at eight, there was a knock at the door. Mary rushed over and opened it. Her heart sank.

"Blue?" she asked. She turned to the three kids who were still working on homework. A short, slim man with long, light-brown hair and blue eyes stood on her porch. He was wearing a black t-shirt beneath his leather jacket.

"Hey, Mary, been a while."

It had been thirty-two years since Mary had seen Blue Scaasi, the last time she had seen him was at their high school graduation.

"What are you doing here?" Mary felt the urge to whisper her words.

"I'm here to pick up my daughter."

Mary's eyes widened. "Did you know that she had been hanging out with my daughter?"

"Not until I knocked on the door and saw your face. How's Johnny doing? Assuming you are still with him."

"He's great, and he'll be home very shortly," Mary lied.

CHAPTER 6

Lovetta had barely smiled this school year. Things were looking down ever since lunch on the first day back to school. Just she and Aldric sat at the table. John Jr. wasn't here, and to be honest, Lovetta knew that if it hadn't been for their newfound powers, she would be sitting alone. At the following table over, they had noticed that Tris was sitting alone. The people he usually ate lunch with were all under Ace's care – Spencer, Regina, Lexi, and Ellen. They would have invited him over to sit with them, but they knew that they'd rather talk about their new powers, which was something that had to keep between them.

Lovetta looked further down the cafeteria where the Viridi Crash Ring team sat quietly as they too lost friends to Ace's home care – Caden and Aldaricus. Lovetta's eyes then traveled to the Alet Crash Ring table, where a group of students laughed wildly. She noticed that Aldric had been looking that way for a while now.

"You can go over there if you want," Lovetta broke the silence.

"*Huh?*" He snapped out of his trance. "*Nah*, the only person I like on that team is John Jr."

Today's lunch special was vinegar turkey. She knew she should've brought lunch. The silence returned. She looked out the window and noticed that the day outside was just as grim as she felt, gray and cloudy. She then looked to another werewolf textbook given to her by her favorite teacher Gower, who, too, had gone away as he was part of the ministry. Lovetta wished that she was old enough to join, but you have to be a graduated Galdorwide High student to apply. She'd do anything to know just what was so important that the ministry had to stay at the mansion. This was the second time this year. The last time they stayed at the manor, the whole kingdom had almost come to an end after an attack by dragons.

The textbook was titled *A Weekend with Werewolves* by Pool Jr. Scaasi and Kenneth Riley. Lovetta cracked the textbook open and propped it up on her Sugary Slap soda can. Aldric had just begun to eat his homemade forest yak meat when a letter appeared in front of him. Aldric slumped back in his chair with confusion after he took the red envelope into his hands.

"What is it?" Lovetta asked, looking up from the book. "Open it! It might be from Gower!" she said, a little too happy.

He began to read, and after reading the first sentence, he made his way to the male restroom to finish reading it privately. He locked himself in the stall and sat on top of the toilet tank, letting his feet dangle on either side of the toilet.

Aldric, I wouldn't be surprised if all your friends and trusted teachers dropped you after discovering your truth. You try to keep it a secret, but you wait. One day, your secret will emerge from the darkness of the moonlight. I don't suppose that you'd care if your disease takes hold of you, making you kill those you love. I mean, if you did care, you would tell them the truth and run off to live with the other creatures of the night.

Aldric's body began to rattle as he sat. His heart sank, his face started to burn with anxiety.

To think that after all this time, I found out your secret only last night, even though you have not met me yet! I'm a watcher of all the sick people in this kingdom. If I can figure out your secret, I'm sure those closest to you will find out – and soon. Your father would die of shame, and your mother of a broken heart. Maybe that's why you hide this secret? He didn't bring you up to live a reckless life. After all, this whole incident would've been avoided if you did not take your nightly walks through the forest. You could've died, but now you are suffering an even worse fate. I am truly disgusted. Your father will face worse punishments than you when I set the truth free. After all, you are underaged in the eyes of the law. Just know that when Gower, John Jr., and Lovetta die, it will be all your fault. You better think twice before you step a single toe out of your bedroom window at night, demon. For I will be waiting for you, and I will slay you!

The silence of the bathroom only grew louder. Aldric took his trembling hands and began to rip up the letter along with the red envelope. He dropped the pieces into the toilet bowl and flushed it down. Aldric felt relieved but only for a brief second before realizing that someone knew his secret. He sat stunned as if his whole body had been lit on fire. He could hear a few people talk and laugh as they passed by the restroom door. The voices grew louder, and Aldric knew that this meant that class would be starting soon.

Lovetta closed up her textbook, threw out her leftover turkey, and placed the tray on top of the rest of the dirty trays by the garbage bin. She walked back over to the table and set Aldric's food back into his lunch tray before catching him outside of the next class that they shared. She knew something was wrong as soon as she saw that his face was as white as a ghost's.

He grabbed his lunch pail out of Lovetta's hand. His insides were burning with guilt. He knew that everything said in that letter was accurate. He knew that he would have to stay away from everyone. He couldn't hurt his friends, not after everything they'd done for him. He had no time to dwell on this after the teacher called for them to enter.

Their teacher was Gemini Scaasi, the new teacher. He was in charge of teaching students the art of taming animals.

Through the green yard, vegetable patch, and eventually, he took the class outside to a wooden barn, where magical creatures were kept for school experiments and training. Aldric looked at Lovetta, who walked with her head down, her tangled, brown hair flowing behind her. He couldn't tell if it was tears or raindrops on her cheek. Aldric began thinking about whether he had to distance himself from the ones he cared about. Discovering the reality that he had to abandon his friends, he still could not bring himself to do it in a manner that hurt any of them in any way.

Professor Gemini Scaasi led them to the barn and entered while instructing the class to wait outside until he had the animals ready. He still hadn't precisely revealed what creature they would encounter. Professor Gemini Scaasi strolled out of the barn and beside him stood a tall man who looked to be in his early twenties. He had blue eyes and red hair and was wearing a brown suit and thick, black glasses. Although his outward appearance was ordinary, his mind was extraordinary. For a moment, Aldric was almost sure he saw the young man's eyes flicker green. Another twinge of guilt panged at his side.

A large amount of dirt was on both Gemini's and the red-haired man's clothes and fingernails. It was an odd sight considering how nicely dressed they were. Aldric looked to Lovetta, whose eyes were sparkling and fixed on the red-haired man.

"Hello there," the young man addressed the class.

"Sorry for the delay." Gemini wiped his hands on his tight, dark blue jeans. "We had to doctor up a few animals as they haven't been tended to for much of the summer break. "This here is Coby Soleil, a student of

Python Seger who is extremely talented in the art of taming animals. He will be helping us this semester as he will be shadowing me so that one day he too can teach this class."

The usually disgruntled Coby had a cheerful smile. There was a murmur of interest. This was the first-ever art of taming animals class any of them had ever taken. After all, this class is mandatory for second-year students only. Though future classes could be taken if students were interested in the study. Professor Gemini Scaasi turned around and pushed open the heavy barn doors. Aldric caught a whiff of damp earth wafting from out of the enclosed structure. Delicate, pink flowers hung from the ceiling. The flowers had big eyes and small smiles. They moved elegantly in what looked like them shaking their head to a tune unheard to a witch's ear. Along the walls were locked doors containing animals. Growling, hissing, and howling could be heard throughout the room. Coby Soleil had been the last to enter, behind Lovetta. He reached his hand out and placed it on her shoulder.

"Can I have a word?" he asked, and as soon as they entered, they exited as the door closed behind them. "You don't mind if you're a couple of minutes late? Professor Gemini Scaasi already knows."

Lovetta now had a closer look at the man who was a few years older than her. Now she could see his large eyes, large ears, and he even had large teeth that glistened a bright white as the sun gleamed down over them.

"It's Lovetta, right?"

Lovetta nodded. It's all she had been doing.

"Professor Scaasi and I are good friends of Professor Silwhet. He told us to keep an eye on you. He explained what happened last semester and just wanted me to let you know that if you have any symptoms like you did last semester, to alert Gemini or me."

Lovetta wanted to pretend that she had no idea what he was talking about. For a moment, she hadn't, but then she remembered that embarrassing, repressed memory of her running straight for Gower's sink in the middle of class. She was embarrassed. It wasn't any of these two guys' business about her health issues, especially when she didn't even exactly know what was wrong.

"I knew you were Lovetta the minute I saw you. You stand out in such a bland crowd, did you know?"

Her eyes remained fixated on his pearly teeth. He had a large smile on his face, and it only seemed to appear when he looked at her.

"You should join me at Python Seger! It is where I plan on learning how to become a teacher. I want to take what I learned there and combine that with what I am learning here to make a better course on animals' taming. I'm betting that you are planning on studying this further and turning it into a career!"

"No, actually, I'd like to teach the art of Terra magic."

"Like professor Silwhet, *huh*? Speaking of Gower, he also told me you had gotten severely sick a few months back. A bad bug bite, if I do recall? How're you feeling now?"

"Better... it *was* months ago."

"I understand. You don't know me fairly well. I expected you to be quite unsure and hesitant about me. You reminded me of myself when I was your age. Gower felt bad about that; you being bitten. I don't see why but I guess it's because it happened just outside of his home." He took a step back and eyed Lovetta from head to toe before looking back to her eyes. "You will go on to do great things, my young darling. You've got a wonderful smile, you know."

She had been restraining her smile until he looked into her eyes. He gave her a wink and turned to open the barn's doors. He strode inside. Lovetta stood still for a moment, her legs weak. Once she regained feeling in her legs, she slid inside.

Professor Gemini Scaasi was standing behind a large, wooden bench in the center of the barn. Piles of red gloves laid on top. Lovetta walked in and took the open spot next to Aldric as they stood behind a large bench that faced Gemini.

"Today, we will be working with phoenix owls," Gemini began. "Now, tell me, what do you know about phoenix owls?"

To everyone's surprise, besides Aldric, Gemini, and Coby, Lovetta raised her hand. "Phoenix owls are long-living owls. They regenerate, becoming born-again, arising from their ashes. Unlike a normal phoenix, these owls are associated with the moon. They often travel alone and are nocturnal. They are a bird of prey. A healthy phoenix owl will have an upright stance, a head larger than its body. Any traits opposite to this suggest that the owl is nearing its time of regeneration. Like an ordinary owl, they have binocular vision, binaural hearing, sharp talons. However, an ordinary owl's feathers are made for a silent flight where a phoenix owl can be heard due to the sparks emitting from the end of its feathers."

"Excellent!" Gemini beamed.

"Phoenix owls," Coby began, "have many aspects that can be used for antidotes. Does anyone know what properties these are?"

Lovetta's hand shot up once again, nearly striking Aldric, who rested his head in his hand. "Both its feathers and its tears are good properties for healing potions."

"Precisely!" exclaimed Gemini.

"Now," Coby began, "as helpful as these animals are, they are also dangerous. Does anyone know why?"

Lovetta didn't even raise her hand this time. Instead, she just began to answer.

"If angered, a phoenix owl can emit a foul-smelling odor whose properties, if inhaled, can be dangerous and give the inhaler symptoms similar to that of Black Death."

"Luckily" – Gemini nodded – "the owls we have with us here, today, are young and will only emit such toxins that will mimic symptoms of a mere cold if angered."

In the middle of the room was a sizable square-like structure covered by a black drape. Gemini nodded to Coby, who proceeded to walk to the form and removed the drape. Everyone leaned forward over the bench to get a closer look.

"Everyone, take a pair of gloves," Coby instructed. "And a pair of nostril clamps."

Everyone began to step on one another's heels as they hurriedly made their way to grab gloves from the table that sat in front of the professors.

"Make sure that there are no holes in the gloves," Gemini began as the students made their way back to their seats. "Coby and I searched them, but a second check won't hurt. You must not take off the gloves or unclamp your nose until the owls are back and secured into the cage."

Lovetta pulled the red gloves over her hands. She couldn't help but feel Coby's stare. She looked around, wondering if anyone else noticed the man's odd behavior, but everyone was too busy preparing themselves. Lovetta blushed before clamping her nostrils shut. She was pleased to see, once she looked up, that Coby's nose was hooked. She rolled up the sleeves of her Caerul robe as Gemini passed her an owl.

She let out a gasp of surprise, Coby noted. She had never seen one up close before. Its two large, yellow eyes were unnatural, taking up the top half of its entire head. Its beak was minuscule and looked almost wooden. It tilted its head as it looked at her. It gave a single flap of its wing as if to show-off. Three feathers stood upright on top of its head.

She laughed as the owl hopped closer to her. It stretched out its wing as if to shake her gloved hand. She accepted the gesture. With another laugh, she looked to see if Aldric was looking. Her eyes widened. Aldric's owl was vibrating as a green smoke emitted from its wings. It was not taking a liking to him.

Coby was walking down the bench handing students vials and tweezers. When he got to Aldric, who seemed to have been the only one to upset an owl, he reached into his pocket and pulled out a handful of dirt. Aldric opened his palm, allowing Coby to pour the soil into his hand. The owl immediately spun its head and began to use its little beak to eat at the dirt. Coby dusted the rest of the soil that had stuck onto his gloves and onto the workbench.

"You are to grab the tweezers and pluck one feather from the owl's wing," Gemini explained, standing in front of the class. "It is essential that you show the owl the tweezer. If the owl is compliant, it will raise a singular feather from its wing for you to pluck. If not, you will have to do some encouraging. Stroke its wing and eventually pick a feather and begin to raise it yourself. If compliant, the wing will stay up. If the feather sinks back down, the owl is non-compliant, and you will have to respect its wishes. Once plucked, you may place the feather in the vial provided to you by Coby. You may begin."

Before Lovetta had even touched the tweezers, a feather on its wing raised. Lovetta squealed and thanked the bird and had a one-sided conversation about wanting to take him home. Aldric showed his owl the pair of tweezers. The owl looked away, and all its feathers remained flat. He then hesitantly reached out his hand and began stroking the sparking feathers. He then reached for a feather and began to raise. His bird was non-compliant, but this was proven in a different way than explained by Gemini. Instead, the owl had quickly turned its head and bit Aldric's gloved hand. Luckily, the gloves were made to be fireproof, which thankfully meant that Aldric didn't feel the owl's bite. Frightened, he pulled his hand back.

A small tree-like plant with apples that hung from it stood behind the professors. With no warning, holes began to appear in the apples. Teeth grew from the top and the bottom of the holes, and a screaming noise came from the plant. The professors turned around.

"Get me some cinnamon!" Gemini instructed. Coby ran off to the supply closet in the back and returned with nine sticks of cinnamon for each of the screaming apples. As soon as he placed the cinnamon sticks in, the apples began to chop them. Once the cinnamon stick had disintegrated in their mouths, the holes disappeared, and they looked as if they had been ordinary apples.

The student next to Lovetta was about her height. He was slim with blue eyes and long black hair that surpassed his shoulders. Lovetta was too busy paying attention to Coby's stares to notice that the boy beside her was staring at her too.

"Clancy Scaasi," he finally mustered up the courage and extended his bare hand to shake hers.

She turned, surprised by the sudden greeting. She smiled and shook his hand.

"Lovetta Annettes, and I know who you are." She blushed. Clancy was one of the most feared students in her grade, and as for the other dreaded students at the school, they were his friends.

Clancy beamed as he noticed that she didn't look frightened of him. Something he needed. Aldric looked over, unimpressed.

"I see that Gemini has taken a liking to you. He's a Scaasi like me but don't ask me how we're related." Clancy laughed as he looked down at his owl, who stretched out a feather for him to pluck. He took it and placed it inside of his vial. "Coby hangs out with us sometimes. He's friends with my bandmate Adolfo." He gave a small chuckle once more. "Coby is a friend of theirs too. He was pretty upset that I didn't enroll at Python Seger after training school, but all of my friends go here."

They didn't have much time to talk after this as they had to collect their owl's tears now. It was a task that required total concentration. Gemini's demonstration made it look so easy, but it most definitely wasn't for anyone who was collecting owl tears for the very first time. Owls didn't cry very often, and they didn't like to unless someone they care about was wounded. If you weren't injured, you were to palpate the corners of their eyes gently. This was something that would often lead them to kick, spit, bite, or even release their toxic odor. Everyone struggled. However, Clancy found a solution. He reached into his pocket and pulled out a black pocket knife.

Popping the blade out, extending his hand, he slit the middle of his palm. His owl immediately hopped over and leaned over his hand. A flow of tears exited the owl's eyes and into his scar. He used his free hand to use the vial and catch the tears. By the time he had collected enough, his scar had faded entirely.

"Clancy!" Gemini eyed the student. Clancy lifted the vial, showing it off despite knowing that his tactics were most definitely improper.

By the end of class, anyone who wasn't Clancy was sore, sweaty, and thirsty. Lovetta had a half-hour break before her next period, in which she devoted time to wash up in the girl's locker room shower. She wasn't as dirty as the rest as ten minutes after still trying to get her owl's tears, Clancy sacrificed his hand once more.

Once she was all cleaned up, she raced to her next class, Terra arts, which Gemini also taught, as he replaced all of Gower's classes. Terra arts was one of Lovetta's favorite courses, but today's lesson required a lot of work. Aldric found it especially hard as it seemed that everything he had learned from last year's Terra arts class had leaked from his head.

"The key to the Terra arts is all in your stance," Gemini began. "Your body has to be ready and strong. Earth is a powerful element. If you want to manipulate the earth, you're going to have to become just as powerful. Today, we will be 'burrowing.' We will be making tunnels in the ground from in here to out there." He pointed to the window where the bright, blue sky hung.

Gemini had gone over the spells, wand work, and all of the burrowing spell requirements. You had to keep your wand and hand by your shoulder and give a robust downward flick of your upper arm. All Aldric seemed to have done was tire out his arm.

Lovetta stood between Aldric and Clancy. She looked over to Clancy, who talked to Amara, who had hair longer than hers and Clancy's. Amara's wand had been bandaged as it was believed to be a bad omen to use a fixing spell on a rod, but by the looks of it, it seemed that soon he would have to take the risk. Crackling sounds along with green sparks all came from Amara's wand. Lovetta had been quite shocked to see his Viridi aura as he always had a big smile and was quite introverted. Viridis were often labeled as the second evilest aura – Hearm, the aura that emits black magic, being the most vicious. However, none of this theory is proven accurate as aurae represent your strengths in magic, not the witch's personality. Every time

Amara cast the burrowing spell, black smoke would emit from his wand. Lovetta could tell that he was self-conscious about this as everyone would look over as they hid their smirks. However, Clancy always managed to laugh things off, and soon enough, they were making strange, scary faces and sounds as if they were creatures appearing from the smoke. Eventually, smoke filled the room and dusted all those present's faces, hair, and clothes. Gemini wasn't pleased but didn't punish the boys he considered friends outside of the school.

Finally, Lovetta correctly cast the spell. *"Crypel!"* A gentle, baby blue ray of magic exited her wand by flicking her hand. A hole, wide enough for only her to fit in, opened, sweeping her through it. Now all she had to do was cast the exit spell, which would shoot her up from the ground when she estimated the proper distance. *"Ablawting!"* She successfully shot up from beneath the ground, covered in dirt. She stood up and waved to her teachers and classmates, who had all ran to open the window and see where she would pop up.

No one else in the class had successfully burrowed by the time the lunch bell rang. Aldric's brain pounded inside of his head. Everyone ran out of the classroom, allowing the black smoke to flow into the hallway.

"Stupid... useless... thing." Amara looked at his wand, shaking it in front of his face.

"You should just fix it," Lovetta suggested with a smile as she pressed her books into her chest. The wand began to make a popping noise, and green sparks flew out of it like a firecracker.

"I don't need any more bad luck in my life," Amara explained. His wand began to make a hissing noise, and he plopped it into his soft, green shoulder bag. *I deserve a rod like this anyway,* he thought.

They went to the cafeteria, where the group said an awkward goodbye before heading off to their usual tables. Lovetta understood. She didn't fit in with Clancy or his friends. She was a bookworm, and they were bringers of mayhem, or so they planned.

Aldric was not in the most fantastic mood. He already had had a rough first half of the day. His owl hated him, he couldn't burrow, and worst of all, Lovetta seemed to have more fun sharing a class with Clancy and Amara than with him. He looked to Lovetta, whose face had blushed like an apple as she stared down at a letter that she had retrieved from her blue cloak pocket.

"What's that?" Aldric asked, resisting the urge to take it from her hand and read it for himself.

"Nothing." She put the piece of paper back into her cloak.

After they had finished lunch, the two walked down by the lake, where they took a seat rather than train their new powers. Lovetta crossed her legs and began to stare down at *A Weekend with Werewolves*. After she finished the chapter, she turned to Aldric, and they started talking about Crash Ring, a sport she was going to try out for this year. A few minutes into the conversation, she stopped talking after getting an overwhelming feeling that she was being watched. She looked behind her to where Clancy had quickly looked down to the dandelion he had been tearing. It was odd. He looked transfixed. In his hands were two white, gold spoons. These were elvish spoons, a type of instrument he played for his band 'Chaos.' When they clanged together, they made beautiful sounds that sound like raindrops on a harp. A beautiful tool when used alone, but their sound is quite haunting when combined with his other bandmates' darker instruments. After Lovetta looked at him, he turned bright red.

Clancy looked back up and took a tentative step forward. "Hi," he began breathlessly. "I was wondering if today, after school, if you'd want to come by and hear the band? We'd be showing you our newest song." He turned to Aldric. "You can come too if you like."

"Hear you play?" Lovetta blinked. The most notorious, the darkest band in all of Galdorwide wanted her – a makeup-less nerd – to come by and listen to their newest song.

"Our journalist will be there. We'd love to get some pictures of the day. I'd love it if you were to be in some of them… both of you. Our journalist is great, he takes pictures of us while we're in motion for his magazine. The camera clicks away as we move and pose, trying to get the perfect shot. We can even sign his next array of posters for you guys to have, for free." He took an eager step forward.

"Why us?"

"My friends and I have taken notice of you two out here, knocking down trees and doing some badass fighting. It's all pretty… evil. We like that. And we've also heard about that werewolf almost killing you guys. Not every kid is running around with monsters. You guys are our type.

"If you want to listen to music, you should come to see us tonight."

Loud cackling came from behind Clancy, who slowly turned around.

When he saw who it was, he groaned with an eye roll. Lonny, Chad, Lilly, and Nichole, members of a band that played upbeat, party songs often played in clubs. Lonny was the leader of the band; he had dark hair and tanned skin. He wore an Alet dress shirt with the sleeves properly rolled down. Lonny and Chad were one of the few boys at school to wear the white uniform slacks. Lilly and Nichole wore fur coats with their Alet uniform skirts. They were the group singers, and they both had awful, large, permed hair and wore thick sunglasses. They walked right up to Clancy.

"We'll see just whose show sells out tonight," Lonny scoffed. "Party music or black magic music with a goblin of a singer."

Clancy clenched his fists, but just before he could speak, Lovetta stood to her feet. "You're just jealous!" the slim girl shouted.

"Jealous?" Lonny asked. "Of what? I don't want my songs to make listeners' ears bleed or a singer whose voice sounds like screaming straight from the underworld." Chad and the girls began to snicker.

"*Scramble!*" Lovetta pulled out her wand and pointed it at Lonny. An irregular, baby blue surge of ripples raced to Lonny's forehead, ultimately scrambling his thoughts, making him become confused and disorientated. Lonny began rubbing his knuckles as he gave Lovetta a menacing glare.

"Be careful, Annettes." Chad sneered at her. "You don't want to start any more trouble." Aldric stood to his feet, his wand drawn.

Professor Adolfo Olsen, a fellow band member of Clancy's, approached. He was wolf-like with sharp, piercing eyes and long, unkempt hair that matched his untamed spirit. His movements were graceful and calculated, commanding attention like a magnet. Despite his fierce and bold nature, there was a hint of mischievous humor in his eyes and a gentle side to his personality. He had a way with words that could charm even the most skeptical people, but he did not tolerate foolishness. His intelligence and curiosity led him to seek new experiences and knowledge, traveling far and wide to explore the world. However, he also had a deep-rooted love for the simple pleasures in life, such as good food, company, and a warm fire on a cold night. He lived life on his terms, embracing his flaws and strengths unapologetically. His powerful presence forever changed those who knew him.

He was wearing a leather jacket over his black Chaos band shirt. It had the word 'chaos' written boldly at the top where the 's' extended downward like a snake over a white drawing of the queen's castle.

"What's all this?" he asked as he strode down the hill over to the students, his hair flowing flawlessly behind him. He looked to Clancy then over to Lonny, who was gripping his head.

Before Clancy could speak, Adolfo placed his arm over his shoulders and began to guide him away from the other students. He nodded Lovetta and Aldric over after noticing that they weren't following. They jogged over and caught up to them.

Clancy was now yelling in Adolfo's ear about how Lonny and Chad were disrespecting the band. Adolfo didn't react but kept the boy close to his side to prevent him from running back over there and causing chaos. He held him tight as they walked so that Clancy's head was restrained from looking anywhere except ahead. Lovetta found it quite helpful because she could see the four students smirking when she looked back, and that indeed would've angered the short-tempered Clancy.

"So" – Adolfo cut Clancy's rant mid-way and turned to Lovetta – "coming by tonight for some music and photos? We will send you signed posters once the new magazine comes in." Lovetta stuttered a yes right before the afternoon bell rang. "Off you guys go, see you tonight," he said his farewell to Aldric and Lovetta as he still held Clancy at his side. He looked down at him. Clancy looked up at Adolfo, who he often referred to as his 'at school dad.' "Want some advice?" he asked as they walked into the building. "I didn't have to get involved there, but I did. I know you could've handled yourself, but it's also important you get an education. If any other teacher were to have caught you, you would've surely been sent to Mr. Bernard's office… who may not give you another free pass for your good looks." He chuckled. They turned down a corridor where students stared at them. "Once you're free from school and you have an education, you're free to wreak havoc on his kingdom. After all, that's what education's for." He gave him a playful shove.

They arrived at Adolfo's classroom, which was conveniently Clancy's next class. Adolfo released Clancy. Clancy straightened his green cloak and took a seat at the back of the room.

Aldric walked in and sat beside him, hoping they weren't overstepping their welcome.

"Did you see the chicks' faces after you scrambled Lonny's brain?" Clancy laughed, relieving them of any anxiety about their new friend. "See, girls like that are a waste in this world. But you get it, Lovetta, life's too short not to show this world your true potential." He leaned back in his seat.

Lovetta blushed. "So what band are they?"

"The Kingdom People." Clancy shook his head.

"Oh," Lovetta said. "I've heard about them. There's a fan club here for them at school. We should start a fan club for your band."

"No way!" He sat upright and leaned closer to Lovetta. "No way, we don't want fans. We make music for a small group of people. The people who matter. The people like us."

When the whole class was seated, Adolfo cleared his throat, which was enough to quiet his students, who sat oddly uncomfortable in their seats as they stared up at the scary-looking man. He picked up a book from off his desk and showed them the textbook cover: *Troll Music and Their Instruments*.

"One of my favorite texts." He pointed to the book. "It is also one of my greatest musical achievements. My musical skills in troll music have gotten me a position in the Troll's Order and Troll School, which takes place in the summertime. I am also an honorary member of the Troll Defense League and a five-time winner of the Troll Music Award. Now, you're probably wondering how music got me there, and the answer is, it's not just music. It's a skill learned through passion, perseverance, as well as education on the troll culture. I see that you've all come prepared with all of this semester's required texts as I had asked, so thank you. Today, we will start with a little quiz all about you. I want to know your interests in music, your strengths, as well as your weaknesses. Learning requires teamwork between both you and me." He handed out the papers. "You have thirty minutes." He smiled before taking a seat behind his desk.

1. *What is your favorite color?*
2. *What are your ambitions?*
3. *What has been your most outstanding musical achievement?*

The test went on for another forty-five questions, each question giving you lots of room to write. Half an hour later, he collected the tests, and he skimmed through them briefly with an interested glance. "I'll shape the semester based on your answers. There's no point in making you learn stuff you don't want to. From what I've seen so far, we have similar tastes. We will be looking at many Yeti music originating from the dear kingdom Polar

Frigemilt, where four of my dear friends are from. As well as werewolf music which has a special place in my heart." He gave a small smirk.

Lovetta was looking at Adolfo in disbelief. Everyone had been so scared to go to Adolfo's classes, but now she could say she officially had no more fear. He was sweet, happy, and cared about his students. Lovetta could've sworn that all the late students who were stuck in the front row were shaking.

"Miss Lovetta Annettes, I must say you and I have a lot in common when it comes to music. Horrid tastes – good girl!" He flipped her quiz over. "Exactly all the same answers as me. Not even Clancy and I matched this well. Quite excellent, my dear."

He bent down behind his desk and pulled up a blanketed object. "We will start with the basics." It looked as if a long, thin rod lay beneath the blanket. He pulled the thing out. "Troll recorder. To many, this is a foul-sounding instrument. As seen on page fourteen, this instrument can be cursed, and its song can become harmful to all those who hear it. Today, I will be teaching you how to protect yourself against an enchanted troll recorder along with many other cursed instruments. This may just be one of the scariest classes on your schedule. However, be calm as no harm will come to you while I'm here."

Clancy leaned forward onto his desk. He looked interested. It was nothing Lovetta had seen before. A young girl in the front row cowered. Adolfo immediately brought his attention to her, placed a comforting hand on her back, and soothed her, explaining the process and letting her hold the instrument to ease her fear. Lovetta let out a low growl that sounded as if it came from a hundred-pound animal. Clancy and Aldric turned. She hadn't seemed to notice the sound that came from deep beneath her throat.

Adolfo walked back to the front of the class. "I must now ask you to scream and make as little noise as possible. It could make your pain worse." The whole class held their breath. "Devilish, the curse put on this recorder."

The recorder was an electric blue color and about eight inches long. Adolfo placed the cursed recorder down and picked up an identical recorder that sat on his desk. "I will demonstrate how a regular troll recorder should sound." He brought the mouthpiece to his lips, and a shrill sound came from the other end. It sounded like female trolls arguing. The sounds began to shake the room; it was pretty bizarre.

"All right then, now onto the curse. You will have to remain calm, cover your ears with both hands as the counterspell is more powerful when used with brainpower rather than wand power. You will have to repeat the spell as you focus." He reached beneath his desk and pulled out a long sword which he used as a pointer for the chalkboard. He pointed to the spell and repeated it aloud. "Edhwierft, it works just as the spell Normalem, which I'm sure you've all used in a spell gone wrong. However, with curses, Edhwierft seems to work quicker. So, place your hands and repeat the spell. Once complete, the sound of the recorder will go back to normal, and I will give you a thumbs up to uncover your ears."

Adolfo brought the recorder to his lips once everyone's ears were completely covered. A wild uproar shook the room, shooting black magic around throughout the room. It raced toward Aldric and lifted him off of the ground. The black magic ran toward the back of the class, where a glass cupboard housed instruments. The spell broke the glass. Books flipped open from the breeze, ink bottles toppled over, splattering the room, knocking over paintings and posters – one of which was of his bandmates posing in front of a white wall. The band member Aksel was giving Amara, who gave a menacing pose, a nuggie. All of the nine band members wore corpse paint except for Aksel and Mike. Lovetta looked at the fallen poster as she repeated the spell. She got nervous, thinking that she was sitting next to the only band member on the sign to have been staring straight into the camera. She grew even more worried as she thought that tonight she would be meeting them all. The black magic began to smash the windows. The students, with their hands still over their ears, hid beneath their desks. Aldric still floated in the air.

"Come on now! Focus on the music and the black magic it sends out!" Adolfo tried to encourage them.

The countercurse was beginning to work. The black magic released Aldric, and he fell harshly on the back of a chair. The misplaced posters and paintings were flowing back into place. The black magic swarmed Lovetta; the cold air bit her ears. It felt as if she was getting frostbite.

Clancy emerged from beneath his desk and pointed his wand at the recorder. *"Freosan!"* An interwoven, green stream of particles exited his rod and struck the recorder, coating it with an ice sheet, causing the black magic to fall like dust to the ground.

"You said no one would get hurt!" Clancy huffed.

CHAPTER 7

Lovetta and Aldric could hear distant, loud, complex music playing as they approached the building. Posters of Chaos similar to that of the shirt Adolfo was wearing were plastered outside the building.

"It's the first time Amara will be performing in front of an audience. He has raw talent, dedication, and an infidel brain that has had a huge influence on all of us," Clancy spoke to them as he walked backward toward the building as if he were talking to a film crew.

He turned around and opened the side door that led behind the stage. More posters hung around the walls inside.

"And it's time to introduce the more evil than ever Chaos to our fellow black magic followers and create some mayhem."

They walked in. Mike was sitting on a leather chair smoking bone dust. Even though he was seated, Lovetta could tell he was tall. He had long, dark brown hair and matching eyes.

There was a couch beside him where Aksel and a fat teenager sat. The small coffee table that sat in front of them was littered with cups, cans, and bottles of Arctic Crush Beer.

Mike rubbed Aksel's head. "Stop!" Aksel pushed his foot off of Mike's leg.

Amara was in the corner of the white room with corpse paint on his face. He was pacing. Lovetta pouted at the sight as she crossed her arms. "He must be so nervous."

Time was ticking before their show began. They walked to the blank, white wall that Lovetta assumed was the same wall they had posed in front of for the poster that hung in Adolfo's classroom.

Lovetta counted and noted that there were only eight members instead of nine; one of them was missing, yet the fat teen, who Lovetta assumed was their journalist that they had been talking about, was taking pictures of them.

Mike bent his long legs as he squatted against the side wall allowing the shorter Clancy to put his elbow on his shoulder. Amara had his head tilted, and his eyes rolled back; that stance mixed with his corpse paint made him genuinely look like he was dead.

"That's sick!" The journalist snapped the photo.

"One more!" Clancy shouted.

"Grab his head!" the journalist suggested.

Aksel wrapped his arm around Amara's neck and dragged him down, similar to the poster that hung in Adolfo's classroom. After taking the photos, it was showtime.

"All right, let's go," Mike said firmly.

"Showtime." Clancy threw on his leather jacket.

"Let's go, let's go." Aksel grew impatient as everyone took their time.

"Good luck, guys!" the journalist called out. "*Faster than a vampire,*" he began to sing to himself as the band members walked up the stairs, leading to their stage.

Lovetta and Aldric stayed downstairs with the journalist who collected his video camera. Amara stood at the microphone and began to scream into it like a goblin from the underworld, an insult made by Lonny, but something was mesmerizing about this sound. Something dark and wicked seemed to have come out of the round-faced, smiley boy. "*Faster than a vampire.*"

The crowd raised their hands and cheered and screamed just as dark as the singer had. Lovetta, Aldric, and the journalist pushed their way to the front. He aimed the giant camera that had to sit on his shoulders toward the stage.

"*Terrifying vampire.*"

Lucian, a band member, began to play his wood elf air horn. The sound it made was similar to chimes with sounds of wood critters in the background. He lifted his hand and let out a scream. Clancy, stood on the opposite side of the stage, began to play his elvish spoons, which, when clanged together, made tunes similar to a Heofsij piano.

"*Enraged like a demon.*"

Mike, who stood closest to them, began to play his nymph organ that sounded like chimes but on a darker frequency. Aksel, who sat at the back, lifted a cobra for the crowd to see before placing it around his neck to begin to play his goblin drum, which sounded like haunting chimes when struck. On his first strike on the drum, green lights illuminated the stage, and the fans cheered. Walter, another band member, began to play his merfolk harmonica, which made deep chime sounds when blown. He raised his hand, acknowledging the eager crowd.

An instrumental solo began. The journalist zoomed in on Clancy. Amara began to bang his head, flipping his long, blond hair around as he felt the music in him. Lovetta's eyes couldn't help but focus on Amara. Something was intriguing about him on stage. He seemed like a whole new witch disguised behind his mask of white and black paint. On each corner of the stage stood two stakes. One held a pig's head. The other had the head of an Aegopithecus, a half-goat half-witch creature whose goat head could be told apart from an actual goat by the narrow nose and face that dropped down to a more witch shape. Male witch hair was still on the back of the deceased head. No normal witch could handle the sight as Aegopithecus are more witch-like than animal-like. Another cobra slithered on the stage. Amara picked up the snake that slithered in front of his feet for the crowd to see. The crowd cheered.

The music grew intense as it anticipated the goblin-like vocals. Amara swirled and banged his head around to the music's beat before placing the cobra down on the stage. The journalist focused his camera back on Amara.

"*Half witch, half ghost.*" The music continued to grow more intense by the moment. "*Kings and queens of feasting, pulling on your time. Twisting, smashing, and stealing your dreams. Blinded by the cold, dead eyes, you'll never awake.*"

Seppo, another band member and older brother of Amara, began to bang his head and play an orc accordion, which sounded like heavy footsteps and heartbeats. This started another instrumental solo. When the crowd couldn't imagine the sound getting more pressing, it did. Amara reached back down and picked up the snake. Lucian raised his hands, acknowledging the crowd.

Amara placed the cobra down and walked toward Aksel's drums. Amara began to roll up his sleeves. The journalist zoomed in. Adolfo began to play his eagle bagpipe, which, as one would guess, makes the sounds of eagles cawing.

Lovetta looked to Clancy, who continued to play the elvish spoons while looking over to his friend. The journalist's mouth dropped in awe. It must've been the first time for him to hear this song come alive. Adolfo smiled as he watched the performer entertain the crowd. Even Walter looked impressed. Amara ripped the Arctic Crush beer bottle out of Aldric's hand and brought it onto the stage. Lucian let out an excited scream, raised his hand, and got the crowd going. Clancy decided to look away and played his spoons aggressively. Lucian screamed again. Seppo looked at his brother, Amara, showing little to no emotion while nodding his head to the music's beat as he played the accordion. Clancy looked back to Amara. Lovetta bit her thumb as she hid a smile as Amara raised his arms. She looked away and gave a little laugh.

"*Just call my name, and I'll hear you scream*," Amara continued to sing. The crowd cheered, and the music grew even more intense as if each of Amara's lines added demonic fuel to the instruments. "*Kings and queens.*"

Clancy looked to Amara with a smirk. The music grew more intense, and the crowd became wild, pushing and shoving one another as they jumped around. Amara walked over to the pig's head as another musical solo began. He ripped it off of the stake and threw it into the crowd. The journalist focused his attention on the pig head, which fell between Lovetta and a teen with long, blond hair. They both caught it. The raw flesh called to her. The teen bit into the head, and she did the same. The music grew intense before it came to an end, the singer raised his arms, and the crowd cheered once more. After the show, the band and the journalist, Lovetta, and Aldric walked to the Sleeping Sprite restaurant, drank beer, and waited for their ordered food. Lucian had been called up to retrieve his food. In one hand, he held a plate and in the other a bottle of beer and napkins. Not having a good view of his seat, he bumped into Aksel before sitting down. The drunken journalist had a good laugh at sight.

Lucian sat down and took pieces of turkey from out of his sandwich. He shoved them onto his incisors to make him look like a vampire, a creature that seemed to mesmerize the band. Aksel brushed the hair from out of Lucian's face so that everyone at the table could get a better look at what he was doing. Everyone laughed.

Clancy was talking her ear off. Lovetta didn't have a chance to communicate with anyone else, not even Aldric, who sat quietly, shifting awkwardly and his eyes mainly surveying his food.

Lovetta didn't take her eyes off of Amara. Clancy took note and looked to see who she was looking at. When he saw his friend, he couldn't help but be concerned.

"How are you?" he asked.

Amara, whose eyes were fixed on his pale arms, only marked by old self-harm wounds, looked up. He didn't reply. He looked tired. Clancy kept his eyes on Amara as he took a sip of beer ordered by the group's adult members.

Lovetta looked to both Clancy and Amara. "You guys are the best band in the world."

"Definitely undead," the journalist agreed with a full mouth and a point of his fork.

"We're not just a band," Clancy began. "We perform not just music but our way of life and our beliefs."

"Order number fifty-two ready for pick up!" yelled the man behind the counter. Clancy stood up and walked over to the counter to pick up his food.

The bell above the restaurant's door rang as a frantic teen rushed inside. He had black hair and wore a yellow sweater and black jeans and had a yellow bandana with black speckles on it around his head.

"Hey! You guys were awesome today! The show was awesome! I mean, I was at the very back, so I couldn't see much, but I must say you guys sounded awesome. My name is Haruto." He took a step forward.

Now Clancy had a better view of the teen; he saw that his sweater had a picture of The Kingdom People in a dome-like structure with rainbows shooting out of it. "Just exactly what band do you think I'm from?"

"The Kingdom People, the after-party is here at the Nightingale."

"This is Sleeping Sprite. Nightingale is the next building. And I'm from Chaos." With that, Clancy threw a punch, breaking the kid's nose.

Haruto spent the next school day avoiding Clancy and the other members of Chaos. When he saw Clancy turn down the corridor, he would be sure to find the nearest exit, whether it was a classroom or broom closet. He had never seen the members of Chaos so much in one day. His anxious, rambling thoughts made him conclude that they had memorized his schedule and were now hunting him down as if a broken and cut nose wasn't enough damage for a slight misunderstanding.

"Hello, Haruto," they'd say, making him jump out of his skin if they had come from behind him.

He would be polite and act casual by replying with a 'hello' as calmly as possible as he tried to work. He couldn't hide the fright in his voice.

Haruto shared almost all of his classes with Amara and nearly screamed each time his wand malfunctioned, letting out green sparks and black smoke. At one point, the rod had flown out of Amara's hand and headed straight for the back of Haruto's head as if the wand itself was insulted because of last night. A large, throbbing, green boil had formed where it struck, causing Haruto to run off to the hospital ward.

Aldric had just exited from the Alet dressing room, where a short boy with brown hair and thick glasses had just begun to walk past the room when he stopped in awe at the sight of Aldric.

"Oh wow! Are you a Crash Ring player? I've never seen a game before! I heard it's one of the most dangerous sports in all of Galdorwide," Beau Scaasi beamed. Beau now walked beside the student, who was much taller than him.

"It'll be boring to watch," Aldric explained.

Beau seemed to ignore this as his face was filled with excitement as he continued to trot beside him. "You're probably a brilliant player. I haven't even learned how to fly a broom, but I'm only thirteen, but I'll be fourteen in five weeks. I still won't be old enough for a broom, though. Is it easy to fly? Is that your broom or the school's?"

Aldric was bombarded with questions that took him a bit of time to process as more questions flew out of the young boy's mouth. "It's not hard, especially not during Crash Ring. The ring does most of the work. Plus, you don't need to be sixteen to play. I'm fifteen, so this is just my training broom. My birthday is in two weeks. Then I can get a real broom." He enjoyed the company, especially after a night like last night.

"I don't get the game," Beau continued to talk. "But I am interested in trying out for it one day."

"Well, really, you try finding ways to knock people off their brooms, using spells. Of course, last ring standing wins."

They walked out the backdoor of the school, which led to the Crash Ring field. Beau tripped on his shoelaces but managed to stay on his feet.

"And you're this year's captain now that John Scaasi is sick, right?" he asked.

Aldric wondered how Beau knew so much. "Yes," he replied as they walked along the lawn covered with orange leaves despite the trees still having green leaves on their branches. "Once he gets better, he'll return as captain."

Beau didn't stop asking questions until he walked Aldric to the Alet team's bench. "I'm going to get a good seat since we're early! Good luck!"

He ran off toward the tall rows of the spectator bench.

Daemon, Tassos, Michael, and Aaron were still upset with the kids for not following the rules. Usually, the Python Seger students would have been happy to reach the weekend, but that wasn't the case for this Friday night. The kids planned to meet their friends who attended Galdorwide High for the weekend, but this was put on hold.

Saturday morning, they were all awakened earlier than any of them would've liked.

"What's going on?" Chris moaned, throwing himself beneath his covers as if it would protect him from the day.

"Class," his father Aaron said sternly before walking over to the bedroom window and whipping both the curtain and the window open.

Chris tossed over and squinted at the window. There was a thin mist hanging below the pink, golden sky. He could hear the birds happily squawking, as if anyone was happy at this time of day.

"Dad," he said groggily and as if he were about to make a plea. "It's the crack of dawn."

"Exactly," his father replied. People often made jokes about his appearance, saying he resembled De Brazza's monkey due to his sharp facial features and intense gaze. He was wearing a black gi which was the new attire for both the students and the teachers. "It's part of our delinquent program. Listen, and you won't have to wake up at six in the morning. Come on, grab your wand, and put on your new gi. It's at the end of the bed. Then meet us all downstairs. Fall asleep, and you'll get another five hours added to your delinquent program," he said heartily.

Yawning and slightly shivering as the cool air rushed into the room, Chris sat upon his bed and threw his legs over the edge. With eyes barely open, he patted his hand around, looking for the gi.

"Good man," Aaron said, almost impressed as his son was out of bed twelve hours earlier than usual. "Meet us downstairs in five minutes."

When his hands finally grasped the gi's fabric, he pulled off his blue pajamas and put on his gi. He threw a black sweater over the top as all the windows in the building had been opened. He walked down the hall filled with statues, paintings, and monuments and down a spiral staircase with his wand in hand.

"What in Galdorwide is this?" He could hear Daemon shout. When

Chris reached the steps and finished wiping his eyes, he could see that Daemon had just shut the door and looked down at a magazine. "Coby!" Daemon shouted and began to look around the room.

Coby had just emerged from the staircase and regretted his timing. He looked to his dad, who held up the magazine and repeated his question.

"Nothing." Coby shook his head.

The top story in the magazine was about his friend Adolfo's band and their performance last night. Coby had been in the first row, and the cover had an image of Amara banging his head, and the back of Coby's head had made it into the picture as well. "I was supporting my buddy's band." Coby walked over and swiped the magazine from Daemon's hand.

"Which friend? I need to talk to their parents."

"Dad, he's a professor at Galdorwide, and I'm pretty sure his parents are dead."

"*Ooo!*" Mamie walked down the staircase with her gi in her hand. "You on the front cover, will you sign it for me?"

"No," he replied, annoyed before brushing past his sister to put the magazine upstairs in his room.

Once Coby returned, the teachers took him to the front of the class and looked at the puffy-eyed students. Chris looked as if he were about to fall asleep where he stood. Everyone took turns yawning.

"Mamie," Daemon turned to his daughter. "Why are you still in your pajamas?"

"I just think that it's sexist that I, being the only girl here, has been given a long-sleeved shirt to wear beneath the gi."

Daemon looked to his friends and fellow teachers, then back to his daughter with a smirk, and shook his head. "Go ahead, put it on without the shirt, go on," Daemon nodded toward the bathroom on the opposite side of the staircase.

"Thank you," she stomped off with a smile.

She walked out without the undershirt. The opening of the gi stooped down below her breasts, barely keeping them covered on either side.

"Look in the mirror," Daemon said with a smile.

"I know I look horrible. I'm tired." Mamie walked over the training floor and looked in one of the many mirrors that lined the wall. "I see your point." She pressed the sides of the gi down and stomped back over to the washroom.

When Mamie returned, Daemon began his speech. "I want to have a quick talk with you all before we begin today's class. The rest of the teachers and I have devised a plan to help keep order in this school. We have decided to recruit three of our good friends to help train you. They will move in and become just as much part of the school as us. They will be arriving shortly. They were once classmates, along with me, Aaron, and Michael. Tony Scaasi trained us – yes, my ex-brother-in-law and his friend Harvester Gold. They were horrible trainers when it came to morals but great teachers when it came to discipline. Today, we will be drawing up classes and activities once given to us by them."

Daemon walked to the room's side, grabbed a diagram, and placed it on the easel in front of the class. It was of the forest. On the chart, many color-coded lines and arrows had been drawn in. Daemon took out his wand and tapped the diagram making the image come to life. The drawings were going plan by plan according to Daemon's words. Chris' head leaned onto Mamie's, and he began to snore.

Daemon spoke about the forest's plan for twenty minutes. He removed it, revealed a diagram of the water outside the woods, and then showed another chart. This one had the image of Skogen Island. All the students had lost interest and barely heard any of the words he was saying.

"So," he said finally, almost snapping everyone back to reality. "Everyone clear? Any questions?"

"I've got a question, Daemon," Chris began as he had only really been awake for the final diagram. "Isn't Skogen Island where the Skogen prison is?" The class began to murmur their worries.

"Quiet!" He glared at all of them. "Now, listen, you all should have been able to accomplish your last mission with no problems. You guys make a great team. But, unfortunately, due to poor behavior and greed, your mission was utterly unsuccessful."

Chris, Ken, Horus, and Mamie shifted guiltily. They had wanted to run off and collect gems in Gimmian to gain riches rather than arrive at the head elf's castle with Coby, Stephen, and Brad.

Daemon took a moment to regain control. He could feel Tony Scaasi's temper and words fighting to escape him. The thought of his students going out of their way for their greed and pleasure tormented him, especially when his son Ken and his daughter Mamie were involved.

"You will train harder than you ever have before. Okay, so head to the forest and begin the first step in your mission."

Stiff-legged and yawning, the students exited the premises. The sun was beginning to rise. Mist hung above the grass. As they walked into the forest, they saw three men standing as if they were waiting for them – which they were; the students would've known this if they had paid attention. They introduced themselves as Python Seger's new teachers.

The man in the middle was tall, bald, and had blue eyes. He was wearing a blue priest-like robe. He introduced himself as Alburt. The man to the left was tall, athletically built, with blue eyes and light brown hair. He wore a green robe. His name was Bozidar. The man who stood on the right side had neatly styled brown hair that fell to his shoulders. His facial expression seemed menacing. He wore a blue robe. His name was Costas.

"Please tell me you have breakfast for us." Chris was exasperated once they had finished their introductions. "Or at least some caffeine quake."

The three men looked at one another. "Your mission hasn't even started yet," Bozidar replied slyly.

"Today," Costas began, "you will learn new spells."

"First," Alburt began to speak, "you will have to mount your brooms and make way to where Daemon has instructed. We are here only to evaluate. So, if you please…"

The students mounted their broomsticks and kicked their feet off the ground while Horus transformed into his bat form. The early air whipped their faces as they soared upward. It seemed to wake them up. It felt terrific flying, but they were all nervous about what was to come next. They flew around a high circle of trees, landmarking the middle of the forest.

Mamie was in the back of the group. She could see their mouths move, but she couldn't hear them, which was odd because she seemed to be at a close enough distance to be able to listen to their muttering, at least. After straining her ears, she noticed that she couldn't hear anything at all, not her cloak flapping in the air or the wind brushing past her ears.

"Guys!" she yelled out, but she couldn't even hear her voice. The boys looked backward, hearing her call. "I can't hear anything!"

Their eyes widened. They began to look slightly to the left of Mamie's head and looked to have been saying, "Lookout!" She turned to where they were looking and saw a culfer. A creature from another kingdom. It had the body of a dove, the face of a shrew, and red tentacles surrounding its body. When at a close distance, all noises are muted.

Frightened by the ugly creature, she lost balance, and her broom began to spin out of control as she fell downward. Horus removed himself from bat form, swooped down, and helped her regain balance as the boys shot spells at the creature.

"*Grama arodscipe!*" A vibrant, baby-blue wave of particles exited Chris' wand, surrounding his wand and turning it into a black blade filled with demonic energy. He flew closer to the creature and struck it, allowing it to fall to its death.

Down below, Amara Johansen was walking with his little sister Diana. The creature fell perfectly in front of them.

"Cool." Amara bent down, picked it up, and placed it inside of his green bag.

"We've got company," Stephen pointed downward, and it wasn't at the two blond siblings.

Several Tuscels marched on the forest floor. Tuscels were creatures with the bodies of a witch and the head of a canine, their chests were bare, and they wore yellow skirts or kilts depending on the gender. In their hands, they carried large, silver staffs used as walking sticks. At the tips were carved canine faces.

"I don't believe it!" Chris hissed in outrage.

"Daemon said this would happen. You would've known if you had listened," snipped Stephen. They approached Amara and Diana.

"We'll just see about that." Coby lowered his broom to help a friend of a friend.

Coby shot to the ground, landing hard just in front of the siblings. The rest of the Python Seger delinquents followed.

"Tuscels!" Coby bellowed. "This is Galdorwide, home to witches. You shall return to your hometown of Scape. Now!"

The Tuscels stood quite taller than the average witch. Cunning was written over their faces. "Plenty of room here in this empty forest," a male Tuscel replied with a sneer.

Mamie, Stephen, and Brad stomped to Coby's side while the rest formed behind them, keeping Amara and Diana in the middle. Oddly, the two siblings seemed to be quite amused by the unwanted guests.

"The king himself kicked you out of this kingdom," Coby reminded. "The queen stands behind his decision," he spoke sternly with his deep, drawling voice.

"*Ah*, I see," the same Tuscel continued to speak. "Well, we will not leave empty-handed." There were seven Tuscels in total, three female and four male. They all sneered. "Or at the very least, let us give you a gift."

All seven of them aimed their staff at the teens. Coby, being the closest, had a stick placed under his nose. Dust exited the staff and entered Coby's nose, rendering him unconscious. He fell backward. Amara caught him and laid him down on the ground gently as Brad and Stephen stepped closer to one another, once again blocking Amara and his sister.

"Clean is his brain, now," said a female Tuscel. "Clean them all!"

For a moment, the teens froze, unsure of what to do. The Tuscels continued to sneer, letting the anticipation rise. Their eyes were cold and reduced to slits.

"Oh, how intimidating," Brad mocked.

"My brothers, my sisters, and I will take over this kingdom," the female Tuscel taunted. Amara and Diana showed zero fear as they gaped at the sight.

"Soon," the Tuscel continued to speak, "this kingdom will be covered in silver and gold if our mirror is not returned. We'll clean this whole kingdom as we have your handsome boy." She snickered, looking down. They followed her eyes and noticed that Coby's nose and lips were turning gold. "I expect the mirror to be returned to us by dawn." The Tuscels howled with laughter after noting the fearful expressions on the kids' faces.

"Or" – Horus reached into his black cloak pocket – "we can do this the easy way." He pulled out his wand and aimed it at the female Tuscel. "*Scead Clawu!*" A wobbly, purple-black stream of sparks exited his rod and turned into a shadowy claw which rebounded off of the Tuscel and turned to Horus, slicing the side of his head. He fell backward. Amara caught him and lowered him down next to Coby. The Tuscels howled with laughter again. Chris and Ken let out a war cry and jumped forward to attack the nearest Tuscel, but Brad and Stephen jumped in and blocked them.

"Stop!" Stephen shrieked. "Killing them won't turn Coby back to normal."

"Brad, take Horus to the hospital ward. Coby will have to stay here until we return. A doctor won't be able to help him." Brad nodded and bent down and lifted Horus from off of the ground.

"You two," Stephen continued his orders as he looked to Amara and Diana. "Go with Brad."

Diana was very interested in getting answers. "What spell was that? What are those things? Will he and the cute blond die?" She asked an array of questions as she hopped along happily beside the boys.

"The demon energy is digging deeper into his skin." Amara pointed to Horus' blackened wound where smoke stemmed.

"*Ooo,*" Diana said, fascinated.

"Need help holding him?" Amara asked Brad.

"Sure," Brad said before handing the smaller boy Horus' body.

The two of them took turns holding Horus as they made their way to Galdorwide High. Brad had insisted they go to Ace's, Daemon's nephew, but Amara was adamant that he had suspicions of Ace and that Notleaf and Morgan had yet to disappoint. He also reminded him that another Scaasi, Dr. Caressa, would be at Galdorwide High.

"Nearly there, Horus," said Brad as the school came into view. "You'll be all right in a minute."

They were twenty feet away from the school when the doors opened. A knot formed in Amara's stomach when he saw Ace exit. He was striding out wearing a leather jacket.

"Quick, hide," Amara, who held Horus, hissed. He ducked behind a nearby bush, Diana and Brad followed.

Brad was contemplating whether or not he should stand up and call for Ace's attention. He didn't seem to understand why Amara was so afraid. After all, it wasn't his friend who had been injured.

Behind Ace was Caressa, who remained on the step-like porch with her arms folded. She wore a black turtleneck which made her blue eyes pop. On her hands, she wore black gloves. Caressa was tall and slim with dark brown hair that today was fashioned up in a bun.

"It's all a matter if you know what you're doing," Ace spoke loud enough for the whole realm to hear. "If you did, Notleaf would've entrusted your brother's care to you and not me." He walked off as Caressa stared at her distant relative with burning eyes.

They waited until Ace was out of sight. Amara pushed Horus onto Brad's shoulder, who placed a hand beneath his friend's back and the other beneath his legs. He stood up, and they emerged from the bush. They walked over to the backdoor leading to the hospital. Caressa had already marched off inside. They knocked at the door urgently.

Caressa opened it, looking quite upset. She must've expected it to be

Ace returning for one last comment. Her expression lightened when she saw that only people who needed her help were at the door.

"Come in, come in." She moved aside, allowing Brad to carry Horus inside. "Sorry about my earlier expression. I thought you were someone else. Over there." She pointed to the nearest hospital bed.

Amara and Diana noticed that the hospital had gone through some changes since they had been there last. Beside each bed was a fireplace with a red button and a blue button to emit either fire or ice, depending on what temperature would better aid the patient. Caressa hadn't seemed too concerned when Brad had walked her through what had happened – of course, leaving out the fact that Tuscels were involved. Brad lowered Horus onto the bed. Caressa raised the head of the bed with a twirl of her wand.

"I'll be back, just going to fetch a potion," she explained, briskly walking over to her office. When she returned, she held a green-tinged potion bottle with brown liquid inside. The label read: Puke Potion. She handed it to Horus. "Demonic toxins are coursing throughout your body. You will need to drink this to eliminate them from your body. It won't be pleasant, but the toxins are better out than in."

She bent down and reached into the bottom of the cabinet drawer. She pulled out a silver basin and placed it on top of the vampire's lap.

"There's not much else we can do." Caressa eyed, taking note of the young boy's face as he held up the potion to the light.

Horus looked up at her. She motioned her eyes to the potion. Horus pinched his nose with one hand then placed the bottle to his lips with another. He took one consecutive sip before bending over the basin and vomiting out a mix of brown, green, and black substances. "It's a difficult curse you have performed. Where did you learn such a spell?"

"Python Seger," Brad answered for him. "It's where we've been taught ever since training school."

"My Uncle Daemon works there. How's he been?" She smiled.

"Good, excellent, especially now that Aisley has been revealed to be alive."

Caressa furrowed her brows as she tilted her head.

"I'm sure you already know," added Brad awkwardly.

"No," she said dimly before sparking a cheerful attitude. "I didn't know, haven't talked to much of my family for years besides my siblings. I assume my father hasn't told any one of them either."

Caressa hopped off over to the entrance of the hospital ward, where a counter displayed caffeine options. She began to brew them all tea. She also returned with a vial of a thick, creamy liquid.

She grabbed a cloth and began to wipe the blood from the cuts on this side of his head. Once it was all clean, she plopped the liquid onto her gloved fingertips and began to cover the wound with it gently.

"Can't believe that, Ace," Caressa said as her guests sipped their teas while she patted Horus' wound. "Coming into the office, giving me advice on client care. I mean, he's not the head doctor here. Notleaf is. Ace acts like I don't know what I'm only doing because I had been a high school dropout, but I came back, earned my diploma, and excelled in the art of healing magic. If only he knew just exactly what I'm capable of. Ace acts like he's the only doctor that this kingdom needs, yet his patients are in his care for years. I mean, it's hard enough to gain trusted patients, but here he is, snatching each one of them." She removed her gloves and reached into her pocket, and handed Horus a toffee. She quickly removed her hand and tilted her head. "Is there something you guys aren't telling me? About the incident? Who exactly were you trying to curse?"

They all looked to one another guiltily, wondering how to reply. "Things are just wild in the forest. You heard it was banned. It's banned for a reason," Brad lied.

Caressa crossed her arms. "A curse is not a go-to self-defense spell against a mere common creature." She looked pale and sweaty, as if she already knew what danger they had encountered. "Who or what were you attacking!" Horus leaned over his basin as a sea of black particles emerged out of him. Caressa was outraged. "Answer me," she growled.

"Tuscels," Brad finally confessed. "Tuscels, they came here, wanting to take over, threatening that they would turn the whole kingdom silver and gold. That's when Horus attacked them. Now they've ordered our friends to find their mirror. A mirror we've never even heard of or seen before." Horus burped just before another wave of puke exited him.

Caressa, instead of looking frightful, looked pleased. "Tuscels, disgusting creatures, aren't they?" She wiped her sweaty brow. "Dirty animals they are. It's ridiculous that they would try to take over the kingdom. Half-dog half-witch," she scoffed. "Can you imagine the first-ever relationship to create those freaks of nature?" Horus retched into the basin once again. "Well, I don't blame you for trying to curse them, Horus," she had to say that loud enough for him to hear over the sound of him vomiting. "Maybe it's a good thing it backfired. I mean, a cursed Tuscel would have meant war for the kingdom."

"What tea is this?" Diana asked as if the whole conversation was meaningless.

"Toffee Tea."

"Get this," Diana turned to Amara. "The next time you go to the market."

Amara smiled and began to rub his little sister's head, messing up her already wild, blond hair. She smiled and laughed, showing her large teeth.

"I've got a bone to pick with your oldest brother, Stuart." Caressa pointed to Amara, wagging her finger. "He needs to make up his decision about where Diana will be going for her studying and surveillance. I do hope he picks me. Diana is such a sweet girl. I'd love to care for her here."

"I hope he picks you too. I know Diana would be in your care if it were me making the decision. I mean, just because he's the eldest doesn't mean he should be making the decisions on her behalf. After all, I'm the one who watches after her most of the time. If he doesn't pick you, I sure as the underworld do not want her in Ace's care. But, unfortunately, I think that is the route he is heading. You know what they say: Scaasi men have a charm."

"You can say that again, all we Scaasi women get is being labeled as pushovers, but that's all thanks to Aisley. I mean, the Scaasi before her were strong, both blood and those married into the family."

"Please," Brad spoke up. "Don't talk about Aisley like that. She's been staying with us. She's important to my father. I grew up hearing stories of her strength, so don't put that label on her. Maybe you think that about Scaasi women because you are one – a pushover."

"I beg your pardon?" She spoke in shock as she crossed her arms.

"I'm sorry." Brad genuinely went to pat her on the back, but she reeled backward.

"Don't touch me!" She freaked. Brad reeled his arm back.

She straightened herself up and lifted her chin. "I don't like being touched," explained Caressa. "Fudge, anyone?" She tried to relieve the tension in the air.

"Me!" Diana raised her hand as if she were in a classroom.

Caressa smiled before looking down at Horus, who hadn't vomited for a few minutes. "How about you? It may help with the taste." He nodded. She looked back at Diana. "Wanna come with me? The doctors here just got a new greenhouse where we grow medicine as well as healthy food."

"Yeah!" Diana jumped from off of her seat.

They exited the building and headed to the school's side, where the greenhouse could be seen. Diana wore colorful, striped gloves on her hands which she wrapped around her coffee mug.

Inside the greenhouse were dozens of rows with different plants. To the right was a row of fudge plants. Green bulbs hung from the branches, and when plucked and peeled, a circular piece of fudge could be found inside. The fudge trees in the greenhouse grew much more significantly than those that grew in the forest. Here, they had all they needed to grow to their fullest potential. Diana looked around in awe.

"Pretty nice in here, yeah?"

"You grow pumpkins here too." She pointed to the very back of the greenhouse.

"Yes, good eyes. Once they're fully grown, each of the students will go home with one. Would you like one too?"

"Sure!"

Caressa looked over her shoulder. She had to admit that she was a bit on edge after the Tuscel revelation. She looked back to Diana, whose teeth pulled on the fabric of the glove and danced around awkwardly as she felt Caressa's stare.

Caressa smiled before looking down at the ground. "See those" – she pointed – "those are bligs. They were the first living things in Galdorwide, before the grass, before the trees."

Bligs were slimy and looked a lot like an eel. Its body was made of surreal shapes and was missing a tail.

"Watch your step. Bligs are kind creatures, but they don't like it if you get too close. They'll give you space, and in return, they like when we do the same."

It was nearly noon, and Stephen and the rest of the Python Seger students had not had breakfast. They were all keen on getting the Tuscel situation and their mission over with so they could go home and eat homemade food made by Aisley. She said it was the least she could do for them for all their help. Stephen had branched off with Chris while Mamie and Ken were sent in the other direction. The groups said goodbye and said that if they didn't find anything within five hours to return to where they met the Tuscels hoping that the other team had better luck. Stephen and Chris were heading to the ministry's mansion in hopes of finding answers. They wanted to appear professional and responsible in front of the queen, the emperor's son, and the ministry, but Chris began to hiccup as soon as they got to the door.

They were barely stepping through the archway of the mansion's front entrance when they saw the queen approaching with brutal steps and a stern face. "This is a private building," she stated loudly. Chris, nervous already, let out another hiccup.

"You do know there is a punishment for trespassing. You will become my servants for five days. Wiping every inch of this mansion as well as the castle, that might sound like a fun break from school but not when the rule of my servants is that they can't use magic. Magic can miss the small details."

Chris gulped while his younger brother looked somewhat composed. Nobody wanted to be a servant of the queen. Being a friend of hers could even be scary.

"You would also need to help me mail all of my important paperwork if your reason for trespassing is non-valid." She raised her brows, waiting for the two young boys to speak. "I'm going to need to hear a reason for all of this," she said after noticing that her glare was not enough to get that message through to them.

The boys slouched and felt small in front of the intimidating authorities of the kingdom.

"There are some kiwi fruit and strawberry yogurt in the kitchen." Adelaide kindly motioned the boys further into the castle.

Chris and Stephen didn't enjoy the food as much as they would've liked. They felt worse knowing that the kingdom rested on their shoulders, and potentially telling the ministry may cost them their mission and give them another long lesson like today's, and even with that.

"There are about a hundred cups in this room I could have you two go through and clean thoroughly." Bella crossed her arms before reaching into her purple cloak and pulling out a pile of envelopes which she tossed onto the table. "They need licking and stamping."

Saturday afternoon melted into the evening. It was five to eight when the queen dragged them to her office at the castle while the ministry was ordered to settle the Tuscel issue. The boys gritted their teeth, angry that she was still upset with them and even more upset with knowing how their father would react. She pushed the tall, white doors open.

"Lick, stamp, that's all you'll do. Maddox here" – she gestured to a tall, slim man who had blue eyes and down the left side of whose face, from forehead through his eye to cheek, was a deep scar; he had long, black hair – "will be here, watching you two and making sure there's no peeking in any of the envelopes."

Shining brightly on the marble walls were lit candles, flickering in the otherwise dark room. On the walls were portraits of the previous rulers, including her father, King Delanie Carter. Two large piles of envelopes were laid on her desk.

The minutes snailed. The two boys restrained themselves from talking in fear of the large man that stood by the door. The candles along the walls burned lower and lower, making them dance over their still faces. Stephen moved his hand to grab what felt like the two-thousandth envelope.

It must be nearly time for the day, Stephen thought to himself, *we must be almost done for the day.*

When asked the time, Maddox replied that they had been working here for nearly four hours. Chris wanted to complain about child labor but bit his tongue.

Shortly after, the queen arrived and said that the boys could return home and come tomorrow at six in the morning for more work. When they got home, it was so late that only Horus, Tassos, and Tassos' wife Sheryl were awake. Horus sat on one of the living room's navy-blue armchairs, cradling his still store stomach. Stephen and Chris went straight up to their room after being informed that the ministry had solved the Tuscel situation quite quickly, considering they had the mirror they wanted. It had been used to bring forth the dragons months ago. They had taken the mirror and had brought it back to Doryu Edjer's church. Chris and Stephen walked into their shared bedroom and found that Brad was in bed waiting for their arrival; they slipped into their pajamas and got into bed.

"The queen explained she was making you guys do chores on behalf of trespassing on ministry property. What did she make you guys do?" Brad asked.

"She made us stamp and lick envelopes," Stephen moaned as he rolled to look at his brothers as he wore his blue silk pajamas.

"My muscles have all ceased," groaned Chris, who lay in the middle bed. He rolled onto his back and allowed his body to sink into his soft mattress.

Lulia was alone in her room when she heard a young boy's voice come from thin air. She was sure it was a ghost.

Come to me – help and tear me from this dark world I'm in… Lulia… you're my only hope.

Lulia initially hesitated, but the voice sounded so desperate that she couldn't ignore it. She cautiously approached the space where the voice seemed to be coming from and asked, "Who are you? How can I help you?"

The voice replied, "I need your help."

Lulia didn't know what to do but felt a strange connection to the boy's voice. She closed her eyes and focused on reaching out to him. Suddenly, she felt a surge of power flow through her body, and she opened her eyes to find herself standing in a different place altogether. Lulia suddenly found herself in an unknown place, realizing she had been transported to a different world. A young boy stood before her, grateful and hopeful. Lulia knew she had to embark on this unexpected journey and help the boy in any way possible.

"Thank you for coming," he said. "I knew you were the only one who could help me." Lulia didn't understand how she had gotten there or what was happening, but she knew that she had to help him—

Upon awakening, she felt disoriented and confused, only to soon realize that she had fallen asleep while studying.

Feeling dazed, she walked back to her bed, lifted her homework books, and placed them into her backpack before crawling into bed.

The next day after school, Lulia explained to Flower and Beau about the about the dream she had. It wasn't like her to dream things in general, let alone a dream so vivid, no matter how tired she was.

"Did you recognize this guy?" Flower asked.

"No." Lulia shook her head as she spoke softly and trembled as they sat in her bedroom. The dream had left her feeling uneasy and disoriented. She couldn't shake the feeling that it meant something, even though she couldn't remember all the details. Flower's question only added to her confusion, as she couldn't recall ever seeing the man in her dream before. Lulia's fear was palpable as she spoke, and Flower knew the experience genuinely shook her. As they sat in silence, Lulia tried to piece together any clues that might help her make sense of the dream. But no matter how hard she tried, nothing seemed to fit. She only knew that this dream had left a lasting impression on her, and she couldn't shake the feeling that it held some significance. As they continued to talk, Lulia felt a sense of relief wash over her – knowing that Flower was there to support her made all the difference in the world.

CHAPTER 8

October arrived, sending foggy, chilly nights around the ministry's castle. Ian Morgan, a ministry member, and the ministry's doctor, didn't have to worry about taking care of the patients' colds back at work. Instead, he was kept busy here with the ministry. Adelaide Nillag, looking pale, was bullied by Ian to take his potion, which would cure her potential cold. If it worked, he would know that her paleness was from a cold and not a concern for her unborn child. Falling asleep instantly is a side effect of the potion coming in contact with a patient's cold. If Adelaide were to fall asleep, it would be a good sign. If it were not a cold, the potion would not do anything. Luckily, as soon as Adelaide drank it, her body sunk into the salmon-colored couch. Raindrops, the size of bullets, struck the windows of the mansion. Despite this constant, rainy weather, Bella insisted that everyone train as they did not know what they would have to face when the prophecy comes true. Everyone, besides Adelaide, stood outside, muddy and drenched.

Along with tonight's rain was a gush of constant, cold winds. Inside, after she awoke, Adelaide was looking solemnly out the window, wishing she could train and help her fellow ministry members. They assured her that she was okay. After all, she was typically the bookworm and interviewer of the team.

"Hello, Adelaide." Kenneth walked in. His beige cloak was glued onto his skin from the rain.

"Hi." She looked over to him then back at the window.

Kenneth began to look around the room. He was wearing a dashing, plum-colored hat on top of his long, curly hair. Before today's training, he wore a beige tunic with a ruff he had taken off before going outside.

"You look as pale as smoke," he said. "You may need another potion. If you were any paler, I would think you were a vampire!" Vampires often have skin so pale that it is see-through, allowing people to see their red veins. "You look troubled," said Kenneth. When she didn't respond, he continued to speak as if he were some psychic, understanding how she felt. "*Ah*, I understand how hard it must be not to join us for some aching muscle training."

Despite his airy tone, Adelaide could tell he was not taking a liking to her silence, not something he was used to.

"I'll tell you a story to prove to you that I know how you're feeling. Pregnant, left out, and scared sick. One time, I was in search of a headless horseman. When I found him, he brought me to his past to understand how he felt and why he was so enraged. With this transportation of my soul, I endured the pain of getting slashed in the neck forty times until my head was severed, and then... I was brought back into my own body. You can read about the event in more detail once I release my book. I mean, the experience opened my eyes. We're all made to believe that decapitation is just one swift blow to the neck with an ax, but no, I was in a lot of pain. Anyway, I bring the story up because recently I received an anonymous letter. I suppose it's from an avid fan. Inside was a drawing of the decapitation of the headless horseman, but it had my face, which is odd because it's a story I had never told anyone. I can still feel what it felt like to have the last skew of skin attaching my head and neck before the nothingness that was soon replaced with an overwhelming feeling of relief when I saw myself standing back in front of the headless horseman." He took in several deep breaths while a tear seemed to be forming in the corner of his eye. "Enough about me, but I hope this little tale helped you a little."

"No," Adelaide said simply. "You just compared my pregnancy to decapitation."

Adelaide's temper was just about to explode before the mansion's front door had been kicked down. From the corner of Adelaide's eye, she could see a pair of gigantic yellow eyes out the window. Her heart dropped. Outside was a giant black cat.

At the door was Arthur. "Get away from the window! Go upstairs!" Adelaide held onto her stomach as she ran up the stairs. Kenneth went to follow. "Kenneth!" Arthur corrected. Kenneth headed toward Arthur to go and help.

Suddenly, Samantha Scott, a woman who the ministry had helped a few months back, popped out from behind the tapestry in Adelaide's room. Adelaide almost didn't recognize the woman. After all, Adelaide didn't spend much time with her, and her hair had grown longer. She was wearing a red t-shirt and looked calm and comfortable even though she shouldn't have been in Adelaide's room.

"Hi, sorry, I forgot your name," said Samantha. She looked down. Her eyes popped. She looked crazy as mud dripped from her clothes. "I know what you're thinking. I'm a mess. I must've gone amuck. I've just had enough of this stupid queen. To ruin the surprise, I was a follower of the king before you guys even helped me. I was a distraction, you see. One of your henchmen was hurt – the hot one. That was unfortunate. I was hoping it would've been one of you broads who got hurt."

Gloom filled the room. Samantha had lied to them and caused Krum's injury that severely affected his performance come the day of the dragon attack. Adelaide began to wonder how the woman had found her way into this dingy, windowless room. The room was lit by a single oil lamp, adding to the uneasiness of the situation. The ceiling hung low. Adelaide was tall and had to hunch down whenever she stood, but Samantha, who stood eight inches shorter than Adelaide, didn't have a problem standing upright. A faint smell of roasted horse filled the room, a sure sign that the dinner Adelaide had been cooking before she had fallen asleep was beginning to burn. Wooden cabinets lined the room. Adelaide was wandless and was looking for anything that would help her in this situation. Chains and hooks hung from the ceiling, it was an odd sight, but this had been the butcher's room before the abandonment of the mansion. Adelaide was extra careful when walking around the room, making sure not to penetrate the sharp metal through her skull, but neither she nor Arthur cared enough to rid the objects. They would only be here for a few more months before they could go back home. If Adelaide were allowed to stand upright, she would've taken Samantha and penetrated the hooks through the woman's ankles.

Adelaide reached for a quill while Samantha went on a rant describing her and the other ministry members as she approached. "Pirate dictator, foolish plonker, infidel, crap sample, I'm sick of all of you."

Adelaide went to bring the quill to Samantha's neck, but it was stopped by a pale, silver-outlined hand. The king. Adelaide backed up in fear. His spirit was getting powerful. He was able to touch, which meant that he was able to kill.

"Hurting the future queen is a crime," spoke the king in a deep, scratchy voice.

"The future queen?" Adelaide asked, repulsed by the very thought.

"Yes, my future queen." The king turned to Samantha. "Take her to the dungeon!" Adelaide shivered. "I will decide her sentence."

The king unpleasantly squinted as he watched Samantha grab hold of her arm. A great bang came from the ceiling causing the oil lamp on the nightstand to wobble. Before anything could stop her, Samantha transported herself and Adelaide to a place that no one even knew existed.

Samantha threw Adelaide into a black cell where nothing except for a moth-eaten chair, bucket, and blanket was laid.

"The king's prisoners are treated better than the queens. You have two options for entertainment: a book or an instrument that's enchanted for only your ears to hear, so don't think that you'll annoy your way out of here with a trumpet."

"A book," Adelaide said as she crossed her arms and sat on the chair. "And by the way, I'm pregnant, you know."

"Well, looks like we have something in common." She smiled.

"Does your future husband know?" Adelaide was mortified.

"Why, of course." Samantha locked the cell door.

After a few moments, Adelaide could hear Samantha's shuffling feet. Through the cracks, Samantha tossed her a book. It fell on the ground in front of her feet. Adelaide bent forward, picked it up, and was immediately displeased. *Quick Magic* by Kenneth Riley.

"Don't think about using magic. It won't work down here," stated Samantha before walking away. Adelaide could hear her footsteps rise as she headed upstairs.

Lovetta stood in Aldric's room. He had gone off to greet Clancy and his friends. Lovetta was sitting on the chair in front of Aldric's desk, littered with homework, much like her own desk. However, something caught her eye, a red envelope, which had arrived for Aldric in the middle of lunch, which made him act differently for a long time afterward. She sneaked to the bedroom window and looked out. Aldric was still standing by the oak tree in his yard, waiting for the guests to arrive. She reached over, opened the envelope, and took out the letter. She read it and was horrified. What secret was the writer talking about?

She heard the laughter and chatter of the boys walking up the stairs. She stuffed the letter back inside the envelope and tossed it onto the desktop. She tried to act normal and pretended that she had been looking casually at her nails this whole time.

She looked up and greeted the boys. Aldric's eyes quickly darted from her to the red envelope that now sat on top of his homework papers. His face grew a bright red, and it wasn't from embarrassment. He looked angrier than Lovetta had ever seen before.

He stomped toward her. Lovetta flinched as he stretched his arm out and over to the envelope he raised. "Did you read it? Did you?"

"No," Lovetta lied in fear.

"If you read this, Lovetta – I swear!"

Lovetta was staring up at him. She had never seen him look this mad before; his eyes were popping.

"I want you to go."

Lovetta gathered her backpack and scarf and brushed past Clancy and his bandmates. Lovetta raced down the stairs, through the hallway, and out the door.

"Lovetta! Lovetta! What was that?" Clancy had run outside.

"Stay out of it." Lovetta had planned on being harsh but immediately regretted it, so her words came out mumbled.

"Did you read it?" he asked when he caught up.

"No," she lied. She couldn't let her truth come out in case it'd get back to Aldric. The two of them set off down the road, heading toward Lovetta's house.

"Is there anything I can do to help with your next show?" Lovetta asked, breaking the silence.

Suddenly, the air became icy cold. "It'll be on All Hallows Eve. I wouldn't want to take that night from you."

"No, I'd love to come and help."

"Great, it'd be our five hundredth show!" Clancy stated excitedly. "It's just going to be held in my basement enough to fit the fans who matter. Aldric and your brothers are welcome to come," he added. "It's also my birthday hence why it's also important for it to be close people. No gifts required – besides you and the group, no one knows about my birthday. It's kind of a sucker thing to care about."

Lovetta smiled. "I'm sure my brothers would like to come. After all, I went home the other night and told them how frightening and interesting your show was. I'll probably have to shield my youngest brother."

"Yeah... good idea." Clancy talked with his soft, drawling voice as if each word needed to go through a proper decision process of whether or not he should say it.

"It was passionate and scary. It moved me. True art, I'd say."

"Well… then… my dear… Lovetta, you're one of the few to believe that my friends and I aren't insane." He gave a slight bow of appreciation. "I mean, I don't mind scaring people. Gets rid of all the weak, fake friends."

Lovetta opened the front door to her empty home. She threw her bag down by the front entrance and headed to her bedroom. She began to scramble through her drawers. She turned, holding a clump of clothes. "Do you mind?" she asked.

Clancy turned around. He could feel a burning tingle in his throat that went down to his chest. When she gave him the all-clear, he turned around. She had slipped out of her uniform and put on a white dress and her blue cloak. The two of them spent the evening working on their art of potion-making homework.

"That sounds depressing to me," said Aksel as Clancy described his evening with Lovetta. "I mean, you were in a house – alone – and no sex? Zero sex?"

Rain lashed on the windows of Aksel's living room that displayed the ink-black night sky. Inside, the house felt calm as oil lamps flickered on the side tables. The fireplace was lit, sending a flickering glow throughout the room. Plenty of squishy armchairs filled the room, it was pretty cluttered, but it was enough for most people to sit comfortably. There was a free chair, but Amara, wearing a green velvet fedora, was seated inside a cardboard box. His knees were squished up to his chest. He looked up at everyone with his brown puppy eyes. Walter, Seppo, Lucian, and Mike were all on the chairs working on homework. Nicholas, a member of the band Misfit Crew, was trying to kill insects with fire spells. Who would've thought that Nicholas was from a royal family, the Snowballs? Unlike the rest of his family, he had dark brown hair instead of white-blond, but that's because he used a spell to change the DNA of his hair. Darren and Frederick, fellow members of Misfit Crew, gathered along with Rabbit to watch Nicholas burn the insects.

Mike looked up from his homework. "Good on you, Clancy. Premarital sex is a sin. This is a time of romance and courting."

"Yeah." Aksel smirked. "Be more like Mike and marry your girlfriend at eighteen and knock her up."

Mike smacked the back of Aksel's head playfully. In each band, they had a member called the 'dad' of the group, and for Chaos, that was Mike. In Misfit Crew, Gavin – who was at his house sleeping after he kicked out his bandmates to stay here and make noise until they were ready to come home and sleep – was the oldest out of everyone in all of the groups. He was thirty. The 'dad' of the band Imaginary Kings was Terry, as he was responsible and in charge for nursing his reckless friends back to health after dumb stunts.

Sparks followed a loud bang. They looked over to see the four boys who were killing insects covered in black smoke and dust. Mike had looked over, concerned until the four of them began to laugh. He rolled his eyes then looked back to his homework. Anne, Mike's pregnant girlfriend, who lived at the house with Mike, Aksel, and Walter, had stomped down the stairs. She began to bellow herself hoarse as she yelled at the men who had caused the incredible explosion.

"Mike," Frederick began. "Silence your lady friend."

"Excuse me?" she shouted even louder. "No one can silence me and especially not Mike!"

Mike stood to his feet. His eyes flickered with anger. "No one speaks to my wife like that, you badly drawn alien!" Mike took out his wand. "Go home, all of you." He looked at the four men.

***

By the time Halloween arrived, Lovetta was happily anticipating Clancy's show. His basement had been decorated with dead, hanging bats and Jack-o'-lanterns large enough to be used as seats. Adolfo had also enchanted real skeletons from graves they had dug up to dance.

At seven o'clock, Lovetta, Aldric, and her three younger brothers arrived. Lit candles lined the staircase rails, directing them to the event. All the candles were lit with black flames casting a ghostly shadow on everyone's faces. The temperature in the basement was cold, on Amara's request to help him tune in with his dead, vampire stage persona. Lovetta shivered as she brought the sides of her blue cloak closer together. Everyone's breath was visible in the extreme temperature of the basement. It was as if they had all crowded themselves into a freezer.

It was an incredible sight. Some people sat on pumpkins while others enchanted their feet to hover above the ground so that they could dance like spirits. Behind the stage was a black drape to cover the white painted walls. There was a black, dazzling chandelier hanging in the middle of the ceiling. It was large and looked to be holding a thousand black candles.

The set began with what sounded like nails scratching a chalkboard. "Hello, dear friends. Welcome, welcome, so glad you all could make it. Before we begin, give it up for the person who has been by my side and a part of this band from the beginning – nymph organ player Deceased-Slaughter!" Clancy bellowed a scream into the microphone motioning to Mike, who screamed as he stuck out his tongue and acknowledged the crowd who cheered.

"And give it up for everyone's favorite drummer – Aksel!"

Aksel raised his snake-green drumsticks in the air. The crowd cheered once more.

"We are Chaos!"

He pushed the microphone, almost making it topple over, but Amara swiftly caught it and began to scream his goblin-like vocals into the microphone. Amara bowed and swiftly whipped his green, velvet fedora hat into the crowd. Lovetta caught it. He smiled and winked. He looked kind despite the dark sound his throat was producing. Clancy was the first to start the music with his elvish spoons, followed by Aksel on the drums, then Mike on the organ. Progressively, the other members began to play their instruments.

People were waltzing to the beautiful, dreadful music. This song was particularly chilling as the music sounded like saws grinding against each other.

"Should we dance?" Lovetta turned to Aldric as she placed the green, velvet fedora atop her head. Aldric was confused at first, but Lovetta explained that it would only be a means to warm themselves.

Lovetta, Aldric, and her brothers rose above the crowd. They began to dance. In the corner was a tall, slim blonde girl with green eyes, dressed as a slutty nun for the occasion. She danced – alone – provocatively. Her eyes never seemed to leave Clancy. Lovetta let out a low growl, sending Aldric reeling back. A ragged teen was in the opposing corner. He was draped in chains. In another corner, the band's journalist was taking aerial shots of the band and the crowd. A teen boy in close range wore a royal knight costume. In his forehead was an arrow.

When the song was nearing an end, from the corner of Lovetta's eyes, she could see a young brunette girl bouncing to the beat. Next to her was a blonde girl who looked quite frightened. A red-haired girl was on the opposite side dancing. Behind the girls was a small, scared boy.

When the song ended, the young brunette shouted, "You guys suck!"

"Get out of here. You shit graduate!" Clancy shouted as he pointed up the stairs.

"Get out of here. You shit graduate!" the young girl mimicked.

His friends, both on stage and watching, laughed at the young girl's mimicry. It was someone they all seemed familiar with. They seemed joyed by her presence while Clancy was growing impatient.

"Amara." The blonde girl looked at her brother. "Is your throat okay? Do you need medicine?"

After the show, Aldric took Lovetta's brothers home so that Lovetta could stay, only to be disappointed as Clancy spent time with the slutty nun. She had a camera around her neck and was an aspiring journalist, and he was urging her to go upstairs and take some pictures. Upset, Lovetta took off the hat that Amara had tossed her during the show. She walked over to Amara, who was sitting alone while giving those around him a puppy-eyed look.

"I believe this is yours." Lovetta stretched out the hat with a small smile.

Amara looked up, almost shocked as if he was not expecting anyone to talk to him at all this night. He waved his hand in halting.

"It's yours. I own like ten. Are you okay? You look very numb."

Numb wasn't the word Lovetta would use to describe how she felt, but she knew that he had read her emotions perfectly after hearing it. She crossed her arms, her eyes filled with tears, and her bottom lip began to tremble. Amara stood to his feet and began to rub her upper arms in a comforting matter. He bent down so that he could look into her eyes.

"I want to show you something," he said hesitantly before a wide smile spread on his face. He grabbed her hand, and they began to walk up the staircase. He pushed open Clancy's front door, and they walked over to his house that he shared with his siblings. A loud snore could be heard from one of the rooms, but other than that, the house was utterly silent. He lit the lanterns with a wave of his wand. Continuing to hold her hand, he brought her to his shut bedroom door.

"Okay." He smiled wildly. He opened the door.

The room was larger than expected in the tiny home. Amara explained that he got the enormous space to help contain the smells. The wall by the door was made with black paneling. The furthest wall was made of wood paneling. There was a mattress with a yellow blanket draped along and a white pillow on the ground. On every wall were excellent, dark sketches of dead trees, cemeteries, demonic creatures, ghouls, and vampires. A single lantern was hung in the middle of the room, creating only a dim light. The Chaos band logo hung on his wall, the center of all of his drawings. Dirty clothes littered the floor.

"Look at this." Amara motioned her over. He pointed to a picture. It was a black and white picture of a young boy with shoulder-length, light hair. Next to him stood a young girl. She had the glummest-looking face Lovetta had ever seen before. On her face was a pair of thick spectacles.

"Ainsley Moan. She died exactly five years from today. I almost died with her."

"I'm so sorry." Lovetta placed her hand on Amara's shoulder comfortingly.

To Lovetta's amazement, a ghost slowly emerged out of the closet door over to them. It was Ainsley. Amara smiled and walked over to his green bag, where he pulled out a dead bat. He tore off one of the wings and walked over to Ainsley, who opened her mouth. Amara plopped the wing into her open, silver-outlined mouth and she began to chew.

"You can eat?" Lovetta asked. The girl nodded as she continued to chew.

"Ghosts can only eat carcasses," explained Amara. He leaned in closer to Lovetta while Ainsley turned away to sit on the bed. "They don't get hungry, but eating can act as a comfort."

Lovetta smiled. She felt special being introduced to this other side of Amara. Any other person may have felt sick with the smells and the sight of a dead girl eating a bat's wing, but he trusted her.

Lovetta walked over to Ainsley. "I'm sorry, I didn't properly introduce myself. I'm Lovetta."

"Hello," the young girl said cautiously.

"More nibbles?" Amara asked the ghost sweetly. Lovetta's heart fluttered.

The girl shook her head. He placed the remainder of the bat back into his bag.

Ainsley crossed her arms and looked at Amara. "I heard them talking rudely about you again today. They're lucky I can't touch mortals! Why do you hang out with them?"

"They're my neighbors and my bandmates. I don't consider them friends. I don't need any friends. They're just something to do and people to hang out with while I'm at school."

Ainsley sniffed. "They were talking about you," she continued sulkily. "Saying how—"

"Saying how great your performance was," Lovetta said. She glared at Ainsley. If they were talking poorly about him, it wasn't something he needed to hear.

"No," she objected, looking at Lovetta suspiciously. "They were making fun of you."

Lovetta turned to Amara. "I didn't hear one person talk badly about you all night, I swear."

Silver tears rapidly ran down her face. "Yes, some of them had nice things to say, but some were just awful." Tears now flooded her face.

"It's okay, both of you. I know what they say behind my back. They call me ugly, scrawny, dead-looking, and depressed. It's fine. It's all true anyway. No need to get upset over it."

Lovetta was shocked. "Amara, I'm so sorry. I never heard anyone talk bad about you. And if I had, I would've knocked them on their feet! You're not ugly – you're perfect. You're adorable. You're sweet. If they are saying those things, it's because they're jealous. You're tall. You look mature. You have a strong, manly face that doesn't allow you to look like a girl with all of that hair, unlike some of them." Lovetta laughed. Each word she spoke came out as fast as her angry heart's beats.

"Enjoying yourselves?" A familiar drawling voice came from the bedroom entrance.

"Yes, we are," Lovetta snipped at Clancy.

"Not a bad turnout for our small show," said Clancy. "My friend Sky came from Udonid. I was just going to give a speech when I noticed you two were gone. I was worried – terrible things happen on All Hallows Eve." He looked to Amara and Ainsley. "You two know that especially."

To Clancy's amusement, Ainsley began to sob in anguish. He then brought his focus back to Amara.

"We planned another set. Are you going to join?"

Before Amara could reply, a hunting horn sounded. "Oh, no," Amara said numbly.

"So much for my speech." Clancy smirked.

Amara grabbed Lovetta's hand as the three of them ran outside. "Wait! Where's our sisters?" Amara looked to Clancy, who shrugged.

"Diana!" Amara shouted. "Diana!" He screamed.

Through the forest trees that sat just off the property, a giant, six-headed turtle emerged. "Cool," Clancy said with a dark smirk.

The turtle was an icy blue color. The night was cold, Lovetta was hungry, and she would not let one giant creature get in the way of snacks. Her teeth chattered, and she would do anything to be back inside. Lovetta hurried toward the beast. She thought about her father's traditional All Hallows Eve pudding that would be waiting for her when she got home.

***

Lulia had fallen asleep. And, in her dream, she had seen the young boy once again. "Go outside," Lulia heard him say. She awoke sitting in Flower's bedroom; Beau was working on his homework with Diana, and Flower was dancing to inaudible music. Lulia rubbed her eyes, trying to shake off the drowsiness from her dream. She couldn't help but wonder what the boy's message meant. Was he trying to tell her something important?

"I had another dream," the red-haired girl said.

Flower immediately stopped dancing and turned to face her friend. "Did he say anything?"

Lulia nodded.

"What did he say?"

"He said to go outside."

"Well, we can't do that," Diana said as if there was no question about it.

"Yeah, Diana's right – for once," Beau began. "The warning alarm just went off. Who knows what's out there, especially on a night like this."

"*Go outside.*" She heard the voice even though she was not sleeping.

"Listen! Did you hear that?"

Beau and Diana froze, looking up at her. They seemed frightened. Flower, on the other hand, was quite intrigued.

The voice continued to tell her to go outside, but the voice seemed to be slowly fading out. A mixture of fear and excitement gripped her. Maybe she would finally know who this guy was. Was it a phantom? A witch using a telepathic spell?

"Come on!" Lulia shouted, motioning her friends to follow as she rushed out of the room and over to the front door. She sprinted outside. Diana and Flower ran after while Beau continued to sit on the bedroom floor, contemplating if he should follow them or not.

Lulia's stomach dropped. Outside, she could see Clancy, Amara, and Lovetta attacking a giant turtle.

"*Help them. Or someone will die!*"

The three girls stood on the porch, bewildered. Beau finally caught up after deciding to follow. He jumped up to see over the heads of the taller girls. When he caught sight of the animal, he fainted. Lulia began to run toward the creature, leaping three steps at a time. She could barely hear the boy's whispers over the sound of her pounding heart and feet. By the time Diana caught up, she was panting.

"What is this thing?" Flower shouted over the creature's whaling.

"Look!" Lulia pointed to the neck of the creature, where a collar with a letter inside hung. The collar shimmered in the moonlight.

"It's an ice creature!" Flower shouted. "Use fire, you fools!"

"*Ad*!" Clancy cast as he took a vital step forward. His aim was off after his front foot slipped in a puddle of mud, sending his legs to split further apart than he would've liked.

At the sight of the fire, the creature grew angry. Amara grabbed Diana and backed away.

"*Ad*!" Lovetta cast, striking the creature's head.

The creature went up in flames, almost as if it had disappeared, which at first is what they thought had happened. That was until they approached closer during the dark of night. Laying on the ground was Brad Silvermaul. He was stiff. His eyes were wide, cold, and staring up at the sky. His skin was deathly pale. The side of his head was burnt to a crisp. The collar hung around his neck. For a moment, none of them moved.

"Let's get out of here," Clancy suggested hastily.

"What? No!" objected Lovetta. "We need to help!"

"You just killed someone! We have to get out of here!" he protested.

It was too late. Running feet approached from out of the forest. Lovetta fell to her knees, crying over the body of a boy she didn't even know. Angel,

Daemon, and Aaron emerged from the forest, smiling. They loved the thrill of a chase, but when they got close enough, Angel screamed. Tassos joined the sides of the adults.

"Lovetta!" Daemon ran over to his temporary student, who cried over the body of his friend's child. He tried pulling Lovetta from off of him.

"No!" she shouted as she tried to shake the boy awake. Daemon pulled her back. "No!" She fought forward back over the body. Her whole body flailed on top of Brad's body.

"What happened?" Daemon asked as he walked around to the opposite side to look at Lovetta's face.

"I killed him! I killed him! I killed him!" she repeated in disbelief. "It was a giant creature, but after I killed it, it turned into a boy. I didn't mean to. I didn't mean to," she cried.

Daemon clasped his hands around Lovetta's face. "It's okay. It's all right. You're safe. It's all over." Lovetta began to sob.

"What happened?" Aaron asked from afar. His friends turned and looked at him with solemn faces. He began to pace forward, his heart beating. "What happened?" He began to run. His friends parted, allowing him to make way for his son. As Aaron ran toward his son, he couldn't help but feel a sense of dread. His mind raced with all the possible scenarios that could have led to this moment. Was his son hurt? Had he gotten into trouble? He saw his son lying motionless on the ground as he ran closer – dry tears on his son's face. Aaron's heart sank. He rushed to his son's side, feeling fear and sadness. He gently lifted his son's head and checked for any signs of injury. His heart pounded in his chest as he waited for a response. There was no response. Aaron's mind raced as he thought about what to do next.

"Summon Ian!" he shouted.

"It's too late," Angel croaked.

Aaron's heart sank as he realized his worst fears had come true. He had lost his son. Tears streamed down his face as he struggled to accept the reality of the situation. Lovetta moved out of the way allowing the grieving father to cradle his boy. "Brad!"

Lulia began to cry. Diana buried her head into Amara's side while Flower wrapped her arms around Clancy's waist tightly. Daemon walked back over behind Lovetta and pulled her back. Weak, her body fell into him. "Go inside," he insisted. "All of you." He looked at the kids. Daemon stood

Lovetta to her feet and walked her inside Clancy's home, where the rest of the kids followed. Once inside, Daemon could hear Aaron howl in agony. He ran back outside to comfort his friend. Amara took both Diana and Lovetta into his arms.

"It's all right, I got you," he said as their tears sunk into his shirt's fabric. "I got you."

Lovetta could still hear Aaron's howls, each one digging through her soul.

CHAPTER 9

"You!" Aaron screeched. "You killed my son!"

"Aaron!" Daemon growled. "Come with me. You too, Lovetta, Amara, and Clancy." He led the four of them back over to Brad's body.

Amara had his arm wrapped around Lovetta, while Clancy looked as though he felt unnecessary. He also looked excited and didn't even try to hide it. They joined with Angel and Tassos. Daemon bent down and examined the body, eventually taking note of the collar and the letter attached. Lovetta and Amara exchanged tense looks. He unrolled the paper and began to read it. His eyes narrowed, looking up to Angel. Clancy tried not to smile, but he could feel the drama rising.

Aaron continued to sob dryly as there were no more tears to be shed. His face was in his hands as if to shield him from all the heartache that laid beneath him.

Lovetta barely knew Brad and Aaron, only seeing them occasionally at Python Seger. She felt terrible for what she had done. She was also scared, knowing that the men of Python Seger were not ones to mess with, and she feared what the letter would say or if Aaron wouldn't accept the truth.

"Did you know about this?" Daemon asked Angel.

"No, of course not."

"Well, this suggests otherwise," he stood and tossed the paper at her.

Angel looked at the letter. Her jaw dropped. Daemon took out his wand and began to mutter all kinds of spells that could've been helpful in a situation like this. He even took off the necklace that prevented him from dying and draped it around the boy's neck. Nothing happened.

"This amulet should be working." Daemon shook his head. He looked up to Angel. "Are you still here? Because I wouldn't be if I were you."

The blonde woman clenched the paper tightly, bit her lip, held back her tears, and then ran off. Daemon stood to his feet and looked at Aaron. "None of this was Lovetta's fault."

"It wasn't?" Aaron choked the words out before slowly lowering his hands off of his face. "She said she killed him."

"Brad had been cursed, turned into a Frore Byrdling. He was unable to control his actions. Instead, his actions were controlled by the king. He was ordered to attack the kids of Galdorwide. The letter was assigned to Angel by the king. This morning, he had given her a choice, either save Brad or let a secret of hers out, and she chose to ignore the choices. By choosing neither, he chose for her. She's the reason why he's dead." Tears began to stroll down Daemon's face; he had been tough for everyone, and his emotions were starting to seep through. "The amulet's not working because the king knew of our Arcane magic and counteracted its powers. This was a personal attack."

"So much for asking for Angel's help," Tassos scoffed.

The men of Python Seger had noticed Brad's disappearance and asked for help from the ministry. Angel volunteered because she already knew that it'd be on her if something happened to Brad.

"I'm so sorry." Lovetta turned to Aaron.

"It's okay." Aaron's face was now purple. "You were just at the wrong place at the wrong time. You protected yourselves. I cannot blame you." Aaron then looked to Daemon. "But why my boy?" he croaked.

***

"You have to admit, the circumstances are suspicious," Dr. Notleaf began as he stood on Ace's porch. "No visitations and no communication besides letters. Only one of your patients has been discharged, and that was Tris Smith – who praises you highly. But you've had patients in your care for years, and none of them have left yet. If they're not dying, I suggest you release your patients before I get the ministry involved."

"Why don't you join us for dinner – tonight? Come in." His eyes sparkled in the moonlight.

Dr. Notleaf's heart began to thump rapidly. If he said no, he would never know for himself if Ace's patients were okay and if he said yes, was he putting himself at risk? "I'm exhausted," he tried to make an excuse.

"Without supper?" Ace smiled wickedly.

"I'm not hungry," Dr. Notleaf objected right before his stomach let out a loud grumble.

Ace's smile widened. "I suggest that if you're not willing to come in and see my patients for yourself, then there's no need for the ministry to get involved. After all, you can't be too concerned if you keep on making excuses."

"Really?" Dr. Notleaf snapped.

"Well, the proof of my excellent care will not only come from Tris' words but now in physical proof if you come in now."

Dr. Notleaf began to search Ace with his eyes. His piercing blue eyes looked up and down Ace's body. With little knowledge of magic, Ace was sure that Notleaf was using some x-ray vision on him.

"I will eventually be able to cure all my patients. That is the goal. After all, I need some more time. Please, remember that I took the complicated cases. I am working on Mr. Hall, but I do think some magic will be needed, a certain potion, I can't recall the name, but once you take a look at him, I'm sure you'll exactly know what it is that he needs."

There was a long pause as Notleaf contemplated what action to take. He took a step back off of the porch. He turned away and began to move quickly, all while trying not to look as if he were running away. Notleaf made way to the office at Galdorwide High.

"Do you think I should've gone in?"

"No," Caressa replied with no hesitation. "You followed your gut, and that's a force stronger than any magic."

"So you do believe Ace is up to something too, don't you?"

"Of course I do. Most Scaasis are."

"Do you think you can ask your father?" he asked. Caressa eyed him. "Just this once?"

To Notleaf's surprise, Caressa snickered. "Oh boy, you owe me so much, you know that? I'll call him at the witching hour. He'll only answer if he's concerned." The kingdom's town clock rang just as soon as she had finished her sentence. "Really? Already?" She groaned. "Fine."

***

"Turn back, turn back," Haruto ordered his friends in the hall. "These Chaos guys are everywhere."

"Chaos guys?" one of his friends asked.

"The gang of long-haired dudes that are in a band called Chaos, a fitting name in my opinion. They're ruthless. The spoon player in the band broke my nose because I thought he was a band member of the Kingdom People." There was still a visible cut on the top of his nose.

They walked into the cafeteria and held up their trays for the Ixicia lunch ladies to plop on their food. They took a seat at their lunch table, which was now clothed in a black, velvet fabric for the final day of Samhain. The food on their plates smelled disgusting. The main course was a rougarou licorice salad. There was still fur attached to the meaty licorice.

For days, the school could only talk about the trio of second years who had been responsible for a Python Seger's death. The rumor had started true, at first, that it had been Lovetta who had killed him accidentally, but eventually, it became twisted. Everyone believed that Lovetta had a love triangle between Clancy and Brad and that Clancy had found them naked in the woods. Angry and heartbroken, Clancy deliberately killed Brad. Lovetta dismissed this rumor every chance she got. A relationship with Brad would've been illegal, he was in his twenties, and Lovetta was only fifteen. Lovetta's objection only twisted the rumor that instead, her father had found them in the forest and killed Brad. In red paint on Lovetta's locker was the word 'killer' spelled in a way to look like blood. Before she could open the door of her locker, a large hand pushed it shut. Frightened, Lovetta jumped back.

"Are you new to the school?" a handsome student with long, brown, curly hair down to his shoulders asked. His blue eyes never left hers.

"*Uhm*, no, I'm not. I'm pretty well-known." Lovetta motioned to her locker.

"Then why were you sitting alone at lunch today? I'm Varg, by the way."

Lovetta blushed. She wished she had met Varg before killing Brad because she didn't walk around with squelching red eyes from constant crying back then. Lovetta was both disturbed yet infatuated.

"I'm a huge fan of what you did. I hate those Python Seger students. We're better off without them."

The small smile that had briefly appeared on her face faded. "I didn't mean to kill him. It was an accident."

"You don't need to deny killing him to me. I see the evil in you." He brushed past her.

After school, Lovetta met up with Amara and Clancy and began to walk in the direction of their houses.

"What took you so long?" Clancy asked her.

"Coby Soleil made me stay after class. I don't think he forgives the whole Brad situation. He made me clean the barn, and by clean the barn, I mean clean up all of the animals' literal crap – without magic."

"What an ass!" Clancy threw a rock. Kids from the training school that had been walking in the direction of the three students turned and ran away. "Yeah!" Clancy shouted. "You better run!" He laughed. Amara shook his head and looked to Lovetta, who rolled her eyes.

They finally arrived at Clancy's home. They threw their books and homework onto the ground.

"Can you believe the extra work Coby gave us?" Clancy shook his head. "An extra three papers. Like who gave him authority over Gemini?"

"I know, what an ass," Lovetta said as she opened her *Art of Taming Animals* textbook.

"I say we torture him to death."

"Clance," Amara's tone came out in half warning half question. His nostrils flared.

"He's a spitting sod rider!" Clancy defended his suggestion. "Look at this!" He lifted the pile of homework Coby had assigned to them.

"I have to leave early today." Amara changed the conversation. "I have to say goodbye to Diana. Stuart chose to put her under Ace's care, which pisses me off. I don't trust Ace, I don't even think Dr. Caressa Scaasi trusts him, and she's his niece."

"What exactly makes you not trust him?" Lovetta asked.

Amara sweetly bit his lip. "I don't know. But don't you ever get that bad feeling in your gut?"

"Yup, whenever I'm with Clancy." Lovetta laughed, but she meant it.

"Lovetta," Clancy, who had been scratching his head looking at homework, interrupted. "Can I look at your homework?"

"No, you cannot," she swiped her papers after he desperately leaned over to look at them.

"Oh, come on! You let Aldric copy off you all the time!" Clancy whined.

"Yeah, but that's because, in return, he lets me copy off of him in other classes."

"Fine, you can copy me in music class, deal?"

Lovetta nodded and handed him her papers. The next day at school,

Lovetta and Clancy walked Amara over to the doctor's office to address his concerns about Dr. Ace Scaasi. Caressa took the three of them to the office, expecting Amara to be ready to talk to her about his depression or delusions, but her jaw dropped after hearing that he, too, had felt uneasy about Dr. Ace.

"Can you tell me exactly what Dr. Ace does at his home care? I'm not buying the sales pitch that he told Stuart. I'm worried about Diana. I only wish that I could at least visit with her and make sure that she's okay. Being a year apart, the two of us have always been close. I can't bear to be away from her, especially over some illness called ADHD, which to me explains a young child."

"ADHD is a bit more than a child being a child. You see, we believe she failed training school because of this condition. Luckily, they allowed her to pass her second chance. ADHD causes her to have a hard time focusing and trouble when it comes to paying attention. She also acts on instinct without thinking, and she has a hard time sitting still."

"I get it, sure she's ill, but that doesn't change my opinion about Ace. My brother Stuart says I'm irrational and that my fears are ludicrous, but something tells me that you feel the same."

The three students waited impatiently as every second felt like a minute as Caressa tried to form a professional response before saying it aloud. "Back before anyone in this kingdom could remember, a certain doctor had taken patients from out of the public eye. It became an expectation of the healing community that each of the four doctors had in-home care, taking patients with conditions correlating with their specialties. This, however, was banned after it was found out that the doctor whose idea it was to have in-care patients was mentally and physically abusing them, treating them more like prisoners than patients. Ace has been the only doctor to do home care since. The late king had lifted the ban after Ace's explanation of fear of working around magical witches, with him being a Nullum and all. He explained that he could only be of help if his fear of magic were kept at bay, and due to Ace's great demonstration of healing skills, the king obliged. Despite the king's acceptance, Notleaf, Morgan, August, and myself all share a disagreement." Caressa pursed her lips, holding back a rant. "I do have to admit that I do fear that some horrors are occurring behind those doors. Especially because I don't believe he truly has a fear of magical beings. After all, he only brought in patients after his own son's accident.

Fourteen years of having worked with magical beings, and he still literally works here. He fooled the king with lies that he's not even trying to pretend is true."

The room fell silent. Everything pointed to Ace being corrupted. There was an uneasiness in the air that even Clancy felt, yet Clancy wanted to hear more specifics of what horrors she believed to be happening behind Ace's closed doors.

"Besides a few people's suspicions, Dr. Ace's home had been investigated by the ministry in the past once, but I have contacted my father, and he spoke to the ministry, and they are looking back into the case."

"Sorry," Clancy interrupted. "Earlier, you mentioned that you fear some horrors are occurring behind those doors. What exact horrors is it that you fear are happening?"

"I believe he is a monster, like the many Scaasi that created the reputation we have today," she replied. The three students exchanged nervous looks. "The ministry will investigate," she continued. "And if these horrors are shown to be true, all matters will be handled. One thing we know for sure is that no death has occurred under his care, so that will be a relief to us all."

"But," said Amara, "if he's been investigated in the past. What if he hides the truth and continues to work his horrors right beneath our noses?"

"I highly doubt Ace could mask his horrors, being a Nullum and all," Caressa objected. "And… this time, the ministry will have someone else working with them and it will be hard for anyone to hide anything from them."

"Who?" Lovetta asked eagerly.

"Me." The woman smiled.

A wide smile grew on Amara's face. "It's true; the other day, you knew Brad, Horus, and I were lying!" His heart leaped with excitement while Lovetta's plummeted upon hearing her victim's name.

"But," said Clancy, "what if he is doing his job? How will you know he's not lying?"

"I've got my ways," Caressa said slyly. Clancy eyed the attractive, confident woman with a satisfied smile.

"I always knew Ace was a twisted lunatic," said Amara as the three of them pushed their way through the crowded corridor. "Stuart wants to put me under his care, he thinks I'm delusional or something, but you couldn't pay me to stay in his house for one minute. Honestly, if my brother tries to force me under his care, I'd get on my broom and fly back to Polar Frigemilt."

Clancy nodded in agreement while Lovetta remained in a daze as her heart still sat in the pit of her stomach. Lovetta wanted to talk to Clancy and Amara more about her feelings on the matter of Brad, but Clancy always dismissed and said, 'The first kill is always the hardest. From now on, it'll come with ease.' Amara's responses were usually along the lines of 'He's better off dead, this world is cruel, cold, and abysmal plus, if he wants to, he can probably return as a ghost.' These responses had not comforted her, so she decided that there was no more point in talking to them about the matter. She could still remember killing Brad as if it were yesterday. She could still hear Aaron's howls in her head and his voice shouting, *'You killed my son!'* Lovetta, ever since she could remember, felt relieved knowing that criminals, more often than not, were associated with the Scaasi name, but here she was, an Annettes and a killer.

"Hi, Lovetta." Varg joined the group as they walked down the hall.

"Hi, Varg." She blushed.

"A kid in my class today was talking about a theory he had about you. That you're a Scaasi."

"Rest assured, there are none of the seven Scaasi birthmarks on my shoulder." They turned into the cafeteria and sat at the 'Chaos' table. The four of them were the first to arrive.

"Can I see?" Varg grew excited. "Just to make sure?"

Lovetta rolled her eyes; he was handsome, but she didn't care for pigs.

"No," Clancy piped in protectively. "But you can see mine." Varg's sly smile faded. "Beat it." Clancy banged his fist against the table.

"Fine." Varg pushed himself up from off of the table and walked off.

"Thanks." Lovetta smiled at Clancy.

"No problem." He took his brown paper lunch bag out of his backpack.

"So," Lovetta began, "do you think Ace is up to no good?"

"I mean, only one person had been discharged from his care. He has yet to cure the rest of them. Some have been there for years, so yes, it is quite the cause for concern," said Clancy, taking a bite from his sandwich.

The three of them walked over to Clancy's after school. The nights were growing longer. Walking to the house in the dark reminded Lovetta of the night of the kill. She stopped and stared at the ground where Brad's body once laid. Clancy and Amara did the same. On the grass in red spray paint meant to look like blood was the word 'killer.'

They looked at each other. There was no one in sight.

"Someone needs to keep guard," Clancy stated firmly.

Amara got to his knees and began to inspect the ground for any clues. He began to crawl. "Over here!" he shouted.

Clancy and Lovetta ran over, eager, only to be disappointed. The two of them looked at each other. There was a trail of spiders leading into the forest.

"Spiders?" Lovetta asked dimly.

"Be serious," Clancy added.

"I am," Amara objected, lowering his head to the ground as he watched the spiders in awe.

"Big deal," sighed Clancy. "We need to find who's spray painting the word killer everywhere Lovetta walks."

"Lovetta." Amara ignored Clancy. "Didn't you say that the day someone spray-painted your locker and that millions of tiny spiders crawled within it? Maybe the dude who's spraying is some kind of spider freak?" There was a long, silvery thread that the spiders had seemed to follow. "Spiders don't usually act like this," Amara added. "Something's up."

"Are you okay?" Lovetta asked Clancy, whose whole body seemed to be growing tenser the longer they looked at the trail of spiders.

"I – don't – like spiders," he replied through a puffed chest as he seemed too frightened to exhale.

"Really?" Lovetta asked, almost in shock. "You never seem to have a problem in the art of potions class when spiders were the ingredients."

"I don't mind them dead," said Clancy, which seemed to pretty much sum up his preferences on most anything. He lifted his eyes from the spiders, hoping that his fear would ease up if he weren't looking at the tiny eight-legged creatures. "The way they walk... gives me chills." He shivered. Lovetta giggled. "Shut up, it's not funny," he said sternly, turning his focus onto his classmate.

"You're a witch." Lovetta ignored his tone. "Witches, especially of Viridi Aura, are usually very comfortable with nature." She spoke with respect despite wanting to laugh once again.

"Maybe we should just wash up the spray paint. This poser isn't doing any harm," Clancy suggested.

"Wow," Lovetta said in fake shock. "How forgiving of you, Mr.

Scaasi."

"Whoever is doing this" – Amara ignored his two friends – "knows where Brad died. The words are in the exact spot."

The three kids used a cleansing spell on the ground to eliminate the paint and cleansed the death spot.

After studying, Lovetta walked over to Amara's to pop in and say hello to Ainsley. Amara went to reach for the doorknob of his house's front entrance but withdrew his hand as if it had been burned.

"What is it?" Lovetta asked.

"Stuart's home," Amara said as his heart sank. "We walk in, then go straight into my room, okay?"

Lovetta nodded. Lovetta liked spending time at Amara's. She felt, in a way, that her presence brought a little more happiness to Amara's home life. After all, his house had to be one of the gloomiest, depressing places that she'd ever gone. The bathroom mirror had a large crack down the middle, and the sink was chipped. The floor in the whole house was damp from the leaking wooden ceiling. The bottom of her socks was always browned by the time of returning home. Stubs of remaining candles were the only things lighting the home; the wooden doors in the home were scratched and flaking. Seppo's bedroom door was barely dangling off its hinges. They headed for Amara's room.

"Hello, Ainsley," said Lovetta.

Amara shut the door behind him. The ghost was floating above his bed.

"I just wanted to come by and say hello," Lovetta explained.

The ghost was staring at a dirty, old mirror that sat on top of Amara's dresser. "Hello," she choked through tears.

"How are you?"

"People need to realize that ghosts were once human and should be treated with the same respect and understanding as the living. They are not to blame for being trapped between life and death." The girl lowered her head into her hands.

"What're you talking about?" Amara asked, lowering his green bag to the ground. "Did you happen to go outside today? Did you see anyone who doesn't live in these five houses?"

"Has someone upset you?" Lovetta fired another question at the dead girl.

"My life had been nothing but misery before my death! And now people continue to pain me," she wailed.

"Who hurt your feelings?" Amara asked protectively. "Stuart?"

She shook her head. "The boy who sprayed the grass." She gave a tragic sob and dived down toward the bed, her body floating inside the mattress. Her moans became muffled.

"AMARA!" A loud voice boomed from his bedroom entrance. Stuart was standing at the doorway, his hands on his hips and an angry expression on his face. "Where were you?" he asked.

"Studying at Clancy's," Amara replied simply.

Stuart's face began to swell with anger. "I had to shoo off some kid spray painting the lawn. He didn't put up much of a fight up once I came striding toward him. How are you not bothered by this? Do you know how bad this looks? We just moved here, and the last thing we want to do is be labeled as killers."

"Why should we care what people think?" Amara asked hotly. "It's not the truth. You believe that, don't you?"

"Not with those kids you and Seppo hang around. Do you know how traumatized Diana was after that night, how she begged to be taken to Ace's away from the monsters?"

"That's not true. You can't lie to me, Stuart! I know Diana would never want to go under Ace's care, and that's something you would know if you cared to listen!" His face was reddening with anger.

"Lovetta, go home. You won't be able to come under this roof until Amara has learned his lesson," Stuart said tensely. Stuart strode off, the back of his neck red.

Lovetta wasn't too upset. Stuart couldn't control them seeing each other at school or Clancy's. Amara, however, was still tempered the next day at school. He kept ripping the quill through his homework requiring new sheets of paper every three minutes when the thoughts of Stuart would creep back into his mind. At one point, his sheet of paper caught on fire just from his intense stare. Suddenly, fed up with trying to focus on his homework, he shut his *Art of Standard Spells* textbook. Lovetta and Clancy followed suit.

"Your brother Stuart saw who was spray painting. Who was it?" Clancy asked.

"He gave a very undescriptive description. It was a boy with long, brown hair down to his shoulders."

Clancy immediately looked to Lovetta. "Do you think it's your boy toy?"

"Who? Varg?"

"Who else could it be?" Clancy asked. "No one else in this kingdom is male with hair as long as ours who isn't Varg or one of our friends, and Stuart would've recognized it if it was any of us. Has nicknames for us all."

"He seems proud of the kill. Why would he try to shame me?" Lovetta asked skeptically.

"Look at his family," he continued to debate on behalf of his suggestion.

"I don't know his family. I don't even know him."

"You will know once I tell you who his brother is – Keegan Thorn. The kid who shot off a firework spell in the middle of mass, not to mention tried killing his cousin Rachel when she won the student council election. The Thorns have been close friends with the Scaasi bloodline for centuries. They even are related if you go back like five generations. He could easily be a Scaasi descendant. Even if not, they're evil."

"Well," Lovetta began. "It's possible, but I don't see why when he seems to be obsessed with me. Merlin knows why."

"We just need to find some proof," Amara added.

"I think I have an idea," Lovetta lowered her voice to a whisper after looking around the room. The boys instantly grew intrigued, leaning closer. "It will be difficult and very dangerous. We will be breaking the law."

"Get on with it." Clancy grew impatient as his excitement grew.

"Well, we will have to go to Varg and ask him a few questions."

"Okay." Clancy waved his hand as if it would speed up her explanation process. "What's so illegal about that?"

"We would be using a truth potion. If we do this, he will tell us everything. Getting a hold of the recipe will also be very difficult."

"Sounds a bit dodgy to me." Clancy leaned back in his chair, no longer impressed by what she had to say. "I've never heard of such a thing before, just the myths."

"Just trust me, okay. That'll work but again, getting the recipe and ingredients will be very difficult. It will be at the library, at the back, it's best if we don't check it out so that people won't trace that we had used it. After all, getting a book from the back of the library will require permission from the queen herself."

CHAPTER 10

Since the disastrous event with the troll recorder, Adolfo had no longer brought in cursed objects. Instead, he made the class take turns reading out of the textbook whenever a cursed instrument was the day's topic. He often chose to start the readings in front of the classroom on the left side so that if the unit were short, Lovetta, who sat in the far-right corner, would not have to read. Two volunteers would then act out a scene. One would play an instrument, and the other would use the counterspell from the text and act as if the device was cursed. So far, the demonstrations this semester included a vampire accordion, a yeti bagpipe, and a vampire banjo.

Today, Adolfo had dragged Clancy and Varg to the front of the class when the two usual volunteers had not come to school. Clancy was to play a werewolf bass while Varg would demonstrate the counterspell. If Adolfo hadn't been a band member, Clancy would have told him to shove the demonstration.

"Clancy, you know how to play it properly, and it's more than strum," Adolfo, who took a seat by Lovetta, instructed.

"Refresh my memory." Clancy was not amused.

"Howl – pounce forward. A cursed werewolf bass would need to be brought to the neck level of the victim. You would have to put all your power into the instrument. Howl again. At this point, Varg would be growing werewolf fangs."

Clancy did as instructed. The class gasped when Varg turned, and real fangs were visible. Fur began to grow along his face and hands. The students screamed in terror.

The bell rang, and all the students besides Varg, Clancy, Lovetta, and Amara remained. Aldric had left. The remaining witches stood to their feet. Adolfo had forgotten all about the homework he was going to assign the students.

"Remain calm." Adolfo raised a sword. *"Normalem!"* he cast. The magic exited through the tip of his blade.

Varg's fangs shrunk, and the fur retreated into his skin. Lovetta looked on, her body trembling. Adolfo smiled wildly, trying to act as if everything was completely okay.

"Think you're so clever?" Varg turned to Clancy.

"Did I just pull off a curse?" Clancy turned to Adolfo with a wicked smile on his face. "Am I like the best student you had?"

Adolfo raised his sword and motioned his bandmate out of the classroom. "Get out." He shook his head with a revolted face. Clancy took this as a 'yes' to his question.

Clancy smiled and brushed past Adolfo. Varg, shaken, picked up his bag and headed for the door. Lovetta stepped in front of him.

"He's sorry, you know," she said.

She decided to spend lunch with Aldric, a friend she hadn't paid much attention to after being introduced to Chaos. "Tomorrow's the first game of Crash Ring for the year, right?" She tried to start a conversation that wasn't about Chaos or Brad.

He slowly looked from his lunch. "*Second*," he hissed.

"Oh, time goes by fast, *huh*? You guys are playing against the Viridi team, correct?" she asked. Aldric shrugged instead of nodding. "I heard they made you captain. Congratulations." Lovetta tried to continue the conversation and keep her polite tone despite the attitude she was being given. "You know, I was thinking of trying out for the Caerul Centaurs with Spencer, but I never got around to it with our new powers and all. Professor Silwhet, when I was staying with him to reveal my power, had urged me to do so once this was all figured out, but I guess I have to try again next year. I wouldn't mind if you trained me before then." She smiled.

Aldric brought his attention back to his sandwich. Lovetta pushed herself from off of the table and stomped toward the Chaos table. Clancy and Amara sat at the table with fellow bandmates Walter, Mike, Seppo, and Lucian. They were the only six members in high school, and Mike's pregnant wife also sat at the table.

"I don't believe it." She squished herself between Amara and Clancy. They all looked at her, confused but with smiles. They liked her fire. "He said one word to me, and it was him correcting me. I *hate* being corrected."

"Same," said Annie, who sat relatively short next to her husband. She glared up at him; he didn't acknowledge her, but he had a smile on his face.

"Don't worry about Aldric," Clancy began. "He's a Milf Blender."

They all laughed then looked over to Aldric, who sat alone. He was looking. Lucian gave a taunting smile and wave. Aldric, hurt, grabbed his tray and left the table that once used to be his, Lovetta's, and John's. He walked over to the Alet table. Lovetta didn't know why, but a pit in her stomach began to grow.

She sighed, then looked to Amara and Clancy. "Ready to go to the library?" she asked.

"Damn right." Clancy rushed to his feet. Lovetta and Amara did the same. They began to run off.

"Hey!" Mike shouted. "You have class in fifteen minutes! The library is forty-five minutes away! Don't fly! You don't have licenses! Guys!" Mike lowered his head and pinched his nose as everyone in the cafeteria besides Clancy, Lovetta, and Amara had gained his attention.

The three of them dropped their voices completely as they entered the library. The thin, irritable librarian stood behind the front entrance desk. This reminded Lovetta all too well of the last time she went to the back of the library with John Jr., only to walk out and be chased by a royal knight. She shivered. At least she felt more secure with Clancy and Amara at her side.

The witch nodded them inside despite looking at the students who should've been at school suspiciously. The three of them walked to the back of the library, passing by a table of three young children who eagerly sat looking into a crystal ball and staring at it as if something spectacular was about to happen.

"Flower?" Clancy whispered angrily.

Beau, Flower, and Lulia rushed to cover the crystal ball with the scrying cloth.

"*Shh!*" Flower brought her finger to her lips and motioned to the 'no talking' sign.

"Don't you shh me." Clancy walked over, his voice a tad lower than before.

Amara and Lovetta shrugged as they continued to look for the book while Clancy lectured his sister to be at school. Lovetta had finally found it – a large, moldy book. Amara lowered his green bag to the ground and slowly unzipped it, looking over his shoulder to make sure the librarian wasn't looking. He took the book and threw it inside his bag.

"Are you seriously putting a book in that bag?" Clancy looked on appalled and as if he were about to puke.

"It doesn't look like that's the worst thing this book has been through." Amara defended his bag.

The three of them now walked toward the door along with the three children, who were, for once, quiet. Lovetta swiped a random book off a shelf to not raise any more suspicion. She checked the book out, and with that, they exited with the book they needed.

After school, they walked home. Flower and her friends branched off to her home while Clancy and Lovetta followed Amara into his. Amara assured Lovetta that his brother Stuart was not home and that his room would be the best place for privacy as no one liked going into his foul-smelling room, and Ainsley tended to depress anyone who entered. The three of them leaned over the book.

"This is some messed up book," Clancy mused. The first potion would have the drinker's skin peel off until they were wholly skinned alive. "No wonder why the queen doesn't want a commoner to have this book."

"Here it is." Lovetta pointed to the page titled *Riht Potion*. The page was decorated with drawings of the stages of the potion. First, the man stood tall, his face calm. The second, his mouth looked to be forcefully shut as if he were fighting an impulse. The third was of the man sweaty, his mouth no longer closed, as he couldn't resist the potion's impulses. "This is the most complicated potion that I have ever seen," she said as she scanned down the list of ingredients while ignoring the images. "Blessed water by someone with a religious background, drop of a grandmother's blood, bee honey, a four-leaf clover, a drop of Tuscel blood, a cherry, and tree bark. If brewed correctly, it should look like a colorless liquid. Oh, and we will also need a lock of the drinker's hair."

"That last ingredient won't be too hard. All you'll have to do, love, is ask." Clancy laughed.

Lovetta picked up the heavy book and began to smack Clancy with it repeatedly. "Anyway, it'll be easier than just asking him. He was probably shedding fur in Adolfo's classroom. Wolf fur is just our DNA of natural hair grown through every pore, so that'll work," Lovetta said as she placed the book down in the middle of where they sat.

"I'm concerned," Amara began. "About the grandmother's blood, like what? Poor thing."

Lovetta's heart fluttered. "No, it'll be okay, my grandmother. I can prick her when I help sew her a dress tonight."

"You evil little girl." Clancy laughed.

"Shut up. Anyway, I'm concerned about the Tuscel blood."

"Don't be," Amara piped in. "I know a vampire who collects all kinds of blood. I can ask him."

"*Hmm,*" Lovetta pondered. "I'm not sure if that's such a good idea. He'd probably want something in return."

"That's what I'm hoping for," Amara smirked.

"Okay, what about the blessed water? That's the only other difficult ingredient." Lovetta looked to the boys.

"Mike," Clancy began. "He's in training to become a pastor or priest or something."

Lovetta's brow furrowed, her forehead creased. "You mean to tell me that a member of Chaos who performs with creature heads on stage is in training to be a part of the church of Galdorwide?"

"Yep." Clancy nodded as if it wasn't a weird concept.

"Okay," Lovetta said, still surprised, "I guess now we have to go on a mission."

"Full steam ahead." Clancy stood to his feet eagerly as he had the most straightforward mission that didn't involve collecting blood.

***

Aldric woke up early Wednesday morning. He lay awake, worrying about today's Crash Ring match. The Viridi team always played dirty. The Viridis were worthless. His thoughts about the Viridi team became thoughts of those with Viridi auras as a whole. He never hated Viridis more. If anything, they should be the ones fearing to face him. His insides churned. The whole school would be watching today's game since it was the two best teams facing off. After forty minutes of staring at the ceiling, he finally got up, got dressed, and headed downstairs for breakfast.

When lunch came, he saw the Alet team huddled together in the cafeteria, looking uptight and tired. The game replaced the final class of the day. The bell rang, and the teachers led their students out to the Crash Ring field. It was a muggy day suggesting a storm was brewing for later that evening. Lovetta rushed over to the Alet locker room to wish Aldric luck despite his harsh behavior toward her lately. The Alet team began to put on their protective gear, layering their team's varsity jacket over the top. Being team captain, it was up to Aldric to give the team a pre-game pep talk.

"The Viridis have always been labeled the better team," he began. "But that doesn't matter because we play by the rules, which means that more likely than not, tonight, the Viridis will be disqualified. Us, we've trained harder these past few days. Unlike them, we've practiced even on days where the practice should've been canceled due to harsh weather. Today, let's make the Viridis rue the day they put us and all the other auras down! It's up to us. We have to win."

As they walked on, they could hear the teachers and those with Alet, Caerul, and Pure auras cheer them on. However, the boos from Viridi students could also be heard. Coach Abbey instructed Aldric and the Viridi team captain to shake hands, which they did, with a little too much strength as they glared into one another's eyes.

"Get to your circle and onto your brooms," she instructed.

Once each circle was filled with the required members, the rings rose, taking the team off the ground. The teams ducked their heads, allowing the captains to be first to draw their spells.

"*Nebula!*" Aldric cast. An intricate red stream of particles struck the Viridi captain's eyes, causing his eyes to cloud over, making the world look heavily fogged. Aldric knew it was best to stick with elemental spells with his new powers.

"*Clingan!*" the Viridi captain cast. A bright, green blaze of fragments rushed toward Aldric. He dodged it, which was good as that would've shrunk him to the size of an imp.

The team began casting spells. All of them seemed to be aimed at Aldric, which didn't make sense as the circle rotated in a way that would make each target fair game no matter the player's intention. He dropped his head and moved his body each possible way to avoid getting hit. He ducked and used his next spell as a shield. Every spell from the Viridi team passed the Alet players and struck the shield. His guard began to fade, and the spells seemed to be magnetized toward him. The weather started to take a turn for the worst as the rain started to befall the game's field. His teammates worked hard to strike the other team hoping to get them down, while Aldric repeatedly used a shielding spell to protect him by the variety of dangerous spells targeting him all at once. Such an occurrence could quickly kill him, depending on the mixture. *Someone must be tampering with the ring,* Aldric thought.

"*Stillan!*" an Alet player cast. A violent, red flash of sparks exited his wand. It successfully struck one of the Viridi players' forehead, causing his mind to be pacified. The player toppled over. Coach Abbey raised her wand, caught the student's fall, and safely lowered him to the ground.

"We need a time out!" Aldric shouted after casting another shielding spell. He waved down at the coach, trying to get her attention.

She got the message and blew her whistle. The circles lowered each team onto the ground.

"What's going on?" Abbey asked, looking to Aldric. "You kept shielding yourself. That's not a very captain thing to do."

"I was trying to keep myself from getting murdered! All the Viridis' spells were being aimed at me!" Aldric replied angrily. "Something's wrong with the ring. Not one spell was aimed at anyone else. I'm guessing the rotten Viridis messed with it."

"The rings were checked before the game," Coach Abbey drawled.

"Okay, it's fine. I won't shield myself. I'll take the hits, and hopefully, I won't die."

"Don't be ridiculous. The ring won't let two spells strike you at once," Abbey scoffed.

The Alet team looked to one another, not so sure.

"We'll try to get their team down," an Alet player reassured Aldric.

"That's crazy," a female Alet player spoke up. "Coach, it's not safe for Aldric to be playing. Something's not right. You can't let him die for a stupid game."

"He won't die. Everybody, prepare to be shot back up," Abbey ordered. Everyone turned to Aldric, worried, but Aldric wore a look of determination on his face. "All right," Abbey said, feeling good about her decision as the 'endangered' student looked confident. She ignored everybody else.

The rain was beginning to fall heavier. The rings raised at Abbey's whistle.

"*Cunnan cunnan hemming til mec!*" A Viridi player summoned their owl familiar. It raced toward Aldric and began to fly around him, smacking his face with its wings and pecking him with its beak.

Aldric grew dizzy as spells raced through his body, but he was still breathing, and that was all that mattered. *"Scead arodscipe!"* Aldric's wand turned into a blade made out of shadow energy. He struck the familiar which fell. Abbey cast a spell that lowered the owl to the ground. The school doctors and specialized teachers were there, ready to collect the game's next victim. Professor Gemini carried the owl inside.

"*Bled*!" a rounded, multi-shaded green twisting wave struck Aldric's broom, causing it to turn into a blooming flower.

"*Deor!*" A Viridi player casted. A gentle, green surge of particles exited the player's wand, striking Aldric and successfully turning him into a yellow fox. He fell off of his flower. Abbey caught his fall.

The Viridi magic now seemed to be targeting random players. The crowd began to cheer as players fell from the ring. Currently, only one Alet player remained on the broom. The Alets won.

Aldric fainted from the array of previous spells cast on him. When he woke up, he found himself still lying on the field, his skin still covered with yellow fur.

"I can't seem to fix him," Caressa said reluctantly, turning to Notleaf.

Aldric tried to stand, but aching pains shot through his body. Maybe he *was* dying. He *did* warn Coach Abbey.

"Lie down," Caressa stroked the top of the fox's head. He lowered his body.

Notleaf looked to Caressa and leaned in to whisper into her ear. They both looked solemn before their eyes traveled up to Ace. A strange sensation roamed through Aldric's body, starting at his head and going down to his paws. It felt as if his body was becoming deflated. He didn't want to, but he closed his eyes. Lovetta had pushed her way through the crowd that surrounded her friend.

"He'll have to come with me," Ace said.

Ace took the fox into his arms and began to walk with him to his house. He had his daughter Abigail create a room for Aldric. Once the room was finished coming together, Ace lay the animal onto the bed.

"Can you go into my lab and grab me my bag of medicine?"

Aldric's consciousness was slowly coming back. "How can you cure a magical condition with Heofsij ways?" he asked weakly through a whiskered mouth.

"It's not your animal condition that the other doctors and I are concerned about. You were struck with many spells, and more spells would do more harm than good," Ace explained to the animal kindly. "Unfortunately, you're going to have a rough few weeks until all your conditions are cured."

Abigail returned with a piece of luggage filled with medicine bottles. Inside was an empty baby's bottle. He began to pour a clear liquid inside of it. He brought the bottle to the fox's mouth.

"It's going to be quite harsh going down, but you must drink it all."

Ace was right. It was harsh. Aldric's whole mouth seemed to be burning. He pulled back, coughing. Dr. Ace Scaasi was patient as he helped Aldric take his time between gulps.

"Good game," the doctor made conversation. "An odd game, but you guys won nonetheless," his friend's uncle said. The fox grinned. "I will have to speak with Mr. Bernard. Unlike Coach Abbey, I do believe that someone had tampered with the ring."

Ace left Aldric alone in the room. The silence intensified the stabbing pains that shot up his limbs. Eventually, he fell asleep.

After a few hours, he woke up in pitch blackness. He gave a small yelp as his senses returned. His body felt as if many tiny nails were being penetrated throughout his whole body. A natural, pleasant feeling was caused by his furry face being sponged with warm water.

"Who's there?" he asked, disoriented.

"Abigail, Ace's daughter," a voice replied in the dark.

A tiny source of light came in through the four sides of the shut door. Aldric could make out half of her face. He could see a tear stroll down her short nose.

"You shouldn't be here," she whispered solemnly. "It's all my fault."

Aldric looked up at her. "What do you mean?" His voice croaked.

She brought the sponge to her lap. Her bottom lip began to tremble. Aldric's heart began to race. He grew immediately concerned.

"My father, he made me—" She began to sob. She began to shake her head vigorously as if it'd help erase the past. "He hid me beneath the bleachers. He made me tamper with the Crash Ring. I did this to myself, as punishment." She lifted her forearm to the light where dozens of cuts bled. "I didn't know why he wanted me to do it – until now." She was rocking nervously back and forth. Aldric had never seen such a troubled girl before. "I saw that you had been hurt," she began to scratch her other arm, causing it to turn red, breaking the skin.

Aldric lay his head back onto the pillows trying to make sense of it all. "You nearly got me killed," he said fiercely. "You better get lost."

"All you'd have to do is ask nicely!" She wiped her nose with the back of her hand. She continued to sob. She looked pathetic, but Aldric couldn't help but feel sorry for her. She was a victim too.

"Why'd you do what he said?"

"I'm a slave." She wiped her nose once more. "He says that if I help him, I'll be free one day, but I always help, and I'm never set free." She wiped her eyes now. "He uses my sister and me for our magic. You have to help us get out of here. Please, before somebody dies. You're injured, but he won't expect it. He won't know that you know about this place's horrors! You need to save us!"

"Oh, is that all?" he asked angrily. "I don't suppose you have a plan?"

"If you only knew how many times we've tried. I've been in this basement my whole life. Only let out when it's convenient for him," she groaned. Tears dripped from her cheek onto her lap. "If only he knew what he was doing, but he's blinded by trying to find out what makes us witches while he is stuck as a Nullum. Ace is at his worst when it comes to violence and punishments. I worry that the three in the room beside you are already dead. They've been locked in that room for days now. I don't think they've had any food. It's like I can feel their fear. I can't stand it any longer. He treats us all like vermin because he envies us and our magic." She began to dry her face with her non-bleeding arm. "We want our lives to be normal. I'm surprised that any of us are still alive. We need to break out of here. Please, you're our only hope. We need these dark days to end. Terrible things are going to happen if we stay here any longer. Perhaps something terrible has already happened. I can't let him hurt you, not when you're only here because of me."

A shadow blocked the light swimming in from the hall. Abigail jumped, her head snapped back to look at the door. Beneath it, she could see the outline of someone's feet. Abigail reached into her pocket, pulled out a match, and dragged it along the night table, igniting it. She dug it into her scratched skin, and Abigail winced. The fire burnt out.

"I'm sorry," she whispered to herself. The feet turned away. She looked back to Aldric, whose eyes were on the burn mark on her arm. "I am Ace's daughter. I should be loyal to him. This is the first time I've ever betrayed him. I deserve to be punished."

"I'll help you," he whispered, looking up at the broken girl.

"I need to go before he grows more suspicious. But know that going against my father could cost you your life. If anything, save yourself. You don't deserve to be here." Her body quivered. Footsteps rushed toward Aldric's bedroom door. She was terrified. She clenched her fists as if bracing herself for more pain.

The door swung open, she flinched. To her relief, it was Adam Hall. He looked frantic, and she could hear urgent, panicked voices coming from the hall. He was breathing heavily.

"What's going on?" Abigail asked.

"It's Lena. Ace attacked her on the stairs."

"I thought he liked Lena."

"She's on the stairs, not moving, and Ace isn't helping."

Her stomach turned. If he could hurt Lena, he could do worse to everyone else in this house. She rushed past Adam and the crowd of people that stood around the still girl whose eyes were plastered wide and opened.

"I can't find a pulse," Ellen whimpered, removing her fingers away from the girl's carotid artery.

Everyone shuddered. They all stared down at Lena. A jet stream of smoke left her body, her soul. Upon death, her bowels and bladder relaxed.

"What happened?" Abigail asked. "Why would he do this?"

"I think… he's gone mad – madder than he already was," Crispin Cherish said hesitantly.

Diana ran out of her room, pushed her way through the crowd, and clasped her hand over her mouth. "Oh my Merlin!" the young girl shouted in disbelief. "Is he going to kill us all?"

CHAPTER 11

Chris woke up Sunday morning in his room that he once shared with both of his brothers. He rolled onto his side to see Brad's bed, empty and made, untouched as it had been for days. Blazing sunlight shone through the window. Aisley came bustling into the room with two breakfast trays. It had been something she'd been doing ever since the incident for all the students who stayed at Python Seger.

"How are you, boys?" she asked as she placed trays with a bowl of harissa and date yogurt in front of them. The boys shrugged as they sat up. "Your father wants you downstairs in the training room once you've finished your breakfast."

After breakfast, Chris and Stephen hurriedly dressed and headed downstairs, wanting to be as far away from their gloomy bedroom as possible. They wanted to meet up with the Soleil kids, who could hopefully distract them, but they weren't downstairs in the training room. Instead, their father told them that class was still canceled until further notice and that they could go about their day in the kingdom.

They threw on their winter jackets and headed outside, wondering where the Soleils went off to. As the two of them passed the library, Flower and Lulia exited, looking quite excited. They were speaking high and fast. They lowered their voices as they passed the boys, and once they were behind them, they continued speaking rapidly.

"Wait!" Chris called after them. The two girls turned around. "Lulia, have you seen your cousins?"

"Which ones?" Lulia asked.

"We have about a hundred," Flower added.

"Not a Scaasi. Have you seen the Soleil siblings?"

"Oh yeah, they were on the way to visit my brother," piped up Flower. "I think they're chilling at Amara's place."

The girls walked out of sight. He couldn't see why the Soleils would be visiting Clancy or Amara. They headed up Amara's stairs and pushed open the door.

"Hello?" As Chris had pushed him in front of him, Stephen called out, scared of all of the residents who lived in Forest Edge's five houses. "It's Stephen… and Chris," he added after knowing that his older brother wouldn't speak for himself.

A splash and a gasp came from the bathroom in the hall. A silver shadow raced into Amara's bedroom, and they followed the shadow and headed toward Amara's room. They reached for the door handle when a voice called out for them.

"We're in here!" Mamie shouted from a bedroom whose door was off its hinges.

The boys walked in. Mamie, Ken, Coby, Clancy, Amara, and Lovetta sat around a cauldron. Seppo lay on the bed, snoring and drooling. His arm hung off the bed next to Amara's head. Lovetta was writing the name 'Varg' on a piece of paper as the cauldron crackled.

"They're working on a truth potion." Mamie turned to the boys, who looked on with confusion. "They think Varg's behind all the strange occurrences."

"We've decided to work here," Clancy began. "Stuart's out of the house, and well…" He looked up to his snoring bandmate. "He won't hear a thing, and if he does, well, he won't care." He looked back to Stephen and Chris. Amara seemed stiff and quiet.

"I think we should use this on Ace next." Lovetta looked to Amara. "To make sure your sister is in good hands."

Amara's eyes remained fixed straight ahead. It was as if he wasn't even in the room. He snapped out of his trance and looked to Lovetta, and he gave her a slight nod.

"I already know Ace is bad news," Coby began. "None of the staff at Galdorwide High trusts him. Except for his brother."

"The sooner we get a confession from both Varg and Ace, the better," Lovetta said. "We all agree that we have a bad feeling about the both of them, right?"

Everyone nodded except for Stephen. "My dad said the king is the one responsible for Brad's death."

"The king?" Clancy laughed. "The last time I checked, the king was dead."

"No." Lovetta nodded. "That could be true. Remember when the ghost of the king brought forth the attack of the dragons?" She began to pour honey collected in a small container into the cauldron. "Are we sure it's Varg we want to target?"

"Yes," Clancy replied instantly. "Even if the king is the one behind his death, we need to find out if Varg had a part of it. And if not, why he's so obsessed with Brad's death and why he keeps harassing you."

"He's harassing you?" Coby asked angrily.

Lovetta looked up, her mouth opened, surprised by the student teacher's response. She shrugged. "Yeah… he has this weird obsession with me, and *uh…*" She looked around the room. "He thinks I'm some murderer and the thought of that only fuels his attraction for me."

Suddenly, an attractive blond man ran into Seppo's room. It was Rabbit Carter. "There's something I need to tell you." He pointed to Clancy. "And you." He pointed to Amara.

Amara pointed to himself in question. He never spoke to Rabbit much. He was intimidated by his good looks and assumed that that would make him an automatic asswad.

"And him." Rabbit pointed to the sleeping man.

"Can't you see we're busy?" Clancy motioned to many people that sat in Seppo's room as well as the cauldron.

"It'll be quick," Rabbit promised. "It's a residential meeting. Come on! Over to my place!" Rabbit ran out.

Clancy stood to his feet, Amara followed suit. "Come on, hey! Get up!" Clancy kicked the side of Seppo's bed, startling him awake.

"Wh—what's going on?"

"We're leaving." Clancy and Amara began to walk out of the room.

"What, where?" Seppo anxiously asked as he threw on his black boots that sat on the floor beside his bed.

"Let's go! Now!" Clancy shouted. Seppo grabbed his leather jacket and stumbled after them out the door.

The band members from all three bands sat around in Rabbit's living room of the house that he shared with his bandmates, Elio, Theodolphus, and Terrance.

"I didn't want to tell you guys this." Rabbit stood up and paced in front of the small crowd of his friends. "I was told, a few months ago, that the queen would need my help sometime soon, but the longer I sit here waiting for that unknown day, the more fearful I get. As the only male Carter, I am the only one who can defeat some giant creature that the king will conjure from his grave. I'm not sure what creature it is."

"Kinda ironic, isn't it?" Terry smirked through his mop of brown curls. "I mean, you're frankly scared of everything."

"Funny," Rabbit said before moving on. "I should be training with the ministry to prepare, but it seems as though the king has forgotten my existence and believes his plan to be foolproof. So I pretty much have to stay invisible. On the battlefield, I will also have to disguise myself. To completely cover my existence as a male Carter, the queen suggests I dress up as a woman – AND if any of you are to laugh now or on that day where I am dressed as a woman, you too will come to the battlefield dressed as one. Understood?"

The men held back their laughs with their hands in surrender.

Clancy and Amara left the house and let out their laughs as they headed back to Seppo's room. Seppo decided to stay back and hang out with his friends. They walked into Seppo's room to find Lovetta, who sat putting a four-leaf clover and cherry inside the cauldron.

"You see," Lovetta continued the conversation she had been having with the Silvermauls and Soleils, "two of my friends are now in Ace's care, yet to be discharged."

It was announced this evening that Ace's patient Lena Baxter had died while in Ace's care. The news spread like wildfire throughout the kingdom. The air in Galdorwide was suddenly thick as rumors spread as well as suspicion as Ace refused Michael Nichols, the mortician, to take a look at the victim as he 'already knew the cause of death – overdose on the illegal songbird drug given to her through the mail.'

The Galdorians walked around, frightened. Two deaths had already been experienced shortly after one another.

***

Diana sat at the kitchen table, distraught. The evening before Lena's death, she had sat next to her. Everyone was too solemn to cheer the young girl up as they were bothered by the event. Last night, she had had a terrible nightmare, and she didn't have any of her three brothers here to comfort her. She wanted to write a letter, but Ace had immediately turned down her question.

She wished that she could wear her gloves, enchanted by Amara that would ward off all danger, but Ace had confiscated them after Stuart had explained that they were magical objects. Eion, a boy who had grown up friends with Diana's brother, assured her that she was in no danger as she was his friend and that if his father laid a hand on her, he would have him, her three brothers, and members of all three bands to worry about.

"He hurt Lena," Diana spoke to Eion as they walked down the steps. "And he liked her a lot, and he doesn't like me all that much." Her face was filled with fear. "Is it the first one he's killed?"

In the second week of December, the truth potion was almost done brewing, and Clancy had yet to get the blessed water from Mike. They still also needed the tree bark and lock of Varg's hair. Clancy felt that Amara would be the best to ask Mike as Mike grew up with him in Polar Frigemilt and had always been close to the kid.

"He will expect that I'm getting it for a bad reason. You have to be the one. If you don't ask" – Clancy looked to Amara as they walked down the school's corridor heading to the art of potion making – "at the very least, we need a distraction, and we can just take the blessed water."

Amara and Lovetta looked at one another nervously.

"I think I'd do good at stealing." Lovetta looked back to Clancy. "I mean, I could look about in the church while you two talk to Mike. He won't expect me to be stealing."

Clancy smiled feebly and just wished that Amara could muster up the courage to ask Mike, who once had been his best friend, instead of potentially causing mayhem in one of Galdorwide's churches if Mike was to find out. Angering Mike, despite him becoming a pastor, was like awakening a demon.

The potions took place on the first floor, above the dungeons once used for detention. Today's lesson had proceeded as usual. Cauldrons were placed on each of the thirty desks. The pots were steaming as Olly's replacement teacher paced around the room, observing the students' work and not saying much. Varg had spent much of the day throwing salt at the three students. The teacher remained feeble and pretended not to notice. Once Clancy had had enough of the torment and had seen the embarrassed and frightful expression on Amara's face, he pulled out his wand.

"*Crypel arodscipe!*" An interwoven, green rush of small waves exited Clancy's wand, striking Varg and draining all of his energy from him. The student fell over.

The quiet teacher immediately gave the long-haired student a detention slip he seemed to have been holding in his hand from within his pocket. The teacher had two students carry the burly student to the hospital ward and instructed Clancy to finish working on his potion.

Clancy's sum glimt into se eftwyrd potion stayed a flat plum color rather than having the purple liquid emit gold sparkles up into the steam, but how could he concentrate with someone like Varg tossing salt at him?

"All right, class," the teacher instructed, "if your potions emitted the gold sparkles, feel free to bottle them and take them home. Remember, if you want to see a glimpse of the future with this potion, drink it before bedtime on a full moon, the next full moon is in ten days, so mark it on your calendar!"

Later that evening, at the church, Lovetta was waiting for Clancy's signal. When Mike began to go off on a rant about Clancy's detention, Lovetta caught a glimpse of Clancy's eyes, and he gave her a nod.

Lovetta nodded to Amara, who sat outside the church, looking in from behind a bush. *"Cunnan cunnan hemming til mec!"*

Amara ducked from the window, and a bat began to flutter around him. Amara stood and whispered to his familiar. The bat took off with its command, flew straight into the church's entrance, and smashed into the towering glass fountain filled with blessed water that sat next to the large, black-clothed table that sat at the front of the church.

With the bat's weight and the impact of its dive, the glass broke. The tube exploded, showering everyone in the room with the blessed water. Mike shrieked at the shock while Lovetta and Clancy tried to act just as surprised. The water struck Clancy's face, and it began to swell. His fingers expanded to the size of hockey pucks. Mike calmed himself and turned attention from the flowing water that flooded the room. Mike swam to Clancy after making sure that Lovetta was okay. Through the confusion, Lovetta took out a glass vial and scooped up the water.

Lovetta stuffed the vial back in time as Mike turned to give a panicked order. "Go get Terry! Tell him we need a de-swelling potion!"

Lovetta did as told. Her makeup smeared from disaster as she swam with the current out of the building.

Amara tried not to laugh when he dived inside and began to swim toward his friends. Water continued to flow from the tube as if an infinite amount of water had been inside. Clancy's face was now the size of a watermelon. Amara should've felt concerned, but he didn't. Clancy was a friend, but he had his moments of going too far when teasing him. A part of Amara hated him for it. His arms had swelled to that of a bear's. His thin lips had puffed out. His clothing began to stretch.

Lovetta returned with the tall, athletically built, blue-eyed, and dark-haired Terry wearing a white dress shirt whose most top buttons were left open.

Terry helped Mike and Amara guide the swollen boy out of the church onto the front lawn, where no water traveled. He had Mike pull Clancy's fat lips apart and poured the beige-colored potion into his mouth. Clancy's various swellings subsided. Once Clancy's body returned to normal, Amara pushed his legs through the flooded church and picked up his bat, who had been flapping enjoyably in the water.

"Is that your familiar?" Mike asked when the young boy returned, cradling it in his arms.

Amara nodded and tried to make a face that wouldn't cause suspicion. Mike's eyes locked onto Amara for what felt like thirty minutes before looking away.

"He knows something up," Amara began as he walked with Clancy and Lovetta while his bat laid in his arms, now cradled in his jean jacket. They hurried to Seppo's bedroom. "I can tell. He's never looked at me like that before."

Lovetta poured the water into the cauldron and began to stir feverishly. Seppo laid on the bed snoring. "It'll be ready soon!" she said happily.

"Listen." Clancy turned to Amara, who he could tell was panicking. "Even if he knows we're up to something, he'll take it out on me, not on you. He loves you." Clancy patted his friend's shoulder. "Plus, Mike's punishments are the equivalent of a training school's teacher when his anger passes at least."

A week later, Lovetta, Clancy, and Amara walked down the main hall, where they saw a cluster of people blocking the path. They were looking up at the bulletin board. Walter, Aksel, Seppo, and Abner were amongst the group. When they locked eyes with the three of them, they beckoned them over while Mike stood, pinching his nose.

"They're starting a Crashnet club," Aksel explained excitedly. "The first meeting is tonight."

Clancy's face beamed. "We should all go. We'd *kill* the other team."

"Yeah." Aksel laughed.

Mike looked at his friends with disgust.

"Come on, Mike," his pregnant wife began. "It could be useful. You heard what Rabbit said about the *giant creatures*," Annie whispered at the end of her sentence as not to cause alarm in those uneducated about the kingdom's possible demise.

The group of students headed to the cafeteria.

"So, shall we go?" Annie looked up to Mike with pleading eyes.

Aksel raised his brows, something he did whenever something shocking or awkward had happened or had been said.

"No!" Mike, Clancy, Amara, Abner, Seppo, and Walter shouted. Their shout echoed throughout the large hall.

Lovetta chuckled as her friends had seemed to get attention from the cluster of students pushing their way toward the cafeteria.

"You're two months' pregnant," Mike began to scold. "You and I will go, but just to spectate."

Everyone else in the group was all for going to the meeting. So at eight o'clock, they all returned to school. They rushed into the gym, where two golden stages were placed in the middle about three feet apart. Thousands of candles were lit and floating by the ceiling. The ceiling was velvety black, along with the rest of the school. In the gym was their group, along with a few clusters of ninth graders. Everyone in the room had their wands in hand while Mike and Annie walked over to the navy blue stands against the far wall.

"I wonder who will be teaching us," Abner began. "I heard the Alet teachers tend to be the greatest at these sorts of things."

Just then, Coby Soleil walked onto one stage while Gemini Scaasi walked along the other. Coby wore a dark green velvet robe while Gemini wore a deep red.

"Gather 'round, everyone." Coby waved the students toward the stage. "Now, Mr. Bernard has been kind enough to allow this sport to be practiced during this year in response to the previous incident of the dragon attack a few months back. This class is to teach self-defense so you can protect yourselves, especially after the incident with my good friend Brad

Silvermaul."

Lovetta let her messy, brown hair fall in front of her face as she looked down and began to rock on her heels. When she looked up, she saw that Coby was giving her a small, genuine smile. She returned it, and her breathing went back to normal, and she could feel her body cool off as her fear released its hold.

"So, before we begin," Coby continued, "Professor Scaasi and I will perform a demonstration."

"Wouldn't it be cool if one of them gets seriously injured?" Varg suddenly said as he walked up behind Lovetta and spoke beside her ear.

Lovetta gave a quick look over her shoulder, narrowing her eyes. The boys did the same, practically growling at Varg, causing the teen to take a few steps back.

Coby and Gemini turned to each other and bowed. They then raised their wands like swords, pointing them at one another.

"As you can see, we are raising our wands in the combative position," Coby began to explain, projecting his voice to make sure it could be heard throughout the large gym. "On the count of six, we will cast our spells, none of whose purpose will be meant to kill."

"I wouldn't get too comfortable," Lovetta told Varg with a sly smirk.

"One – two – three – four – five – six!"

Both of them brought their arms in then shot them out, screaming their spells.

"*Wanung Andmitta!*" Gemini cast. A violent red wave of tiny particles exited his wand.

"*Fleotan!*" Coby cast simultaneously. A jumbled, green blaze of particles exited his wand.

The magic from both spells struck each other. Each of the attacks fought the other to make its way through to the target. Gemini's stage remained still while Coby's was being pushed toward the net violently. The stage smashed into the netted wall, and Coby fell forward off of the stage. Gemini's spell had won, and Coby was beginning to lose weight. By the time Dr. Caressa Scaasi entered the gym, he had become skin and bone. She, along with Dr. Notleaf, aided him down to the hospital wing.

Varg cheered. Lovetta and all her group looked around, concerned, hoping that their friend hadn't been injured permanently.

"Do you think he's all right?" Lovetta asked, looking to the boys.

"Who cares?" Varg laughed.

"Well, there you have it." Gemini turned to the crowd. "Both spells used to cause no permanent harm. In this sport, it is not the spell you use. It's the power and strength you put into it that matters. That's all for demonstration. You six look like a good bunch." He pointed to Lovetta and her friends. "Get on Coby's stage. The rest of you onto mine."

"Dream team." Aksel stood with a smirk as he took his place at the end of the line, looking down at his friends who stood alongside him.

"Great," Clancy moaned, looking across from him. Flower waved tauntingly.

"So much for *killing* the other team," Aksel leaned over and whispered into Clancy's ear.

Varg stood in front of Lovetta, Lulia stood in front of Amara, everyone else was paired off with random students they had never seen before. Beau sat next to Mike and Annie, who shared their popcorn with the young-looking student.

Across from Aksel was a large girl with a square face and heavy jaw. Aksel smiled and gave her a flirtatious wink. She sneered. Aksel's eyebrows raised, and his eyes roamed the room, hoping to get the scary girl's attention off of him.

"Face your partners!" Gemini instructed from the side of the stage. "Bow!"

Lovetta barely gave Varg a bow. Instead, she slightly inclined her head.

"Wands ready!"

The twelve students raised their wands like swords.

"When I count to six, I want you to cast your spells."

Gemini counted down.

The students drew their arms back then shot them out, casting their spells. Lovetta's stage was shockingly being pushed back, but the other stage began to head toward the net after their team put more effort. Lovetta's knees were shaking as she fought with all her might.

A haze of greenish smoke began to fill the room as most of the students participating were Viridi aura. Abner's face had turned an ashen color as all his energy was beginning to wear out.

Lovetta was whimpering as the muscles in her arms began to ache. Aksel wasn't too shocked that his partner was beating him. After all, she was much larger than he was. Walter's nose began to bleed, as did Amara's.

Amara brought the sleeve of his black cloak to his nose, making him look vampire-like.

Flower was flustered as she thought her brother would go somewhat light on her. Lovetta looked to Varg, whose black eyes glistened demonically.

Amara's bat familiar flew into the gym after sensing his struggle. Lulia's already pink face turned red. Clancy gave Flower a twisted smile, and she smirked back. Abner looked nervously at his partner. Lovetta and Varg stared into one another's eyes angrily. The large girl hissed as Aksel's power was beginning to outweigh hers. Amara's bat flew alongside Amara, its fangs exposed, unsure whether or not he should help.

Everyone on both teams was either grinning, looking puzzled, scared, or angry. Clancy gave his younger sister a calculating look. When did she get so powerful? He didn't like it.

Lulia began to lose focus as she faced off against Amara. She could hear a boy's distant mutters bounce off of the walls. She felt something pat her bottom. She turned and looked and saw no one or nothing that could've been the cause. Her stage began to push back. Soon, her whole table had been forced to the net.

Varg toppled off of the table, with Lovetta's spell striking him, rendering him temporarily blind. The large girl had gone rampant as she had been turned into a demonic creature of sorts. Lulia had become temporarily deaf due to Amara's spell, and Flower's memory had been wiped. The other team had won.

After being treated in the hospital ward for over five hours, Flower and Lulia were fully restored from their afflictions. Caressa insisted that they spend the night, but Lulia was eager to tell Flower all about the new strangeness of her new 'ghost friend.'

They ran to Flower's house, with Beau struggling to keep up. Once inside Flower's room, Lulia pushed her and Beau onto two armchairs that sat by the bedroom window.

"Did you guys hear any muttering bouncing off the walls near the end of the duel?" Lulia asked.

Beau and Flower looked to one another before turning back to Lulia, shaking their heads.

"And right after I heard the voices, I felt someone touch me," she pointed to her backside.

"He what?" Flower practically jumped out of her chair, screaming with excitement.

Aksel opened the bedroom door peeking his head in.

"I got a little distracted with the girl in the hospital wing that I went to apologize to for turning into a demon. Do you know where your brother is?" he asked.

Flower shook her head.

"And what's all that screaming about?" he asked a question he'd soon regret.

A wide smile spread across her face as she couldn't contain her excitement. "Our ghost friend touched her ass!"

Aksel's eyebrows raised, and he shut the door.

"I know!" Lulia shouted excitedly. "I mean, it's the second time he's made physical contact with me. One time, I could feel his breath on my cheek as I was trying to sleep."

"I mean, it's not that much of a big deal." The short boy shrugged in the tall-looking chair. "Ghosts make contact all the time. Diana's brother has a ghost that he sees all the time."

Flower was puzzled by the strange phenomenon. She knew that regular ghosts couldn't touch anything, so she wondered what this entity was. She noticed a small beige fabric sticking out from under Lulia's blue pillow and decided to investigate. Flower pulled the fabric toward her and found a small stuffed bag. She opened the bag and discovered a small crystal inside, which glowed a faint purple in the dimly lit room. Flower was intrigued by the energy emanating from the crystal and picked it up to examine it closely. The crystal's surface had intricate patterns etched into it that shimmered in the dim light. Flower had never seen anything like it before, and her heart raced excitedly. Holding the crystal in her hand, she felt a strange energy pulsing through her fingertips. Suddenly, she realized this might be a sleep satchel – a mystical object that could induce deep and restful slumber for its possessor. It could even allow the maker to enter the dreams of those who slept with it.

"Maybe we should get rid of it," Beau suggested. "What if it's something evil?"

"He's not evil!" Lulia shouted angrily.

"Whatever, this is all too creepy. We don't know a single thing about this ghost. We have no clue what this could be," Beau continued but decided to tread more lightly with his tone.

Both Lulia and Flower looked as if someone had died, they knew their cousin was right, but neither wanted to believe that *he* was some terrible being.

"He hasn't harmed anyone." Lulia crossed her arms.

They heard the front door open. Flower listened to her parents walking in with goods from the market.

"I can make a lucidan pouch – one that will help me control my dreams – and if I have the right amount of control, I can ask him who he is. I've always been fascinated by lucid dreaming, and the idea of being able to control my dreams has always intrigued me," Lulia began in a hushed tone now that they weren't home alone.

They heard Blue's heavy footsteps approach. They felt panicked. None of them wanted this discussion to end, but it was a school night, and Blue was most likely coming to take Beau and Lulia home.

"For all we know, you could be right," Flower whispered.

There was a knock at the door. "Time to go home."

***

Lulia laid awake for hours. Her eyes drifted from Spencer's empty bed over to the window where snow drifted blissfully. She let her mind wander.

Could this boy be dangerous? She didn't know anything about sleepwalkers after all.

Quietly, Lulia tried to speak to her ghost friend, all while trying not to wake up Olivia and Harriet, who laid asleep in the room. She didn't receive a response. Maybe it only communicated when it wanted to. But he couldn't be evil. He seemed so lovely. But most people put up an excellent front only to reveal the harsh, dirty truth.

Lulia turned over. The next day, she'd work hard with her friends to find out the truth about this boy. He wasn't evil. She punched her pillow.

***

The snowfall that had started in the evening had transformed into a blizzard mid-day. The art of musical magic with Professor Adolfo Olsen had been canceled. Adolfo didn't trust that his student friends would go straight home, so he walked them all home and made sure they arrived safely.

Theodolphus and Annie suggested that everyone get together at the Misfit Crew's home, since it was the largest, and sit by the fire. Gavin and Terry sat playing a Heofsij game called chess while drinking caffeine quake.

The house was darker than usual as harsh weather often impacted fire and light magic, dimming light sources. Thick, gray snow swirled outside of all the windows. Flower, Beau, and Lulia shivered. Adolfo had insisted that they walked with him as well. Annie began to shout at Amara, who had turned Darren into a dog. Little did she know, Darren had been bothering Amara fooling around, saying that Amara 'should kill himself.' Mike, Annie, Beau, and Lulia took this time off to work on homework.

Lovetta, Amara, and Clancy hovered over the spell ingredients list and began to focus on how much longer until they could use the potion. Lovetta went off looking for the bathroom. She took a wrong turn and ended up in Gavin's room; the walls were lined with high bookshelves.

***

While walking through the school's halls, Lovetta could still hear students mutter about the incident between her and Brad, saying that they were sure it hadn't been an accident and that she'd kill again. She'd clear her throat as she'd pass. They would all stop and stare, petrified. She hated what they spoke about, but she loved the sight of their fear. The color drained from the frightened students' faces.

Today's discussion was quite different than the ones prior.

"It wasn't an accident," said a stout student.

"You think so?" a girl with blonde pigtails, named Lynn, asked anxiously.

"She's always been strange," the stout student continued. "I've seen her cutting down a tree with her bare hands. What a freak! She probably would have no problem killing Brad. She could probably kill any of us with a single wave of her foul-smelling, dog-like breath."

A tear fell from the rim of her eye as she stood around the students' corner, feeling too foul-smelling to walk by.

The students shared some laughter after this.

"We're not the only ones to think she's a killer. You saw what someone painted on her locker," the stout student continued. "Plus, the girl is always covered in dirt and hangs out with that Chaos group. She's not all right in the head."

"She always seems so nice," the blonde girl defended. "So do all the Chaos members except for maybe Aksel and Clancy. They're half and half, in my opinion."

"Some say that Clancy is the one who cursed Eion the night of his Crash Ring incident. Eion used to be a spy for the king, who made Clancy jealous and spiteful. They also say it's because Eion's power went to his head, as evidenced by Eion punching Abner after being told a compliment to show that he was not one to mess with. Rumors say that Elio has stabbed Clancy before and that Clancy cursed Elio to no longer see, causing him to slowly become crazier and crazier as if he's some lab rat in an experiment. They also all party shooting off guns in the middle of the night, giving everyone within walking distance a heart attack. Seppo is believed to have all sorts of mental issues. Walter is said to have a dark secret, and Aksel is, well, Aksel. I say she kills Varg next. She and her whole group have issues with him."

Lovetta finally gained her confidence. She turned the corner and cleared her throat. "Have any of you seen Varg?" she asked.

It was as if all their fears about her had become true. They all looked at her as if they were afraid for Varg's safety.

"What do you want with him?" a stout student asked in a quivering voice.

"I want to tell him I'm sorry about his defeat during the Crashnet duel. I heard his condition took the longest to heal out of his team members."

The stout kid bit his lip white. "Just leave him alone. We heard what happened at the duel, how you made him go blind."

"It was just a game," Lovetta reminded strongly.

"He was traumatized, trembling for days."

"It was a game!" she shouted.

"Before you get any ideas about coming after me next, I'll have you know everyone will turn to you as a suspect, and you will be tried and executed if you lay a single finger on me!"

"I'm not going to kill you! But if you keep this up, I just might!"

"So you did kill Brad?" The stout student tested.

"His family knows it's an accident, and that's all that matters to me."

Lovetta spun on her heels and walked off. She looked down at the old spellbook that seemed to glisten in her eyes. She gripped it tightly.

"You know, I was thinking about getting a new wand tomorrow." Lovetta approached Varg, who sat on the snowy ground, looking up at the sky.

She figured that maybe she should try getting along with him, perhaps he'd open up to her about his involvement, and maybe people would stop acting as if she were plotting to kill him.

"Maybe the four of us can go shopping. Of course, there are all the restaurants nearby too."

Varg was staring off into the forest.

"I'm just saying. Maybe it can do us some good, go out together." She flapped her lips. "I'm not trying to force anyone." She sighed.

She positioned herself next to him with her legs wide open. She propped her head up with her hand as she leaned back. Varg kept his face turned.

Lovetta stomped down the corridor with no concession to anyone around her and no longer knowing where she was going. She was confused, and her body was shaking with nervousness. The result was walking into Adolfo. The impact nearly knocked her over.

"Oh, sorry." She calmed herself in his presence.

The majority of his face was covered by a thick scarf dotted with snowflakes. But she could recognize him by his thick eyebrows, leather jacket, and confused, blue eyes. Next to him was Amara, who carried a dead rooster in his bare hands.

Adolfo pulled down his scarf. "You all right?" he asked. "Class is that way." He pointed behind her, knowing that she was in his next class.

"Oh, right." Lovetta squeezed her eyes as if it'd help organize her thoughts. She then turned to Amara. "What's that for?"

"Class." He gave a happy nod.

"For a charm," Adolfo added.

Adolfo peered at her more closely through his snow-covered eyebrows. "You sure you're all right?"

Lovetta couldn't repeat what those students were saying about her, especially the thing that hurt her feelings the most, her 'dog breath.'

"Yeah, it's nothing, I promise." She gave a limp smile before walking off to class with them. Her mind was filled with everything that they had said about her and her friends. Was it all just rumors? Like how she killed Brad was just a rumor?

***

Later that night, students were waiting for their parents to come in carriages or on their brooms to take them safely home in the harsh weather. The majority of the students sat waiting in the cafeteria, enjoying muffins.

Varg sprinted out of the stockroom. "Go! She's right behind me!"

The burly woman Aksel had faced during Crashnet gasped before tearing off. They ran side by side down adjacent corridors, panting. At the far end, they stopped and stared as they spotted their friend Lynn's lifeless body lying on the floor. They gasped. Varg and the burly girl looked at each other.

A man with a sack on his head, carrying an ax, roared behind them. The man buried his ax in Varg's skull. The burly girl screamed as Varg collapsed.

Adolfo had seen the burly girl running toward him. He decided to run where she had come from. He saw Varg and Lynn. Standing around them were Lovetta, Clancy, and Amara. He sent five kids to run to the hospital ward and call for help.

Lovetta wanted to run, but she knew she had to face this. Would anyone believe that she had nothing to do with this?

Doors swung open throughout the hall. Kids and teachers alike had heard the chaos and had come running over. Teddy, Selena, and Gabriel Jr. from the ministry had been summoned. They had enchanted handcuffs and placed them on the three students and Annie and the rest of the Chaos band members who were conveniently still present at the school. They were brought down to Mr. Bernard's office. The front entrance of the school burst open. Ministry members swarmed in, followed by Mike.

Seppo walked out of the cafeteria with no knowledge of the incident before being pinned against the wall. In confusion, he even tried fighting Gabriel Jr.

By the time they were all brought to the office, everyone had been panting after trying to fight.

"Caught in the act." The stout boy who had been in the hall came into the office, pointing her finger at Lovetta. "I saw how her eyes were fixated on the two."

"That will do," Selena said sharply.

Clancy looked down, grinning. He'd always loved mayhem, and he began to sing the dark words of Chaos' new song happily. "*In Transylvania...*" Clancy looked to Amara, who smiled and joined in.

"*In Transylvania, we are fighting!*" Aksel joined.

"*With swords and knives...*" Walter was the next to be influenced.

"*And guns and spears!*" Abner smiled and added his voice to the mixture.

"*In Transylvania...*" They all looked to Seppo, who shook his head. Mike pinched his nose as the boys finished singing. "*In Transylvania. We're in Transylvania!*"

Clancy leaned over to Lovetta and kissed her cheek.

"That's enough!" Mr. Bernard screamed.

Aksel raised his brows before allowing his eyes to roam the room awkwardly.

"Varg and Lynn have been brought to the hospital ward, and all of you better hope that they survive this attack."

"Mr. Bernard, I swear we didn't do anything," Lovetta pleaded.

"This is out of my hands, love." He looked over to the three ministry members.

Amara's bat flew in and perched itself onto his shoulder. It must've sensed his fear.

"Follow us." Selena opened the office door.

The students stood to their feet and followed Gabriel Jr. and Teddy out of the room while Selena followed behind them. They were brought to the ministry's black tower, astonished by its black mirrored interior. Despite their gloom, they couldn't help but be amazed. They heard the office door thud behind them once they took a seat around the long, u-shaped table. Slightly dizzy, Amara placed his head down onto the table, to Mike's concern.

CHAPTER 12

The door opened silently, and Angel entered. "My sister will be here shortly," she spoke softly.

The three arresting ministry members had instructed the boys, Lovetta, and Annie to remain quiet as they waited for the queen. Clancy looked around, many sly comments raced through his head, but he was humbled after hearing just how much trouble they were in for. He wanted to remark about how Galdorwide was ruled by a dictatorship, a queen suppressing everyone with her words and actions. She already claimed the forest was forbidden and ruled out unauthorized magic for all training students. What was next? However, despite his hatred for the queen and the ministry, he had to admit this black room was attractive. If he hadn't been handcuffed and stared at by Gabriel Jr. and Teddy Scaasi, he would've roamed about the room pleasantly.

It was a large, black, circular room. Filled with silence, everything that did make a noise echoed throughout. The table in the middle stood on spindle legs. The black chairs they sat upon had clawed feet. Now finding awkwardness by the stares and the silence, Clancy decided to speak.

"Can I have a smoke?" Clancy asked. Gabriel and Teddy shook their heads, unamused by his question and trying to keep silence in the room. "All right."

The walls were covered with portraits of all of Galdorwide's rulers. Most of them were all men besides Bella and Despina, Bella's great-great-grandmother who ruled after her husband Heath Carter had met an untimely death shortly after their marriage. Clancy looked at Bella's portrait. She was beautiful despite how tired she looked.

His eyes trailed to the front of the room, where a golden light illuminated a large, brown shabby witch hat in a glass case. His eyes widened. "Is that Merlin's hat?" He nearly jumped out of his seat.

"Yes, one of them," Angel answered. "Though not from Galdorwide, he was extremely fascinated by how our magic here worked, with our auras and all. He came by once upon a time and gave the ruling king his hat as a thank you."

"He gave a hat as a *thank you*?" Aksel asked, almost offended.

Angel gave the boy a quick look. "He *is* one of the greatest witches of all time. The hat was said to give him and my family good fortune."

"Come! Quick!" The ministry member, Dorothy, burst through the door. The three ministry members immediately followed her.

Clancy slid off of the chair and onto his knees. He sat on the ground and slid his handcuffed hands under him, so now they were in front of him. Mike made a disgusted face as he was currently unable to pinch his nose. Clancy stood onto his feet and walked around the desk. He brought his hands to the glass case.

"It's not even secure!" Clancy grew excited. "Aksel, help."

Aksel did the same maneuver and walked toward the glass case. They each slowly raised the glass off of the hat with all their strength sent to their fingertips.

"Put it on my head." Clancy lowered himself.

Aksel picked up the hat awkwardly and lowered it onto Clancy's head. When he stood upright, the oversized hat fell over his eyes. Clancy stared at the black inside of the hat. He nearly jumped out of his skin when a voice rang in his head.

"Got a question there, Clancy Scaasi?" The voice of an older man echoed throughout the hat.

"*Uh*... Sure?"

"*Ah*, I see, you're wondering if your band will be the greatest in the whole world. Yes, Chaos will be one of the greatest bands and the greatest in your genre of black magic music. But it will come with difficulty. Your music will inspire generations to come, and your music will be considered a classic. However, I must say that this will all be due to your band's infamy. I see suffering, mayhem, and death in yours and your friend's future."

Clancy's stomach plummeted. He whipped off the hat that now hung limply in his handcuffed hands. He put the dull, grubby hat back on the pedestal. He felt like he was going to be sick.

"You're wrong," he mumbled to himself. He looked back to the hat that lay still and quiet. A gagging noise came from behind him.

Standing at the door was a bleeding Teddy. "There's a time for everything." He lifted his wand and said a simple spell, and the handcuffs on the prisoners were released. "I'm going to need your help."

The prisoners, except for Annie, ran down the stairs of the ministry's office. They raced outside to find a giant bird, almost the size of the building, that looked like a half-plucked turkey. It stared at the ministry members whose attacks seemed to only feel like mere scratches for the creature. The creature looked ill as if it had been mistreated its whole life, its eyes were dull, and it wasn't putting up much of a fight. A few feathers fell from its tail.

Mike struck the beast with a spell containing holy magic, and the beast combusted into flames and then to ashes. Everyone screamed and backed away as the creature's fiery flesh and feathers fell from the sky, nearly striking everyone in sight. Lovetta let out a yelp before Clancy moved her out of the way. The flames remained, beginning to spread throughout the grass. Bella took out her wand and diminished the fire with a purple fountain of water flowing from her wand. Bella turned around, looking very muted.

"My Queen." Mike bowed. The rest followed, including Clancy, who was taken by her beauty. "I'm sorry about the fire." He straightened himself up.

To everyone's astonishment, the queen smiled. "No need. It's about time. We had been fighting that creature for eight minutes too long." She chuckled as everyone looked at her stunned. Had they expected her to be stricter or crazier? She would've been, but that wasn't her current mood. Instead, she was pretty pleased by the men in front of her. "However, my concern is that this was no ordinary bird. It was a phoenix. They rise through their ashes. This may be the creature that will be Rabbit's problem."

Mike looked down just in time to see a wrinkled, tiny newborn bird. The newborn was vibrant in color and had all its feathers, looking much fresher and healthier.

"It's a shame. She's so cute." Bella bent down and picked up the bird. She looked over her shoulder and over to Mike. "That spell, I had never heard it before. What was it?"

"Gangwuce Estmere, ancient Galdorian for holy water, Your Majesty."

"Are you a holy man?" Bella asked, almost flattered yet concerned as he wore his Viridi uniform.

"I am or training to be at least."

"Training? But you're still in high school." She stood to her feet.

"I'm very dedicated to my school and work. They gave me an early year start."

"What's your name?"

"Mike Hansen."

"Well, Mike, I may need you to stick around. None of us can perform such a spell."

"I'd be honored."

She smiled before looking back at the bird. "She's ravishing with her red and orange feathers. They are fascinating creatures and make loyal pets. Too bad this one belongs to my father."

With the shock of the attack of the phoenix, they had all almost forgotten why they had been here. That was until the queen led them back up the steps to the ministry's office. They all sat around the table where Annie had been anxiously waiting. The queen took her seat at the front and gave each of the arrested students a glare from her icy, green eyes.

Before Bella could say a word, Adolfo, wearing his thick, furry winter clothing, burst into the office. He was carrying the dead chicken that would be used in the following day's class. "It wasn't them! My Queen." He lowered his voice having realized he was standing in the presence of the actual queen. "I know them all, they may look bad and act bad, but they ain't bad. Especially not Lovetta. She wasn't raised like we were. Varg had many enemies. It could've been anyone at the school or even out of it considering the other deaths."

"The only other death was Brad, and that was at the hands of Lovetta."

"And Lena Baxter."

"Lena Baxter?" Bella furrowed her brow. "Who's that?"

"She's one of the patients at Ace's home care. She was killed, but he says it was from someone from the outside, though, poisoned her through the mail."

"How do you know this?"

"Caressa Scaasi works at Galdorwide High, and she said that her sister Damaress had just received Lena's body. I already told the members downstairs that they were needed at the morgue. Please, it wasn't Lovetta. You can give them all a truth potion, then you'll see."

"Who are you?" She halted with a swift cut of her hand.

"Adolfo Olsen, I'm a teacher at Galdorwide High and bandmate of

Chaos. But can we get back onto the topic? You have the wrong people."

"I don't think they did this either. Their eyes are innocent despite what their music wants you to believe, maybe not you, though." Bella turned and pointed to Aksel. "Your eyes tell a different story, but I still don't think you did it either."

"Oh, thank Merlin." Adolfo turned to the boys. "I'll be right outside waiting." He closed the door to the office.

"You don't think it was us?" Lovetta asked hopefully. "You have no idea how quick everyone is to blame us for these sorts of things."

"No, I don't." Bella smiled before anxiety rushed through her, returning her somber look. A burning rush went from her shoulders to her chest. "But I still want to talk to you all."

They all waited anxiously for Bella to speak. Her long, slim fingers came together.

"I would like to ask you all if you have anything you wanted to tell me. Anything at all."

They all looked to one another, wondering what it was the queen could have been talking about. They hadn't done anything illegal that they could remember.

"Can you give us a hint?" Aksel asked.

"A boy I once knew was a true enigma. He had an air of mystery about him that drew people in, but he never let anyone get too close. I feel his presence strongly around you. But the last I heard, he was in another world. Does anyone have any information?"

Lovetta, Amara, and Clancy looked to one another. They had no idea who she could be talking about.

"No, nothing at all," Clancy stated.

***

Despite their release, the double attack on both Varg and Lynn had turned the school upside down as they feared Lovetta and the Chaos group. Many students opted out of going to any of the classes that they shared with them. Most of the day's classes only had seven students rather than the usual twenty-five. Everyone whispered about how terrible they were to do that to two students they barely knew.

"At this rate, soon the only people in the school will be the teachers and us, or maybe just the Scaasi and Adolfo," Clancy said almost happily. He had to admit, he liked the halls no longer being a stampede. He hated people and loved the fact that they feared him, so all in all, it was perfect.

There were rumors that the band composed of vampires and werewolves, and every time someone passed them in the halls, they scurried past as if they expected them to grow fangs or cast a deadly spell. Clancy had fun with this, so much so, he'd cough a word into his sleeve as people passed, and they would scream as if they had just seen a vampire.

Clancy, Walter, Aksel, Amara, and Lucian soon began to have fun. Shouting things like 'you're next!', 'I'm going to kill that one,' amongst general growls as people passed by, sending males and female witches alike running. At one point, Amara walked down the hall with a tall, plastic scythe, fake vampire teeth, and a black cloak. Amara, Clancy, and Walter wore their corpse paint to school.

Mike was disapproving of their behavior. "This is not a laughing matter. People *died*," he scolded coldly. "It's sick. They were our classmates, and now they're *dead*."

"Who cares," Clancy replied sternly through his cold, blue eyes, not liking the tone Mike was giving him. "It's not like they were our friends. They were rude to Lovetta."

"Still, this is *so* wrong."

"It's supposed to be wrong. People are supposed to hate what we do. They're supposed to fear us. People are supposed to think that we're fucked in the head." Clancy pointed to his forehead.

"Well, you fucking are."

"Oh, have some fun, Daddy." Walter patted Mike's shoulder. Mike couldn't help but smirk.

"Yeah!" Clancy shouted. "Let's burn down the demented school!"

Mike's smile faded. Annie wasn't approving of this behavior either. They usually listened to her, being pregnant and all, but nothing she said worked any more. They were out of control.

"Oh, don't say that," she wailed. It had been all she had said to any of them. Lately, she was beginning to sound like a broken record.

Lovetta didn't mind, they were having fun with something that would've made her even more upset about the incident with Brad, but instead, she was laughing and having fun, making use of the fear that surrounded her. She didn't feel like an outcast any more. She felt like the school's queen, and Clancy was the master at all dark and evil things, real or not. But their antics seemed to get on the nerve of Theresa Thorn, better known as TT, Varg's twin sister.

"You should feel bad, you're parading on her brother's death—" Mike added as he looked over to the burly TT.

"Wait," Aksel interrupted. "That's Varg's *sister?*"

"Oh, hey, isn't that the girl you faced in Crashnet?" Clancy asked. He looked over at her with wide eyes before quickly looking back at his friends.

"How could you not tell?" Mike asked, exasperated. "They're practically identical, good for him but not so good for her."

Aksel still had a stunned look on his face. Mike waved his hand in front of his friend's face. Annie's eyes widened. "Oh, don't tell me," she said. Aksel looked up, guilty.

"Hey," Clancy interrupted, not catching on to the drama show revealing in front of him. "We should use the truth potion on her. Maybe she knows something. Then we can prove Lovetta didn't kill Brad."

"But do we still think Varg killed him?" Annie folded her arms. "I mean, he did die, himself. It could be anyone."

"It's worth a shot." Clancy shrugged.

They decided to wait until the end of the semester before using the truth potion on her. The silence was as deep as the snow-filled kingdom. Amara found it peaceful, finding the gloom intoxicating. But no matter how much he loved melancholy, he did whatever he could to stay away from the house, which meant playing knockout of law, a form of fighting, with the three bands as well practicing Crashnet in the Misfit Crew house's basement.

Mike often locked himself and Annie in their bedroom after deeming all their behavior as childish. He often came down to check on Amara, who felt like a younger brother to him. After all, he had known him before moving to Galdorwide when the two of them had lived in Polar Frigemilt. He did say that if they ever needed him because Amara was bleeding to death, or if Lucian got punched in the throat, or if the fighting got out of hand, he would come and help, all of which had happened prior.

Saturnalia morning dawned, bright and white. They had all spent the night at the Misfit Crew house. Mike woke up his Chaos members, Terry woke up the Imaginary King members, and Gavin woke up the Misfit Crew. They all headed downstairs in their pajamas, where they would exchange gifts. They were now just waiting on Mike and Seppo.

"Wake up." Mike opened the blinds to the guest room where Seppo was sleeping, allowing the bright light, illuminated by the white snow, to shine in.

"What?" Seppo shielded his eyes from the light. "What's going on?"

"Happy Saturnalia to you too." Mike laughed. "We're going downstairs to open presents," he added. Seppo sat up, suddenly awake.

Downstairs, Clancy leaned over to Amara. "I've been adding the last ingredients to the potion all morning. It's ready."

"Are you sure?" Amara whispered.

"Positive," said Clancy. He shifted his black cat familiar that kept trying to get out of his arms. "I say the best time to do it is tonight."

At that moment, Amara's bat familiar swooped in through the living room window, carrying a letter beneath his fangs. "Hello," said Amara as the bat landed on his lap. "Are you speaking to me now, after the incident at the church?"

The bat looked up at him affectionately. Seeing his bat again was a far better gift than the one he had received. It was from his parents who remained in Polar Frigemilt. A letter explaining that he got into the art of art magic class in the graduating school up North. Amara didn't want to go; sure, he excelled in art class, but that didn't mean he was willing to skip the next two years at Galdorwide High and go to a school with people he didn't know. He couldn't go back, not after what happened following his and Ainsley's attack.

The rest of Amara's gifts were far more satisfying. Mike had gotten him the latest *Travels with Vampires* book, and Clancy had given him a Tassos Rudd T-shirt. Aksel had brought him a vampire-themed mug that had moving, real blood flowing from the rim's edges. The last gift he had received was from Seppo, who had bought him socks designed with images of vampires, hand-knit by Seppo himself. He kept all the letters they had written him and placed them on top of his dresser where Ainsley admired and could read and study his new belongings.

***

No one could have a good time spending Saturnalia dinner at Ace's. Despite the gloom everyone felt, the upstairs looked magnificent. There was a frost-coated tree by the door. A wool wreath hung on the backing of the door, and red candles were lit all around the room. Ace ordered Abigail to enchant the ceiling to allow warm snow to fall from above. He insisted that everyone sing carols, which made the cheerful songs sound depressing. Everyone grew tense as Ace hadn't noticed Abigail trying to enchant the front door. They all looked to the door, their eyes going back to Ace to make sure he wasn't growing suspicious. To keep the attention off the door, Aldric, now in human form, created a distraction by idly talking about Ace's usual white dress shirt. With a bit of luck, they may get out.

They all ate three rounds of dessert to keep the enchantment going when Abigail locked eyes with all the patients, giving them the signal to prepare. The door burst open, and everyone ran for the door. Spencer, John Jr., and Aldaricus were the only ones to make it out before Ace slammed the door and began to lock all of the locks.

***

"We're going to need a lock of TT's hair before we can give this to her," Lovetta said as she pulled her cloak around her after the boy's sudden arrival at her place. "It'll be best if I do it. She doesn't seem to like guys too much."

"She seemed to like Aksel." Clancy sniggered.

"Well, we can't trust Aksel. Who knows what stealing a strand of her hair might turn into. We'll also have to make sure that our interrogation of her goes uninterrupted. This potion is illegal when used without authorization. If anyone finds us, we can get in trouble. The queen was already more generous than before when Varg died. If we get caught, we may… have to become the evil we've all been pretending to be."

Amara and Clancy looked at one another, almost excited. "I don't think we have to worry," Clancy began. "She has no friends, and her family is low-lives."

The steely glint in Lovetta's eye faded. "Well, then, before we worry about that, we have to figure out a way for me to grab a piece of her hair."

"How about her brush? Like if you ask to use her washroom or if it's in her room," Amara suggested.

"Does it look like she uses a brush?" Clancy laughed before looking up to Lovetta, who crossed her arms as her busy hair fell around her. He stopped his laughter.

"We're not meeting her at her house. She and her family are poorer than the three of us negatively combined. She'll be having dinner at the village hall. I had heard her speaking about it to Professor Gemini."

Lovetta bustled back inside as she reviewed Clancy's additions to the potion. Amara glumly looked to Clancy.

To Amara's utter amazement, the first step in the plan went smoothly. The three of them lurked at the entrance hall after the Saturnalia tea had been passed around. TT stood up from her table and headed out of the dining hall. The three of them hid behind a royal knight statue that stood next to the door's arch.

Lovetta followed her, a wand in hand, to the city hall bathroom. They entered the bathroom. To Lovetta's relief, the bathroom was empty. She raised her wand and pointed it at the back of TT's head. "*Cnyll butan!*" A modest, blue flash of sparks exited her wand and struck the rear of TT's head. She fell over, unconscious. Lovetta quickly bent down and grabbed a long, curly, brown strand of her hair that fell across her forehead. She plucked it and placed it into her vial.

She sprinted out of the bathroom, over to the boys, before running over to Seppo's bedroom. They could hardly see inside the house as black smoke emitted from the still brewing potion. They covered their noses with their sleeves.

"Seppo?" Amara asked, concerned for his brother's health if he had decided to return home for a nap.

Seppo emerged from the smoke, shiny-faced. Behind him, they heard the *gloop* of the potion. "Did you guys get the hair?" he asked. Lovetta raised the vial where the long strand of hair sunk, looking as if it was desperately trying to hang to the top of the glass.

"I thought it best to get you new clothes to wear. In case you get caught," Seppo explained, focusing on one word at a time as his thick accent fought against the words. He held up a small sack filled with Pure cloaks.

They smiled, taking their sizes before walking into the room and staring into the cauldron. The concoction was a thick, dark-green liquid.

"You sure you've done everything right?" Seppo asked.

Lovetta grabbed out the potion book and re-read it all nervously. "It exactly looks as it's described. Once she's drinking it, we will have exactly one hour to get all we can get out of her."

"Now what?" Clancy asked.

"We put it into a glass and give it to her as a gift to apologize for our behaviors."

"How do we expect her to drink that thing?" Clancy asked, almost angry. "It smells awful. That'll never work."

"Not if we mask it with a spell that'll make it appealing to her cravings." Lovetta smiled, pleased with her plan.

Lovetta ladled three large dollops into a glass bottle. Her hand trembling, she added TT's hair into the potion.

The potion hissed loudly like a boiling kettle. The brew frothed before relaxing into a greenish-black color.

"Yep, TT would turn the potion black." Clancy laughed, reading what the color change after the hair meant. "Black potions mean the user is troubled, dark, and a victim of psychic abuse. It could also mean that the hair taken is from someone possibly attached to a malevolent spirit."

Clancy, Amara, and Seppo turned to Lovetta. She only looked up once the silence in the room had become deafening.

"What?" Lovetta asked angrily. "You were with me! I didn't kill her brother!" She sighed. "You boys ready?"

"Ready."

"Now, things will go smoothly if she hadn't seen me, you know, knock her unconscious today."

The second step in operation also smoothly went as they stood on her doorstep. TT's eyes immediately landed on what she saw to be hot sherry. They pushed her into the house, which was luckily empty, which meant no evil-doing had to occur. TT's insides began to turn as if they were being spun on a wheel. She kneeled over. She wanted to puke, but the potion disabled her gag reflex so that the brew would remain in her body. A burning sensation spread from her stomach to her head. She felt as if all her insides were beginning to melt.

As suddenly as it had started, it stopped. TT lay faced-down on her rotting, wooden floor. With difficulty, she stood up. Her hands were trembling. She brushed her wild hair out of her face.

"Are you okay?" Seppo couldn't help but ask.

"Yeah," her response came suddenly and uncontrollably.

TT stared at them with her cold, black eyes. Clancy scratched his head uncomfortably. Her long gorilla arms rested on her knees as she tried to hold herself upright. "This is unbelievable, my brain – it can't think."

"No more wasting time." Lovetta's voice grew unusually high as a rush of energy went through her, along with a wave of anxiety mixed with guilt. She looked at her blue watch. Five minutes had already passed. She looked out the window to make sure no one was coming.

***

John Jr., Spencer, and Aldaricus headed down stone steps that led to an underground tunnel. If Ace were looking for them, he'd expect they'd be out in the open especially heading to Spencer's home that was close by. However, they walked into the darkness of the tunnel, hoping to lose his trail. Their footsteps echoed louder than any of them would've expected. The second part of escaping wasn't going to be as easy as they thought.

The tunnel was composed of a labyrinth of passageways. They walked deeper and deeper underneath the kingdom. They were constantly checking over their shoulders, making sure that Ace wasn't sneaking upon them. After a quarter of an hour, they were convinced they were lost. Just when they were losing hope, they heard footsteps coming from up ahead. They were excited and fearful of moving toward the noise.

"*Ha!*" Spencer whispered excitedly. "Could be someone who can help up ahead!"

"What?" The deaf John Jr. asked a bit too loudly.

Spencer held her finger in front of her lips to quiet him. A figure was emerging from the dim light in front of them. They had spent so much time with Ace that they could at the very least recognize it wasn't him. This figure was shorter, broader, and had longer hair. Their hearts sank, it wasn't anyone they knew, and he didn't look much older than them. It was Rabbit Carter.

"What're you guys doing down here?" he asked, not used to seeing anyone besides his friends using the underground tunnels to avoid the normal witches of Galdorwide or authority.

"We need help," Spencer admitted desperately.

"Wh—okay, what can I do?" Rabbit asked, deeply concerned.

"We need to get home, to my parents. It won't be safe for us wandering about in here for much longer."

"Okay, you'll be safe as long as you're with me. Where do you live?"

"606 Living Lane," Spencer replied. Joy filled her entire body as if a whole new feeling had been introduced to her.

A voice suddenly echoed behind them. Ace was strolling toward them. The joy left her body like air in a balloon that had just been ripped apart.

"There you guys are," he drawled, looking at his escaped patients. "Have you three gone mad? I've been looking for you three all day. Had me worried sick." Ace glared witheringly at Rabbit. "And what deranged lies have you filled into this boy's head?"

Rabbit looked outraged. "You might want to show a bit more respect to a Carter. I must acknowledge that this situation doesn't look favorable. I have always had suspicions about you, and, now, it's challenging not to believe I was right. Your behavior isn't the only thing that's concerning me. Several inconsistencies need clarification. The stories you've shared with me in the past don't align with what I'm observing now. Furthermore, you've been avoiding my recent inquiries about Diana. I don't want to make assumptions, but I can't shake the feeling that something is happening here that I'm unaware of. My sister was supposed to go under your care, but my gut told me no, and now I see that I was right to do so no matter how much you tried to persuade me otherwise." Rabbit puffed his chest. Ace sneered and motioned his patients to follow him. "Over my dead body." Rabbit whipped out his wand as the patients fearfully began to follow the doctor.

"Now!" Ace shouted.

Abigail emerged from behind him. Her wand drawn, pointing at Rabbit. "*Hwuendlio cwaltt!*" A plain, purple blast of particles exited her wand and struck Rabbit. She was successfully making him temporarily dead.

Spencer fought back the urge to run to check up on Rabbit, but she didn't want to experience her uncle's wrath twice the amount she was already going to receive. Spencer, John Jr., and Aldaricus reluctantly followed him.

"That Rabbit Carter," Ace sneered to himself.

"Rabbit?" Spencer asked. "The cousin of the queen?" She tried to hide her smile.

"I've noticed him sneaking around lately, and I bet I know what he's up to. He thinks he's going to impress his cousins and join the ministry." He laughed.

Spencer looked to Aldaricus and John Jr., and their looks at her showed that they felt the same. Ace was underestimating the young royal.

Ace paused by a stretch of a bare stone wall that emerged from the rest of the tunnel. He looked to Abigail, who looked up at him worriedly. He eyed her.

"You know the spell, don't you?"

She nodded, almost holding back tears. She raised her wand, pointing at the lock while keeping her eyes on her father. "*Gypung*!" A uniform, purple ray of particles exited her wand and struck the wall. It began to push out.

Ace gripped Aldaricus' arm tightly and threw him in. John Jr. and Spencer were tossed in immediately after.

"*Handgestealla!*" Abigail cast, the wall pushed back, slowly muffling their screams.

When Rabbit awoke, he walked over to Chaos' new music store Grornhof, Galdorian for Underworld. The store at this time was closed. He took out his skull-head key and opened the door. He entered it and locked the door behind him. He passed the cash register and headed down stone steps that led to a long, low underground room with rough stone walls and ceiling from which black candles hung from chains. The flames crackled beneath the mantelpiece where the three bands' names were carved in black. Several band members were seated on black chairs with high backings.

He took an empty seat, closest to the lowest hanging candle. He tried his best to look at home despite what he was about to ask Theodolphus. He reached into his red-colored cloak and pulled out a newspaper clipping. He thrust it under Theodolphus' nose.

"I need your help," Rabbit said. He saw his bandmate's eyes widen as he read.

SUSPICION AT DOCTOR'S HOME CARE

Caressa Scaasi, a doctor at Galdorwide High, was fined fifty-two feohs for harassing Dr. Ace Scaasi, after relentlessly trying to break into his home, having suspicions about

his home care facility.
Mrs. Angel Scaasi, princess of Galdorwide,
insists that Caressa resign from her position
as a doctor at Galdorwide High.
"Ms. Caressa Scaasi, it has brought distress to both the ministry and Mr.
Scaasi," Mrs. Scaasi told the reporter. "She is unfit to care for
patients and her attacks on Mr. Scaasi
must stop."
Ms. Caressa Scaasi has not yet spoken
to the press or given Ace Scaasi an apology
but her boyfriend has warned the press
to no longer swarm outside their house.

"Well?" Rabbit asked as Theodolphus handed him the newspaper clipping back. "Are you in? His niece has the same suspicions I have had all along. I saw three of his patients today who asked me for help before returning, and he had a patient of his use a temporary death curse on me. Diana is there, and so is Nicholas' sister," Rabbit explained. Theodolphus' face contorted with fear. "So, what do you say?" Rabbit asked his best friend desperately.

"I say, I think I'm going to be sick."

"Well, puke it out, then come with me. We need to kick Ace's ass. You know, the newspaper should be talking about how only one of Ace's patients has ever gone home. Who knows, some of them could be dead for all we know. I suppose the ministry has this all under hush, and I bet they're behind it all, with the ministry associated with the Scaasis now."

"Elio is a Scaasi," Theodolphus replied smartly, referring to their band's lead singer.

"Elio is also legit ancient. He existed before all the Scaasi went mad.

"Come on, Theo, they'll all be dead soon if we don't help, Diana and Lexi included. My gut has always told me Ace is the worst thing to happen to this kingdom since the king. He's a Nullum and a kidnapper. And a decent ministry would not let something like this happen under their noses if they gave a single shite about us. Come on, Jaxon can take our pictures, and he could write an article and make us sound like heroes! Girls will be all over you!"

"I don't want girls to be all over me. I'm quite happy with Camila.

Thank you very much."

"Okay, well, I'm sure Camila would like to be dating a hero. Do you know how many people would want to have your autograph?"

"You mean like how Imaginary King fans do already?" Theodolphus replied smart once again.

"If you help me, I'll do whatever you want. I'll be your slave." Rabbit got onto his knees and began to beg.

Theodolphus leaned back into his chair with a smirk. "I do like the sound of that." He crossed his left leg over his right and raised his hands to the back of his head.

"You're sick." Rabbit helped himself back into his chair.

Theodolphus laughed.

"So, Saint Theo, do you accept? I know your heart is too good not to help."

Theodolphus sighed and nodded, slumping his body.

***

"I don't know who killed Brad!" The truth potion spilled from TT's mouth during the interrogation. "I can help you find out who did, just—just stop this pain!"

Their mouths dropped. They were just as clueless as TT was. Maybe it was the king, but what would explain the spiders?

"You must know something!" Lovetta, befuddled, stated angrily, wanting to know who tried turning her into a monster.

"A masked man wielding an ax killed Varg! He might've been behind Brad's death! But there's also a rumor that the king was behind Brad's death," TT shouted, still bent over, holding her stomach. "That's all I know! That's all I know! That's all I know!" Her last shout ended with a high screeching, heart-breaking sound. "I don't know who did it! I hope that whoever killed him and my brother are killed slowly and tortured first with a potato slicer against their tongues."

Lovetta was clenching her free fist, worried about the masked man. Amara gave her a concerned look.

"Whoever did this will be caught. The ministry's on the case," said Amara.

"For all we know, they may have a part in it. Acting so innocent, pretending to care for the kingdom when they don't," Clancy argued.

"Let's go. We will go to prison if someone sees us in the act. Let's not get any more mixed into all this. Worst-case scenario, Mike's working with the ministry. Maybe he can insist they look into these deaths further."

TT fell forward. The potion was wearing off. The group looked to one another before running off, fearing the manly girl's wrath.

They sprinted out and hurled themselves inside Amara's house and dashed into his house. They hoped TT didn't know where any of them lived despite her living a block away. They crashed onto the floor while Amara threw himself onto his bed. Muffled music could be heard coming from the Misfit Crew's house. They took off their shoes and tried to relax.

"Well," Clancy began. "That was a waste."

"But who's the masked man? She couldn't have lied about that?" asked Amara.

Lovetta began to think back to the last conversation she had with Varg and how he felt like someone was after him. Ainsley sprinted out from beneath the mattress through Amara.

"Hi, Ainsley," Amara breathed into his pillow.

This was the happiest she had ever seen Ainsley as she wore a smile. Though, suddenly, she began to sob.

Amara quickly sat up and looked at her, then at his friends. "Hey, can we call it a night?" His friends nodded solemnly.

When they shut the door behind them, Ainsley looked to Amara, pouting. "I've been teased something awful today by a young girl and a *spider*."

CHAPTER 13

TT was brought to the hospital ward by her mother. There was a flurry of rumors surrounding the Chaos group saying that they had been trying to kill her. Everyone, of course, turned to Lovetta. Though she had been the reason why she was in the hospital, she hadn't tried to *kill* her. TT had denied all visitors except for Aksel.

Aksel had gone to see her every morning since she had been admitted. He brought her homework, and she ended up showing him how it all worked.

"You know, if I were in the hospital, I wouldn't be doing homework," Aksel admitted. "Grorhorn, I barely do it now."

"Don't be silly. I need to do my homework." TT had a soft side around the naturally tanned boy. Her spirits had been greatly improved since Seppo, Lovetta, Amara, and Clancy explained that Aksel had no idea what they had been plotting. "I don't suppose your friends have any new leads on who killed my brother, do you?"

"Nothing." Aksel shook his head.

"I was so sure it had been Lovetta behind the killings. The whole school was, but I know that the person I saw couldn't have been her."

"You think?" Aksel laughed before looking at her pillow, where something green poked out. "What's that?"

"Just a get-well card." She tried to push it further underneath the pillow.

Aksel plunged for it and began to read: '*To Miss Thorn, wishing you a quick recovery from your concerned friend, Acwulf.*'

"*Acwulf?* That weird, nerdy werewolf kid?"

"Yes, he has a crush on me, all right?" TT swiped it back.

"Okay then, now why is it under your pillow?"

"He's just sweet." She brushed a strand of her thick, curly hair behind her ear as she smiled down at the card.

"And who has the crush? Have you two… ever?" He let his question trail rather than asking.

She laughed and looked up at him. "You're cute when you get jealous, and no, but he has seen me without a shirt."

"Wha—how?" Aksel asked, confused.

"He asked me to take my shirt off."

"Wha—and just like that?" he snapped. "You take your shirt off?" he asked.

She shrugged. Doctor Notleaf carried in her file with her prescribed potions on top. Aksel stormed out and joined Clancy in the hall. "That Acwulf kid, we should smoke him out, honest. I hope he's next. D'ya think if I wish it enough, it'll happen? I mean, though, I wouldn't mind knowing what it'd feel like to penetrate a knife through his werewolf heart."

"You should try it," Clancy said, almost emotionless.

"Yeah, maybe I should."

Adolfo had given them so much homework that Aksel had needed to get some of it done. Aksel thought that Adolfo would go easy on him, considering Aksel wasn't a second-year any more, but, nope, the work just got heavier and heavier. Aksel was just on his way to Lovetta's class to ask her where he could find a werewolf killing knife when a bone-chilling scream came from the second floor above him.

"That's Adolfo." Clancy turned to Aksel. They immediately headed back up to the stairs. "You don't think someone else has been attacked, do you?" Clancy asked as he jumped up the steps.

"If it is, let's hope it's Acwulf."

They ran up and turned the corner to see Amara and Adolfo arguing. "You skipped today's class because your ghost friend was upset? I should tell Mr. Bernard you lied and weren't sick!"

"Yes, and go right ahead, I just need to find Clancy or Lovetta."

"Right here," said Clancy. "Just Aksel, instead of love."

"Okay, that'll do, come!" Amara began to run down the steps down the other side of the hall.

They had followed Amara back to his house. When they entered, they could already hear Ainsley's crying. The floor was more damp than usual, with a few puddles of her tears silver gathering upon it. Stepping over them, they headed into Amara's room.

"A young girl was throwing stuff at me when I sat outside last night." She was talking as if they had already asked her what was wrong.

They walked closer to her, wishing they could comfort her rather than stand around, arms at their side awkwardly as she sobbed.

"What did she look like?"

"All I remember was her red hair. I didn't get a good look." She was growing impatient. She had already explained this all to Amara. "I minded my own business, and then she decided to pick on me! What is so wrong with me?"

"I mean," Aksel began, "if she threw stuff at you, it ain't so bad. I mean, you can't feel right?" Aksel asked before dragging his hand down through her head and her neck before he pulled it out.

"I can feel feelings! And they hurt! And put your hand through me one more time, and I'll possess you!" the angry young girl warned. "I had just been outside, thinking about my life when it went through my head from behind. I got a quick glimpse, and it was a large creature with eight legs standing beside a young girl with red hair. The spider had told her to throw it," she explained.

Clancy shivered and began to scratch his neck, where he started to feel the sensation of tiny legs walking. "The shoes are still outside, follow me." She floated toward the door, and outside, she pointed to it lying in the front yard beside a bush.

Amara bent down and picked up the shoes that emitted a silver glow. They were drenched from the previous night's rain.

"Merlin!" Clancy was exasperated as Amara touched the thing.

As Amara picked up a pair of shoes, he wrinkled his nose at the strange, musty smell and noticed cobwebs covering them. He couldn't imagine why anyone would want to wear such creepy shoes that seemed like they belonged in a horror movie. Upon closer examination, he saw tiny spider legs sticking out from the seams, making him uneasy. Amara asked his friend how old the shoes were, but they were unsure. They both agreed that the shoes looked like they had been through a lot. Despite his curiosity, Amara quickly put the boots down, feeling a sense of revulsion. He wanted nothing to do with the creepy shoes or their owner. He flipped the shoe over and examined the inside of the tongue and found the initials LS scribed at the top.

"Now—what redhead do we know with the initials LS?"

"Lulia," Clancy said.

"You think?" Aksel asked, throwing his hands in his pocket before his eyes widened. "Yeah, yeah." He wagged his finger. "I walked into Flower's room one day, and she was talking about how a ghost..." He thought about what they had been talking about and decided not to describe what he heard. "Just talking about a ghost. Something weird must be going on with her."

"I wonder why she would've thrown it at Ainsley. I mean, everyone likes her and all."

After turning the shoes over, he carefully inspected their soles. He noticed the grooves had worn down, and the rubber started peeling away from the leather. "It has the royal crest." His fingers trailed over the indented image of the four-tiered crest of a dragon, hound, mermaid, and fairy – the only four familiars worthy of being given to a royal.

"This must've belonged to a royal before it was theirs. Maybe Nicholas or Rabbit gave it to them?"

"We can ask." Clancy shrugged.

TT finally left the hospital ward at the beginning of February. On her first day back, Aksel had her meet up with his group, where they showed her the shoes, the only lead they believed to be connected to the murderer. Nicholas and Rabbit had denied giving it to the girls, and the girls refused to talk.

"It may have powers." TT took the shoe into her hands to study it closely.

"If it has, it's not very obvious," Aksel said in a way to make sure her hopes didn't go up too much. "Pointless holding onto it. I mean, it's just a stupid shoe, and Lulia probably just made a weird spider friend."

"A spider friend who may have an army of tiny spiders responsible for the deaths. Did spiders follow the axman?" Amara asked.

"Not that I remember," TT replied.

"I say we don't rule out the shoes just yet, maybe we can do some research on royal boots and see if they're special, or maybe Rabbit and Nicholas can work on cracking what power it has. Maybe they're the only ones who can use it, being royals and all. I mean, the girls aren't, but maybe that's why they got rid of it. These boots could tell us everything about the murders. I mean, they're royal boots. What if the ministry is just as corrupt as we always sing it to be?"

"That's brilliant!" TT exclaimed. "I think we're onto something!"

"Except this could just be ordinary shoes." Aksel sighed.

"Well, as Amara said, this could be a thing only royals can use, or maybe we can crack its secret."

"I think I'm with Aksel on this," Lovetta began. "I mean, we already tried the geswutelian spell, and auras don't mean much. It's just a myth."

"But a blood spell could be locking this," TT replied.

***

"Ow!" Rabbit drew his hand away from the knife that Amara had dragged across his hand without warning. "You finger licker!" The blood dripped onto the shoes. Nothing happened.

"*Hmm*," Amara pondered, ignoring his friend's rage, "maybe it's Snowball blood." He went to walk toward Nicholas.

Nicholas drew out his wand. "I swear I'll burn you if you come near me with that thing." He backed onto the couch like a gargoyle.

"I'm telling you," Aksel began, "there's nothing to find in those dumb shoes."

"How about" – Clancy's eyes lit up – "we torture the girls to tell us the truth about the shoes!"

"You're sick," said Walter, who sat on the floor going through records.

"Yeah, no," said Lovetta. "How about… the truth potion."

"*Hmm*, the potion put TT through a lot of pain. So that's a no as well."

"Pain?" Rabbit cradled his bleeding hand. "You had no problem hurting me! You worm piper!"

***

Lulia couldn't find the shoes. It had been placed at the foot of her bed a few nights prior, and she was sure that they had been a gift from AC. She had been able to communicate with him, primarily through her dreams, but their conversations were always cut short. She found herself thinking about him even at school. She couldn't shake the feeling that there was a specific reason why he chose to talk to her. As the days went by, she became increasingly curious about AC. AC meant so much to her. It was like he was her friend that she had known all along, but it couldn't be. She hated making new friends, and the boy spoke more maturely than the kids her age. He spoke with grace.

Nevertheless, without the shoes, she still wanted to find out more about AC. Along with Flower and Beau, she had skipped school to head to the museum where AC said was one of his favorite places to go before he had met his doom.

They had searched the library for three hours before she had found a purple shield hanging with the initials AC inscribed at the top. Next to it was a purple medal.

"He seems like someone important," Flower stated.

***

The sun was beginning to shine weakly on the school building. Inside, the students had returned to classes and became more hopeful as they saw TT working alongside the Chaos group. There had been no more deaths since Varg and his friend.

TT, however, never indeed left her grim state. She wished that there was a spell to bring him back. Perhaps, Varg's death had a more significant meaning, hopefully considering it could've been at the hands of a royal. There had not been any more deaths. Maybe he was the last one that they needed to kill. Perhaps, they knew that they were on their trail and thought it was best to lay low because they were on high alert.

Some were still convinced Lovetta was behind the killings, but Jaxon had done his best writing about the hunt for the killer, trying to help prove her innocence. He was just as tired as the Chaos hearing the school talking poorly about their friend.

The ministry, concerned about Bliant's lost son and the king's creatures, still worked on the killing case, and since it had stopped, they decided to focus on the first two problems. 15 February came around, and the school cafeteria had never been more awkward. It was Lupercalia. No teen the night before had gotten much sleep, knowing that the school would be decorated with aura-colored anatomically correct paper hearts along the walls next to strung flowers the next day. Constant confetti fell from the ceiling. The Chaos group looked sickened, along with TT and Lovetta, unlike all the girls blushing, staring, and giggling with their crushes.

They all looked around, their faces contorted as if they had just tasted something awful. They shook their heads as if they were listening to heavy music as they tried to get the confetti out of their hair.

The day's events began in potions class, where they were taught how to make love bug potions. Later in the day, the Chaos group, though in separate classrooms, reacted the same when tiny, flying babies with arrows floated into the rooms. They ducked under their tables.

"Please!" Clancy looked to Amara in the art of music class. "Feed me poison!"

"So, Lovetta." Clancy turned to her as she also sat beneath her desk. "Any love cards to you?" he asked. She shook her head, almost embarrassed. "Good," he said.

Unwilling to cope with other classes filled with bombarding fluff balls of fairies, Clancy, with the help of Amara, shoved himself into his locker, where he would remain until the final bell of the day rang.

When the final bell rang, the Chaos members bolted out of the rooms, their books covering their heads. A letter appeared in front of Lovetta. Clancy stopped in his tracks, eyeing it and her. She took it, opened it, inside was a letter from someone with the initials MB. She stuffed it in her backpack.

"Who's it from?" Clancy asked sternly.

She shook her head. "I honestly don't know."

He eyed her before accepting her reply with a nod. They continued to run. She ran numbly, as her body was filled with joy, guilt, and confusion all at once. Clancy grabbed her hand to help her run. Two angels of love chased after them relentlessly as they desperately ran away.

An arrow struck Clancy's knee. He kneeled. "Oh no, it's got me." He grabbed onto Lovetta's arm, his eyes wide. His face ashed over, and he began to act robot-like. "Roses are red, and violets are blue, the scenery is romantic, and so are you."

He gasped in fear, ripped the arrow out of his knee, which oozed pink liquid, and struck it into Lovetta's side. He needed to know if he was her love too. The arrows worked in ways similar to truth potions, making lovers confess their love and bring people together – a kingdom-wide fertility technique.

"Ow!" Her face washed over. "Daisies are pretty, daffies have style, a beam is illuminating, and so is your smile." She clasped her hands over her mouth. He removed the arrow.

Clancy would've given all his fame away if it erased this moment from existence. He stood to his feet which he couldn't feel.

"Well, off I go," Clancy said awkwardly. "See ya." He saluted.

"My house, it's uh… that way too."

"Well... I'm going back inside to uh... study." He rubbed the back of his head feverishly as he passed her.

Lovetta bent down and picked up the notebook she had dropped when he struck her with an arrow. She crossed her arms as she tried to convince herself that she didn't care.

"Sad on Lupercalia?" A gorgeously handsome man approached from behind, watching her watch Clancy walk into the school. "Guess he doesn't like you very much."

Lovetta covered her face with her hair and turned to walk away. The allure of the man was strong, but something was unnerving and disturbing about him.

"What? Didn't you like my valentine?" he asked.

She turned around, snarling. Clancy ran back out of the building to see her wand pressed against the much older man's throat. Clancy ran over, pulled her away, and they ran off.

"Who was that?" he asked as soon as the man was out of sight. They stopped running.

"I don't know, I don't believe I know him, but I do feel like I know him – somehow."

He turned her face to his. Their faces close, they could smell the sugar lion drink from their lunches lingering off their breath. He had only expected to look at her face to see if the love he saw when the arrow was in her was still there. They were overpowered by their senses, feeling a rush that neither had felt before. Like a force, they pulled in closer. Their eyes clenched as they locked lips.

It wasn't until the heat faded when Lovetta noticed something odd about the shoes that now lay on Clancy's bedroom floor. The shoes had zero water damage from the rain that had soaked it the night before they found it. She had only noticed as it lay next to her book, which she had spilled some water on when the angels first invaded her classroom. Some droplets could still be seen. She tried to explain this to Clancy, who only responded with moans and groans as he lay in bed half asleep.

She brought her knees up to her chest as she examined the shoes. She threw her legs off the bed and carried the black blanket around her. She bravely walked toward the desk and sat down, daring to do what everyone else was too afraid to do – she put the shoes on her feet.

"Hello," a boy said in front of her. He was short and slim, with blue eyes and dark brown hair. He was wearing an outdated purple Galdorwide High uniform.

Her heart fluttered. It worked.

"Who are you? How did you come across the Haunter Shoes? Where is Lulia?" His body would fade in and out of view as he spoke.

She was taken aback by his sudden appearance and barrage of questions. She hesitated for a moment before responding.

"My name is Lovetta. Lulia threw them at my friend. She's at home." She was eager to hear his reply. The boy's expression softened as he listened to Lovetta's response.

"I see," he said, nodding slowly. "Thank you for answering my questions. I apologize for startling you." He paused for a moment before continuing. "Bring the shoes to Angel Carter so I can help her and her kingdom. She's my only hope. Lulia hasn't been hurt by one of the king's creatures?"

Lovetta breathed a sigh of relief as the boy's demeanor relaxed. She shook her head in response to his question about Lulia. "No, she's safe for now," she replied. "If I bring these shoes to Angel, what shall I tell her?" Her heart was hammering. The shoes were given to her friends by a giant spider, perhaps one of the king's creatures. Could this boy help, or was he just another pawn in the king's game? Lovetta took a deep breath, trying to calm her racing thoughts. She knew that she had to tread carefully in this dangerous world.

'Please tell her that the shoes are a gift from an old friend. I know the princess very well if I were to explain – well – you wouldn't believe me. My existence in this kingdom had been wiped away with a single lie. When I turned eleven, I was attacked and nearly killed by someone I trusted very well. I wished that the woman would've been caught and tried, but I hear she's doing very well for herself. You may have heard the lie about me, Prince Aidan Carter, who had gone missing in a freak accident while traveling with his younger sister, Princess Bella Carter.

'Let me show you something,' the boy said.

She glanced nervously over her shoulder and to Clancy. What was he going to show her?

The boy retrieved his wand from his pocket as the room grew darker. Purple light emitted from it as he pointed it at the wall, revealing a concealed door. The girl stood up, her legs slightly shaking, and followed him inside.

Inside, she saw a young boy with dark brown hair and piercing blue eyes wearing a purple schoolboy suit completed with a jacket, shorts, and knee-high socks. Beside him stood a young girl with thick, bushy brown hair and thick eyebrows. She was wearing a dark purple dress with white lace cuffs and a collar. Suddenly, Lovetta recognized the young boy in front of her as Aidan Carter, the eldest child of Delanie Carter. However, he appeared much more youthful than he should have been, still wearing the same uniform. This realization was followed by a dreadful thought that she might be witnessing his death, as he had not simply disappeared. Something more ominous must have happened. They stood in a circular room, Lovetta recognized it, the ministry's office. On the walls hung the paintings of previous rulers, Bella's picture yet to be fastened on the wall. Unlike the present day, bookshelves lined the walls, and the glass floor was tiled.

"I said I was sorry," the young boy said in a sophisticated tone. In his hands, he had been holding the diary. Bella had been staring at the ground, frowning, her fists clenched. "Honest, Bella, I'm sorry. I didn't mean to disturb you." He sighed before he walked over to the small, rectangular window. His eyes widened when he saw that the sky had turned a deep red. He looked back to his sister, who was wiggling her fingers.

The door began to rattle. His hair blew around wildly as a wind picked up in the room.

"Bella!" he scorned angrily rather than frightened.

Bella didn't move. The nervousness began to show on his face as it grew tighter.

"Sit down," he tried to order. "I hadn't read it. This is a journal that my father had given me. I was joking. He gave us the same book." He explained. She tightened her fists. "I was lying saying Dad would send you to an orphanage if he read it because I didn't even read it, but now, with this reaction of yours, I am curious to know what you wrote in yours. I mean, we've only had it for a half-hour, mine's empty." He lifted his journal.

Her back was still turned to him, her face reddened. "You weren't lying about the orphanage," she said through gritted teeth. "I heard Father telling you the truth about me, how he's not my real father. Father doesn't want anyone to know the truth. I guess I'll have to live my life as a Carter."

"Carter or not, you're still my sister and the princess, as long as I have a say about it," Aidan tried to reassure her, his confidence returning as his sister was finally talking with an ounce of sense.

"She even named me after that Nullum, Isabel. She gave me the middle name Ashford, the name of the village he lived in. Isabelle Ashford Carter, but who knows what my true last name would've been, probably something that started with O' or Mc. Isabelle Ashford O'Sullivan."

"No matter the circumstances, he doesn't want anyone to know. As far as we're all concerned, you're a true princess of Galdorwide."

Lovetta's heart leaped. She didn't want to miss a single thing.

"Precisely." Bella drew up her head. "My dear brother, you must see how foolish I'd be not to take this opportunity to bring a new reign to the kingdom, in light of a recent tragedy – the disappearance of the poor, eleven-year-old boy, meant to be king one day. Don't worry. You'll be safe."

Aidan's eyes widened. "Bella! Stop it... you're starting to scare me."

"What do you mean?" Bella asked with a squeaky voice as she slowly turned her head to face him.

"Bella," Aidan said quickly. He sank back into his chair. "As the prince and soon to be king, I order you to leave," he spoke, more humbled than usual.

Bella scorned before slumping out of the room. The room began to follow the young Bella as she walked down the steps from the ministry's office.

As she emerged out of the building, a large hound was waiting outside for her. The hound looked at the girl who froze in position as her brain wandered through many thoughts, plots, and schemes. She bit her lip and furrowed her bushy brows.

Then, as though she had finally made a decision, she hurried off, the creature followed behind her. They didn't see another person until she reached the entrance hall of the castle when a tall witch with long, sleeking light-brown hair called for her from the other end.

"What have you been doing up so late? And where's your brother?"

Lovetta gaped at the sight of the man. It was the young king who, to her, looked a lot like Clancy and his father. They all shared the same height, long hair, and piercing blue eyes, but the king had a much lighter color of hair and a few years on both Clancy and his father.

"We went to the office," Bella answered, not giving her father a complete answer.

"Well, hurry off to bed," ordered the king, who gave the young girl a penetrating stare as if his look would make her act out his order immediately. "Best not to roam about the kingdom this late anyway, not with all that's been happening."

He sighed, bid his daughter goodnight, and strolled off, trusting she would listen. Bella watched him, waiting until he was out of sight, before moving quickly through the dining hall, and then down the steps to the dungeon. She was in hot pursuit.

She walked down, unlocked a cell with a key her hound had fetched, and opened the cell. Inside was a young girl who looked to be in her early twenties with long, brown hair. She was huddled in the corner, sleeping. Bella blew out the torches that lit up the cramped, black cell. She didn't shut the large, metal cell door completely as she poked her eye out to get a view. She stood statue-like, peering out of the cell as she watched her familiar leave.

Lovetta's eyes grew heavy as the room had remained still for two minutes straight. All she could see was Bella staring out the door, waiting for someone or something. And just when Lovetta began to wonder just how long the room would remain like this, something beyond the cell door could be heard.

Someone was creeping through the dungeon. The footsteps approached the cell, and Bella backed herself against the wall so that when the door opened, the door would cover her. She remained as quiet as a shadow. The door creaked open, and a hoarse whisper could be heard from the entry.

"Tonight's the night, Teej. I'm going to get you out of here." There was something familiar about the voice – it was Aidan.

Suddenly, Bella jumped from out behind the door, her wand drawn. The room was dark. She could only make out the image of the bushy-haired girl with her wand pointed at the outline of her brother, who now crouched closer to the girl who was startled awake.

"Hello, brother." Bella sneered.

Aidan jumped to huddle the girl who still lay on the floor, shocked. "What're you doing down here, Belle?" he asked.

Bella stepped closer. "I'm going to have to do something. I need to know if given a chance, Father would let me be queen over Angel."

"What do you mean?"

"All that matters is I'm not going to hurt you. I want to make sure that I am worthy in our father's eyes. I just need to exercise how far he thinks of me as his daughter."

"You don't have to do anything crazy. Just ask him!" He backed against the wall, no longer protecting Teej, knowing that he was the one that Bella wanted to harm. He drew out his wand, refusing to not put up a fight.

"You or the girl?" Bella brought her wand down to point at Teej.

"You're crazy! Me, do whatever you want to me."

Bella drew her wand back up. "You were always so good to our sister." She eyed Teej before flicking her eyes to her brother.

The spell she cast lit up the entire dungeon. The magic was so powerful it sent Bella flying out of the cell. Teej screamed in desperation as she saw her brother's body slowly dissipate. She couldn't believe that he was gone forever. Her pain and sorrow were overwhelming, and she didn't know how to cope with it. She had always been close to her brother; now that he was gone, she felt lost and alone.

Bella rubbed the back of her head, then stood, ironing her dress with her hands. She placed her wand back into her boot and paced over to Teej. The girl shook her head as tears rolled down her cheeks. Bella smirked at her older sister before running out of the cell.

"HOW COULD YOU?" Teej called out as she tried to chase Bella out, but she was too late. Bella had slammed the cell door on her face.

The edges of the room faded until Lovetta was staring at a black abyss as her stomach turned.

Before Lovetta, trembling and shaking, could regain her breath, the door opened. Amara and Aksel walked in. With a raise of his brows, Aksel raised his hands in surrender and walked out.

"There you two are," said Amara, relieved. "Everything okay?" He noticed his friend nearly naked and distraught.

Amara's eyes traveled to the ghostly shoes upon her feet.

CHAPTER 14

The Chaos group had always known mayhem to follow the queen, hence why they adored her despite complaining about how she ruled things. During her first year reigning, Galdorwide was attacked by a swarm of dragons only to be saved from a pirate that Bella despised. They all knew that she took her power seriously and would take down anything that got in her way. The previous year, rumors of her killing her father had circulated but now, with proof that she was why her brother disappeared, her killing the king sounded even more likely and would explain his promise to bring down the kingdom from beyond the grave. They could all believe the story Lovetta had described, but they also had to question whether or not the ghost was a trusted source. After all, who was the girl Teej that the siblings had addressed as a sister?

Lovetta half-wished that she had never discovered the truth of the shoes. She repeatedly recounted the same story to the nine Chaos members, answering each of their questions that she had almost always heard before.

"Bella might have done this," said Lucian. "Maybe even her killing the king could be true. It'd explain his constant attacks on the kingdom."

"How much longer do you think we should wait until we give Angel the Haunter's Shoes?" Aksel eyed the shoes.

"We always knew that the queen had been power-hungry," Lovetta said miserably. "To me, everything makes sense."

"Bella seems like a whiny crybaby. Why did she care whether or not the king saw her as a real daughter? I mean, she was a princess, wasn't that good enough?"

"Speaking of," Mike began, a tone of concern in his voice, "who was the girl in the dungeon? Queen Elizabeth had only ever been pregnant three times. How could that girl be their sister and show less resemblance than Bella, who was at the very least still Elizabeth's daughter?"

"All that matters," Lovetta continued, frustrated, "is that we know what these shoes are."

"I do understand her frustration, though," said Walter, adding zero to the conversation and more to the pile of random things being blurted out. "He joked about sending her to the orphanage because of her not being a Carter. I'd be pretty hurt and angry too."

"Enough to hurt someone you loved?" Mike challenged. "I can't believe the queen would do that. How can we feel safe under her care if she's willing to hurt her own family?"

"Mike," Lovetta turned to him. "You've been working closely with the queen. How does she seem?"

"Nice. Crazy nice. Maybe a little too nice."

"Oh, nice?" Annie challenged. "Is she nice?" Mike smirked before wrapping his arm around his stiff wife.

"How about…" Amara began. His voice was hesitant. He never usually talked much during big group situations. "We try to save the kingdom without Angel's help?"

Mike made a disgusted face. "Could you imagine what that bloke's attitude might be if he finds out he ignored his one wish?" In the end, they decided that they couldn't trust the ghost.

***

Lulia, Flower, and Beau found themselves bored, no longer hearing the disembodied voices or feelings AC's touch. Instead, the two girls got to watch their brothers and their friends obsess over the shoes. TT had almost entirely gotten over the anger stage when it came to grieving her brother.

The school went back to feeling only a little fear toward the Chaos group, and everything seemed to go back to order. The Chaos members' concerns about Brad's death, Varg's death, and the shoes had now been transferred onto the fears of what programs they'd be taking next year.

"I'll take whatever you take," Amara told Lovetta.

"We're going into our third year, Amara. What we choose has to be based on what we want to be in the future," Lovetta explained.

Amara shrugged and began to select all the ones Lovetta and Clancy had checked off so that he'd at the very least be put in with one of his two friends. All of them were putting checks next to the variety of new open programs while Annie and Mike were checking off which apprenticeships they wanted to take.

"I don't want to take the art of healing." Lovetta sighed.

"Understandable," Mike said with a kind smile. "You don't have to do anything you don't want."

"*Hmm*, I do want to go on to teach Terra arts when I graduate, so maybe Terra arts defense?" she pondered. Mike nodded with a smile.

"Mike," Annie began in a sing-song voice. "So you're apprenticing for the church, right? And you're also a part of the ministry and in a band. Well, what if I become a stay-at-home mom? Please, and I can just not worry about filling out the job applications."

He looked at her and kept his smile. "Sure."

She gasped and brought her hands to her face in shock. "Really? You're the best!" She wrapped her tiny arms around him. The rest of the table watched on with smiles as they watched their 'mom and dad' share a cute moment.

Mike looked back to Lovetta. "Anyway, you don't need to worry about the art of healing. Both me and Terry are masters in it. You'll be safe with us."

Aksel was the only one who didn't converse during the selection. He had his forehead buried in his hand as he looked at the papers with stress, not knowing which classes to take. Heck, he didn't even know what he wanted to be in the future besides being a musician. However, Mike had encouraged them to master in at least one other class besides the art of music. Lucian had his eyes closed and would drop his finger onto the page at random and put a check next to whatever class his finger had landed next to.

"Lovetta!" Amara exclaimed. "Are you seriously checking off every program? Are you trying to kill me?"

"Good girl." Mike winked. Mike then noticed Aksel's evident struggle. "Aksel, choose whatever you want. I'd recommend art of the gangwuce as I had." The table burst with laughter. "All right, all right," Mike calmed everyone. "I think it could straighten you out. You could take Heofsij studies. I think that every witch should try to learn about other realms. We aren't just limited to this one. You may even want to take up a career they have in the other realm. Or how about the art of taming animals? You like being outdoors." The table snickered. "Sorry," Mike began sarcastically. "Galdorwide High doesn't offer dark arts, necromancy, or Chaos magic. Anyway, Aksel, pick out what you want and play to your strengths. Maybe pick the classes you had this year that had the best marks."

But the only thing Aksel felt like he was good at was music. In the end, he decided to check off the classes that TT had chosen, so at the very least, if he didn't like the courses, at least he'd share the course with her, and if she was good, she could help him out.

***

Lovetta's good mood didn't last long. When she got home, she was greeted by her two brothers waiting outside of her bedroom.

"Don't get mad," said Justin through his missing front teeth.

"We—we don't know who did it, but we swear it wasn't us," said Hugh.

Watching their sister fearfully, they pushed open the door. The contents of her dresser had been thrown all across the room. Her favorite gray jacket had been torn apart. The sheets of her bed had been ripped off. Contents that once lay in her bedside cabinet now rested on her bed.

Lovetta walked toward her bed, her mouth open. She was treading on some ripped paper from *Travels with Werewolves*. She began to place all the objects that were once in her nightstand back inside. Her two brothers helped her make her bed as her father walked in and bit his tongue as his brain fought to swear.

"What happened?" he asked.

"No idea." She looked back to him, worried. His eyes trailed to her cloak that lay on the floor, its pockets out-turned.

"Someone was looking for something." He stalked in. "Is anything missing?"

"Oh no." She bolted to her closet door that had been open, and to her horror, she knew what was missing, the shoes. "My shoes, they're gone."

"What?" Her father grew angry.

Lovetta hurried to pass her father and out the front door. She barged inside Amara's house to find him sitting in a cardboard box reading *Vampirism Made Easy* as a green, velvet fedora sat on his head.

He was aghast as she explained what happened.

"But… who would know you have it? It has to be someone who we talked to."

"I know."

***

Lulia, Flower, and Beau walked down the school's marble steps when AC's voice returned. *"Get... Me... Out."*

Lulia screeched, sending Flower jumping back and making Beau stumble down the five remaining steps. "His voice! I can hear it again, can't you?"

Beau shook his head, wide-eyed, as his heart struggled to relax. Flower, however, clapped her hand to her forehead.

"I forgot to tell you." She looked around cautiously before continuing. "Come with me to the library," she said as she sprinted out of the building.

"What did she forget to tell us?" Beau asked, concerned.

"Who knows, but hopefully, it's something about AC."

"But why do we have to go to the library? Why can't she tell us now?"

Lulia shrugged. As they ran after Flower, Lulia kept her ears strained, hoping to hear his voice again. Soon, Lulia's ears swarmed with the sound of panting and the breaking of twigs beneath them, along with the sound of air whooshing.

As she ran, her mind was still on the disembodied voice. She was taking off her baby blue cloak as she began to sweat. Her only comfort was that they were almost at the library.

***

Aksel, Walter, and Lucian had arrived at the gym for tonight's Crashnet game. They were short on players, but TT offered to join their side to face off against the other team's four players, as Lulia and Flower didn't show. Today was the first official game, and great, roaring cheers stemmed from the stands. Before the match began, the four of them brought themselves to a huddle to think up a game plan.

Just as the two teams readied their wands, Mr. Bernard stomped in. He projected his voice so that everyone in the gym could hear him. "Everyone is to go home! The school will be out for both today and tomorrow as, yet again, the school has suffered a loss. I ask that everyone leave the gym except for you four." He looked to the Chaos group. When everyone exited the gym, Mr. Bernard approached the students. "Do any of you happen to know where Mr. Clancy Scaasi is?"

"Home, he's sick." Walter failed at hiding a smirk.

"Well, I suggest you go straight to the Scaasi home and alert Clancy, his parents, and his siblings that Miss Flower Scaasi has been attacked off the school properties. She was brought to the hospital ward a few moments ago, and it is not looking well. I suggest that one of you stay."

"I'll stay." Lucian gave a stern nod before hopping off the stage, his legs weak.

Students were swarming the waiting room, trying to catch a peek of the hospital ward as doctors and nurses flew in and out of the room. Most of them looked eager with curiosity, while others stared on, worried. Lucian walked up the marble staircase, his body slowly growing numb with each step. He couldn't feel his face, and the corner of his eyes burned with tears. His heart pounded, hoping only to be able to comfort his young friend.

Lucian entered the waiting room, where Dr. Caressa was awaiting him with a clipboard. "There's been another attack, a double attack," her voice was soft. "It's quite a shock, your friend, so young. We're doing everything we can."

Lucian's stomach somersaulted as Caressa pushed open the door. The ward was empty besides the two beds; a man in his early fifties laid in one of the beds. He was swarmed by plenty of people, including a royal knight with long, black hair with a scar down his cheek. Next to him stood a short man with blue eyes and light brown hair. Three other males and one female student stood around the bed, crying. A lively woman with short blonde hair cried over him, her wails making it evident her heart was breaking. One of the boys, dressed in dirty clothes, was patting her back. Lucian looked at the other bed across from the man to see Flower laying still, nurses working all around her.

"When her two friends brought us to her, we found her on the path just outside the library. She was covered in wounds which we tended to at the scene," Caressa began. "She lost a lot of blood." Lucian looked to the young girl he considered a sister to see her chest covered with pads set in place to soak up the blood. "We brought her here on a carriage. It was too risky for her to go on a broom or through a transportation spell. We're unsure what has attacked her, and her friends claim that they hadn't seen anything. They said they heard her struggle, and when they caught up to her, they saw her on the ground, with multiple wounds to her chest and neck. No suspect in sight."

"Caressa." One of the nurses tending to Flower looked to the doctor. "She has a resp of 23, BP 80 over 60."

"Okay." Caressa looked down at her chart. "Grab 1 liter of O Neg blood." She looked to another nurse. "Give her half a liter of an adrenalizing potion." The two nurses dispersed, leaving seven more around her.

Flower began to cough as an oxygen mask covered her face. Lucian ran to her side and grabbed her hand. "You're okay, you're okay," he repeated like a mantra, trying to hold back his tears and remain strong for her.

"Quick!" Caressa called to the nurses, looking to the nurse across from her. "Our main concern is the wound on the side of her neck." Looking to Lucian, she said, "We're going to need you to wait outside the curtain. We're going to operate."

Reluctant, Lucian released her cold hand and stepped away, allowing the nurse to close off Flower's bed with the curtains. He bit the nail of his thumb anxiously. He looked at the opposing bed, where the man's face was now covered with a blanket. Only the weeping woman and the young girl remained. She was rubbing the sobbing woman's back. He turned his gaze away and over to the curtain.

"Patient has agonal rhythm," he heard one nurse say.

"Grab an intubation tube," Caressa ordered.

A nurse rushed from out of the curtain and over to the storage room beside the offices. The nurse who had to grab the blood finally returned, she entered the curtain.

Once Flower's condition stabilized, Lucian was allowed to see her, but she was still unconscious. He stayed by her side, holding her hand and praying for her to recover. The day's events had shaken him, and he couldn't help but wonder who could have been responsible for what had happened.

***

Seppo awoke to loud bangs on his front door. He sat up in his bed, not wanting to move. He had a bad feeling in the pit of his chest.

Amara, who was showering, stepped out and wrapped his lower body in a brown towel. He dragged his fingers through his long, wet hair. At the very least, he wanted to look presentable for whoever was eagerly knocking at his door. Amara slipped off the towel and put on a pair of baggy shorts as he hurriedly put on a short-sleeved green dress shirt. He headed toward the door as he buttoned it up. Amara passed by the fireplace mantel that held his band's music awards, glancing at them proudly. The knocks continued and grew wilder as if tons of people were knocking on the other side. Amara tried following the sounds of the lapses, some came from the top, and some came from the bottom.

"Seppo! You lazy hole wiper!" He heard Walter shout.

Amara backtracked his steps and entered his brother's room to find him sitting on the bed, staring at the wall across from him. "Hey." He tapped his shoulder, Seppo continued to stare. "Hey." He began to gently shake Seppo's shoulder. He snapped out of his trance and looked up to his younger brother. "I think Walter's here. Sounds important." Seppo gave him a nod, and Amara walked past the dirty kitchen back to the front door.

Clancy lay in bed, his arm around Lovetta. Stirring awake, Clancy rubbed his eye then placed his arm back around her, gently pushing her off him. He sat up at the edge of his bed and scratched his head. Clancy inhaled deeply, reaching over to his nightstand where his wand lay. He picked it up and walked to the washroom. Placing the rod beside him on the sink, Clancy turned the tap and began to wash his face. He looked at the mirror with a grimace on his face as a knock came from his front door.

Lucian woke up suddenly in the hospital waiting room and heard a commotion from behind Flower's curtain. He was frightened to see a group of people gathering around. He rushed toward the curtain, his heart racing with fear. Lucian tried to make out the chatter from the nurses.

"*Elektrisch*! *Elektrisch*! Start chest compressions."

"She's in asystole," said one nurse.

"I need a scalpel," Caressa ordered.

Lucian regretted it, but he looked to the floor where blood began to pool. The puddle extended toward his feet.

"Her color is coming back," said one nurse.

Blue and Alexis, Flower's parents, were spending a blissful morning on the beach. The tiny, athletically built woman with hazel eyes walked up the stones of the beach, naked. Tattoos of black flowers were printed beautifully along her back. The wind howled. Blue lay beneath wool blankets wearing a gray t-shirt and green beanie. With his long hair, he looked almost identical to his son. He stirred awake, looking behind him. He furrowed his brows, sat up, and looked over to his wife, who was putting her sundress back on. She wiped her arms off with a towel and began to walk over to Blue, who took off his beanie, creating a stir of long, black locks to fall below his shoulders.

"Good morning," she greeted.

He ran his fingers through his hair. "Good morning."

She began to dry off her long, blonde hair with a towel. He stood and wrapped his arms around her waist.

"How come we didn't go home last night?" he asked.

"You were out cold," she explained.

"I was pretty wasted, *huh*?"

"Yeah, two bottles of honey badger blitz will do that to you." She chuckled.

"*Mmm-hmm.*"

"*Elektrisch*! Everybody clear. *Elektrisch*! Get me another adrenalizing potion. Check her pulse."

"No cardiac activity," a nurse replied solemnly.

Caressa sighed. "Time of death, 9.10 a.m."

Before she could open up the curtain, Lucian fell to his knees.

Rabbit bit his nails as he sat in the Misfit Crew's basement. "How?"

"I don't know," replied Lucian hoarsely. "Caressa said she'd been... she'd been attacked."

"By who?" Rabbit asked, starting on a new nail.

"Her friends who had been with her hadn't seen what happened," Lucian replied.

"Flower's dead," Lovetta said aloud numbly.

"Where're your parents?" Lucian glared at Clancy.

"They went out last night to some bar. They never returned."

"Have you tried contacting them?" Lucian asked.

"Yeah." He stared vacantly.

"Did they leave around the same time Flower had been attacked?" Amara asked.

Everyone in the room looked at him. Clancy glared. "What's that supposed to mean, Amara?" he asked. Amara shrugged and leaned back into his seat. "My parents didn't have anything to do with Flower's attack."

"Okay," Amara said quietly.

"What?" Clancy turned around angrily, making everyone's hearts jump.

"I said, okay." He spoke clearly and oddly didn't seem as afraid as everyone else.

"You need to find your parents. They need to know." Lucian turned to Clancy, his voice stern.

"Should we be afraid?" Lovetta asked as two streaks of mascara ran down either side of her face.

"I think so, love," said Seppo. "Four people dead. Who knows who could be next?" he asked. Lovetta began to cry again.

"What about her friends?" Rabbit asked. "They were with her."

Lucian nodded. He looked to Clancy. "Go find your parents. Rabbit, let's go talk to the kids." He began to walk up the stairs, Rabbit followed. Clancy stared at the table.

Mike and Alexis began to cry. It was always hard watching someone so strong be hurt. Blue shuddered and shook his head. "Who—who attacked her?"

"We don't know," replied Gavin. He, too, fought against his tears. He remembered going to the hospital ward when Alexis was giving birth to her fourth child.

"We can't let them cut her up, man." He began to cry and turned his back to everyone. He buried his face in his hand as he sniffled. He could barely breathe as mucous streamed out from his nose. "Head bastard!" he shouted before picking up a twine bar stool and chucking it to the other side of the yard, breaking the seat into pieces. He groaned then wiped his face. "Merlin." He buried his face once more and began to sob.

Alexis stood up from the poolside, her face red, and began to stroke her husband's hair. Gavin stood and placed a supporting hand on his friend's shoulder.

The gate to the backyard creaked open. "Lucian?" the voice asked. Caressa peeked her head through. "Hi, I'm so sorry, I meant to find Lucian, but I think this actually will be better in one of your hands. It's her belongings." The Haunter's Shoes were inside a clear bag that she held up.

Clancy stood to his feet and eyed it. "Thanks." He outstretched his arm and took it from her.

Rabbit and Lucian strode to the back of John Scaasi's backyard, where they saw Lulia and Beau crying by the poolside. Walking over to them, the kids looked over their shoulders at them with wet faces.

"Is she okay?" Lulia looked up to Lucian but immediately knew the answer when she saw his bloodshot eyes and stiff face. "I couldn't stay by her side. I ran for help." She shook her head and sniffed. "When Caressa got to her, she was still alive, and when she was in the hospital ward, she was still alive."

"Did you see who did it?" Lucian asked.

"It all happened too fast," she explained. "Merlin, I can't believe she's dead." She stood to her feet, her hand cupping her mouth as she sobbed. She brushed her hand back through her red curly hair. Lucian embraced her.

"Beau, I'll walk you home. You kids have to be more careful."

***

The queen returned to her castle from the ministry's office. She stood on her balcony and held a meeting. "As of late, this kingdom has suffered four losses, varying in age. We can't say who's safe. Everyone must respect the new curfew. They must be in their homes by nine in the evening. After that time, no one is to leave the walls of their home. At school, the ministry members will escort the students from class to class. No student will roam the halls without the supervision of one of the ministry members. All after-school activities are to be postponed as well as any evening events held at local businesses."

The Galdorians packed outside the queen's front yard listened as she rolled up the scroll from which she read. She then addressed the crowd, her eyes forward and meeting her civilians' eyes.

"I feel that I must add that I have never been so distressed. The school will likely close if more attacks occur, whether on the property or not. It is not safe to be roaming about even during the day. I urge anyone that has any idea who may be behind these attacks to come forth. If so, upon entering the castle, Maddox will not be there to greet you as he is mourning his brother's death. You will meet with Eldoris, a servant of mine. Also, Teddy will be taking time off to mourn this death as well. So, if you have news, you will be greeted by Mike. If you have no useful information, you may all go home as you are dismissed."

She awkwardly turned away from the crowd. Mike, who stood behind her to her right, saw her cringe. She always had a hard time concluding her meetings. She sulked inside her bedroom that once used to be her father's.

As she left, the crowd immediately began to speak to one another. "That's two Viridis and two Caeruls down," said a student from Galdorwide who held up two fingers on each of his hands as if he were keeping score.

"I say we question the queen, no Pures have been hurt, and we know she's a fan of Alets who she claims to be brave," said Walter. "I mean, I don't think it's a coincidence with how much stress Galdorwide puts on our auras. Who knows, this could be a scheme from the ministry or the king. I say we put a stop to the Pures!"

The crowd nodded and cheered. Mike looked down from the balcony, eyeing his friends; he was looking pale and stunned. Typically, Mike was the kind of person to let his views be heard, but he remained quiet.

"Mike's in shock," Clancy whispered to his friends. "Maybe we're onto something."

Lucian was only half-listening. He couldn't wipe the image of Flower lying still and gray on the bed like a statue. Lucian could still see the pool of blood that stained his knees as he fell. If whoever did this wasn't punished, he'd surely go mad. Lucian's stomach turned as he looked at all his friends. He couldn't bear to lose anyone else.

"What're we going to do?" Amara asked in Clancy's ear. "Do we suspect the queen? The king's followers?"

"We've got to go and talk to Mike." Clancy nodded, making up his mind. "I honestly don't think it's the queen, but Mike looks ill. Maybe he knows something that we don't."

"But how will we speak to him?"

"I think…" – Clancy did his usual dramatic pause – "we have some information about the case we'd like to tell him."

It was their only chance to get into the castle without raising suspicion or too much attention. They waited until everyone who went into the court to speak to Mike had left. If they were going to talk to him, it was going to be without a line-up.

As soon as they entered, Mike eyed them and motioned them to follow him. They walked through the dark corridors of the castle in areas not meant to be trek. It wasn't as glorious as one would hope.

The castle was crowded for this late in the day. Royals, knights, and servants roamed the halls. Clancy and Amara began to think that they wouldn't find any private place to speak. Mike turned around and hushed them after Clancy ungraciously swore after stubbing his toe on the base of a displayed suit of armor. Just ahead of them stood a brooding knight who eyed the denim and black-clothed boys. With relief, Mike opened an oak door with ease. A large, black hound growled, and crossbows lined the walls.

"Woah!" Amara's jaw dropped.

"What is this place?" Clancy asked.

"Nothing... Nothing... Just ignore everything, all right? Sit down. I'll make tea."

Mike made tea almost every day, but they had never seen him struggle as his long, slim hand trembled, almost knocking everything off of the small counter space and almost spilling the boiling liquid all over himself.

"Are you okay?" Clancy asked. Mike continued to zombie around.

The two of them exchanged worried glances before looking up to their friend, who was usually the only one with a good head on his shoulders. He walked back over to the counter and began to slice into a mince pie. Mike was cutting two slices before there was a knock at the door.

Mike dropped the pie as Amara and Clancy exchanged nervous looks before being ordered to hide in the back corner of the room behind a couch. Mike walked toward the door and turned to look at the corner to make sure they were hidden. He reached for the nearest crossbow then opened the door.

"Good evening, Mike."

It was the queen. She entered, looking deadly serious, and was followed in by Arthur and Ian Morgan, whose hair was rumpled. He was wearing a green pin-striped suit, an emerald tie, and the black ministry cloak.

"I have to sneeze," Clancy whispered. Amara nudged him harshly, queuing him to be quiet and fight the urge to sneeze.

Mike, who had gone pale and sweaty, dropped himself into the chair his friends crouched behind. He looked to the queen and then over to

Arthur.

"Too bad." The queen roamed about the room, her arms folded. "Four people struck down by monsters at the hands of my father. The kingdom can't know this, and for now, if I don't want a riot to break out. I will need to arrest someone, just until the matters are handled."

"I know what you're thinking, but not me! I'm a nobleman, I plan to be a pastor as well as a ministry member, I can't let people think that I'm some killer!"

"I want it understood that by doing this, I guarantee you a spot in the ministry after it's all settled. I didn't want to do this… but after the meeting… I heard some nasty stuff about overthrowing me," she explained. Mike rolled his eyes, knowing it was his friends who had been talking ill of her. "A queen can never be too cautious."

"But, why me? My wife is pregnant. I have to be there for her when she gives birth. She'll never forgive me if I'm not." His brown eyes were full of a fire that no one had seen in him before. "How will the kingdom feel if they think a ministry member was the one who committed these crimes? There'd be mayhem."

"Are you questioning me? This will be a test, one where I will know if you'll do what's asked of you come time to be a part of the ministry. I have been told that we only have one more creature before the final one. It is the final creature that your Gangwuce powers will not be able to destroy. So after you destroy the next beast, I will throw you into Skogen prison, where you will remain a prisoner until the final beast is defeated. I can't have my people turn on me. Another creature for you to defeat has been foretold to me in a dream to come tonight. A spider. I am putting you and your friends on this mission." She peered over the couch and over to Amara and Clancy, who slowly lifted their heads. "I want to see their potential."

Amara quickly stood to his feet. "Put me in prison, not him."

Bella stretched out her hand to caress his face. "Aww… aren't you just the sweetest. Fine. After tonight, you will be arrested on account of the monsters and will be freed once your friend Rabbit defeats the final monster."

There was a loud rap at the door. Bella motioned the boys to sit back down in their hidden position. She walked to the door and answered it. The boys peeked and gasped when they saw Kenneth Riley walk in.

He was wearing a long, black cloak and a cold but satisfied smile. The hound in the room growled once more.

"What are you doing here?" The queen sneered.

"I have the unfortunate news that the emperor has signed the agreement to have you step down from your throne. We feel that you don't have the right touch. There have been four attacks in less than a year in your kingdom. Two just yesterday, correct? At this rate, we'll lose half of this kingdom's population, not to mention all those who were lost during the attack of the dragons. We all no longer want this kingdom to suffer any more losses."

"Oh, now see here, Mr. Riley," began Arthur, looking alarmed. "She will be making an arrest tonight."

"Oh." Mr. Riley smirked and looked as if he were hiding a laugh. "Nonetheless, the de-crowning of the queen is coming from the emperor. She has had attacks happen to her people, all of which were fatal," said Mr. Riley smoothly.

"See here, Riley," Arthur began, trying to keep composure despite the sweat dripping from his auburn mustache. "Five attacks in one year isn't too bad. I mean, Galdorwide isn't known for its pleasantry. If not her to stop these attacks, then who?"

"That remains to be seen," said Mr. Riley with a nasty smile. "But twelve people, including the emperor, have agreed to this, signatures and all."

Mike leaped to his feet, his curly, brown hair scraping the ceiling of the small room. "But you don't have the signatures of the queen's ministry. I say they should have a vote!" He started nervously but ended strong.

"Dear, dear, the temper of you Chaos boys will get you in trouble one day. I'd advise that you do not show that attitude toward the Skogen guards when the day comes. Surely, they won't tolerate it."

"You can't take Bella!" shouted Mike, ignoring Mr. Riley. "Take her away and the kingdom won't stand a chance!" Mike's shouts sent the hound cowering behind the couch along with Amara and Clancy.

"Calm yourself, Mike," said Bella sharply but with a smile. She looked at Mr. Riley. "If the emperor wishes my removal, I surely will agree."

"But..." Arthur stuttered.

"No!" Mike growled.

Bella had not taken her emerald eyes off of Mr. Riley's icy blue ones. "However," Bella began, speaking unusually soft, "you will find that even if I am not queen, I will be willing to help my people at any cost." Bella, from the corner of her eye, looked to the space where Amara and Clancy huddled.

"Admirable sentiments," said Riley as he bowed. His mood had changed now that Bella wished to step down from the throne. "We should all miss your... er... unique way of running things, Bella. And we only hope that your successor will be better equipped to prevent these killings."

Mr. Riley strolled to the short door and bowed Bella out. Arthur, fiddling with his red bowler, waited for Mike to go ahead of him, but Mike stood his ground, took a deep breath, and said carefully, "I will kill tonight's creature. Any idea of where I can find it?"

Arthur raised an eyebrow at Mike's request but quickly regained his composure. "Ah, I see you're ready for your first ministry hunt." He nodded. "The creature you seek is a rare one indeed. It's been spotted in the forest just beyond the old mill, but be warned, it's not to be taken lightly. It's said to be able to control minds and manipulate reality itself."

Mike stared at him in amazement. Arthur tipped his hat and walked out. Mike turned to face the chair behind which the hound and his friends sat. "All right, let's get going." He pulled on his lynx fur overcoat. When he saw that only Amara stood, he smirked. "If it makes you feel better, Clance, we can take the hound."

Clancy stood to his feet. "We're in trouble now," he said gravely. "No Bella. We might as well head to Polar Frigemilt and start a new life there. The risk will be greater with her gone." The hound started howling and scratching frantically at the door.

***

The Duke of Galdorwide read from a decree. "Her Majesty the Queen to give and to grant unto Her Royal Highness, Princess of Galdorwide, the style and titular dignity of a queen of the Galdorwide kingdom." A crown was carried on a pillowed cushion. "The Princess of Galdorwide shall henceforth be known as Her Majesty, Queen Angel Carter."

Angel, wearing all of her medallions, kneeled before her sister. The royal sword was held above her as Bella placed a gold stash over her shoulder. She placed the crown on Angel's head. Another ceremonial cushion followed, she took the small vial from off it, and she anointed her sister's hand, then lightly touched the royal crown. Bella took a scepter from another cushion and handed it to Angel. A golden robe was placed around her shoulders. Bella tied the ties in the front, and for a moment, their eyes met with demonic intensity. Bella stepped back and resumed her stance. Angel gazed at her as she mounted the podium where she stood in front of the smaller throne. The giant throne she stood next to had an embroidered 'A' beneath the royal crest. Angel stood next to Bella. Bella sat down first. Then Angel sat side by side beneath the royal crest that sat above the thrones. As Bella sat bolt upright, the epitome of dignity, Angel glanced at her, and with weary eyes, she contemplated the assembled court. Her ex-husband Lewis, her cousins – Rabbit, Elizabeth, and Anahita – and all the gathered lords and ladies watching her in respectful solemnity. Nobody moved.

Later, in an empty chamber, royal artist read as Angel posed awkwardly for her first official portrait. "O, the famous daughter of Galdorwide, this is she. Great by land and great by sea. Thine island loves thee well, thou greatest princess since our world began." He painted his first stroke. "Quite marvelous, ma'am. Now to the roll of muffled drums, to thee, the greatest soldier comes. For this is she, O give her welcome. This is she, Galdorwide's greatest daughter. She that gained a hundred fights, nor ever lost her Galdorwide wand." Angel's confidence grew. The painter stroked some more. "Quite magnificent, ma'am. Quite marvelous." Angel eyed the portraits of her ruling ancestors lining the chamber.

CHAPTER 15

Amara, Mike, and Clancy advanced through the dense forest, their wands at the ready, passing the old mill. As they delved deeper into the woods, they began to feel uneasy.

Clancy spotted something. Several giant spiders were scuttling over the ground on the glass path. Amara looked to the track after noticing Clancy freeze while his face faded into a ghostly white. He saw that the spiders were walking in an unusually straight line. Amara began to smack Mike, who was knelt looking in the opposite direction.

"Ouch! What are you—" Mike turned around.

Amara pointed to the spiders. The sight would've been hard to see if it weren't for the moonlight reflecting off the glass path.

"Can I go back?" Clancy gulped.

"You don't have to, but the queen sees potential in you, both of you."

Clancy sighed. Amara fixed his eyes on the spider and looked in the direction they were heading to. "It looks like they're heading further into the forest." Clancy looked even unhappier about that.

"Oh, come on!" Mike exclaimed sarcastically while he playfully nudged Clancy. "I thought you were the master of this shit. We'll be fine. We have Bella's hound with us. It's her familiar." He jerked his thumb toward the basset hound with prominent jowls that were almost touching the floor.

"Right… but aren't there like… werewolves… in… the forest?" Clancy anxiously twirled his wand between his fingers.

A wide grin grew on Amara's face as he and Mike shared a knowing look. Mike turned back to Clancy.

"Can I tell you something?" He leaned over to Clancy's ear before receiving an answer. He whispered, and Clancy's eyes widened.

"What? Adolfo is a werewolf! Since when?"

"Since birth," Amara answered for Mike.

"What? I mean, how is it possible you two know this and I don't? I mean, I've known him longer than you two have."

"Well," another voice called from behind them. It was Terry. "The signs were obvious. He was born on the 25th of December. He has to pluck his unibrow, shave his hairy palms, his index finger is longer than his middle, and he eats raw meat and only raw meat."

"Thanks, Doctor August." Clancy rolled his eyes.

Amara smiled wide at the sight. Terry was one of the few non-Chaos members he felt comfortable with. "What are you doing here?"

"The queen sent me. I mean Bella."

Mike smiled, then looked back to Clancy. "There are good things in here too, like unicorns and…"

"Ants," Terry added when Mike was at a loss for words.

Amara had been in the forest before, especially at night, and more so after it was deemed forbidden. His bat, Bugsy, would follow him. It was where he could be alone with his thoughts. He always felt that he had belonged to the woods. It was there where he wanted to die, when that time comes, whether at his own hands or someone else's.

Clancy swallowed hard, he stiffened, but as his friends followed the spiders, he did too. Mike and Terry lifted their lanterns. Mike's magic cast a white flame into the lantern, and Terry's had conjured a purple flame. Terry's color was no shock to the boys as he had been ordained a purple aura after saving the life of Nicholas Snowball five years ago. However, Mike's white magic was a shock to them all. Typically, it was green as he had a Viridi aura.

"Woah!" said Clancy.

"What's that mean?" Amara asked, taking a closer look at the ghostly flame.

"Gangwuce aura, a holy aura. I got it two weeks ago after a ceremony at my placement at Galdorwide's church of Astradung."

Terry and Mike continued to hold the lanterns out in front of them, illuminating the spiders as they trekked their paths. Mike and Amara walked on one side while Clancy and Terry walked on the other. Clancy was walking too close for Terry's comfort. Terry stopped in his tracks, causing Clancy to bump nose-first into his back.

"Wait," he called out, causing Mike and Amara to stop. "Look." He pointed. Up ahead, every other spider was branching out into two separate lines as they hurried into the shade of the trees.

"Okay, let's split. Come on, Clance." Terry nodded as he headed right.

Clancy followed before stopping and looking at Mike.

"Can we take the hound?"

With a smile, Mike nodded. He handed Clancy the leash. After a few tugs, the hound finally gained the courage to hop over the row of crawling spiders.

Clancy held the leash tight. His muscles grew tense as he unknowingly gripped so hard that his hands blanched. The hound scampered alongside him in the forest, sniffing the roots of trees and leaves. Clancy looked up ahead, where Terry's purple glow illuminated the army of spiders. They walked behind them for about fifty minutes, neither of them talking as they strained their ears to see if they could hear anything besides the rustling of leaves and breaking of twigs. Soon, the trees became thicker, so much so that not even the stars above them could be seen. Terry's purple light shone brighter as the sea of darkness grew black. The purple light allowed them to see that the spiders were now taking a new path.

Terry paused, causing Clancy to bump into him once more. He wanted to see what was up ahead, but he couldn't see much beyond the circular, purple illumination. Terry had never been this deep into the forest. Now, he wished he had Amara at his side. Terrance gulped as the spiders began to go off the dirt path into a part of the forest not often trekked. Nonetheless, he knew he had to do as Bella requested and follow the spiders despite his fear. Even though they suspected she wasn't the queen, they didn't let their fear stop them from doing what was right – helping the kingdom.

Something cold and wet touched Clancy's hand, causing him to jump back, only to realize it had been the hound's nose. His slobbery mouth was getting slop everywhere.

"REALLY?" Terry shouted after he had jumped in fright in response to Clancy's needless yelp. He took a deep breath. "So, partner, ready to follow the not-so-beaten path?"

"We've come this far." Clancy was gaining confidence as so far he had not encountered any real threat, just the odd shivers and scratching as he looked at the tiny spiders. He felt as if they had decided to stop following their path and crawling all over him instead. However, every time he looked, there was nothing there.

They followed the speedy shadows of the spiders through the trees. They couldn't walk as fast but considering there appeared to be six hundred spiders behind them, they didn't feel the need to catch up. They were all going to the same place. Clancy reached into his green cloak pocket and handed Terry a machete which Terry flinched at the sight of.

"Why the treachery are you flinching? I'm not Eion." He laughed, remembering Eion's violent tendencies.

Terry ripped it from Clancy's hand and began to chop the branches that stood in their way. "Why in Galdorwide are you carrying around this?" Terry asked as he used it.

"Giant. Creatures," he replied. Terry looked ahead with a smirk.

Everything was nearly visible by the time Terry's arms got tired from chopping and lifting his lantern high in front of them. Clancy found comfort in the hound's hot breath that blew on his hand every so often. Terry crouched down, aiming the light at the ground as his eyes struggled to see the spiders. Noticing they were still on track, they continued to head further into the forest.

They walked for at least what seemed to be twenty minutes. Their robes were beginning to snag on the thorn bushes beneath them. After a while, the boys saw that the terrain began to slope downward. The trees were only growing thicker.

Suddenly, the hound let out a fantastic big bark, causing both of them to flinch. They stared out into the dark forest. Clancy kept a tight grip on Terry's elbow.

"There's something over there," Terry breathed. "Listen, it sounds like something big."

They listened. To their right, still at a distance, they could hear the sound of large branches snapping as if something big were making its way toward them.

"Oh no," Clancy winced. "I thought we'd sneak up on it, not the other way around!"

"*Shh*, you don't want it to hear us."

"It already heard this stupid hound!"

"Shut it!"

The darkness seemed to be blinding them as they looked to their right. They stood terrified until Clancy saw something from out of the corner of his eye. He backed away as he trembled.

"Terry… just… trust me." Clancy shivered. Terry looked back to Clancy, his brow furrowed.

Clancy clenched his fists as well as his eyes as he tried to gather up the courage. Once gathered, he bent down, took off his shoe, and took it into his hand. He brought it up above his head before giving a hard slap to Terry's behind.

Terry blinked in confusion as he looked at his friend. His face blushed as he wore a glare on his face. Clancy struggled to put on his boot. Noticing that his friend was still staring at him, he pointed to the ground, where a giant spider, the size of Clancy's head, laid curled up. The back of Terry's cloak was covered with spider guts.

"You're welcome." Clancy bowed before shivering.

Terry heard a crack in front of them. He raised his lantern to find that the final spider was almost crawling out of sight. He plundered after it. They tripped and fell as they struggled to keep up. Before they knew it, they entered a large clearing.

They found themselves in the middle of a circle of thick trees. Clancy had to admit, he was relieved seeing that the spiders had stopped traveling and remained in the ring. Maybe Amara and Mike were stuck with the beast while they were stuck at a large gathering held by minuscule spiders.

They looked at one another, relieved. The sides of their faces were scratched and covered with mud. The hound didn't seem as keen about the situation as the two smiling men did. He kept close to Clancy. Clancy looked down after feeling the hound's warm body quiver against his leg. Clancy, after his breathing finally slowed down, placed his wand into his cloak's pocket.

"And we thought we'd be facing a giant creature!" Clancy laughed as he leaned on his much taller friend, who stood only three inches shorter than the average door. He patted Terry's shoulder as if they deserved it for all their courage.

"We followed the trail. Let's go back and see if we can find Amara and Mike," said Terry.

He went to walk away when he saw that Clancy's eyes were fixed straight ahead, his lips quivering and his face pale. He looked mortified. Before Terry could turn around to see what Clancy was looking at, he felt something sharp and hairy reach around his torso and lift him as if he were some kind of feather. The thing raised him in a way that had him hanging upside down. Struggling in its grip, Terry saw Clancy's feet leave the ground. Terrified as the grip remained stiff no matter how much he moved, he looked to the ground again, where the hound was howling and whimpering. Soon, the creature swept them toward the trees.

Terry looked down to see that the creature walked on six hairy legs while the front two held him and Clancy high into the air. They were moving toward the very heart of the forest where last year's dragon attack had occurred. Behind them, they could hear dozens of other, smaller spiders following after them. Terry could overhear the hound wrestling through the army of spiders, trying to reach the men who he had been ordered to protect. Terry looked to Clancy, who looked back at him. They were both happy to at the very least have each other but couldn't yell or even scream as their voices had seemed to leave them.

They had been in the creature's clutches for about ten minutes before the sun began to rise, letting the two men see the swarm of spiders that followed the massive one that was carrying them. Terry craned his neck and saw that they had reached the ridge of the forest's gate. The monster pushed it open with its thick, hairy body. Stars shone down as the sky lightened. Terry and Clancy kept their eyes on the spiders, the sizes of carriages, as the view slowly became more apparent. Clancy shivered at the sight of the many eight legs and eight eyes that belonged to the creatures. The gigantic spider that held them continued forth toward the misty opening. However, the forest was not how they remembered it. It was now matted with spider webs. Terry's eyes widened as he realized that they were being brought into a trap. The spiders were crawling all over them. They almost looked... excited. Insects of all kinds and forest fauna were trapped within its web.

A bearded man lay motionless in the web. Terry reached for Clancy's hand when he spotted the bearded man.

"Come on!" He motivated Clancy to try and fight instead of giving up.

Clancy spotted the man. "Who's that?"

"I don't know!"

"Oh, jeez." Clancy winced.

The spider dropped both of them into the sticky web. The hound jumped in as if to save them, but soon, the nets strangled its brown fur legs. Soon, the hound's howling had turned to whimpers. Clancy looked exactly how Terry felt, but Terry tried to be strong for both of them. Clancy was frozen, his mouth wide as if he were screaming with his eyes popping out of his head. Terry tried to snap him out of his trance but to no avail.

Terry looked up to the creature that had dropped them; it was a spider the size of an elephant. Its eight eyes shone through the misty air. There were gray hairs mixed in with the black of its flesh. When Terry squinted to get a better look at the creature, he noticed that each of its eight eyes was the colors of clouds. He was blind.

The giant spider moved closer, its milky eyes wandering the ground beneath him as if he were trying to get a better look at its next meal. Terry was sure that at the pace his heart was going, he'd die of a heart attack before the creatures could kill him. The spiders moved in on them.

Terry, at first, thought about trying to struggle against the web but then thought against it; he didn't want to anger the spider. He tried to remain still and calm. Terry grew sick with fear. He couldn't reach his wand, and Clancy was practically stone. Terry gathered what remained of his courage. His thoughts were drowned out by the loud rustling of legs heading toward them. Large, black shapes shifted all around them. Terry tried to regather his thoughts and keep his composure. He began to think, what were spiders most afraid of? Terry took his wand into his hand with a tight grip. He looked to Clancy as he saw a spider's leg reach for his friend's face. Filled with worry and fear, he was able to pull out his wand.

"*Fugellim!*" A uniform, purple intertwining duo of coils exited Terry's wand. A flock of birds formed from the waves. The spiders now grew more intent on killing the birds. "Sorry, birdies," Terry said as he had thought the birds would have won the fight. "*Padder*!" A light, purple twisting stream exited his wand, forming toads.

Most of the toads were eaten immediately, but one toad had eaten one of the carriage-sized spiders. This spider, in particular, had tried to play dead, and it almost worked until Terry ripped his foot from the web and kicked it. This toad was more giant than the spider, and it was the only large one summoned along with the normal-sized toads. With an outstretched tongue, it pulled in the spider.

Terry shouted with excitement but was displeased entirely as soon as the giant frog, now full, hopped away. The spiders moved in on him and Clancy once more.

"*Efeta!*" A bright, purple spike of particles exited his wand, forming lizards. Clancy awoke from his state and began shivering.

"It's beneath you!" Terry shouted at the singular, giant lizard from the bunch of thirty that were summoned. The spider was crawling toward him, so he tried to fight his way back through the web. "You're missing the spider, girl!" He spoke to the lizard that had allowed the spider to crawl from beneath it.

"Come on!" Clancy cried, watching the spider approach his friend. He kicked the lizard from beneath the cushion of webs that wrapped around his feet. "Get him! Go on! Go! Go!" Clancy shifted his body in the direction of the spider, hoping to draw the lizard's eye to it. "Go on! Get the spider!"

"Get it!" They shouted at it as if it could understand their words.

"It's right there!" Clancy grew frustrated. "It's over there! I will cheer for the spider in about a second!"

"Oh, don't say that!" Terry was beginning to sound like Annie. "I just want the spiders to die! Come on, girl! Can't you see the big spiders? Specifically, the one heading toward my face?"

"*Eurgh!* Come on, Liz!" Clancy grew disgusted watching the spiders scurry. The lizard, who had been staring at the two shouting men, turned its head in the other direction.

"You're looking in the wrong direction!" Terry's fear and temper rose. "Come on, girl!"

Suddenly, the spider stopped moving as it sensed the danger. The spider turned back under the lizard, and as soon as it passed the lizard's face, the lizard brought it in and began to chop down on its body. The boys cheered.

"Summon another creature! One that can kill them all!" Clancy yelled.

"I only know those and…" He tilted his head and shrugged, unsure of his next conjure. "*Apa!*" A wild, purple shaft exited his wand and out sprung monkeys and apes of all sizes.

The monkeys began to swipe at the spiders, pushing them throughout the web. Some monkeys were afraid of the charging spiders and ran off. Meanwhile, some monkeys leaped toward the enormous spiders. The spiders, when facing the monkey, lifted themselves onto their hind legs. The monkeys mostly just smacked them back down as if the spiders were misbehaving children. The monkeys looked as if they were petting the spiders, but they were scratching at the creatures. Once they finished scratching, the monkeys would lean down and bite into the spiders. *Pop!* One monkey successfully chewed off the spider's head while holding the rest of its body in its hand.

Terry twisted and turned, pulling himself from the web. He ran over to Clancy and helped untangle him. Then they hopped off the web. Feet away, spiders fell from the trees surrounding the gated clearing. Their reflective eyes gleamed from their ugly faces.

Even as Terry held his wand out, he knew it would be no good. There were too many of them. As he prepared to cast out a spell, rustling leaves to their left could be heard. A white light followed the noises.

Mike and Amara were towering past the trees on their broomsticks, in Amara's case a training one. Lanterns glaring into the semi-darkness, Mike and Amara struck the spiders with spells, knocking them out of their way. The endless black bodies and tiny legs flew through the air. Mike and Amara screeched to a halt on their brooms in front of Terry and Clancy.

"Get the hound!" Mike ordered, knowing that if something were to have happened to the queen's familiar, she'd indeed have his head for her next feast. He looked at the giant spider, the one who was the 'giant.' He pointed his wand. "*Gangwuce estmere!*" The creature turned to ash.

Clancy dived onto the back of Mike's broom while Terry retrieved the hound, carrying its shaking, heavy body in its arms as if it were a beautiful princess he had just wed. He ran over to his friends, his mop of curls flapping wildly behind him.

"Give Clancy the hound," Mike ordered. "Amara's broom has a weight limit."

Terry obliged and passed the whimpering dog onto Clancy's lap. Clancy held his hand tightly around the dog's body and kept another tight grip on the broom. Luckily for him, the dog seemed familiar to broom rides, so despite its large frame, he steadied himself without much support needed from Clancy.

They flew off, striking more spiders with their spells. They sped through the forest, crashing through branches until they were out and back into town.

Mike looked back to Clancy, whose mouth was still open as he gave the odd shivers, still picturing the spiders. "You okay?" Mike asked. Clancy stared straight ahead, unable to speak.

They squeezed past two thick oak trees. The hound wailed as if singing full of joy, as it sensed that they were getting closer to home. After twenty minutes of flying, they could finally see the patch of sky as they entered the backyard of the castle.

As soon as Mike and Amara landed their brooms, Terry and Clancy jumped off, almost falling over with excitement to see civilization. The hound fought itself out of Clancy's arms and raced toward the dog door in the castle's back door. After a few minutes, Clancy regained the feelings in his stiff body. All the tense, statue-like straining would surely bring him muscle aches the next day. Mike gave Amara a proud pat on his back. Clancy became sick, vomiting into a nearby bush.

Clancy spoke between gags. "Screw the queen – never again will I do something for her even if she does see *potential* in me." He mimicked her voice as he spoke the word 'potential.' He gave a lovely, feminine gesture of his hand as he mocked.

"I bet she's got a plan for us," said Mike enthusiastically. "I mean, now that none of us died."

Clancy gave a punch to the castle wall. He was still shivering uncontrollably. "I mean, now she's going to send Amara to some prison cell!" Mike frowned. He had forgotten about Amara's fate.

The boys headed to their homes. They each entered their own homes quietly, trying to make up for the squeaky doors. Amara entered his room and held his breath. The ministry could come any time now to make their arrest. He threw a log into the fireplace that sat at the side of the room. "*Ad!*"

He took off his green cloak and put on his black Chaos shirt and black shorts. He put on his black boots and waited by the fire. After forty minutes of waiting, Amara decided to fling himself onto his bed in hopes of getting some sleep, considering he wouldn't get much during his nights at Skogen. However, despite wanting to sleep, he wasn't able to. Amara pulled himself to the side of his mattress that remained on the wooden floor. He was too busy thinking about everything that happened.

He would have to remain in prison until the final monster was defeated. In this case, it could only be killed at Rabbit's hands. He was his only hope of getting out of prison. Even if destroyed, would they be able to capture whoever was behind the killings, or would he remain Bella's scapegoat? He threw his legs back onto the bed and lay down, staring without blinking at the ceiling.

There was no point in thinking. Amara chose his fate, which was better than Mike being in his position.

***

In the school gym, Mr. Bernard stood at a podium applauding a troop of cheerleaders as they concluded their performance. The crowd cheered.

"Students, faculty, and staff. Before we inaugurate Mike Johansen as student council president, rise for our Galdorwide anthem."

The student body stood, placing their hands on their hearts, as Mahnoor Anderson stepped up to the microphone.

"Warriors are we, whose stories are vowed to Galdorwide. Galdorwide! Galdorwide! In everything and loan of call, while this land was fair and blooming, our heroic ancestors planted the roots of which our dignity was sprung. My homeland, my homeland," she sang.

Annie and Lovetta smiled brightly at Mike, who stood on the stage to Mr. Bernard's right. Mahnoor continued to sing. Amara cracked a wide smile. *"Come on, Galdorian witches, come on to freedom!"*

Nearby, Clancy pumped his fist toward Mike discreetly as Walter and Lucian smiled at each other.

"With thy might hand sustain us. Still, our rugged pathway trace, Astradung, our hope, protect and cherish, Galdorian lands and Galdorian race!" Grinning, Amara glanced at Mahnoor. *"Oh, beautiful Galdorwide!"* His smile faded slightly, and his brow furrowed as he spotted what looked to be the king's shadowy silhouette in the distance. *"As the wych elm atop the hill stands firm, unchanged through wind and frost, as if wrapped in armor, so shall our resilient spirit."* She concluded the song.

The ghost king flashed him a smile. Looking toward the doors, Amara saw Queen Angel barging into the gym with Krum and Gabriel in toe. The student body grew restless, throwing puzzled glances at each other as Angel strode toward Amara. Krum and Gabriel cuffed his hands behind his back.

"Queen Angel, what are you doing? I thought since Bella's gone, maybe—" Amara was cut off.

"You're under arrest for the murders of Varg Thorn, Bliant Cherish, Lynn Denmark, and Flower Scaasi."

Amara's friends watched on with confused expressions as the ministry members escorted him away. A shell-shocked Amara glanced at Lovetta, Annie, and Clancy in the stands, who gaped back at him. As he was marched toward the exit, Amara's gaze fell on the king, who stood in a corner, giving the teen a solemn nod before turning and leaving. Annie threw a shocked glance at Lovetta and Clancy in the stands, who watched in open-mouth horror as Amara was led out of the gym.

***

Summer was creeping around the grounds of the school. The sky and lake had turned a neon teal. Neon flowers that were as large as pumpkins began to bloom along the lake. But without Amara, it didn't look or feel the same. He couldn't be seen roaming the forbidden forest with his familiar flying closely behind or seen in his living room, sitting in a cardboard box, or wearing his green velvet fedora. Things seemed wrong without him. Clancy and his family, with the support of their friends, buried Flower.

"We're taking no more chances," Blue began severely as the ceremonial pastor enchanted the casket and lowered it into the ground. "There's every chance that the attacker can come and attack any one of us."

With Bella gone, fear had spread, unlike before. The sun didn't seem as bright, and the air didn't seem as fresh. There was barely a face to be seen at school as many parents chose to keep their children at home in their eyesight. For all those who were at school, their faces were tense and frightened. Any laughter would come to an abrupt stop as it sounded so bizarre along the school's dark corridors.

Mike constantly repeated Bella's last words in his head, *You will find that even if I am not queen, I will be willing to help my people at any cost.*

The Chaos group was more than annoyed when it came to being shepherded by ministry members to and from class in large groups. Everything seemed more cramped as people tried their best to be the one closest to Krum out of fear. He often told the Chaos group to hurry up.

Everyone in the Chaos group, besides Mike and Annie, enjoyed the atmosphere of terror and suspense. They were strutting around the school as if they had all been crowned Galdorwide's new rulers. People were so confused why they seemed to feel on top of the world. After all, the queen was gone, Amara was arrested, and Flower had died. Walter was most pleased.

"I always knew Bella wouldn't last as queen. She has to be this kingdom's worst ruler yet! Maybe Angel will be a decent ruler," Walter spoke loudly to his friends at their lunch table.

"Maybe she will put an end to these attacks once and for all." Clancy nodded.

"Well, Angel won't last long either," Mike began. "She's only filling in until Bella is allowed to rule again, and I hope she returns."

"Rabbit or Nicholas should apply. They're royal. Then we'd be the new ministry!" Clancy exclaimed eagerly.

"Now, now, boys," Mike said through a thin-lipped smile. "Bella has only been suspended, not permanently removed. She will be back soon enough."

"Yeah, right." Aksel smirked. "That little girl..." He shook his head.

"If Rabbit or Nicholas ran, they'd have our votes, and we can intimidate the rest." Clancy laughed.

Annie and Lovetta looked at one another and stuck their fingers in their mouth in disgust.

"I'm surprised not every student, 'sides us, haven't packed their bags and moved out of the kingdom." Walter looked around with his dark eyes. "I bet the next attack will be on one of those dumb Crash Ring players or the cheer squad. Too bad Aldric didn't die during that Crash Ring game."

The bell rang, Lovetta leaped off the bench. Clancy caught her arms. Mike gave her a sympathetic look with a shake of his head. Walter scrambled for his books and didn't notice Lovetta's attempt as she lunged for him.

"Let me at him." Lovetta now fought against Clancy and Lucian's grasp. "I don't care. I don't need my wand. I'll kill him."

Teddy, who had returned to his work as a ministry member, approached the Chaos group to lead them to their following classes. Each of their schedules was in their hands. "Speed this up immediately," he ordered politely.

Clancy and Lucian kept their hold on her as Lovetta still fought to get loose. They were only safe to let her go once Teddy had dropped Walter off at his classroom. Teddy led Lovetta and Clancy last to their outdoor class for the art of taming animals.

The art of taming animals class was very subdued; there were only two other students besides Clancy and Lovetta. Probably because Lynn, who had been killed, used to sit in this classroom. Professor Gemini Scaasi and Coby Soleil handed each student a dreaming worm that they would clean dirt off of. If a successful witch/animal connection is made, they could hold the worm, and it'd grant them one wish, except for giving or taking a life. Though, outside of school, dreaming worms can grant such things. After cleaning up her worm, Lovetta looked up and found one of the two students standing in front of her, their eyes wide.

"I'm sorry that I ever suspected it was you behind the killings. It's just the accident with Brad, then your hatred for Varg, but now I know it wasn't you, I know you'd never hurt Flower." He held out his pudgy hand, Lovetta shook it.

The two students began to work at Clancy and Lovetta's station rather than fearing them like usual and working at the station furthest from them.

"That Walter character, though," the student began as he cleaned the dirt off of the worm. "He seems very pleased about all this, doesn't he? D'you think he could be behind the attacks along with Amara?"

"No," Clancy said sharply, keeping his sparkling blue eyes on the worm. The two students stared at him.

When class was over, Gabriel Scaasi came and escorted the students to their following classrooms. In Clancy and Lovetta's case, the art of music magic. Clancy and Lovetta lagged to the back of the group to be out of earshot.

"I wish we were able to visit Amara," Lovetta began. "I hope he's okay."

Clancy nodded but didn't say much. Adolfo bounded into the classroom and stared at the two of them. Every teacher looked grimmer with each day, but Adolfo always seemed happy. He was always able to see the positives in all things, including the worst of people.

"I know, everyone, these days seem to be getting harder and harder, but in my class, I want to rid you all of these long faces."

Lovetta raised her hand. With a flow of his sword, he allowed her to speak. "How can we rid of our long faces when three of our classmates' seats are empty because two are dead and one is… in prison?"

"I know, everyone's been through a lot this year, but the year's almost over, and I trust in the ministry to handle these things."

Lovetta knew he meant good, but she couldn't handle any forms of cheeriness, not when Amara was wrongfully imprisoned, and they all had to go along with it and act as if the threat was gone. It still did Bella no good; the crown still sat upon Angel's head.

Lovetta loved Adolfo. In many ways, he reminded her of Gower. However, she wanted to throw her *Intro to Ghoul Music* text right at his head.

***

The Python Seger classes had been full these past months, as many witches, all ages alike, wanted to prepare and strengthen their skills just in case they became the next target. After classes, Tassos, Michael, Aaron, and Daemon gave speeches that would make the students feel prepared and safe, and they also told them if they were ever being chased by some creature, no matter how big, to run straight to Python Seger where they would be.

It was so crowded now that Aaron made a strict rule that none of his, Tassos', or Daemon's children could leave the building until all matters were resolved. They, too, didn't believe that Amara was behind the incident; the article was odd, and his photo was endearing with his quirky smile and green fedora.

Hating being locked away and wanting to do something about Brad's death, the kids got together and schemed a plan. They decided to wait in their rooms until they could hear their dad's loud snores. Michael and Aaron had challenged the kids to a game of Forbidden Mask, and Aisley sat watching them. To Aaron's heartbreak, she had seated herself at Brad's usual chair in the living space, but he knew it was time not to let little things like that bother him any more, even if he knew Aisley would happily move to another seat. The six kids were losing on purpose as they were trying to finish the game early so that everyone could hurry up and go to bed. Even so, it wasn't until four a.m. until everyone besides Tassos and Aisley had gone to bed. Instead of following, the two of them descended into the basement.

The six kids waited until they could hear the distant sound of the dungeon-like basement door before simultaneously joining in Coby and Ken's room to perform the invisibility spell and climbing out their bedroom door.

It was another difficult journey for the Python Seger students, dodging all the ministry members outside who ensured the curfew was followed. At last, they reached the moonlit forest. They reversed the invisibility spell to help them see better.

"What are we even looking for?" Chris yawned as they strolled through the dark grass.

"Chris," Coby began, annoyed. "We've been talking about this for days."

"Yeah, but he fell asleep every time." Mamie laughed.

"Didn't they arrest Amara?" Chris continued to complain. "I mean, sure, the likelihood of that cute kid killing four people is small, but what if he did?"

"Well, the lyrics of his songs are pretty… gruesome," added Mamie.

"Well, we'll find out tonight when we find the Great Pixie." Coby lit his lantern with a red flame.

They approached the Great Pixie's cabin that looked like a tiny house with crooked windows. After Coby knocked, the short door pulled back. A little pixie in a gray dress with matching butterfly-like wings and socks peeked from behind the edge of the door. The slim sleeve of her dress had fallen to her elbow due to her awkward positioning. Her long, red hair fell in front of her face, allowing large pointed ears like horns to pop into view. Butterflies flew around her, and two gray fairies with faces of foxes flew beneath her feet, snarling at the guests. Coby reached into his backpack and pulled out a plastic bag filled with five apples. She stretched out her arm and took it, allowing her arms to drop with weight. She let them enter inside.

The fox fairies growled.

"No," the Great Pixie warned them sternly before gently patting their heads. "Thank you for the apples. What would you like in return?"

"The kingdom… is in danger," Coby began, breathing heavily. "That's why we're here. We want to know who's behind all of the recent attacks on our friends and family."

"Attacks?" asked the old, wise pixie who looked relatively young considering she was as old as the kingdom.

"The ministry thinks that they've found the attacker; though they could be right, we seriously doubt it. I mean, we know the kid. He's super sweet and quiet. But they already took him to the Skogen prison."

The pixie tapped her chin furiously, which seemed to echo in the tiny house that was too big for the fairy and the furniture. "*Hmm*, I think I can help answer this mystery," said the pixie fretfully. "Years and years ago, I was given the gift to uncover mysteries with a simple wish. I'm sure you know that; after all, that gift probably made you come here tonight. I also, for your barring of five apples, will allow two answers to two questions."

"So you were given the Great Magic?" Chris asked, cold sweat dripping from his forehead.

"They don't call me the Great Pixie for nothin', darling." She smiled. "I, despite popular belief, was not born in Galdorwide. I'm from Nisse Island. I was a princess there but not next in line for the crown, and I am unlike the rest of the pixies from Nisse. First of all, I had been born from a red egg instead of regular birth. I was taken in by my uncle, who had been an only child. He cared for me. I was hidden inside one of his cupboards. I never knew why until my uncle explained that a prophecy foretold of a pixie born from a red egg would be given more power than the rest of the species. For years, I never knew, and I was fed scraps of food once a day. I was nothing but wing and bone. Nonetheless, my uncle is a good friend, a good man, who did what he could to protect me from those who wished me harm. When I was finally out in the world, I was blamed for killing a girl, but my uncle had defended me. I have lived here in Galdorwide's forest ever since. My uncle still visits, as I grant him..." She paused, noticing the necklaces that hung around the kid's necks all besides Horus. "Undeadlic Healsbeag. Arcane magic, one magic beneath Great. Who are you?"

"The Soleils and the Silvermauls, and that's Horus." Coby nodded in Horus' direction. "He doesn't need one. He's a—"

"Vampire," she answered for him simply with a nod. "I see."

"Our families are the only ones to practice arcane magic. Unfortunately, we were only gifted these necklaces by our fathers after the death of Brad Silvermaul," Coby continued.

"So" – Chris looked at the pixie – "that legend of you killing a girl isn't true."

She shook her head. "I never hurt anyone. I was wrongfully accused. So, this friend of yours, you believe that he's been wrongfully imprisoned?"

"Yes, so, can you find out who is behind the killing?" Chris asked. "Because if it's not Amara, there will be another attack."

The pixie closed her eyes before flying down to her littered table and grabbed a red candle. With a snap of her finger, the wick lit up.

"*I ignite this candle to symbolize myself. It lights, as does my soul. It depicts myself concerning everything.*" She reached for two white candles and placed them on either side of the red one. With a snap, she lit them up as well. "*These hold the symbols for truth. They are urged of Faline furthermore to me will bestow every truth. I ask to know who is behind the attacks on Varg Thorn, Lynn Denmark, Bliant Cherish, and Flower Scaasi.*"

The fairy sat in front of the three candles, her eyes closed for what felt like thirty minutes before her eyes shot open.

CHAPTER 16

It was daytime at the Cherish house.

"Mom?" Andreas asked telepathically.

"Yes, sweetheart?" Telepathically, Agrona answered.

To speak to Andreas, you needed to talk telepathically. She was born deaf and struggled to read lips. But her telepathic communication abilities were excellent.

Agrona stitched a black dress in Andreas' bedroom while Andreas sat next to her.

"What happens after we die?" the eighteen-year-old asked.

"Hmm, what do you mean?" replied Agrona.

"I mean, where do we go?" the eighteen-year-old elaborated.

Agrona clarified that she could only speak for witches and assumed the eighteen-year-old was interested in discovering where her father went. "Most witches become ghosts and continue moving among the living after death. Depending on their beliefs, they may go to limbo, Grorhorn, or Boldwela, while other witches remain in their bodies and continue to dream, receiving another life."

The eighteen-year-old asked if dying was painful and if Aunt Aisley, Agrona's sister, had described it.

With a grin, Agrona responded that the pain experienced during death depends on the weapon or spell used.

"How does Aunt Aisley come back to life? Does she use magic, or is she under a curse?" asked the curious teen.

Agrona chuckled and clarified that there was no curse involved. Instead, Aisley possessed a necklace that Agrona also owned. The chain was a gift from Uncle Daemon, which Agrona was hesitant to keep, as she wished for her children and Andreas' father to have it. However, Daemon assured her he would make more, and Andreas would receive one soon. The necklace was a family secret shared among the Soleil, Cherish, Silvermaul, and Scaasi families. Daemon and Aaron had discovered the spell for the chains and planned to keep it in the family for generations. Agrona finished making a special magic-infused dress for Andreas and handed it over, explaining that it would protect her and grant her the strength to face any challenges. She encouraged her to wear it confidently, as they were now part of a legacy that spanned generations.

They stood to their feet. Andreas exhaled deeply and stepped into the dress.

"I'm helping you into your dress, Andreas," said Agrona as she assisted Andreas. As Agrona zipped up the dress, she said, "I understand why you asked, but your father doesn't possess the necklace. We have no other options. With the necklace, it was easy; without it, it's impossible." Andreas nodded, acknowledging Agrona's words. "It's not a witch's responsibility to revive the dead," Agrona added.

"Don't worry, Mom. I haven't had any ideas," Andreas responded, looking elsewhere. "Even if I did, I wouldn't be able to do anything once he's buried. All we'll have left of him is his clothing."

"I'm sorry." Agrona sighed heavily, embracing Andreas tightly. Andreas reciprocated the embrace, recognizing Agrona's grief.

"We'll keep his memory alive and cherish it." Andreas assured her mother. The two stood there, finding comfort in each other's company as they prepared to bid farewell to their beloved Bliant Cherish.

Downstairs at the Nicholson Mortuary, mourning people came for Bliant's service. Solemn organ music played.

Thor Cherish stood next to his older brother Casper next to the front door. They wore suits and ties. Agrona greeted Dr. Michael Nicholson.

"I'm here to pay my respects, Agrona. Bliant used to visit and assist in the morgue, but now..." said Dr. N, looking down as he spoke slowly. Andreas was seated in the hallway.

Agrona made a clicking sound with her tongue and replied, "I'm sure he'd be glad you showed up. It's beautiful."

Daemon Soleil entered the room and spoke telepathically to his niece, "Doesn't it warm the heart, though?" He turned to face Andreas and continued, "That's magical kingdoms for you, with the strongest stock. The entire Galdorian nation is supporting one of their lost civilians. Andreas, I know your father passed away too soon. When I learned of his passing, I was afraid for this kingdom as a whole."

"The kingdom seems to be doing well, but my father is not. I wish those protection necklaces were finished sooner," said Andreas. Her uncle asked if she knew about the necklaces, and she confirmed with a nod.

Casper Cherish moved closer to his Aunt Aisley to express his thoughts. "Oh, Auntie Ais, we often fail to appreciate the present moment while it's happening. People rarely stop to think about how valuable those fleeting moments are."

His aunt sighed and replied, "It's unfortunate that most people are too preoccupied with their own lives to notice the beauty around them. That's why art and literature exist, to remind us of what we often overlook." Casper agreed with her statement and realized the importance of cherishing every moment and living life to the fullest.

"Are you crying, Auntie?" he asked Aisley.

"It's just allergies," she snorted, wiping her tears. "Let's finish up."

Thor walked over to Casper, and they walked into the parlor. Isabella, the youngest of the Cherish siblings, sang for the gathering. "*It began on a May night. I was the smartest soldier and him, the kindest. He was my father, my smart father, my soldier,*" she sang. "*We used to smile so well back then. We wanted to talk together, all around the world. We wanted it all.*" Andreas sat next to Thor in the front pew.

"It's your turn, Thor," said Agrona. Thor stood up and made his way to the podium. He appeared hesitant as he struggled to find the right words.

Meanwhile, Andreas watched intently, admiring her brother's qualities. Silently, she cast a spell to empower him to become stronger and more confident in his public speaking.

Thor sat up straight as the wind howled and began his eulogy for his father, Cherish Bliant. He wiped his nose with the palm of his hand and struggled to find the right words. "I am at a loss for words. Giving a eulogy is just crazy." Casper's attention was drawn to Thor as he spoke. "He always described me as his 'nerdy' son." Thor chuckled. "But he did buy school supplies for all eight of us children every year. He and I talked about everything. He shielded me from the world's evil and cruelty. During a conversation, I once asked about his life goals, and he replied that his dream was for all his children to achieve their dreams. This truly speaks to what a wonderful person he was. I miss him deeply." He let out a deep breath. "Thank you."

As Casper stood next to Andreas, Thor walked past them. "My father, Bliant Cherish – nicknamed Brilliant – was a good man. He placed high importance on family and duty above all else. He always fulfilled requests and did what was best for our family. He knew the risks of entering the kingdom but knew that Galdorwide was where we belonged. My father loved Galdorwide."

Thor stood up just as the mourners turned to look at him. "He didn't," he stated.

"Boy—" Casper started speaking, but his younger brother interrupted.

"Casper, our father wanted to leave Galdorwide. He was forced to stay here because of your attachment to some girl." Thor became angry, and Casper approached him with a heated demeanor. "Dad might still be here if it weren't for you," Thor retorted, struggling against Casper's grip. "You refused to let us go." Casper tried to calm him down, but Thor's frustration was evident. "Dad was trapped here because of you and your stubbornness," he spat out. "If only you had listened to him, maybe he would still be alive."

The room fell silent as the argument between the brothers escalated, and the tension in the air became palpable.

Casper shoved Thor with a grunt. Thor pushed back, causing Casper to knock over the display. A vase shattered, and the coffin clattered to the floor. Everyone gasped. Bliant's wand fell to the floor, and Thor ran out of the parlor. Andreas' mouth gaped before following him.

Melissa approached the wand and held it in her hands. Andreas rushed outside, calling for Thor. As he leaned against the wooden fence, Thor breathed heavily and expressed his inability to coexist with Casper. Andreas apologized to Thor, who revealed Casper was responsible for their father's death. However, Andreas disputed the claim. Thor then pulled a letter from Drenerth, the Polar Frigemilt High School. Andreas read the letter in surprise.

"It's an acceptance letter for Isabella and me. He applied for us six months ago. We could've gone. He wanted to go. I found it in Dad's room while looking for pictures for the funeral."

"I don't get it."

"We could have left this desolate kingdom, but he stayed because Casper was reluctant. He always followed his children's requests. I am aware of it. Casper murdered my dad." Thor knelt on the ground. "He murdered our dad." Andreas supported him. "What am I going to do?"

"You're going to develop bravery. You're going to do that." Casper gasped as he drew near. "You think it's acceptable to degrade me in this way, do you? In front of everyone, tainting their memories of him?" He took Thor in his arms once more.

"You have to understand the consequences of your actions, Casper," Thor said, tears streaming down his face. "We can't just pretend like nothing happened."

"Let go of him, Casper," Aisley instructed. The other funeral guests followed her.

"I wish it were me," Casper replied, trying to strike his younger brother, Thor. A magical force intervened and held Casper back, preventing any harm.

"Casper, this is your father's funeral. Let's honor his memory and compose ourselves. Our guests are leaving, and we should follow suit," Aisley urged, releasing the spell.

Thor began to walk away, but Andreas followed closely behind. "Please leave me alone, Andry," Thor pleaded.

Daemon comforted Aisley as they watched Thor walk away. "Andreas, let him go," Daemon said softly. "Thor needs time alone to process everything. We should respect his wishes and give him space to grieve." Aisley nodded in agreement, sympathetically watching Thor disappear into the distance.

Andreas and Daemon were sitting in a booth at a café. Daemon expressed his concern for Thor, stating that he might not be able to survive without their father. Andreas agreed, saying that it was true. She sighed and looked away. Daemon asked what was on her mind. Andreas said she was considering the possibility of her father's return. She mentioned a resurrection spell and asked if Daemon knew about it.

"Come again? Uh…" The man glanced behind him, whispering, "A resurrection spell?"

"Uncle Daemon, you saw Thor. He needs his father to return."

"Of all the arcane magics, necromancy remains the most serious and profound. It deals with death magic. It's forbidden. To carry out such an act, you would require permission from the queen and the emperor."

"I love him dearly. And even though I can't do much for him as his sister, as a witch who adores my father, I can fix this. Why shouldn't we if I—if we can reduce his suffering? Daemon, you witnessed Thor's desperate plea for his father's return. The seriousness of his request cannot be overstated."

"Well, there are laws, and it's a risky mission. Time, heaven, and eternity are not to be messed with if precautions weren't taken during the deceased's life."

"Why is it so difficult?"

"It's not difficult for me. I have an enchantment that is easy to use and produces great results. I've seen the outcomes myself. But I implore you not to try it."

"Do you have the charm?"

"It's in my office at Python Seger. The Practice of Resurrecting the Dead has many resurrection spells, but a portion of the spell is unspeakable even if you were to use it."

"What portion?"

"I can't say, even telepathically. The spell requires an offering to work. The force must be balanced."

"So, someone else must die to bring my dad back?"

"Yes, that's the unfortunate truth. The spell requires sacrificing life to bring another back from the dead. It's a heavy burden and a decision that shouldn't be taken lightly."

***

As she approached Tassos in the entrance hall of Python Seger, Aisley humbly requested, "Your Excellency, if you have a moment, I would like to speak with you." Kneeling before him, she explained that she needed spiritual guidance. Tassos kindly escorted her to the living room and urged her to share her thoughts. Aisley took a deep breath before confessing, "I worry that my family has strayed too far from a moral path."

Tassos nodded sympathetically and invited her to elaborate. Aisley opened up about her concerns regarding the erosion of values and principles within her family. She spoke of the increasing focus on materialism and lack of empathy, fearing the negative impact it could have on future generations. Tassos remained attentive and reassuring throughout her worries, providing comfort and peace.

He extended his hand and indicated the ground. Aisley sighed after kneeling and kissing it. "I struggle to keep the Scaasi and the Soleils focused." She took a deep breath. "But our family has fallen apart. Half-criminals, half-abusers, and half-immortals. There are times when I want to return to Tony." She was looking up at Tassos while holding his hand. "Tassos, I'm failing." She groaned. "I'm failing you and my family," she said.

Tassos looked at her with understanding in his eyes. "Aisley, you're not failing anyone," he reassured her gently. "We all have battles to fight, and sometimes it feels overwhelming. But remember, you are strong and resilient. Together, we can rebuild our family and create a better future. The Dark Lady Mania accepts our imperfections. She understands that we are mortal failures. We are like this by nature, Aisley." He squeezed her hand between his own while leaning in. "I also comprehend pain and dread. I was once kidnapped, buried underground, and then found by a normal witch who didn't think of me as a monster. Their kindness and acceptance gave me hope and the strength to overcome my past. Like me, you have the power to rise above your struggles and find solace in the support of those who truly understand you. Remember, Aisley. You are never alone in this journey toward healing and growth."

Her eyes started to tear up. "Tassos."

"Aisley."

After falling from his chair, Tassos gave Aisley a fervent kiss. They were panting and making out on the floor as the fire crackled behind them. Their bodies intertwined, their passion igniting like the flames that danced in the fireplace. At that moment, nothing else mattered except for the intensity of their connection and the desire that consumed them both.

***

Melissa paused before talking to Andreas and started, "I know this might sound strange, but do you recall when your father's coffin fell over? While you were chasing after Thor, I picked up his wand, and something odd happened. One moment, I was at the funeral parlor, and the next, I found myself elsewhere. I had a peculiar vision, and I'm not sure how it's related to your father's wand, but it was about your ex, Andrew."

Immediately after their conversation, Andreas marched over to Gideon's home on a goat farm, and when he opened the door, he asked, "What do you want?"

"Revenge," Andreas replied.

"I can support that," Gideon said. "Against whom?"

"Dad's dead," Andreas replied, her voice heavy with grief and determination.

"Yeah… We know who committed the murder; after all, Amara was already detained for the attacks. What else would you like?"

She uttered, "I want Dad back." Gideon scowled at her. "You owe me for protecting you from Annie and Mike on the night of their bachelor parties." Gideon gave a small smile. "And I have a strategy."

At Galdorwide High, Andreas and Gideon approached Andrew, Andreas' ex.

"Andrew!" with her telekinesis, Andreas called out, focusing her words on traveling to Andrew's mind only.

"What's wrong, Andreas?" he asked telepathically.

"Admit the truth. Why did you ask me out? I know you and your royal family were once close with the king, high and mighty. Why would you ask a girl like me out? And don't bother lying. Because I'll know if you do, trust me."

Isabella poked out from behind Andreas. Andrew folded his arms. "You think that the love I had for you wasn't true? A love for a pretty girl like you. You're the one who broke up with me, Andry. But I guess anything's possible." He smirked. "I asked you out on a dare, but I didn't mind. You are adorable."

"You see?" Andreas turned to Gideon, who she allowed to tune in. "He admits it."

"It was a lie all along?" Gideon asked. "Since the day you bumped into her at the cafeteria?"

"Going soft, are you, Gideon? Your legacy at the school says you're just as sly as me when it comes to the ladies."

Gideon turned to Andreas. "You're right. Something needs to be done."

"Since nothing was natural about Father's death, then this raging arse will help us balance the scale. A life for a life. So, you agree?"

"Andry, you don't have the stomach to kill anyone."

"No, but you do." Andry's voice trembled as she spoke, her eyes filled with fear and uncertainty. "I've seen the darkness that resides within you, the way you effortlessly manipulate others to do your bidding. It's not just about physical strength, it's about the coldness in your heart that allows you to take lives without hesitation."

Gideon smirked and stepped toward Andrew. "How dare you treat my sister with such little respect! Now, who dared you?" Gideon locked eyes with Andrew.

"It was just some friends of mine. Listen, I don't know how your sister found out, but I cared for her. It was their idea to make it a bet, I would've done it without it, but I guess the bet was my motivation. I'm just sorry I couldn't get as far as I would've liked with your prude sister."

Andreas smacked Andrew, who, in return, gasped. Her skill at reading lips was improving. She communicated telepathically with her brother and asked him to bring the person who owed them a debt to the forest tonight. She was determined to settle the score and smiled mischievously as they silently exchanged their plan. It was understood that the meeting in the woods would end her ex-partner's debt.

Gideon laughed and said, "Murder and rebirth? That's not possible. You're not my sister."

"I'll do anything to support the people I care about," Andreas declared as Thor entered.

"When is it?" He approached Gideon. "I think you're talking about necromancy. What time does it start?"

Gideon smirked. "The ritual begins at the witching hour. Get ready for a show like no other."

Thor's eyes widened with excitement. "I'll be there on time. I don't want to miss this."

At Python Seger, Daemon's office door hinges creaked. Andreas entered Daemon's office. Using her wand like a flashlight, she shone the light over books on tall, wooden shelves. Andreas turned around and searched through a smaller, wooden bookcase. She pulled out a slim, black textbook and rushed out of the office, the door creaking as she exited.

As Daemon emerged from the shadows, he couldn't help but think that the child had taken yet another step toward darkness. He compared her to one of Aisley's children and watched as she disappeared into the night, her innocence slowly fading. As he witnessed the scene, a sense of sadness overcame him. He realized that his assistance had led her to become entangled in Soleil's sinister web.

At night, Andreas led a procession down the forbidden forest. Gideon and Thor escorted Andrew to the clearing with his hands tied. A gag covered his mouth as he mumbled, and Isabella followed in the distance. Candles surrounded a pentagram made of red and brown twigs. Items belonging to their father lay in the center.

"As an A student," Thor started, turning to face Andreas, "I strongly suggest that you read the text aloud, word for word. We can all end up dead with the smallest mistake. The Right of Resurrection consists of three phases. We first summon the hounds of the underworld," Thor said, handing her the spellbook with the page he was referring to already open.

Andreas started to read the passage. "Followers of the above, lovers of the below, supporters of Galdorwide, guardians of the gateway, we invoke thee to aid in the restoration *of your fallen descendant.*" She nodded then they all began to chant. *"Dilynwyr syfulm se bufan, tilhengere sylfum se ceorl, entusiaster syfulm se Galdorwide, beskyttere mo runga se inngangsport, wit cigan dig till fultuman se eftforgiefnes sylfum din trus byre."*

Hounds could be heard barking and howling after they finished the chant. "Infidel amputee, it's working," said Thor in astonishment. Andrew whimpered.

According to Andreas, their next task was to locate the divide separating the living world from the deceased's world. "We humbly pay our respects to the gateway and request that its location be revealed peacefully."

They all began chanting. *"Wit knele yn wynebu se geat at separerar se rike syfulm se wtecscipe fram se rike syfulm se gastleas. Tomiddes sibgedryht ar, wit gebedmann at hit isrbodung awrigen."*

They stood in the shape of the five-pointed star. Suddenly, with a whoosh of the wind, the candles blew out. The wind blew through the darkened forest. Suddenly, it stopped.

"Wait for it," Thor whispered. The creaking of a gate followed the heavy chains unlocking. "The entrances are open," Thor declared.

Andreas introduced the third and final stage, "The Offering."

Gideon held a knife in hand and asked, "Do you want to perform the honors?"

Approaching, Andreas replied, "Pleased to." She took the knife as Andrew whimpered, his heavy breath complementing his impending doom.

Andreas made fun of him as she stepped behind Andrew, kneeling.

Isabella fixed her gaze on the dirt and reminded him, "You brought this upon yourself."

Andreas initiated the third and last spell while her siblings chanted with fierce determination. As they chanted in unison, the air crackled with energy, and their commanding voices grew louder with each repetition. Sparks flew from Andreas' fingertips, amplifying the spell's power. The forest shook under the might of their combined magic.

Daemon spied on them from behind a tree. Andreas braced herself and wielded the knife.

"Are you certain about this, Andreas?" Gideon arched an eyebrow.

"I've got to be." Andreas cut Andrew's neck after she raised the knife. Blood gushed violently from the gaping wound deeply carved into Andrew's neck, and he gasped. Andrew stumbled and landed in the pentagram's middle. Andreas retreated to her spot on the star with a stoic expression. Daemon kept a close eye. Thor breathed more quickly as he observed Andreas.

They all joined her and said, "These followers were summoned. The gateway was made available but at a price paid in blood. Dear Bliant Cherish, please. Rise, rise, rise." Daemon chanted along with his nieces and nephews. As the chant continued, a surge of dark energy emanated from the pentagram, causing the air to crackle. The forest grew colder, and a sense of foreboding hung heavy. Daemon's eyes widened with anticipation and trepidation, knowing that what they had unleashed could have unimaginable consequences.

The wind whooshed. Daemon slumped against the tree.

"Now, what?" asked Gideon.

Andreas replied, "We wait six minutes. It is time for Andrew's soul to depart from the body fully."

"And after that?" asked Isabella.

"We bury him. We lay him to rest in the peaceful embrace of nature," replied Andreas, her voice filled with solemnity.

"In a place where his spirit can find eternal tranquility." Isabella nodded, understanding the significance of honoring Andrew's final journey.

Andreas stared at Andrew's mangled body on the ground. She was admiring her work, realizing the newfound power she had. Not forgetting, however, how this was now who she had become – a murderer. However, she couldn't help but be proud of her work. She did it for her father; she kept telling herself. Although she kept thinking back to how Gideon said she was not a killer in the back of her mind, she could not help but ponder, was this the first and only time, or would she ever kill again?

Andreas led them to an open grave. Gideon and Thor, who carried Andrew's body, were breathing heavily. Andrew's corpse was tossed into the freshly dug grave, no longer bound. His body thumped against the ground. Gideon let out a sigh.

Andreas gave her brothers the order to 'cover him up.' Thor gave Isabella a shovel.

Casper arrived suddenly. "Andreas!"

"Oh, no." While the other siblings dumped dirt on top of Andrew, she pushed him to the side.

"Neopaganism, Andreas? This has got to be the most foolish and careless thing you've ever done! What even inspired you to have such a thought in the first place? We can't just randomly kill and raise the dead! Andreas, for heaven's sake."

"Thor was upset, Casper. I had to take action. I couldn't bear to see him like that, so I thought maybe bringing Dad back would help," Andreas pleaded, her voice filled with desperation.

"But necromancy is the most powerful and evil force."

"I followed the ritual strictly, which required a sacrifice for my dad's return. Andrew was the chosen one."

"Why do you keep thinking that the universe will excuse you? Your actions have disrupted the natural order, which cannot be ignored. The order is crucial, and the laws apply to everyone. Trying to manipulate fate or cheat the natural order will have severe consequences. The universe follows its rules, and going against them will cause chaos and imbalance. Understanding and respecting the inherent order governing life and death is essential, as tampering with it can have far-reaching implications. We were taught that in training school, for goodness' sake!"

"If I can't use magic to aid the people I care about, what's the point?"

"Andreas, you've gone too far this time!"

"There is no cause to believe the spell will bring consequences."

To view the grave, they turned around. After turning around, Casper knelt to her eye level. "That's what they all said." Before leaving, he sighed and touched her shoulder.

She called after him, "Soon, Dad is coming back. Everything will be fine. Just wait and see."

He walked toward the forest's exit, throwing his hands in the air. Andreas sighed.

"Everything will be okay," she said to herself. She breathed deeply and reminded herself of her past accomplishments in overcoming adversity. Determined, she committed to confronting the obstacles ahead and believing everything would be all right.

***

The following day, Aisley stood in the Cherish's residence wearing a silk and lace dress. Agrona entered, wearing a costume.

"Good morning, sister. You look lovely today," greeted Agrona.

Aisley chuckled and replied, "Yes, the weather is on my side." Agrona then informed Aisley that she had to leave for work and might be late again tonight. She thanked Aisley for caring for the kids and asked her not to set a plate out for her for dinner. Aisley grinned and went back to reading her newspaper.

Agrona was about to leave, so she asked Aisley what she had planned for the day. Agrona sounded anxious and stumbled over her words, hinting that she had something to say but was hesitant. Aisley replied, "I'll assist the head vampire as he trains Ben." She then raised a piece of paper to hide her face.

Agrona raised an eyebrow, sensing that something was bothering Aisley. She gently asked, "Is there something you want to tell me?"

Aisley remained quiet.

Agrona hesitated, then left. Aisley exhaled.

***

Ben opened his eyes in the basement of Python Seger. He could hear muffled screams.

Tassos asked, "Did you have a dream?"

"Yes, it was a nightmare." Ben, a good-looking man with a beard in his mid-twenties, sat up as he responded.

Tassos then asked, "Was it better than training?"

Ben looked at the elder vampire. Tassos looked like he was in his upper thirties. He had been spending nights with him in the basement. Ben could hear indistinct chatter come from upstairs.

Ben and his mentor, in their training clothes, stepped outside into a gray, grim yard. Aisley, armed, ready to halt things if matters got out of hand, aimed her wand at Ben. He followed Tassos to a line of multiple people.

Tassos said, "They're going to launch an assault."

"Again?"

"Until they are killed."

Ben regarded the people. "Can this be done after breakfast?"

The butch vampire knocked a human over with a clatter. The vampire told the man he had pushed down, "You are in Grorhorn, little man."

The man trembled in fear as he looked up at the towering vampire. "Where is Grorhorn?" he stammered, his voice filled with panic.

The vampire sneered, revealing his sharp fangs, and replied, "Grorhorn is a realm where your kind is at our mercy."

Ben punched the vampire with a grunt. The vampire pushed Ben, who fell into the line of humans. The vampire then grabbed hold of Ben's hair.

The vampire, with ferocity in his voice, proclaimed, "I am Mania." He then grunted and attacked Ben once again. However, Ben managed to get back up on his feet.

"You're not Mania. You're just a maniac," he retorted.

The vampire's eyes glimmered with evil intent as he spoke, "I am Mania, the embodiment of sheer power and unstoppable might. Your tenacity is impressive for a newcomer." Ben's resolve strengthened as he realized the vampire's hostile behavior was simply a way to test his physical endurance.

The brutish vampire swung at him, Ben dodged and head-butted him, sending him flying. Other vampires with scary, rough features lunged at him. Ben rolled down the grassy knoll taking the vampires in the wet, slushy mud. They clamored. He grabbed one vampire and dragged him along the ground by his feet. Another vampire punched him. Ben stumbled backward, then retaliated with a martial arts kick to the vampire's chest. Ben threw another over his shoulder and another over his head. A vampire grabbed him from behind. Ben flung him to the ground, where they wrestled in the gray mud. Ben clambered to his knees to punch another attacker. Aisley rushed forward, firing sparks into the air, allowing Tassos to tackle Ben away.

"What's next?" Ben asked.

He took Ben back into the basement. A dark, stern cell-like room. The door was locked closed behind him.

"Are you that determined to fight these vampires?" Tassos asked. "Take them on individually since they won't be able to harm you due to your near-indestructibility."

"There were, *uh*, six of them. I believed I had to. They would have killed the humans. I had no choice but to confront the creatures. They posed a grave threat to the lives of humans, and it was my responsibility to protect them at all costs."

"Five, Mr. Black," Tassos said. "Humans are the lowest form of life." The tall, well-dressed head vampire emerged from the darkness. "No matter how far you choose, this realm is still too sparse for someone like you to vanish—a wolf, a vampire. In the underworld, creatures like you are greatly feared. I can show you the way."

"What gives you the idea that I need a path?"

"Someone like you chose to come here. You realize that you require assistance in exercising self-control. You have lost your way, however noble your intentions may be."

Ben looked at him weary. "And which route do you suggest?"

Ben laughed and asked, "So you're vampire vigilantes?"

The response was firm. "No, we're not vigilantes. A vigilante is someone who gives in to pleasure-seeking and can face harsh consequences. However, if you push beyond being just a human, a vampire, or a werewolf and become something more, you become all three. When you're determined to pursue your goal, you transform completely into that thing."

Ben was informed that he would finish training the next day. He was also told about a rare black flower that grows on the west hills. He could try to take a flower from there if he was bored with working for the ministry and fighting small-time thieves. He might find what he sought if he brought it back to Tassos.

***

Andreas glanced at the clock again, feeling a mix of anticipation and nervousness. As the minutes ticked by, she couldn't help but wonder if their plan to raise funds for the Alliance of Obscurations would be successful. The thought of making a difference in the fight against evil filled her with determination.

"It's the least we, as a school, can do for the families of those who lost a loved one in this year's attacks. Once the ministry takes care of the situation, it's over in our eyes. However, the suffering will never end for the families." Melissa knew that the families affected by the attacks would forever carry the burden of their loss, and she felt a deep sense of responsibility to support them in any way she could. With each passing second, her anticipation grew, hoping that their efforts would bring some solace to those grieving families.

"Yes, it is terrible." She thought of Andrew's suffering family. She remembered the pain and anguish she had witnessed in their eyes during the vigil for their missing son, which weighed heavily on her heart. Andreas knew that no amount of words or gestures could fully alleviate their pain, but she was determined to be a source of comfort and strength for them in their darkest moments.

Melissa sighed once more as she painted a poster for the fundraiser.

"Do you have visions?" Andreas asked Melissa, noticing her anxious expression. She felt concerned that Melissa might be aware of things she hadn't disclosed yet about her.

As Andreas leaned in closer, Melissa explained that her grandmother Alvina had experienced constant visions after losing her sight and that Melissa herself had a similar ability despite being fully sighted. "It's like having a sixth sense," she said in wonder, adding that it was a real phenomenon among witches. Andreas was intrigued and asked how to unlock this ability, eager to learn more about this mysterious gift. Melissa explained that it affected three out of every nine witches and had to be opened, describing it as an additional sense. Although some might find it hard to believe, Melissa assured Andreas it was a genuine ability.

Andreas nodded, the clock's ticks echoing through her mind, and stared off.

***

Casper and Tassos were sitting opposite each other in the attic. "Casper, my dear, you have many admirable qualities as a young man. Would you like to work with me at Python Seger?" Casper smiled in response.

Meanwhile, Aisley was smoking bone dust in the hallway and waiting for Tassos. She urgently needed to speak with him in private.

He followed her down the hallway, where she opened her old bedroom door and proceeded inside. He paused in the hallway before entering the room, after which he closed the door behind her.

Inside, she presented a box. It contained a creature that somewhat looked like a python. Its skin was covered with red sores that moved throughout its body.

"What does this mean?" Tassos asked.

"Pytonorm Dolg, formed by the soul of someone whose dying emotion was hopelessness. I think it has to do with Bliant or Brad."

***

Andreas returned to the site where the ritual had taken place only the night before in the woods. Hopeful to see her father's belongings gone and some evidence of his return, she had nothing but a gleeful smile on her face, despite the atrocities she had experienced less than a day prior. However, to her dismay, the poor girl saw no proof of her father's return home, as everything lay just how it had been left before the group's departure. Saddened with the anxieties of thinking they may have done the ritual for nothing, the young girl could but only muster up a soft sigh as she lowered her head and decided to return home to her family.

She headed back home to find Casper sitting on the porch whistling as he shined his shoes.

"Hey, what happened to Dad, sweetie?" Casper asked.

"Casper, nothing happened," she replied with a sigh as she leaned against the railing. "It's been a while now, and the ritual failed."

Casper giggled slightly and said, "Think of it as a blessing." Andreas explained that Dad's belongings were still there when she returned to the woods. Casper asked, "Why would you want to return to the woods? Dad's body would be where the soul would return."

"But Thor's ritual didn't say anything about that," she said.

Casper felt a deep sense of worry and fear as his sister toyed with matters of life and death without understanding the basics. Casper's subsequent cruel words hit home, and Andreas couldn't help but focus on the nearby cemetery. His sister walked away, but the gravity of the situation sunk in, and he wondered if she truly understood the potential consequences of her actions. The weight of it all made Andreas feel uneasy.

She hurried past and stopped at the cemetery's entrance to search for any indications of her father. She walked up to her father's grave with a heavy heart. Her father's had completely collapsed, she observed. Andreas scanned the cemetery in fear. Particularly after she saw that her father's coffin had been torn open, she could feel her heart beating out of her chest. *He's gone. What happened to him?* There were no signs of her father, so she wasn't sure where he would have thought to look or if someone had already found him. Andreas was powerless. She had to decide what to do. As panic set in, Andreas realized she couldn't waste more time pondering over her father's disappearance. With determination in her eyes, she made up her mind to search for him herself, leaving no stone unturned. She knew that finding him was the only way to bring peace to her heavy heart and end the tormenting questions that plagued her mind.

***

At the Cherish house, Aisley sat with Isabella, Casper, Thor, Daniel, Oliver, and Jimmy. Before they had time to eat, they heard loud thumping bangs at their front door. Aisley and the Cherish siblings looked over to the door. Thor left his paper napkin on the table and walked to the door. Through the frosted glass, he could see a shadowy figure knocking. The heavy thumping continued. Thor walked toward the door and reached for the doorknob.

CHAPTER 17

At the Cherish house, the knocks continued at the door. Thor opened the door to find Andreas.

She mentioned losing her key as she entered the room and wanted to check on everyone. Thor greeted her with a smile and announced that Bliant had returned after digging himself out of his grave. She was amazed, and Thor hugged Andreas, which was unusual for her younger brother. She asked how Bliant was doing, and Thor replied that Dr. Caressa had examined him and that he was doing great. Thor expressed his happiness and relief but also mentioned that Bliant was still adjusting since his mind had not fully recovered.

"Thor, I'm so… happy and relieved."

Thor sighed. "Me, too. I expect I'll be even more when the stupor wears off within a week."

Andreas' smile faded. "Stupor?"

"Yeah. Trapped in the grave after death and returning to life was traumatizing, but it's not unusual. According to Dr. Caressa, he should soon be able to eat and speak normally again."

"He isn't speaking?" Andreas enquired.

"Dr. Caressa assured me that it was a common side effect after such a traumatic experience and that, with time and therapy, his ability to speak would gradually return. She emphasized the importance of patience and understanding during his recovery process."

Thor shook his head. A creak came from down the hall.

"Is that him?" she asked eagerly. Bliant sat quietly on the bed while her mother closed the bedroom door.

"Mom said he needs to take a break."

She stared at the closed door. Agrona exited the room and walked to the kitchen.

Casper stood in the kitchen, wearing a suit. He asked his mother, "What do you think of my outfit?"

Smiling, his mother exclaimed, "Aww! You look so dashing, Casper!

That suit suits you and makes you look very sophisticated."

"I'm starting at Python Seger tomorrow," he announced. "I wanted to dress up a bit old-school." He spread his arms out. "Is it too much?"

"Not at all," replied his mother. She added that first impressions are important, and you only get one chance to make a good one. Casper grinned. "Okay. The stew is almost ready. Could you set the table and call everyone over?"

"Andreas is going to Uncle Daemon's, and Auntie Ais has been gone forever."

"Oh?" Agrona raised an eyebrow. "I wonder where she went."

"I'm not sure," Casper admitted. "But I think she mentioned going on a business trip. I'll try to find out more for you."

***

"I wish I had known about this confession method earlier, especially since Church of Mania members can use it too."

"In a fire, I feel reborn."

Tassos agreed and said, "The best way to show reverence is to repent from the body. It provides us with both discipline and joy." However, he hoped they could meet somewhere less humid, but they had to keep their devotions private due to Horus' mother's restrictions. He longed for the past when Heofsijs were the only race practicing monogamy, while all other witches embraced polyamory under Astradung's regulations. He wistfully sighed as he adjusted his dark suspenders and reminisced about how societal norms had changed.

"There is a tale to be shared about the experience of journeying with one sole companion through both the joyful and challenging moments."

"As you are aware, Aisley, the arrival of my second child is the most important and life-changing event for me. However, I worry more and more that my wife won't be the mother they need," Tassos admitted. Aisley lowered her eyebrows. "Would you be willing to serve as their Mania Mother?"

Her mouth hung open. "I'd be honored to be your boys' Mania Mother." Aisley's heart swelled with gratitude as she realized the depth of trust and responsibility the head vampire placed in her. She knew that being their Mania Mother would be an honor and a chance to provide the love and guidance that Tassos feared his wife might not be able to offer. Aisley silently vowed to herself that she would do everything in her power to be the best Mania Mother for his second child, ensuring they never felt lacking in maternal.

Mania Mother is a woman who presents a child at baptism and promises to take responsibility for their religious education. In this case, Aisley would bring up Tasso's newborns under the church of Mania, the goddess of the dead, who rules the underworld along with Mantus. She was said to be the mother of ghosts, the undead, and other spirits of the night. She is also the goddess of insanity and madness. It wasn't a surprise that the Soleils worshiped this god. As they die and return often, there is no need to worship any other god. The necklace they used to keep them alive required sacrifices to Mania, hence why the number of necklaces was scarce.

He donned his jacket and expressed concern about his wife's classes at Python Seger and the choir director at the same institution. He requested Aisley's assistance managing them as his wife tired easily these days. Aisley nodded understandingly, maintaining a friendly smile on her face.

"Certainly, I would be more than happy to assist your wife with her duties at Python Seger," Aisley replied warmly. "It's crucial to ensure she doesn't overexert herself, considering how easily she tires. Rest assured. I'll make sure everything runs smoothly for her.

***

In the attic, Andreas told Casper that their ritual had succeeded and "it worked." Overwhelmed with excitement, she immediately shared this news with her elder sibling.

Casper hesitated to check their father's condition, but Andreas reassured him that he was okay. It was unclear whether Bliant fully grasped what had happened to him. Despite Casper's reluctance to speak with their dad, when he went to see Bliant himself, he noticed that his father seemed to be experiencing shock, which Dr. Caressa deemed normal. Casper recommended Andreas get a second opinion, particularly if the doctor was unaware of the type of magic used during the resurrection. Everyone warned them not to go through with it. Still, Andreas was sure that in a week, their father would recover and be able to talk and eat again. Casper questioned why he wasn't eating and realized that they needed to inform their mother and Aunt Aisley about the truth of his return. However, Andreas insisted they keep this between them, as their mother and aunt may not understand what occurred, which could cause unnecessary panic. "Our focus should be on aiding our father's recovery."

"They'll likely figure it out soon. The kingdom is small, so it's a big deal when someone returns to life without a necklace. They probably already suspect something."

"But the truth is, he didn't come back to life – he dug himself out of his grave, but I agree with you. Eventually, they will discover the truth, but it will be too late to do anything about it. Our father will be back to normal by then. Therefore, we should focus on what matters most: that our father is alive and well. Instead of worrying about their anger and disappointment, we should prioritize our family's happiness and unity. Let's not dwell on the past or their reaction. Instead, let's enjoy this moment together."

Andreas left her brother's room to get ready for bed. She brushed her teeth, sighed, then crossed to her bedroom wearing a robe. Her familiar Domino meowed.

Andreas heard Domino meow again and asked, "Is something bothering you, Domino?"

Horus expressed concern. "I think I'm scaring him."

Startled, she asked, "Horus, what are you doing in my room? How did you get in here?"

"I didn't physically enter your room," Horus replied, turning toward the window where a candle with a flickering flame sat on the sill.

"You're astral projecting," Andreas explained.

Horus enquired about her father's well-being, to which Andreas responded that he was fine and up and about.

Horus accused Andreas of lying, which prompted her to request that he leave. With a hurt expression, Horus explained that he just wanted to make sure she was doing okay. Andreas softened her tone and thanked him for his concern but expressed a need for alone time.

They stared at each other as another candle appeared on the window sill that Domino now sat beneath. The flames flickered.

"To risk everything for your family, you must truly love them."

"Yes, I love my family," replied Andreas.

Horus responded, "Oh," before asking if Andreas' family had appreciated her sacrifices. Andreas looked to her right, and Horus noticed they must've been clueless. She acknowledged the danger involved if things went wrong with her father but confidently stated that he was doing well and was a strong and resilient man.

Andreas spoke with pride, expressing gratitude for her father's unwavering support and willingness to do whatever it took to protect their family. She planned to follow in his footsteps and do the same.

"You wish," said Horus before his likeness disappeared. Andreas was surprised by this and stared with her mouth open at the three candles with crackling flames on the window sill.

"Domino, please go to my father and keep an eye on things to ensure our safety," Andreas instructed. Domino meowed loudly, and his tail anxiously swished as he approached the door.

Andreas felt worried as she watched him leave, but she whispered a silent prayer for her father's well-being before returning to the flickering candles on the windowsill with a heavy heart.

The floor downstairs creaked.

Thor noticed his father, Bliant, standing in the corner as he entered the living room. He flicked his wand to light the lantern, igniting it with a purple flame and called out to his father. "Dad?"

Bliant was preoccupied, rubbing his fingernail against the mirror. Thor approached him and placed his hands on his father's shoulders.

With a startled expression, Bliant turned around, surprised to see his son. "Oh, Thor! I didn't hear you come in," he exclaimed, stepping away from the mirror. "I was just lost in thought."

Sensing a distant look in his father's eyes, Thor gently asked, "Is everything okay?"

It had been the first time his father had spoken since the accident. Bliant hesitated for a moment, then sighed deeply. "I'm just trying to process everything that happened," he admitted, his voice filled with sadness and confusion. Thor nodded understandingly, realizing that his father was still struggling to deal with the accident.

He guided his father to sit on the couch. Thor grunted as he sat beside him.

"Would you like to look at some paintings?" asked Thor. "The doctor suggested it could be beneficial." He showed a collection of family paintings. "See, here." Thor pointed to a picture. "You and Mom took us to Teddy Scaasi's last carnival. I got lost on the grounds, and you found me. Remember how worried my mother was?"

Bliant nodded, a hint of nostalgia in his eyes. "Yes, I recall that day. It was quite an adventure. Your mother was very concerned, but we found you and brought you back home safely. Teddy Scaasi's carnival holds a special place in our memories." Bliant's face returned to its expressionless state.

Bliant stared straight ahead. Thor turned a page with a sigh. The photo of Bliant in his green Viridi robe caught Bliant's eye. He stared and reached out to point at it.

"Yeah," responded Thor. "Dad, you were one of the best teachers. Up until this point, you were a teacher. We would always attend each of your formalities. You always had a way of making even the most mundane subjects interesting and engaging. We were fortunate to have you as our guide throughout our educational journey at home and school. Your passion for teaching was evident in every lesson you delivered."

***

Lulia was sitting in her bedroom, conversing with the invisible A.C. as she gazed out the window. The warm glow of the setting sun bathed her room in peaceful hues, creating a tranquil atmosphere. She heard A.C. say out loud, "You were born for this role."

"I can't. What happens if I—?"

"Get caught? Then you flee."

Lulia chuckled. "I'd be grounded if my dad ever found out." A knock rapped on her bedroom door. "Yeah?"

"Lulia, may I enter?" John Scaasi enquired.

"Sure."

Lulia's father opened the door. Lulia was sitting in bed. He questioned, "Who were you talking to?"

"Nobody, Dad." He hung his head, glanced around the room, and put his hands in his pockets.

Lulia could sense her father's concern as he hesitated before speaking again. "I thought I heard voices," he admitted, his voice filled with worry.

Lulia quickly reassured him, "It was probably just the Movey, Dad."

She pointed toward the movey set – a mesmerizing masterpiece of magic and innovation in this fantastical realm. The Scaasis had upgraded their system, which was much better than the video box they had two years ago. It was designed to float effortlessly in mid-air, with a sleek and ethereal look that defied the laws of physics. The screen could morph into any desired shape or size, making it perfect for viewing everything from panoramic landscapes to close-ups of fantastical creatures. This new system could also transmit emotions, making it even more enchanting.

Her father nodded, but there was still a hint of suspicion in his eyes as he left the room, closing the door behind him.

***

At Python Seger, the students chattered. Andreas snuck into Daemon's office. She left the door slightly ajar, crossed to the smaller bookshelf, and took a book from her bag.

As she approached the door, Daemon was waiting for her. "Hello, Uncle Daemon," she greeted him.

"Hello," he replied. "Did you know that last night's bad wind moved through Galdorwide like a flash of lightning? It was as though a veil separating realms had been torn apart."

"I didn't know that," she admitted. "I mostly stayed inside last night."

"But surely you heard the hounds," he said. "All night, it sounded like every dog in Galdorwide was standing and bemoaning something. It was thrilling. It was motivating. You weren't thinking about stealing my copy of necromancy, were you?" Daemon sat down at his desk.

"I wasn't trying to steal your copy of necromancy." Andreas chuckled. "I was engrossed in a book about ancient enchantments. The howling of the hounds must have created an eerie atmosphere throughout Galdorwide. I can only imagine how unsettling it must have been." She looked out the window and noticed that the storm's aftermath had left a sense of mystery and intrigue. Andreas glanced briefly at her uncle before looking away and sighing. "Uncle Daemon?" she called out.

"Yes?" he responded.

Andreas held up a book in her hand and lied, "I grabbed the wrong book. I was looking for The Occultist's Journal." She picked up the correct book from the shelf and asked, "Is it okay if I borrow this for extra credit in

Tassos' class?"

Daemon smiled and said, "Of course. Just make sure to return it once you're finished. The Occultist's Journal is valuable, and I don't want it to go missing."

Andreas nodded gratefully, happy that her request was granted. She was excited to start exploring the pages of the journal and uncover its hidden secrets.

In the hallway of Galdorwide High, Melissa approached Andreas. Kids chattered. Melissa exhaled.

"Is it true, Andreas, what people are saying about your dad still being alive?" enquired a friend.

"People already know?" Andreas responded in surprise.

"Yes, Sir Maddox Cherish claimed to have seen your dad through a window while delivering a package across the street from your house."

"It's a miracle," Andreas announced.

"Or it could be the opposite," said Melissa.

"Why do you say that?" asked Andreas.

"Last night, I had a strange dream," Melissa described. "There was a storm, and I heard the howling and barking of hounds as I wandered further into the forest. Eventually, I came to a clearing, and a group of people surrounded a mysterious object, like some ancient artifact. They were arguing over it, and there was a sense of danger. Your dad was holding the artifact." Andreas looked at her with concern, realizing that Melissa's vision might hold more significance than she initially thought.

Andreas pulled her aside.

"Mel, I need to talk to you about something serious. I'm worried about my family, particularly my father's health. I'm trying to figure out what's wrong with him. Could you help us figure it out?"

"How can I assist you with that?"

"I'm not sure. You have a special ability, right?"

"I'm not sure what you mean."

"You said you experienced a vision when you touched my father's wand. Maybe if you could get close to my father, you could tell if something is wrong with him."

Melissa considered Andreas' suggestion and nodded.

***

"Today was a liberating experience, Your Excellency," said Casper.

In Tassos' office, Benjamin and Casper sat across from him. Tassos said, "I can imagine." He then gave them a gift, a symbol of their shared kinship. "You have been denied a fundamental witch right for far too long. One of your familiars, a goblin with impeccable bloodlines. He goes by the name Behemoth." Tassos went toward a large crate.

As he opened it, a goat bleated. Casper thanked Tassos and said, "Behemoth is magnificent, and I am grateful to have him as my familiar. This gesture strengthens our bond even further, Tassos."

"Casper, these are challenging times for Python Seger. I sense it. I have collaborated with Benjamin to revamp the academy's laws, instruction, and foundation."

"Would you like any help from me, Your Excellency?"

"We'll see. In the meantime, you could help Benjamin translate a ten-volume set of the Traitor Bibles that's been troubling him."

"Sure."

"I'm making my rounds. But you're welcome to spread out." He coughed while standing with his cane.

"Sure. Thank you, Your Excellency. My first day has been productive. I've gained new insights and ideas to create an inclusive and diverse learning environment that promotes innovation and critical thinking. With your guidance, we can make significant changes to benefit the students and the academy's reputation."

Casper bowed his head. Tassos left, and Casper turned to Ben with a grin. Shortly after they opened the first volume, the door opened.

"Where is Tassos?" Elvira asked.

Ben sighed. Elvira, Jiselle, and Horus entered.

Tassos was making his rounds when Horus was looking for assistance from him.

"My friend, Mamie, is currently unwell. She has been experiencing intense headaches and fatigue over the past few days, and we are unsure of the cause. Unfortunately, the doctors have not been able to determine the underlying issue," said Jiselle.

They suspected Casper's sister had tampered with the afterlife and wanted to know if it was related. Horus argued that Andreas' father had returned and was doing well, so they couldn't understand why she was ill. Casper was curious about why Andreas was involved and who had confirmed that his father was all right. Horus mentioned that Andreas had informed him, but Casper shrugged and suggested her involvement was still debatable. Elvira added that they had heard rumors about Andreas dabbling in forbidden rituals, which could be connected to Mamie's strange condition.

"When it comes to elements of necromancy, I'm no specialist, though... I do know someone who is."

***

During their time at the academy, Agrona examined Mamie while Horus explained that her symptoms began the previous night.

Agrona scrutinized Mamie's excrements, searching for clues to identify the cause of her ailment. Horus expressed his concern for Mamie's strange behavior since the onset of her symptoms. Casper observed silently before suggesting that her condition could be related to something she ate. Agrona considered his suggestion and shared her belief that it may be a decompression illness.

Agrona suggested conducting additional tests to verify her suspicion. She clarified that decompression illness may arise from a swift ascent from deep underwater, forming nitrogen bubbles in the bloodstream. It could also occur if someone had recently returned from the dead. Casper nodded in agreement, acknowledging the possibility of decompression illness due to a rapid ascent from deep underwater. However, he questioned the likelihood of someone recently returning from the dead, as it seemed highly improbable.

Casper claimed that people would have remembered if Mamie had died, but Horus rebutted by pointing out that she also did not go deep-diving in the ocean.

Nevertheless, Casper agreed that additional tests would be necessary to confirm Agrona's suspicion and determine the exact cause of her symptoms. Casper asked how they could help Mamie, and Agrona explained that they needed to find a way to stabilize her condition and relieve pressure buildup in her body. She suggested consulting specialists and running further tests to determine the root cause of her symptoms.

Elvira agreed and suggested gathering all necessary medical records and scheduling an appointment with a specialist as soon as possible.

"Wait," Horus interjected. "We may have missed something. There was a day when we didn't see her because she and Daemon had gone camping the night before. According to him, she was sick."

"So let's hold on calling on specialists because perhaps Daemon did revive her on their camping trip. It is important to consider that reviving someone requires expertise and specialized equipment, making it challenging to do so alone. However, Mamie's resilient body has shown the ability to withstand extreme conditions, whether submerged in deep sea waters or buried underground. To help her regain her internal balance, it's recommended to include the four elements in her diet by choosing foods corresponding to each element. For the earth element, include foods that grow underground, such as root vegetables and grains. Opt for light and airy foods such as herbs and leafy greens for air. To represent fire, add spicy or warming foods like peppers and ginger. Lastly, incorporate hydrating foods such as fruits and vegetables with high water content for the water element. By mindfully selecting these foods, you can create a diet that aligns with the elemental needs of a witch who feels unwell."

Elvira fixed Agrona in her gaze. "Is that it? A proper diet?"

Agrona agreed and added, "Apart from a nutritious diet, addressing other aspects of your holistic well-being is crucial. Incorporating regular physical activity, practicing mindfulness or meditation, and spending time in nature can contribute to your overall health as a witch."

As she was leaving and closing the door, Casper approached her in the hallway. "I don't mean to question you, Mother, but you suggested food and drink for a girl who may have survived a serious accident. What made you change your mind about the specialists?"

Agrona pondered, "It will keep them occupied. It was a mistake to transport Mamie back in the first place. Her body is eliminating dirt that feels like gravel."

Casper furrowed his brow, trying to understand his mother's reasoning. "But wouldn't it be better for Mamie to receive proper medical care and attention? I worry that her condition might worsen without the specialists' expertise," he said.

Agrona sighed, her eyes filled with a mix of regret and determination. "I know it may seem counterintuitive, but keeping her here will allow us to uncover the true cause of her affliction. My brother tried to revive her, but it seems like the land wants to reclaim another life in return," Agrona explained anxiously to her son. She begged for an explanation on how both of them were resurrected in one night. The confusion and desperation in her voice were palpable as they both struggled to make sense of the situation. They were searching for a glimmer of understanding amidst the chaos surrounding them.

A stoic expression covered Casper's face.

***

Bliant was seated at the dining room table opposite Melissa and Andreas. Melissa released a sigh. He maintained his gaze ahead. Andreas faced Melissa and nodded. Melissa responded with a slight nod and a faint smile, her eyes showing weariness and worry. Melissa reached out and gently grasped Bliant's hands. She closed her eyes. Melissa usually sensed the emotional burden of others upon physical contact, but when she touched Bliant, she didn't perceive anything. Melissa felt confused and anxious as she opened her eyes and gazed at Bliant's face, desperately searching for any hint of emotion. He remained stoic and unreadable despite her attempts to read his expression, leaving her uneasy. She inhaled sharply and observed a vision that unraveled before her eyes. In a desolate landscape surrounded by darkness, Melissa spotted Bliant standing alone. She became more concerned as she noticed his lack of emotion, realizing something was bothering him deeply.

Melissa was worried about the significance of the vision and realized that she needed to assist Bliant in comprehending the distress he was experiencing.

Melissa's curiosity was sparked by a sound she heard. Melissa followed it and stumbled upon a deserted cottage hidden in the darkness. As she approached, the screams grew louder, tugging at her heartstrings. With apprehension and determination, Melissa cautiously entered the cabin, hoping to find answers and perhaps even a clue to alleviate Bliant's distress. She could hear echoes of far-off whispers inside. The hushed voices came from a distant room, drawing Melissa further into the cottage. The air felt heavy with mystery, and she couldn't shake the feeling that she was being watched.

Nevertheless, driven by her compassion, Melissa pressed on, determined to uncover the source of the cries and end Bliant's suffering. In front of her, Melissa noticed a young man pacing around the cottage. He appeared lost in his thoughts, oblivious to Melissa's presence. His eyes were filled with a mixture of sorrow and desperation, mirroring the distress that Bliant had been experiencing. Intrigued by his presence, Melissa cautiously approached him, hoping that he might hold the key to unlocking the secrets of the cottage and bringing relief to both Bliant and herself.

"Melissa, do you see anything?" Andreas asked.

Melissa shook her head, her gaze fixed on the young man. "Not yet," she replied softly, her curiosity growing. She wondered if he had any connection to the cottage's mysterious past or if he was simply another lost soul seeking solace in its walls.

Andreas' voice came from a ghoulish woman who touched Melissa's shoulder. "Melissa, we must find out more about him." Her voice was filled with urgency. Melissa turned to face the ghoulish woman, her heart pounding with fear and intrigue. She couldn't shake the feeling that this encounter held the key to unraveling the secrets of the cottage and uncovering its true purpose.

"Andreas?" Melissa asked.

Melissa reared back from Bliant's hands with a gasp. She panted.

"What happened? Are you all right?" Andreas enquired.

Melissa nodded, still catching her breath. "I'm fine," she replied, her voice shaky. "But this woman touched my shoulder, and it was like a surge of energy passed through me. It felt strange." Andreas' eyes widened with curiosity, her mind racing with possibilities.

"There's something more to this cottage than meets the eye."

"I encountered your father or at least a younger version of him. He seemed confused and disoriented as if he didn't recognize me. He mentioned a hidden room in the cottage that holds the key to unraveling its mysteries. We need to find it and uncover the truth."

Andreas' heart raced at the thought of discovering the secrets her father had kept hidden for so long. She knew they were on the brink of something extraordinary.

"Was he accompanied by anyone else?"

"No. No, your father was alone."

The front door flung open and shut. Andreas' tall, active brother Daniel

Cherish, who had black hair and hazel eyes, entered. Daniel Cherish's sudden arrival startled everyone in the room. "What's going on here? Where is Thor?"

"The kitchen. Melissa stopped by to see how we were doing."

Daniel's gaze hardened as he studied Melissa, his ex-girlfriend. Memories of their tumultuous relationship flooded back, fueling his suspicion.

"She's helping us," Thor said as he exited the kitchen.

"Like she knows more than Dr. Caressa."

Andreas and Melissa stood side by side, both looking determined.

"I'll talk to you later, Mel," Thor said with a concerned and uncertain tone. Andreas and Melissa exchanged a glance that conveyed understanding.

"Okay, yeah."

Thor turned to face his father after placing his hands on his hips. Bliant remained expressionless as he fixed his gaze forward.

***

Andreas was going through the books in the Cherish residence attic when Agrona walked in. "Casper is dealing with the corpses in the Nicholson's basement that are starting to give off a strong odor."

"I can explain everything to you, Mom."

"No, your brother already went into great detail about it. I felt confused. And you broke my one piece of advice by doing it."

"I think I can fix everything, and I couldn't bear to see Thor suffer like that. I need to reinsert Dad's soul into his body."

"It's too late for that."

Andreas' voice trembled as she continued, "I know it's risky, but I've been researching ancient rituals that could reverse the soul separation. There might still be a way to save Dad and bring him back. Melissa told me she saw my father lost in the misty woods and heard a baby crying. However, it's unclear if the baby's mother was there too. The woods are said to be where the souls of those who passed away before their time and the spirits of unbaptized infants go, regardless of their religion. I need to go there to retrieve my father's soul."

Agrona scoffed and asked, "Will you? Firstly, Andreas, there are two types of exiles: Heofsijs and witches. Secondly, it's absurd for sorcerers to travel across these realms, let alone successfully remove a soul."

Despite Agrona's skepticism, Andreas was determined to find a way to retrieve her father's soul. She discovered ancient texts that revealed a secret passage to the realm of souls, accessible only to those with certain magical abilities. With newfound hope, she begged Agrona to reconsider and join her on this dangerous journey.

"I'm sorry that the witch you defeated to bring back your father is still deceased. You killed someone. Your Uncle Daemon brought his daughter back due to your one-person sacrifice. Mamie and Bliant's health condition is deteriorating. It appears that the Reaper is causing harm to both your Mamie and father. He is expecting to see additional bodies. The suffering will persist until one is laid to rest and balance is restored. I regret to inform you, Andreas, that the issue cannot be resolved satisfactorily. You have permitted individuals to pass between realms! Andreas, you are still a child. What were you thinking?"

Casper came in and announced, "Hey, everyone, you've got to see this!" The room fell silent as everyone directed their gaze toward Casper. As he spoke, his voice trembled, "I discovered a concealed passage behind a cabinet. There is a secret chamber that contains ancient artifacts and symbols." They were perplexed by the discovery. "Finding a solution for the Reaper's curse and bringing back equilibrium is possible. We will have to investigate the mysterious depths of this chamber. It is likely to be a new experience for us."

***

Tassos was captivated by Aisley's conducting skills in Python Seger as he watched her lead the choir. The intense atmosphere suddenly shattered when one of the girls let out a piercing scream, causing another to gasp in shock. Just then, Mamie stumbled into the room, her face filled with anguish as she pleaded for help with a heartbreaking moan.

The students in the choir murmured. Mud covered the front of her white nightgown, and she collapsed. In the choir, Jiselle, Elvira, and Horus gaped at her.

"How did Mamie become a walking corpse?" Tassos enquired.

Elvira said, "Sir, it's all Daemon and Andreas' doing. One of the king's creatures had attacked her father, and she wanted to bring him back to life."

"Andreas brought a resurrection to pass?" Aisley enquired.

"With a book's assistance." Elvira nodded. "As part of the ritual to bring her father back, she slit her ex's throat."

"Afterward, Daemon must have performed the ritual for Mamie nearby, hoping to escape detection by sacrificing just one person," continued Horus.

"But something went wrong," Elvira said.

"Mamie is getting weaker and weaker." Elvira speculated that the failed ritual may have caused Mamie's life force to be drained. As a result, Mamie's health continued to deteriorate. The group grew increasingly concerned for Mamie's well-being and wondered if there was any way to reverse the effects of the botched resurrection.

"I had no idea about that, Your Excellency," Aisley admitted. "I cannot impose restrictions on my family members or children," Aisley replied. "Girls, please take Mamie to the hospital in Galdorwide, where she should have been taken in the first place. I will care for the revived man, fix things, and clean up this mess. If I may, sir," Aisley said, walking beside him. "Andreas is my niece and under my care. I am responsible for her actions. I will make it right and take back anything she did. Please give me a chance to fix everything. I won't disappoint you again. I promise to do whatever it takes to rectify the situation and ensure that Andreas receives proper care and support. I understand the severity of what happened and will take full responsibility for it. Please let me show you that I can handle this situation carefully and diligently."

Tassos fixed his gaze on Aisley. "Go ahead, then."

She took a deep breath. "I'm grateful." She quickly left the academy and ran into the night. Tassos stood frozen, unsure of what to do next. The chaos in the room was overwhelming, but he knew he had to act quickly.

***

"I've prepared a puzzle for you. Why don't you tell me who you are?" "Daniel, you've been drinking since the attack. It's time to stop now that Daddy is back," Thor urged with concern. Bliant sat on the sofa, and Daniel referred to their father as a 'vegetable' and a 'horrible zombie.' Thor corrected Daniel and pleaded with him to ease up on their father, who was not himself. When Daniel asked if anyone was inside, Thor reminded him not to bother their father and suggested giving him space until he was ready for help.

Daniel exclaimed, "It's not my father. I have no clue what it could be." Suddenly, Thor punched Daniel, causing him to stumble back and hold his jaw in agony. The atmosphere in the room became tense as everyone observed the altercation, uncertain of what would occur next.

Daniel punched Thor, and Bliant grabbed Daniel by the throat.

"Dad! Dad! Dad, please stop!" Thor pleaded. The sound of cracking glass echoed through the room. Thor was desperate to put an end to his father's destructive rampage. Fear consumed him as he imagined the consequences of his father's uncontrolled anger. He felt the tension in the air, and the sound of shattering glass added to the chaos unfolding before him.

Daniel choked and coughed. He stumbled outside, and Andreas approached.

"Daniel!"

"Don't enter that house. He's a beast! Not our father, is he?"

Andreas walked inside the home. She panted, holding a jar full of a clear liquid. "Thor?" She questioned, "What happened?" Bliant was grunting profusely.

"I got punched by Daniel," said Thor. "Dad then attempted to kill him."

"What? Are you all right?"

"Yes, I'm all right. I'm trying to get Dad to be quiet."

"Maybe he's thirsty. Here. Give some of this to him." Andreas handed Thor the jar of clear liquid, who cautiously approached their father and offered him a sip.

"Dad, please calm down," Thor pleaded, hoping the drink would help soothe his father's anger.

Bliant sat on the couch.

Sitting on the front steps, Thor observed, "The only time Dad seems normal is when he's asleep."

"Don't worry, Thor. Dad will recover. The doctor said he's in shock," Andreas assured him.

"I'm not so sure. Something's not right," Thor replied with a shake of his head. "I should be grateful, but I'm not."

Andreas placed a comforting hand on his shoulder. "We'll get through this, Thor. But we need to be careful. Dad is asleep now, but we don't know what he might do if he wakes up and feels threatened."

Thor looked at Andreas, a worried expression on his face. "I promise, Andreas. If Dad threatens you, I'll do whatever it takes to keep you safe. I won't let him harm you." His voice shook slightly with the weight of his words.

Andreas headed inside. Shortly after, her mother and Aunt Aisley arrived home.

"Mom? Aunt Aisley?" Andreas groaned.

Aisley yelled loudly, "I need an explanation! Because my niece was using necromancy on her father!"

"Love, she knows everything," Agrona said, trembling.

"And why in Mania's name would she involve her siblings in her rash, foolish, and self-centered schemes?"

"I did it for Thor."

"And tell me, did Thor ask you to perform this task? No, because a person of good judgment wouldn't act as you did. How exactly did you know which spell to cast? According to Casper, he didn't give it to you."

"I didn't," Casper affirmed.

Andreas responded, "Daemon."

"Daemon told you the spell?" Aisley enquired.

"I took a book from his office," Andreas said.

"Oh, I see. You're also a thief. The admission of taking a book from Daemon's office adds another layer to your character, suggesting a lack of integrity and respect for others' property. This revelation further reinforces the negative traits previously mentioned, such as being rash and self-centered. Andreas, this is a serious matter. You and Daemon have disrupted the balance of the universe."

"It was Uncle Daemon's doing. I only killed to bring back my father. Daemon didn't kill anyone."

"But you made the situation worse. What can we do? Blaming Uncle Daemon for upsetting the balance won't help. We need to find a solution instead of focusing on who caused this. We should explore all options and seek professional help to give your father the best chance of recovery."

"I have a plan to bring Dad back," Andreas shared with her aunt. Casper, Agrona, and she had discovered a secret chamber in the old

Nicholson Mortuary building. They had found ancient scrolls that contained a powerful incantation capable of returning the departed.

With cautious excitement, they embarked on a journey to gather the rare ingredients needed for the spell, hoping this could be their chance to reunite with their beloved father again. Andreas confidently stated that the incantation would take her to limbo, and she had researched how to enter and bring back her father's soul. Aisley asked for clarification, wondering what she meant. Andreas explained that she was capable of traveling to limbo.

Aisley expressed her concern explaining that she could make the situation worse. Andreas was determined to do what was right for Thor and her dad, even if it meant going against Tassos. Aisley sighed and acknowledged the importance of her niece's words. She understood Andreas' determination but reminded her that sometimes sacrifices must be made for the greater good, especially when it involves family.

"I'm afraid you don't have the power to breach the wall," Aisley informed Andreas.

Andreas retorted, "You have no idea what I am capable of."

Aisley responded, "You are not a grand magus; you're just eighteen."

Andreas rolled her eyes in exasperation and snapped, "Stop acting like my mother, Aisley. You are not!" But then she took a deep breath and spoke with determination. "Perhaps you underestimate my abilities, but I will find a way to break through that wall. Age doesn't determine one's potential in the realm of magic. So, please step aside and let me prove you wrong."

"I am not your mother, and you are not a child. You are a skilled magician, and it's important that you understand the workings of the different realms. Every action has a consequence, just like Bliant learned the hard way. Now it's your turn to learn from my teachings. If saving your father comes at a cost, even if it means the destruction of the realm, I urge you to consider it. However, please don't fool yourself into thinking it's entirely selfless. Just be prepared for the consequences. I hope you understand that I am unable to assist." Aisley then walked away, warning Andreas not to blame her if things went wrong.

Agrona gave Andreas a look of disappointment. Tears welled in Andreas' eyes. Casper watched Agrona walk away then stared at Andreas.

"I can't do this without a second witch," stated Andreas.

Casper responded, "Please don't look at me like that."

"But you were the one who found the chamber and helped collect the ingredients. Why won't you lend me a hand?" asked Andreas.

Casper took a moment to weigh her words. "It's not that I don't want to help," he replied, carefully choosing his words. "But the magnitude of power required for this spell is immense, and it could be perilous for both of us." Casper looked deep into Andreas' eyes, hoping she would understand the seriousness of the situation. "No one else will be able to assist you."

"Casper, you're wrong."

Casper scoffed as he left Andreas standing in the front hall by herself.

Andreas knocked on Daemon's cottage door, urgently seeking her uncle's assistance. She knew that her uncle's wisdom and experience would be invaluable in solving the predicament she found herself in.

Daemon opened his door. Andreas entered and sat in front of the fireplace. Daemon poured tea into cups. "I must confess that I feel depressed and guilty about taking something from your workplace. However, I cannot regret my actions when I saw how much Thor was suffering, and I could ease his pain. Even though it was a breach of trust and a lie, my motivations were rooted in empathy and compassion."

"I understand. We have all done terrible things to help those we care about. But even for someone like you, a sorceress, limbo is a dying world. The trapped spirits there are enduring unimaginable pain. A Love-Eater that preys on its victims is on the loose. Do you want to risk going there?"

Andreas looked solemn. "My dad would do it for me."

Daemon looked down, then back up at Andreas.

"In that case, I know of a threshold – a portal to limbo. It's a dangerous journey, but if it means saving your loved ones, I will do whatever it takes to get you there safely. Do you confirm that you possess all the necessary components for the incantation?"

Andreas nodded, determination shining in their eyes. "Thank you, Uncle Daemon. Let's be ready for anything that comes our way, and face it together."

Andreas looked down and stared at the table as Daemon stood. The fire flickered in the fireplace. Andreas rose from her chair and stood across from her uncle. Daemon nodded. Andreas nodded. Andreas headed toward the door.

At the Cherish home, where Aisley had resided since her return, Agrona rapped on the door of her sister's guest room.

"Ais?" Agrona walked into the room. Aisley was harming herself. Agrona's heart sank as she saw the fresh wounds on Aisley's arms. She rushed to her sister's side, gently taking her hands and urging her to stop. "Aisley, please, let me help you find healthier ways to cope with your pain," Agrona pleaded, her voice filled with concern.

"No! No, no, no, no," Aisley continued to protest, pulling her hands away from Agrona's grasp. Tears streamed down her face as she struggled to express the overwhelming emotions that had led her to self-harm. Agrona held back her tears, determined to be a source of support and understanding for her sister.

"I know it's difficult, Aisley, but you don't have to face this alone. We can find professional help together and work through this," she said softly, hoping that her words would resonate with her sister.

"Quit it!" Aisley tried to pull her hands away.

"Why would you harm yourself like that, Ais?"

Aisley was out of breath, her face red with frustration and confusion. Her arms had red marks, indicating the pain she had caused herself. "I don't know," she stuttered, tears rolling down her cheeks. "It's like a way to let go, a means to deal with all the turmoil inside me."

Agrona gently held Aisley's hands and spoke with concern. "Harming yourself is not the answer, Ais. There are better ways to cope with your emotions."

Aisley looked up at Agrona with desperation. "I just don't know what else to do," she replied, her voice trembling. She was helped onto the bed by Agrona as Aisley struggled to breathe. Suddenly, Aisley spoke up. "We were wrong."

Confused, Agrona asked, "What do you mean?"

Aisley coughed and whispered, "I made a mistake by allowing you to be responsible for her. Teddy should have been her parent instead of you. It was unfair to Andreas. It's not your fault, but maybe her distress stems from her feeling like she wasn't supposed to be brought up by you and Bliant. It should have been me and Teddy here for her."

Agrona's head shook solemnly as she confirmed, "Tony is not the father."

With a sad nod, Aisley confirmed that Tony wasn't the father. It was Teddy. This news surprised Agrona.

Aisley was trembling as she spoke. "I was too arrogant to believe I could help guide her after all these years." Tears welled up in their eyes.

"She reminded me so much of you. Remember?" Agrona nodded and smiled. Aisley couldn't hold back her tears any longer. "I couldn't give her up. I wanted her to be with you." Agrona smiled and drew her sister close. Aisley's voice was barely audible as she spoke. "I can't bear to let her go. It's too difficult."

Agrona's expression softened as she understood the pain and dilemma her sister was going through. "I know it's hard, but sometimes we have to make tough choices for the ones we love," she said gently.

***

Andreas and Daemon stood before the portal that would lead them to limbo. As they approached, Andreas felt a chill run down her spine. The swirling vortex in front of them pulsed with otherworldly energy, drawing them closer. Daemon, always the fearless adventurer, took a deep breath and stepped forward, determination shining in his eyes. The portal was hidden in an ancient, crumbling temple, untouched for centuries. Its mysterious aura beckoned them to uncover its secrets and embark on a journey like never before. The air grew heavy with anticipation as they took their first steps toward the unknown, ready to face any challenges ahead. Andreas positioned herself between her aunt and her uncle. Agrona had decided to join them on this venture. Andreas took a step forward.

"Not so fast." He pulled out a map from his bag, studying it intently. The intricate markings and symbols were key to navigating the treacherous path ahead. With a sense of caution, he pointed out potential dangers and strategized their route, ensuring they would be prepared for any obstacles. "I know of a portal that leads to various realms. But for limbo, we need specific ingredients. Can you remind me what they are?"

"I have a rare herb called 'Elysium Bloom' and a vial of 'Moonstone Elixir.' Both have mystical properties that can open the portal to limbo. Unfortunately, we only have enough for one person, which needs to be me. I'm determined to undo what I've done. Can you please hand me the map?" Andreas quickly consumed the Elysium Bloom and Moonstone Elixir, ignoring any objections from her family. Daemon handed her the map.

"Recite the words now," he instructed her.

Andreas nodded and turned to face the entrance of the archway. She recited the spell as the wind whooshed and smoke billowed. A grin escaped Daemon's lips as screams echoed from the portal. Andreas turned around, and Daemon stifled his grin. Screams continued from the outlet. Daemon bowed his head to Andreas. Andreas slowly backed away. Andreas looked toward the doorway then back to her uncle.

"I'll be waiting right here for you."

Andreas turned reluctantly toward the portal and disappeared in the billowing white smoke. The screaming continued. She felt a mixture of fear and excitement that made her heart race. The screams served as a clear indication of the possible risks she could encounter. Daemon's bowed head showed his respect for Andreas' skills and his awareness of the gravity of the situation.

Distant whispers echoed around Andreas as she made her way through the dense fog in limbo. The fog engulfed everything, muffling even the whispers and making them more eerie and spooky. Andreas felt uneasy as she traveled on, uncertain of what lay ahead in this enigmatic world. A baby cried in the distance. People wandered among the trees, silhouetted amongst the fog.

Andreas called out, "Dad? Bliant?" Her voice echoed through the dense fog, but there was no response. The silence intensified her unease as she pondered whether she was lost or trapped in this eerie realm.

She looked left and right at the zombie-like people as the wind whooshed. The fog engulfed her as distant whispers echoed. Andreas appeared through the mist as she came face to face with a woman with sunken eyes and matted hair. The girl's eyes widened. There was a distant roaring.

Andreas asked the woman if she was okay. The wind was howling, and a creature growled, warning them of the Love Eater's approach. The woman urged Andreas to stay safe and not let the Love Eater catch them. Suddenly, they heard ominous footsteps, and the woman yelled for Andreas to run. Andreas looked toward the growling and saw a dark figure emerging from the shadows. It was the Love Eater, a legendary being known for consuming love and affection. Fear consumed Andreas as she realized the danger she was in.

The Love-Eater growled and roared. The girl ran, and Andreas chased after her. As Andreas passed through a dense fog bank, the heavy footsteps continued to approach. She looked left and right.

Suddenly, Bliant appeared. Andreas panted.

"Andreas?" Bliant enquired.

Andreas shrieked. "Dad! We have to leave, Dad."

"Where are we now? I was in the forest—"

"Dad, everything will be fine, but we must go."

They heard a girl yell 'No!' off in the distance.

"We must flee!" Andreas sprinted after her father, grabbing his hand. As they ran, the ground beneath them trembled with each thunderous step of the Love-Eater. Andreas could feel her heart pounding in her chest, fear gripping her tightly. She glanced back one last time, catching a glimpse of the monstrous creature's menacing gaze before disappearing into the safety of the surrounding darkness.

A man screamed. The Love-Eater's approach could be heard in the distance, causing desperate cries for help to reverberate. This only increased Andreas' resolve to escape. With each step, the grip of the man's hand in hers grew tighter as their shared fear propelled them to run faster and further away from the imminent peril. A woman screamed. The Love-Eater roared and growled.

"Uncle Daemon! I have my father." She yanked at her father's hand, urging him to keep pace. The Love-Eater's guttural growls grew louder, its presence looming behind them like a shadowy nightmare. Andreas knew they couldn't afford to slow down. Their only chance of survival relied on outrunning the monstrous creature and finding safety. Andreas was sprinting through the treacherous terrain, praying that Uncle Daemon would hear her desperate pleas and chant the incantation to reopen the portal.

Heavy footsteps approached. The Love-Eater growled.

Andreas cried out in desperation, "Please open the portal!" Her father, tears streaming down his face, nodded in agreement. They needed to reach Uncle Daemon's realm to escape the Love-Eater's relentless pursuit and find safety. They pushed forward with all their remaining strength, praying for someone to hear their cries for help.

The Love-Eater growled and roared. A woman screamed, and there was a crunching noise.

"*Brynewielm mec, Exorcista sylfum se Ber, alfhun bemeldian se portal*!" Andreas shouted. "*Arstafas mec agustin nierwett icenhilde-weg ben estmere eorl feorh*!"

The Love-Eater growled. The portal appeared in the fog of Andreas and Bliant as the wind whooshed. They dashed through the archway. Fog disappeared. Andreas entered the other side, holding only Bliant's arm. The Love-Eater shrieked. There was a crunching noise.

"What, Andreas?"

Andreas looked at her hand. "No! No! No. No. No. I have to go back inside, Uncle Daemon. I once located Dad. I can find him once more."

He said, "Andreas, you can't." Andreas halted.

"The Love-Eater appears to have caught him, based on what we just witnessed."

"What does that mean that?"

"Mania is aware."

Andreas bowed her head and fixed her gaze on the floor. She arched her brow. "But I swore to Thor that I would fix this." Andreas started crying as she spoke. She gave a headshake. "His body is still here, though. It's all right."

"It could be trickier than that, I think."

Andreas wiped away her tears and looked up at Daemon. "What do you mean by trickier?" she asked, her voice trembling.

Daemon sighed and replied, "It seems his soul is either stuck in another place or has departed completely."

Andreas stared off. She nodded her head and walked away. Agrona joined her daughter. Tears rolled down her cheeks as Daemon watched them leave. His goat familiar, Billie Goat Armstrong, approached him. The goat bleated.

"Well, it took longer than expected, but it's finally happening. Bliant and Thor, who are Andreas' main connections to her Cherish family, are about to sever ties. Unfortunately, we can't blame Mania for this one," said Daemon. Billy then complained that the Love-Eater had made its way into their realm.

***

As she moved through the plush lounge of her home, she saw her family eating dinner. They were visible to her from an open atrium. Andreas thoroughly looked around, and to her left, her mother was holding a tray of dishes. She looked at her, and her mother looked back. Andreas walked into the atrium.

On the other side, her family ate in an alcove under strings of lights. Agrona approached, taking her seat next to Bliant, who was talkative. Couldn't it be him? Could it? His soul was no more, or was it? Did his soul not come through with her because it returned to his body? At the table with the couple were Thor and Jimmy. They were speaking in ancient Galdorian.

"*Hmm?*" Bliant asked Thor who had been speaking. They didn't look up or notice Andreas until she got very close.

Andreas was startled when she saw a pinkish glow emit from her father's eyes.

"*Benugan incer briw,*" her father said, which roughly translated to English as 'Enjoy your meal.' Her father pointed his wand at his daughter.

"Stay calm," she spoke to her mother and brothers telepathically. "Or we are dead."

"Do you not speak Galdorian?" her father spoke to her telepathically. He could hear her thoughts even though they were targeted just for her mother and brothers to hear.

"I do," she replied.

"Then speak in Galdorian. Eat, eat," he said. He was motioning for her to sit down.

Andreas slowly moved to the table and pulled out a chair. She sat. Agrona and her sons kept their eyes down. Only Andreas made eye contact. Bliant kept his wand on her. Agrona trembled as she looked at Andreas, who stayed still, and then looked at her brothers.

The boys took slow and tiny bites with their forks. They kept their heads down as Andreas stared at Bliant.

"*Unc fyr se wiccung belltid, cenningtid lif be se ber. To niht eyre isrbodung fleam afen.*" 'You walked the witching hour, bringing life to the dead. Tonight will be no different.'

She snorted, then crossed her hands in front of her chin. "*Hwa agustin unc fangennes?*" 'Who sent you here?' Her eyes grew fiery, and her nostrils flared. She scoffed.

"*Se heormheortness berhte.*" 'The grieving daughter.' "*Incer iecend, unc behycgan bere nama isrbodung modgung sylfum hwa unc hwaet godsibb?*" 'Your father, you think he'd be proud of what you have become?' he spoke telepathically.

Agrona squeezed her eyes shut, her body shuddering and quivering.

Andreas looked at him and leaned in. The two brothers looked at her then back at their food. "*Ne beinnan ginto sylfum my broctorgyld.*" 'Not in front of my brothers.' Agrona tried to fight back the tears as she sobbed. Andreas leaned back, her face softened.

"*Estmere be findan Mania.*" 'Time to meet Mania.' Pink magic exited his wand.

There was a clattering around the table. Andreas recoiled as her family dropped dead. Their bodies thudded against the floor as they fell off their chairs. Her eyes got wide and sad. Bliant looked at her calmly, then slowly raised his wand. They stared at each other across the long table. Andreas exhaled deeply. Blood from her mother's head seeped onto the marble.

"*Bedtid ahead alfun betynan icer briw.*" 'Go ahead and finish your meal.'

Her brothers lay at the foot of a grand fireplace. Andreas' face sunk as her eyes watered. Bliant's face tightened with rage. A pink stream of his magic shot at Andreas. She groaned. Bliant stood and pointed his wand at the floor. An archway of branches appeared beneath her body and her family, sucking smoke appropriate to their auras from their bodies. When the archway disappeared, the blood on their skin soaked away, and their wounds healed, the holes in their head from the magic had repaired themselves. Their eyes flickered pink.

CHAPTER 18

In the art of enchantment class, something happened that made almost all the students forget about the deaths. Thirty minutes into the class, Professor Fatinah Genther announced that their exams would start on the twenty-sixth of May. One week from today.

"*Exams?*" Thor howled. "We're still going to have exams?"

There was a loud bang behind Thor that came from Clancy banging his fist off of the desk. Outraged by the news of exams not being canceled, Clancy proceeded to slam his fist loudly off his desk. He then cast a vanishing spell, leaving the classroom. Professor Genther was then forced to resummon her defiant student back to the class, returning him to his seat, positioned at Lovetta's side.

Professor Genther, with a frown, turned to face Thor. "The whole point of the queen – I mean, Angel – not canceling school is so that you students can continue with your education," she said sternly. "The exams, therefore, will take place as usual. I trust you will all study hard."

Study hard? How could he cram hard after what had happened and unhappened to his father? Thor thought to himself.

The students began to mutter angrily, which caused Professor Genther to scowl darkly. "Angel's instructions were to keep this school running properly."

Clancy looked at his wand, which he was supposed to use to bless Lovetta with some gift or a new ability. He thought back to everything he had learned this semester: How to fight monstrous creatures, track spiders and other animals through the ominous forest, craft potions that force the victim to speak entirely truthfully, with the most embarrassing lesson learned that he was allergic to holy water. To his annoyance, all of these lessons were not necessarily exam material.

Lovetta looked as if she had been told that she would have to join Amara at the Skogen Prison. "What about Amara?" Lovetta looked at Clancy. "Will he have to be held back a grade?"

"I'm not sure. I hope he's okay in there. He was never good at making friends – we just adopted him after Mike brought him around."

***

Five days before their first exam, Professor Genther had announced at lunch, "I have good news."

The cafeteria jumped, shouting out answers. "Is the queen back? Have they caught the *real* killer? Exams are canceled!"

"With the strenuous investigating from the ministry, one thing has been confirmed, and that is, Amara is not the culprit. He will be arriving back to Galdorwide as soon as possible. Also, the death toll has decreased by one; it turns out Bliant Cherish is alive."

The cafeteria erupted in cheer with the news of Mister Cherish's return and the pending release of their friend Amara. Lovetta looked especially happy to have her friend returning home. Thor looked over at the Chaos group as he wasn't surprised to see that they, too, were delighted. Their wrongfully accused anti-social friend would be back soon. Mike had never looked so happy.

Mike leaned in at his table once the cheering subsided. "I think we should check in on Amara's ghost friend, Ainsley, but I think he would've wanted us to check in on her now and then. I think today is the best time to go. We can give her the good news that he'll be back home soon, and we can avoid her heretic crying."

"Oh," said Annie, who wiped a tear as everything this past week made her feel emotional. "Is a girl crying such a burden?"

Mike leaned back and comforted her after one too many soft no's. Just then, Lulia walked over to the boys' table. She had a very nervous and tense look on her face. She took a seat next to Clancy as Beau followed closely behind her. She twisted her hands in her lap, something Clancy noticed immediately. It was something Flower used to do when she grew anxious.

"What's up?" Clancy asked, helping himself to a plate of a tenderized hog.

She didn't reply. Instead, she just looked up and down the Chaos table. Beau shrugged. She had a scared look on her face.

"Spit it out," said Clancy, who had waited too long for her reply.

"I've got to tell you something," she mumbled, not looking at Clancy.

"What is it?" Clancy asked. Lulia looked as if she were trying to find the words. "Well?"

She opened her mouth, but no sound came out of it. Lovetta surveyed her before leaning forward and speaking only loud enough for Clancy and Lulia to hear. "Is it about the attacks? Do you know something that we don't?"

Lulia drew in a deep breath. Just then, Walter approached, looking tired. Lulia jumped from out of her seat upon seeing him as if it had just zapped her bottom. She gave Walter a frightened look before running off with Beau chasing after her. Walter furrowed his brows before taking a seat next to Lovetta. He took a sip of his caffeine quake that sat on his tray.

"Walter," Clancy began angrily. "Why is my cousin so frightened by you?" Halfway through a sip, Walter choked. "She was just going to say something about the attacks, but now that you're here, she runs off?"

"Oh... her being scared? That has nothing to do with the attacks." Walter coughed.

"Then why?" Clancy asked.

"Well, *er*, if you must know... the other day, she walked in on me and... someone. So, she probably feels awkward." Walter talked faster the longer he spoke.

"What she walked in on you and... someone?" Clancy laughed. "Who? I was over here thinking you were asexual or something."

"I wasn't having sex," Walter said before sipping his drink.

"Good man," said Mike. Annie nodded.

"With who?" Clancy asked.

"We were just snogging, that's all."

"With who?" Clancy asked again.

"I will turn the floor beneath your feet into quicksand if you ask me that one more time," Walter threatened. Clancy put his hands up in surrender.

***

Mike knew that tomorrow Ainsley would be reunited with Amara, but he still wanted to check in. It was the least he could do for his childhood friend. Mike had gone to school in Polar Frigemilt with both Ainsley and Amara. He didn't talk to Ainsley much, but he panicked when he saw the circle of students surrounding their two bloody bodies. Mike could remember how his magic pushed from out of his body when he was told that Amara and Ainsley had been pronounced dead. It was this magic that brought Amara's soul back to his body – the power of true love. Unfortunately, his love and grief was only strong enough to bring Amara back, leaving a shell of Ainsley behind.

Mike couldn't wait any longer, so as he was being led to Professor Gedwormer's art of energy combat class by Mr. Bernard, who looked as if he hadn't slept for weeks. He snuck out from the back of the line and outside where he would then head to Amara's home. Mike darted across the school field. Just as Mike was about to smile about his sleek escape, he was interrupted.

"Mike! Mr. Hansen! What are you doing?"

Mr. Bernard held his hands up in wonder, shaking his head and placing his hands on his hips. Mike knew that he had to turn back around and face the consequences.

"I was—I was," he stammered, "I was going to visit a friend."

"A friend?" Mr. Bernard asked.

"Yes, my friend Ainsley, I haven't seen her for ages, sir. I thought I'd sneak out and visit her while she was on my mind. I just wanted to tell her that Amara would be home soon and that she didn't need to worry about him any more."

Mr. Bernard was still staring at him, and for a moment, Mike thought that he was about to explode, but when he spoke, it was in a croaky voice. "Of course," he said. "Of course, I know how hard this must be for your friends. With Flower dead and Amara wrongfully accused… I quite understand. Yes, Hansen, you may visit your friend. I will inform Professor Gedwormer of your whereabouts and let him know that I have permitted you to be excused from class."

Mike's eyes widened. He had fully expected to be yelled at and sent to afternoon detention, but he was allowed to leave, free of punishment. He could barely believe it as he walked away. Just before Mike could leave school grounds, a letter from the ministry arrived in front of his face.

Dear Mike Hansen,

Of the various fearsome creatures and beasts that walk our ground, none is as exceedingly unique or dangerous as the Luminaris, identified as the King of the Reptiles. This type of Luminaris may reach a gigantic size and live for hundreds of years. It is produced from a phoenix that lays a reptile's eggs. It finds killing most fascinating. For apart from its dangerous and deadly fangs, the Luminaris also releases a sun-bright light only its victims can receive, inducing their death. It is a Luminaris bringing forth the recent deaths of Flower Scaasi and Bliant Cherish. However, we believe a witch figure was behind the death of Varg Thorn and Lynn Denmark. However, the Luminaris is also the creature that may only be defeated by a male Carter.

Sincerely,
Gower Silwhet

***

"The Luminaris can kill by sending out a bright ray from its skin, a bright ray only its target can see. Only those who the serpent intends to kill can see the serpent," Angel explained to Mike and Rabbit when they arrived and took a seat at the ministry's table. "This explains the mysterious deaths. It was my son who, at the mansion, pointed out a large, yellow reptile. I covered his eyes immediately, and I knew that it was this creature that has been causing the kingdom all its troubles along with my father's devout followers." Rabbit's jaw dropped. Gower passed Angel a large book, which she began to skim through.

"A normal Luminaris can be killed by hearing the crow of a rooster or looking at its reflection. However, this may not be a normal Luminaris as we believe that this is the creature my father has enchanted with the gift of only being defeated by a male Carter. I believe that my father has it someplace and teleports it to the victim of his choosing. That day, when Thomas saw it, it was trying to kill Thomas. I believe my father will continue to try and attack my son. So, we will take Thomas and we will protect him. All of us."

Rabbit grabbed onto Mike's arm and began to look around. He wasn't the only one scared. All the ministry members looked unlike themselves, especially since Bella's departure.

"I know where Adelaide is!" Arthur burst into the room.

Krum stood to his feet. "Where?" he growled.

"The forest, deep in the forest! I saw her through a window in the basement of a large cabin. I couldn't get inside. The cabin was swarming with the king's followers. They were in and around the building. I was almost caught. The cabin, it looks like it's some church – a worshipping place for your father." Arthur looked to Angel.

Kenneth Riley, who had been snoring during the meeting, shot up. "Sorry… I dozed off. What have I missed?"

He didn't seem to notice that everyone was looking at him angrily, including the women who had once drooled over him. Krum brought his face to Riley's.

"We need your help. Your daring expeditions have made you the perfect candidate for the job. We have located Adelaide, and we must retrieve her," commanded Arthur. Kenneth's face went pale.

"You mentioned saving a woman from a group of dark practitioners back home, didn't you?" Arthur asked.

Kenneth stumbled over his words, "Yes, I will help."

"It'll be a great opportunity for you. We have to save the girl *and* defeat a Luminaris," Krum added, still inches away from Kenneth's face. "You were telling me you knew what the beast was and that you wished you had had a chance to stop it before Bella's unfortunate departure. But you wouldn't tell us what creature it is, but we know now it to be a Luminaris."

Kenneth stared around at his stone-faced onlookers. "I-I never… you may have just mis—misunderstood."

"Well, tonight's the night we go."

Kenneth and Rabbit looked out of place as if their hearts were dying to burst out of their chests. They both gazed around the room desperately as if hoping to hear that they didn't have to go tonight. Both their lips trembled, and their bodies shook.

"We all must get ready," Angel addressed. She then looked at Rabbit. "And you know the specific requirements on what you need to prepare, correct?"

Rabbit's nostrils flared. He nodded hesitantly. The ministry members rose and left one by one.

***

"No one laugh, all right?" Rabbit called from inside his sister's room.

"No one's going to laugh, we promise!" replied Theodolphus from the living room with a smirk.

The bedroom door slowly creaked open. With a large exhale, Rabbit stepped into the hallway. Theodolphus, Terry, and Elio all let out room-shaking laughs. The members of the Misfit crew and Chaos all kept their laughs in no matter how hard it was.

Rabbit stood in the hallway. On his head sat a set of long blonde hair with two black bows with purple speckled dots on either side of his head. On his eyelids, he had shaded purple eyeshadow. His eyes were topped off with eyeliner and mascara. He wore his sister's Pure school uniform, which consisted of a white long-sleeved dress shirt, purple and yellow tie, and a black kilt. On his legs were a pair of knee-high white socks that didn't quite fit his muscular legs in the flattering way it did on his slim sister. One of the socks was beginning to fall toward his ankle. Terry, Elio, and Theodolphus continued to laugh.

Tired of their laughter, Rabbit raised his wand. "*Bigenge crudland!*" A violent, purple corkscrew of particles exited his rod and circled his three band members.

Terry found his long, curly, brown hair in purple curlers. He looked down to see that he was wearing a purple silk nightgown along with purple and black striped socks. To finish the entire look, purple bunny slippers replaced his black dress shoes.

Elio found black and green rubber bracelets on his wrists. His brown hair lengthened to his shoulders. However, his mustache was still intact. Around his neck was a green scarf. He was now dressed in a green tank top, pointed bra, and a tiny, tight, leather skirt. Large, circular, feathered, green earrings hung from his ears. He seemed most comfortable in his outfit.

Theodolphus wore a blue bonnet. His brown hair curled and grayed, and he was now wearing a long, blue dress and a thick, blue coat and gloves. The cold weather style outfit didn't quite seem to fit the blue sandals placed on his feet. Pearl earrings were set on his ears. He reached for them. "I didn't even have piercings."

Late to the critical meeting, Aksel stood dumbfounded in his tracks as he caught sight of Rabbit from behind. "Woah, who's the chick?" He practically drooled.

Rabbit spun around. Aksel's eyes widened, and he helped himself back outside.

"Guys, ready to go?" Rabbit turned his attention back to his group of friends. Mike and Gavin nodded.

"Can I at least take off the bunny slippers?" Terry asked.

"Nope. All of that is glued on until the battle is over."

Shaking, Rabbit headed out to the schoolyard, followed by his friends. Rabbit saw that Kenneth was shaking too. The ministry members, including Bella, all stood behind him. He had thought it a good idea to sit in the grass as if he were a tired child. He was picking at the grass.

"I'm glad you all came," said Arthur. The group of misfits couldn't help but feel flattered despite the past hatred they once had for the ministry. "Our first mission is to save Adelaide," Arthur continued. "By the sky, we can expect that tonight we will meet face to face with the creature that you, Rabbit, will have to kill." The clouds that rolled violently through the sky were a deep red.

"Don't sweat the outfit," Krum piped in. "I've been told that my curves and lips will send me on missions unsafe for women – missions that I'd have to be dressed as one. Gower too; he's got the slim physique." Krum nodded toward the dashing professor and winked. Gower hung his head with a shake and a hidden smile.

"Anyway, we must head to Adelaide," Arthur said.

The ministry turned and went toward the forest. The group of boys followed.

"After this, I want to go to Ace's too," Rabbit leaned over to Theodolphus.

The clouds released their bloody rain. They began to hurry to the destination, knowing that the kingdom's impending doom was approaching. Kenneth was standing at the back of the group as Rabbit looked back to see a look of utter terror on his face.

They approached a cabin in the woods; it looked like an ordinary cabin from the outside. They attacked the guards around it. Before going in, they examined every inch of it.

"Now, how do we get inside?" Bella asked.

"Right there," Gower pointed to the back of the cabin where cement stairs were dug into the ground that led to the cabin's basement door. He walked down the stairs before stopping and looking back up at Rabbit. "You first, the creature may be down there with her."

Rabbit took a deep breath in his tight, purple schoolgirl uniform before taking delicate steps down the stairs. He stood in front of the door. He raised his wand. "*Unlucan!*"

A brilliant red light emitted from his wand. The magic began to circle and spin in front of the door. The next second, the door started to unlock and open. The door fell down and out of sight, leaving a large hole in the ground, which appeared to be the only entrance made by the unlocking spell.

Rabbit heard Arthur gasp. He looked over to where he stood on the staircase.

"I'm going to go down there." He had his mind made up.

He couldn't not go down knowing that there was the faintest chance that his wife and unborn child might be down there and alive.

"Me too," said Rabbit, oddly more confident than usual. Everyone else agreed as there was a pause.

"Well, it doesn't seem that you need me, not when all of you are here," began Kenneth. "I'll just—"

He went to turn around, but both Rabbit and Theodolphus turned and pointed their wands at him.

"You can go in second," said Rabbit.

Rabbit turned back to the hole and hesitantly jumped down inside. Pale-faced, Kenneth walked down the stairs and approached the opening. Kenneth lowered himself and sat at the hole's edge, and he slipped his legs inside.

"I don't think—" he started to say before Theodolphus pushed him in with a kick to his back. He fell quickly out of sight, with Theodolphus quickly following afterward.

It was like sliding down an endless, muddy, dark tunnel. The tunnel twisted and turned, sloping steeply downward. Rabbit knew that they were falling further than the cabin's basement. Behind him, he could hear Clancy exclaim as his back scraped against the many stones that were glued inside the soft mud.

Just when Theodolphus was beginning to wonder whether there was an end to the tunnel, he hit the ground beside Kenneth. The floor was damp, and they looked to be inside a stone tube large enough to stand in. Rabbit braced himself as Clancy fell on top of him. Rabbit wrapped his arms around Clancy as he rolled the both of them out of the way just in time to avoid Arthur as he plunged downward.

Kenneth was standing on his feet, with his back stained with mud. He still looked as gray as a ghost.

"We must be miles beneath the cabin," said Rabbit, his voice echoed throughout the black tunnel.

"We're deep." Theodolphus nodded, looking around at the slimy walls.

All five of them turned to face the darkness ahead. "*Beorht!*" An irregular, red shaft exited Rabbit's wand and lit the path. "Come on." He turned to the others.

Off they went, their footsteps slapping off the puddled ground. The tunnel was so dark that they could only see a little ways ahead. Their shadows on the wall looked monstrous in the wand's light.

"Remember," Rabbit said quietly, "any sign of movement, close your eyes. It might help us from the Luminaris if one of us may be its target."

But the tunnel was as quiet as a cemetery. The first sound they heard was a loud crunch from Theodolphus, who had stepped on a skull of a smaller lizard. Rabbit lowered his wand and saw that the ground was littered with all kinds of bones. They tried not to picture what Adelaide might look like if she were down here. Rabbit led them forward, around a deep bend.

Theodolphus grabbed Rabbit's shoulder as they continued their trek. There was a sudden movement behind them. Kenneth's legs had collapsed beneath him. He held his hands over his eyes tightly in fear that the creature was nearby.

"Get up," Arthur said sharply. He pointed his wand at Kenneth. Kenneth got to his feet before drawing out his wand and pointing it at Arthur. "*Nestan!*" Arthur cast. Kenneth began to levitate up in the air, spinning rapidly.

Everyone besides Kenneth continued to trek deeper into the tunnel, remembering that there was no more time for stalls. Adelaide had been down here for months.

The tunnel turned and turned again. Rabbit could barely see as his sweat dripped before his eyes, and he was panting heavily as his heart beat rapidly. He tightened his grip on his wand as it was beginning to slip through his sweaty fingers. He wanted the tunnel to end and to find Adelaide and not cross paths with the creature. He knew he'd have to face it, but he didn't want to have to face it now. Then, at last, the tunnel came to an end, and they stood before a pale, yellow cement door that had large snake carvings drawn into them.

Rabbit approached, his mouth as dry as it had ever been. He raised his wand, cleared his throat. "*Unlucan!*" The cement doors cracked apart. Now shaking uncontrollably, Rabbit stepped inside.

CHAPTER 19

They were standing at the entrance of a very long, dimly lit pathway. Very tall, yellow pillars with carvings of snakes rose to the ceiling, which looked like a night sky. A yellowish gloom filled the place. Seeing the sky and the yellow pillars reminded Rabbit that now was the best time to come face to face with the monstrous beast, for the Luminaris was weaker beneath the moon's light.

Still, his heartbeat was fast. Pumping at a pace that Rabbit had never felt before. The anxiety he felt, knowing how the entire kingdom, and all who resided within, all rested on his inexperienced shoulders. They all stood, listening to the bone-chilling silence. Could the Luminaris be lurking in the corner of the dark shadows? Could the foul beast be lurking deep within the endless corners and eerie dark shadows that consumed the darkened basement? And where was Adelaide?

Rabbit moved forward between the tall, yellow columns. Despite how carefully he placed down his feet, it echoed loudly throughout the space. Rabbit kept his eyes narrow, preparing to lock them shut if he were to see the beast's light. His stomach jolted whenever his senses caught a dull sound or movement. Luckily, so far, that was all because of the group tasked to help him slay the monster.

As they walked, they noticed something lying on the ground. Intrigued, they hastened their steps to inspect it more closely. Upon nearing, they discovered a tall, slim woman with hazel eyes, red hair, long legs, and freckles – Adelaide. Despite her physique, her stomach was tremendous as a baby nestled inside.

"Adelaide!" Arthur shouted as he ran toward her side and kneeled beside her. "Adelaide," he muttered. He placed his wand down and brought his hands to her shoulders, and began to shake her gently. Her face was white as paper. Her skin was cold as ice, and her eyes were opened. "Adelaide… please wake up," he pleaded desperately. Her head wavered from side to side helplessly as he tried to wake her.

"She is unable to hear what you are saying," said a voice projecting from in front of the group. It was the king, who appeared much younger than his actual age. His face was smooth and wrinkle-free, and he had a radiant glow that was hard to miss.

Arthur jumped, looking upward as his knees were cold as they rested on the stone floor. The king was strangely blurred around the edges, it was the king's ghost, but this time he appeared young.

He shook his head. "Don't worry. She's alive. Barely, but alive."

Arthur stared at him. The king was the cause of all of the kingdom's deaths. He was angry yet uncertain of what to do. They had expected to face a lizard, not the ghost of the king.

"You've got to help her, Your Majesty," Arthur said, taking his wife in his arms. "You've got to help the whole kingdom. You don't want to kill hundreds of innocent people."

The king didn't move. Sweating, he went to reach for his wand but found it was missing. When he looked back, the king was twirling it between his gray fingers as he smiled wickedly.

"I've waited a whole year for this – to bring upon the end of the kingdom. Now I know that there will be no stopping my latest creation. A creature that can only be killed by a male Carter." The king chortled.

Rabbit shifted nervously, hanging his head low, letting the blonde curls cover his face.

"Here you are, three men, a teen girl, and… a crone?" The king looked at Theodolphus, who gave a queenly wave. The king let out a high, cold laugh as he felt unstoppable.

The hair on Arthur's back stood on end after hearing the blood-curdling laugh. His mouth had gone dry.

Rabbit clenched his fist, digging his nails deep enough into his skin that'd it hurt for the next few days to come. Anger was coursing through him, as he could barely see straight. Feeling his legs tremble, he began to wonder if he could face the lizard, a real threat, if he were having this much trouble standing around a ghost. He gritted his teeth.

"Your poor friend" – the king turned to Clancy – "being wrongfully accused of something I had done. And now, my weakest link sits on my throne, which I will shortly have in my possession." He started to walk around. Clancy stared at him. The king looked back at Arthur. "There isn't much life left in her. I expected you to come and find her much earlier, but maybe I misjudged the love you had for her. If she were my wife, I would've gone all lengths to find her immediately."

"Yet your wife is dead," Arthur snapped. "Murdered, and you have yet to persecute the person responsible."

"That was because I was mortal, but now that I am dead, I am a God! I can no longer die! I can see all of the past that I wish – and I know who killed my wife, and he'll be on the battlefield come dawn when I release my beast beneath the sun's chaotic rays." There held an irregular purple light within his eyes.

"Is that why you're doing this? To finally avenge your wife? We can imprison him. We don't need any more bloodshed."

"*Tsk, tsk,* you see, the man who killed my wife is now a well-respected ministry member." The king pushed his shoulders back, his chest out, and his chin up like a soldier. "He deserves to suffer a slow, painful death for what he did to Elizabeth – ripping her jaw apart and smashing what was left of her face. And you know why he killed her? Because she was going to kill him for the betterment of our kingdom. He was a dangerous young man who has lived many moons too long after her death. And do not pretend that you have forgotten that not only am I here to avenge my wife's death but also to take back my throne. Not everyone deserves to remain in this realm after death, but here I am, and I am not going to sit back and let my daughters run the show when I am still capable of doing it myself. I am the oldest, with the Carter bloodline running through my veins. I deserve the throne. And why can't I? Just because I have died? Do not forget I was one of the greatest sorcerers in the history of this realm!"

Arthur's brain was jammed. He stared numbly at the king, the king who had been responsible for so many killings during his time as Galdorwide's ruler. At last, he forced himself to speak.

"You're not." His voice was timid but full of hatred.

"I beg your pardon?" The king's triumph turned sinister.

"I said, you're not," Arthur spoke again. This time his voice was louder. "You're not one of the greatest sorcerers." He began to breathe fast. "Sorry to disappoint you, but your daughter, Bella, is a more powerful sorcerer than you. Everyone says so, even those who doubted that she could rule this kingdom. They changed their mind once they heard of her victory against you and your dragons. You know this to be true. Why else would you make this new beast of yours only weak at the hands of a male Carter?"

Rabbit looked back to Theodolphus, who gave a comforting nod.

Rabbit gave a small smile as he held back his tears. Everything was on his shoulders, everyone, and everything.

"Your daughter," Arthur continued, "scares you. You had to prepare for over a year to try and face her once more, but why face her when you could work on making a creature invincible as no male Carter exists."

Everyone knew it was best to pretend that they were still helpless despite never feeling any safer since Rabbit was here – in disguise; a hero that the king wouldn't see coming.

The ugly look remained on the young king's face. Music sounded in the distance as the empty chamber began to twirl around, and the spinning was growing faster. Rabbit's spine tingled as he knew that the night was progressing and that the king's anger was only enhancing his powers. The bows in Rabbit's hair had slipped down as his hair whipped around. His heart felt like it was swelling six times its standard size. Then as the room had reached its highest speed yet, a bright, yellow light encircled them. They squeezed their eyes shut in fear that the beast was near. They didn't relax their eyes until they heard familiar, concerned voices and the warm, wet drops of blood from the sky plopping down onto their faces.

The king appeared in the distance, his laughter echoing throughout the forest. It sounded as if there were twelve of him laughing all at once. "*Do you feel brave? Do you feel safe? Why are you here? No one can defeat my precious creature.*"

No one answered, and no one showed signs of backing down – besides Kenneth, who raised his hands in surrender only for them to be smacked back down by Krum. Everyone else knew that they weren't without help as Rabbit was there. They all stared at the king, not backing down as they waited for his laughter to cease.

"For my throne, dear ministry members and… misfits" – the king was still smiling broadly – "I've been to the future with the fact that no male Carter inhabited a body in this kingdom. I cannot fail at taking back my crown."

Soon, the king was joined by Roman and Daeva Scaasi, along with other followers, including a man with a sack over his head, wielding an ax.

The ministry began to think as they weighed their chances quickly. The king had the numbers, including a giant Luminaris who had yet to appear on this night. Meanwhile, they did have each other, Rabbit, and Bella. Nonetheless, the odds looked terrible. A pit in their hearts grew as they remembered the many casualties that had occurred during last year's battle with the king and his legion of followers. The longer they stood there, the quicker Adelaide's life drained from her body. They knew the sacrifice they needed to make, losing another number to help save the life of Adelaide and her baby – whose name she had decided to be Sophia for a girl and Mark for a boy as she spent her nights in the king's dungeon. Ian took Adelaide from out of Arthur's arm as he teleported her to the hospital.

The king was now in his usual, elder, ghostly form. However, the outline around him seemed to be growing more solid as each moment passed. He was growing more robust and more physical as the moments went on.

Rabbit was shaking like a leaf. Theodolphus wrapped his arm around his best friend.

"I've seen the real you," Theodolphus whispered. "Don't be afraid to bring that side out of you tonight. I know the real you—"

"Watch it," Rabbit said his usual warning line, but this time, it came out soft and desperate, not wanting to have to put up a fight, just to keep his secret quiet.

"You're so powerful, Rabbit. If you embrace yourself, the things you can't change will be followed by many great things. I promise. I know the revelation may be hard for some of our friends to swallow, but I mean, look at us… we're wearing skirts. I don't think they can be any more shocked, do you?"

"It's not that simple. I'm a freak, it's embarrassing, it's not a cool power to have, it's a very, very lame one, one that I never want to reveal. Unless, I…"

"Unless you have to. I know. Just know that no matter what, I'll be with you every step of the way during and after this fight."

Rabbit's face contorted as he could no longer hold in his sobs. He brought his knees to his chin as he pressed his hands tightly against his eyes as if it'd force him to wake up tomorrow after the battle, and he could just relax.

"So what if this power of yours that isn't cool?" Theodolphus continued to comfort Rabbit. "And by a fortunate chance, you were given this gift, and if you nurture it, imagine what you could achieve," he whispered. Terry and Elio watched on, wanting to come over and comfort their friend from a distance but knew that the best person to do that was

Theodolphus.

The ministry stood tense – waiting for the king to give a signal that'd make his followers attack or the terrifying thought of the king calling for the beast. The king's smile twisted wider.

"Now, *Bella*, I'm going to teach you a lesson. My sweet and dearest daughter." His lip curled.

Fear spread up Rabbit's leg. He knew what the lesson was, and his stomach twisted and turned. His body felt like it had been lit aflame. His body grew numb as he looked up. High above them, in the dark of the red night, the king levitated, opening his mouth and calling on his creature. "*Endebyrdnes be mec, Luminaris, tellan sylfum se wrymgeard.*"

Rabbit stood to his feet, staring at the treetops that littered the landscape behind the king. He noticed the trees were swaying forward, first in the distance and at an increasing rate, as the creature made his way closer to his eyesight. He could hear something stomping. Violent hissing sounds projected from the great beast making his way slowly but methodically toward Rabbit's group. Bracing himself for the impending reveal of the dreaded Luminaris, Rabbit could not help but try to focus on all of the kind words everyone used to tell him to encourage him to even take on this endeavor in the first place, that and the thought of innocent people meeting a tragic end at the rays of this beast if Rabbit were to meet his fate motivated him.

"I can see the lizard!" Thomas pointed. Angel immediately covered her son's eyes. Although she didn't want to use her son as bait, it was the only way to know when the Luminaris had arrived on the battlefield.

Rabbit backed away until he pressed up against the wood of the cabin. He shut his eyes tight as the bright light illuminated the forest. Before he knew it, he acted on impulse, doing the absolute opposite of what he wanted to do during this battle.

Rabbit looked to Theodolphus, then to the rest of the ministry, who looked at him with curiosity. He reached for the white school dress shirt that was plenty sizes too small and began to unbutton his shirt, revealing a very unfeminine physique complete with a set of abs and thick biceps – he threw his shirt to Theodolphus.

Rabbit let out a wince as Theodolphus nodded. He let out a massive scream as his back pulled downward. He fell to his knees with his back curled backward as metallic blades began to sprout from either side of his spine. He cried out in pain as rows of blades pushed their way out of him, layering outwards. Rabbit extended his hand upward as his body contorted in pain. He was falling forward onto his hands and knees as he heaved a sigh of relief as the pain subsided. He brought his hand to his knee and slowly stood up. He spread his metallic wings out. He clenched his fists and flew into the air.

Bella gave an amused look before turning back to face her father, who was immediately reminded of his distant, male relative.

Rabbit's legs were still pained with numbness. He looked down at the king, who wore a stone-cold expression as he looked up in the half-darkness to see his relative flying high above them. Rabbit looked down to see that the ministry wasn't charging after the king and that he'd need to make the first move, something he was not yet prepared to do.

"Kill him!" the king ordered his followers.

The massive Luminaris began rushing toward Rabbit. Now Rabbit could see the lizard. Angel pointed her wand at her son and teleported Thomas off of the field.

The lizard's massive yellow scales sparkled as the bloody rain covered the beast. It was letting out a monstrous call as the lizard used its enormous tail to whip those who couldn't see it out of its path as it made its way to Rabbit, who was still taking flight in hopes of maintaining distance from the Luminaris. At the same time, he formulated a game plan to take the creature down.

Rabbit began to fly sideways in a zig-zag pattern, keeping his eyes closed in fear that the monster would set his rays upon him. He was doing anything he could to keep himself alive and in the fight. He tried using his sense of sound to try and help him locate the massive lizard in the hopes of being able to deal with it with a deathly blow.

"Watch out!" Theodolphus called.

Rabbit opened his eyes to see an interwoven jade of fragments race toward him from out of Roman's wand. He was struck with frosty energy, causing him to fall out of the sky. Speckles of frost rested on his hair, nose, and shoulders. He reached upward as his body contorted with pain. He fell forward. He heaved a sigh of relief once the pain subsided. Standing to his feet, his wings of steel spread out as Bella heaved a pleasant and surprised sigh. Theodolphus gave his friend a comforting nod as Rabbit clenched his fist and flew high into the sky once more. His bare knees and hands were stained with fresh blood. The frost began to melt, emitting steam as it mixed with the hot liquid. He could taste the blood that had splashed into his mouth. The reptile was nine feet away from him, and he could hear it approaching as he shut his eyes once more. The wind howled.

There was a loud, thundering, hissing sound coming from above him. Something hard had struck Rabbit's head, so hard it knocked him back down to the ground, laying him flat down onto his stomach. Before he could pull himself back up, Daeva had hit his head hard. She then grabbed the locks of his blond hair and pulled him up to his knees. He couldn't help it. He had to open his eyes.

The enormous reptile with bright yellow scales had lifted its head higher in the air in an attempt to showcase its massive size and deadly prowess. Rabbit trembled in fear, preparing to close his eyes if the monster was to set his primitive, devilish light upon him. It was at this moment that he noticed that something *else* had the Luminaris' attention. He tried to move his head in an attempt to see what it was which proved difficult as Daeva was doing everything in her power to keep Rabbit's face pointed toward the massive creature's foul body, except now the creature was fading from his eyesight as the lizard was focusing on a new, bizarre target. All he could see now was the imprint of the lizard's paws on the red, wet grass.

The wind howled as both the ministry and the king's followers paused, looking over to the beast. In front of Rabbit was an electromagnetic disturbance. Rabbit tried to squirm out of Daeva's grip, but to no avail. She looked over to her husband Roman, who shrugged. No one knew who had summoned the disturbance out from the night sky.

"What is it?" Daeva asked frantically.

"Don't get too close!" Roman gestured.

Daeva quickly stuffed her wand into her cloak and pulled out a knife from her bra. She brought it to Rabbit's neck before standing him to his feet and backing away from the purple-colored energy.

"Looks like some tonnau sioc," Kenneth Riley studied. "Either that or a demon summoning portal."

"Pretty big difference there, genius," said Krum. Electricity crackled from the purple force. "Woah, woah, woah! Everyone, get behind me." Krum huddled the ministry behind him.

"Yeah, get behind us," Bella ordered.

"I vote for running, come on!" Kenneth whined desperately in fear of what was about to happen.

Bella grabbed onto Krum's hand. The electricity continued to crackle. Inside the anomaly, screaming could be heard. Three children appeared within the anomaly before emerging and falling helplessly in front of the Luminaris. The thunder faded, and the anomaly disappeared. The ministry cautiously approached the children and the beast. The middle child wore an outdated Pure school uniform, his eyes closed. Standing to his feet, the boy reached into his pocket and pulled out a Tizeruk fang, and he stabbed it into the Luminaris' heart.

The beast let out an intense, piercing scream as blood spurted out of the beast, covering the young boy's hand and dripping down onto the already bloody ground. The reptile was twisting and flailing before crashing down.

It was dead. There was a silence. The only sound that could be heard was the blood of the beast pooling into the already existing puddle. Those around could see its blood spill.

Daeva released Rabbit's head with a thrust, causing his head to ache as it knocked forward. He felt as if the king was spinning the forest, but no one else seemed to be feeling this. All they did was stare at the boy. Slowly, Rabbit stood to his feet with the help of Theodolphus, who rushed to his side.

John looked at one of the small figures, specifically the one who wore a pink dress and had a set of flaming hair upon her head. "Lulia?" he asked, dumbfounded.

"Beau?" Clancy asked, almost in shock to see his shy, awkward cousin stand beside the boy who killed the beast.

Angel looked to Bella, who had a twisted yet solemn expression on her face. Angel then looked back to the boy who killed the beast. "Aidan?"

***